Also by Anna Gill

The Eastwood Affair

The Tale of Dickie Short

The Sailmaker's Palm

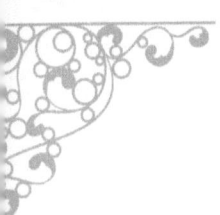

the Island Woman

A CHESAPEAKE STORY

ANNA GILL

CORDGRASS
Publishing

ROCHESTER, NEW YORK

www.AnnaGill.com

Published by:
Cordgrass Publishing, Rochester, New York

Paperback: 978-1-951212-01-8
Mobi: 978-1-951212-02-5
EPub: 978-1-951212-03-2

Library of Congress Data on file with the publisher.

www.CordgrassPublishing.com

Printed in the United States of America

10 9 8 7 6 5 4 3 2 1

This book is dedicated,
with my deepest respect and admiration,
to all women who stand on equal footing
with their men who go out on the waters.
May you always be blessed!

THE MUSEUM

by
Janice Marshall,
A Waterman's Wife

Suppose you went to the museum with your grandchild one day to view all the things and the way people lived at one time while working on the Bay.

On film there was an old Sailing Skipjack dredging oysters out on the Bay and over in the corner was the old oyster dredge just sitting there resting away.

Just over the way preserved in a case is a Jimmy, Soft Crab, and Sook. They all looked so real to touch and to feel but now they only exist in a book.

There's also an oyster preserved in its shell and all sorts of critters too many to say. Like clams and manoes and flounder and grass that used to live in the Bay.

And over in the middle of the room standing strong and proud and tall is the statue of a Chesapeake Waterman — just a relic of the Bay's last call!

CHAPTER 1

Great! Just great!

Siren blasting and lights flashing meant Willa Carpenter's day was about to get worse, if that was possible. Already that morning she had dealt with the most demanding woman in the world, Kit Winthrop, queen of the publishing industry, tyrant extraordinaire. While doing battle with Kit, Willa realized the thump, thump, thumping inside her head was not going away. She was regretting the wonderful wine she'd had to have the night before. Now, having been stopped by one of Washington's finest, she was definitely going to be late to the literary awards luncheon. Yes, today was one of those days the bear was eating her.

"Good morning, miss. Can I see your license and registration, please?"

At least he wasn't so bad on the eyes. She reached over to the glove compartment and got the necessary papers. However, coming back up wasn't so good. She felt as if her head was sideways and she was going to throw up. *Steady, girl.*

"Here, officer. I think these will do. I really don't know what I was doing wrong to be pulled over."

He smiled politely and said, "I hear that all the time."

Did he just wink at me? God, my eyes are out of control, too.

"Well, you were caught on our radar gun going fifteen miles over the speed limit."

"Really?" Willa offered up in a low, soft voice. She knew she was guilty and, at the moment, too nauseous to try to go further. "I won't do it again; I promise."

The young man smiled, exposing a set of perfect white teeth. Willa loved gorgeous teeth on a man. Showed he took care of himself. "I'm sure you won't, Ms. Carpenter."

Willa slouched down in her seat. She knew she was busted and could only pray that one thing would go right in this already lousy day.

"I really don't like to give these out, but you were speeding. Please slow down from here on out."

Willa took the ticket reluctantly but did offer a slight smile. He really was cute and about her age, too. Maybe a date with a . . . nah, she couldn't get serious with a man who hadn't yielded to her charms and who had given her a ticket.

"Can I go now? I really need to get somewhere," she lamented, "although it isn't going to change anything."

The officer grinned. He was definitely attracted to her.

He leaned into the window and said, "Don't rush now, Ms. Carpenter. Wherever you're going and whatever you're doing, it'll wait. Nothing is that important."

He sure was good at summation. "Okay, officer. Will do. You have a good day."

"You try to do the same."

If he only knew what was ahead for her at that awards luncheon, he would have chucked his beat and asked her out to lunch. She would have accepted without hesitation.

Composing herself, she watched the officer get into his nifty police car and drive off. Her mood changed suddenly as she reflected on the last time she had seen the police this closely.

It was the night two of them came to the front door of her family home in Connecticut. She knew the minute she answered the door that something had happened. They weren't inside three minutes before the wonderful life she had enjoyed with two of the best parents on earth had come to an end. There had been an accident. A car was passing another and hit her parents' car head on. It was instantaneous; there was nothing anyone could do. She needed to go to the hospital so she could identify them.

That scene at the hospital would play in her mind forever. You can't ever wipe that out. You go on and do what had been planned—college, friends, life—but that dull, nagging pain never leaves you.

At eighteen, she had become an orphan. She was grateful for the loving aunt and uncle who had taken her in. They had made the best of it and helped her through those dreadful years of separation from all she had known and loved. As an only child, there hadn't even been a sibling to share in the grief. The three of them had been all they had.

When she eventually crawled back up out of the pit of despair, she went on to college and took up writing just like her mother. She found she was good at it—maybe even a little better than her mom. After graduation she began writing romance novels and they were well accepted in the literary world. She was on the *New York Times* Best Seller list right off the bat. She wanted so much to prove to them that she could go all the way. If her famous cartoonist father and famous novelist mother could do it, so would she. And she wasn't about to let some man get in her way. There was no room in her heart for love other than that she had shared with her two dead parents.

Get a grip, Willa! Stop talking to yourself. You have to go to that luncheon. And you know you will be seated with that damned Susan Crandall, who not only copies your stories but is dying to take your place in the eyes and pockets of the lovely Ms. Winthrop. On top of that, you aren't going to win novelist of the year. Your ninth novel was impressive but you've won so many times and they get snarky about that sort of thing. No, they'll give it to someone else just to show you who's boss. But beware: the gawkers will be watching for your reaction. Remember to put on that happy face you hate so much.

Best part is that the high-and-mighty Kit doesn't know the worst of it yet. Her darling of romance has that dread disease that afflicts literary types sometimes: **Writer's Block**. Oh, she's going to love that. She'll be on to Susan Crandall like white on rice, and you can bet that Susan won't wait one minute to rush to her and replace me as her top novelist at old Kitwin Publishing. *Yep, if I don't come up with a cure for this little problem, along with this blasted head of mine, I will be headed for the literary boneyard of yesterday's best-selling writers.*

Now, on to that dreaded luncheon. *Yes, I know what the cute officer said . . . slowly.*

Wheels down and parked in the lot of the hotel, Willa popped out of her car to hurry on in to the lion's den. Only problem was that, when she popped, she snagged her panty hose. When she looked at her leg, a gargantuan run was moving from the bottom all the way up to her unmentionables. Why is this happening? The day just gets better and better. What's next? Oh, we already know that, don't we?

Out of breath by the time she reached the reception table, she leaned over to sign in and heard, "So nice to see you, Miss Carpenter. You look . . . well . . . here's your table number. I personally seated you with all your friends. Have a lovely lunch."

Bitch. She didn't mean one word of that "have a lovely lunch," and she had looked at Willa as if she had two heads. And, come to think of it, she did. One was still trying to find the other after that dreadful wine she'd drunk last night. Geez!

Answering the call of a friend's waving hand and a yell-out to signal where her table was, Willa arrived to the purring delight of Susan Crandall who, by the way, looked as if she had been downing happy pills with vodka. What's that look all about anyway? Bitch. Seems they're all over the place.

"Here's ourrrrr dear Willa," Susan slurred. "Come, sit down here next to me, sweetie."

Sweetie? Willa was perplexed. She sat down, feeling that run in her stocking doing all manner of gymnastics up her leg. She couldn't stand seeing Susan any longer with that stupid look all over her face, so she said, "Geez, Susan, what's in that soup you're eating? I don't think I want any."

Really grasping for words, Susan responded slowly, "Whatever do you mean, sweetie?"

"Quit with that sweetie stuff, Susan, and never mind about the soup."

"Hey, Willa," said her friend sitting on the other side. "So happy to see you made it. I was beginning to worry."

"Have I missed much yet, Gwen? Sorry I'm late. I'm not having a very good day and got held up by one of D.C.'s finest. He was cute though."

"Oh my, Willa. That's not good. Did he give you a ticket?"

"Of course he gave me a ticket, Gwen. That's what they do. The cops give out speeding tickets while the really bad guys run amok. It's just what I didn't need and now—"

A booming voice came from the podium. "May I have your attention, everyone?"

Willa leaned in to Gwen and said, "There she is, Kit Winthrop, the lady of the hour."

"We're here today to celebrate romance and the writers who move us to express our every emotion. They're the best and the brightest, and each year we applaud them."

Willa was so uninterested in Kit's every word that she leaned across Susan to get a roll. She was so craving carbs by now. Susan was doing a little leaning herself, only it wasn't in the direction of the rolls.

Willa glanced at Gwen and chuckled slightly. She and Gwen had become good friends since meeting at a book fair a few years before. Both in their early thirties, they had much in common, but the one thing they especially shared wasn't their writing. It was the fact that Gwen had lost one of her parents, too. And, while Gwen's mother was alive, she wasn't a candidate for mother of the year, so, after college, Gwen had made the break with her forever. Thus, they never had to explain to each other blue days or feeling lonely.

The thread, however, that held them together even more than that was their shared sense of humor. They both always got the joke and both loved to laugh, usually at someone else's expense. And, today, that someone seemed to be Ms. Susan.

"Looks like I really didn't miss that much, huh, Gwen? As we know, nobody speaks before Kit Winthrop, so I made better time than I thought."

"I hope everything's okay with you. I have to tell you that you look as though you've been rode hard and put away wet."

"Boy, did you hit the nail on the head with that one, Gwen. It's one of those days that, from the minute you hit the floor, you know it's going to go downhill from there. And, to make it all the better, I got into a bottle of wine last night for inspiration and the only inspiring it did was make me fall into bed and crash."

"Poor baby. Why didn't you just piss off on today? This luncheon isn't going to make you feel any better. You and I know that."

"Yeah, I know, but Kit's been riding me pretty hard lately and I haven't given her what she wants. I'm stuck right now. I need something wonderful to happen, and, while I thought that might take the form of the hottie in the police uniform, I passed on that fantasy and came here to this fun instead."

"You might regret that decision."

"Hey, I know what's going to happen here. We're all adults, or"—she looked at Susan—"we're trying to be."

"She's such a mess, Willa, but it's going to be a hell of a lot of fun if she wins top novelist award. Seeing her try to get out of that chair will be worth the price of admission."

"Yeah. Wonder how many steps in she'll be before she trips the light fantastic."

Kit finished pontificating, finally getting to the part they had all been waiting for. Or, at least, waiting for it to be over. As always, she was dragging it out so all eyes were on her for as long as she could hold them.

"This is agonizing, Gwen. She's taking forever. Can I go now?"

"Hush, Willa. Behave."

Finally, with yet more drama and fanfare, she did it. She flashed her perfect set of implanted teeth and said, "Best novelist of the year goes to . . . why, it goes to one of my own: Susan Crandall."

The other women at the table practically swooned over Susan as Willa quietly said, "What a surprise. She's so original in her plot lines, isn't she?"

"That's not nice, Willa," Gwen whispered.

"Maybe not, but she won't remember I said it. I don't think she can even get up."

Finally, after an impatient second announcement by Kit, Susan made it out of her chair and began her long day's journey into night on her way to the stage.

Willa began to giggle so hard, she couldn't stop. "This is really too good to be true, Gwen. This day might be changing after all. This isn't going to be pretty, but oh so much fun."

Willa stood and clapped with everyone else, and then, for some reason or no reason, she shouted out, "Bombs away, Susan!"

At this point Gwen couldn't hold it in anymore and broke into a belly laugh as she watched Susan weave right out of the room. "Where is she going, Willa?"

Willa was doubled over. "She's off the radar and headed to the Potomac. Someone needs to go fish her out and give her my award."

By this time, Gwen and Willa had lost it completely. And, it might be added, many others had, too. "I needed this, Gwenny. I thought today was going to be the closest thing to burning in hell, but it's turned out to be one of the best of my life. Thank you, dear friend, for being here to share it with me. Too bad our other dear friend, Prue, had to work. She would have fallen on the floor laughing."

"I know. But, when you tell her, I'm sure the story will get even better. I just wish I could say I was responsible for this joy, but, finally, Susan Crandall has risen to the occasion. Oh, look, Willa! Someone went out and steered her back into the room with a firm grip on her so she can't go AWOL again."

"I can't stand any more, Gwen. I'm going to pee my panties. Let's get out of here."

"Roger that one. Lead the way."

With that, the two of them made a hasty exit before the crowd could sit down from their standing O for the fool of the year.

What a day!

CHAPTER 2

"I don't care what ye say, ye ain't goin' out in that derned boat today. Do ye hear me, James?"

"Ye got yerself all worked up, missy. I know when ye call me James, I'm in a heap of troubles, but I have to go out, rain or shine. You know that. Now don't fuss at me any more, woman."

"Ye will catch yer death if ye do."

"Then so be it, Franny girl."

"Don't ye 'Franny girl' me. Ye be yellin' with the fever by tomorrow."

"Nah, I won't. Now come on over here and give me a big hug before I take my leave."

"Derned if I will, Jimmy. You make me so riled up, I could scream. That water will kill ye yet, but, if yer mind is set, then please make sure yer clothes are on ye heavylike."

"I will, pritty lady. Now come on and give me a hug. I got to get goin'."

"Ye do make me mad, ye know. Ye must be the stubbornest man on the water, but, if it's a hug yer lookin' fer, then a hug you'll get. Take heed out there today, Jimmy. That Bay kin turn on ye faster than anything."

Smiling at his wife, he got his hug and opened the door.

"I will, hon. Be back for dinner a little after noon. Then I have to get on down to the shed. It needs working on before the spring comes and the crabs start to run."

"Be careful out there, and pick me out some oysters for our meal. I love ye."

His old worn cap on his head and wearing a warm wool coat, Jimmy gently closed the door before the sun was even in the sky.

Miss Frances poured herself another cup of strong coffee from the old percolator on the stove and sat down to begin thinking about the day ahead. But first things first. She bowed her head and prayed that her husband's catch would be good and he would be given safe passage on the water. This, Frances Ruth had been doing faithfully for the past forty-five years without fail. Her husband, Jimmy, and her only child, Nellie, were her entire life, though her friends and neighbors were almost kin to her, too. They were all bound by a common life on the island and a common purpose on the waters. A hard life it was, but a good one that they couldn't imagine ever coming to an end.

I know, Lord, he is a stubborn man, and I am a stubborn woman. But isn't that how ye made us? It's how we survive on this island and bear the hardships of a life different from the rest of the world. Please watch over him, and, if I'm not asking too much of Ye, please let my Nellie know we love her, and please protect her while she is way off in Washington, D.C., studying, working, and trying to help us poor folks out back at home. Bring her back to us soon, dear Lord. We miss her terribly. Amen.

With that morning ritual out of the way, Frances Evans began to make her lists. Those lists kept everything in her world running smoothly and kept her from forgetting all she had to do before her Jimmy came through that door looking for his dinner. It was the noon meal that was the biggest one of the day, so that was her first chore, and she was glad that, for once, she had all her fixin's for the meal. However, she would still have to "go off" to go shopping at the big grocery store across the water on the mainland.

She decided to make some fried chicken, cabbage slaw, and mashed potatoes for their dinner, a meal most of the world called lunch. She would also make the sweet potato pie that her Jimmy loved so much. She never knew when someone would come a-callin', and she always wanted to have enough so she could serve them if there was a need. She had cut back some on her cooking these days with her precious girl aways off now across the Bay in Baltimore, working part time and going to college. She missed her so much. They were a close family and their daughter was the center of their life.

Frances had wanted more children but they didn't come. So they accepted what the Lord gave them and were thankful for it. Helen, or Nellie as they called her, had always made them so proud, and she knew that, one day, her daughter would go on to do something really meaningful for their people. She was just that kind of child: always trying harder than anyone else and working until she dropped.

When Nellie called to tell her she was chosen to make a presentation before a congressional committee, Frances smiled and thought back to when she had done the very same thing. But not as a college girl. Frances was born and bred on the island and thankful to have finished high school. Her education came from hands-on experience living with a waterman, which is about all the experience one needed to talk about the Chesapeake she loved so much.

Like mother, like daughter, she thought. However, Nellie's presentation was likely going to get a might cantankerous because, whenever somebody tried to explain things from the islanders' or watermen's point of view, the fur surely began to fly. The folks on the Eastern Shore, let alone the islanders, didn't like being told too much of anything. They did it their way, and, now that the politicians were getting into the act, all that was changing too fast for anyone to keep up. The regulations coming from Washington now made it all worse for them, and they saw no reason for most of these new, intrusive rules. Seemed that all they knew that had been passed on down to them, meant nothing to the bureaucrats and politicians. They thought the watermen were an uneducated bunch of idiots.

Frances's hope was that her daughter would just keep calm and talk slowly. She shouldn't lose her patience or get ruffled. This was going to be an ongoing discussion and would continue until, one day, someone got smart enough to understand that the people who do the work know what they're doing.

However, the days of the commercial fishermen were dwindling, and everyone was afraid of what the final outcome was going to be. Lord knows, Frances had tried when she had sat on the board of one of the water commissions, but it had all fallen on deaf ears. Now her daughter was going to get a chance to tell them what they should know anyway. Maybe she could explain the challenges better and maybe they would listen harder to a college gal. They held stock in educated people. A lot of them didn't give a darn about people who fish. They want what they catch but they don't want to hear from them.

Nellie was an educated girl and was studying marine life in Bay areas at the University of Maryland. That should count for something, right? Frances and Jimmy had saved for years to allow for their daughter to go to college—something they themselves could never have dreamed of—and now it looked like all that scrimping was paying off.

Well now, Frances Ruth, no use to worrying your head about it. Nellie will do what she will do and you can't change a thing. Best you get to the boat to go off and get to that food shopping. It isn't going to jump onto the stove without buying it first. Our girl will be home soon for the holiday, and then she can talk to you about it for hours before she heads back over there.

And maybe one day she'll come back for more than a visit. Maybe she'll come back home to the island to stay.

CHAPTER 3

By the time Willa got back home and settled in, her head was still hurting, but hurting less. Being with Gwen had lightened her spirits and made her realize that not winning that award was not the end of the world. She would rebound, and, when she did, it would be with something wonderful.

However, she would have to deal with Kit. In many ways she was intimidated by the woman. She shouldn't be, as Willa brought a lot of money in to the publishing house, but Kit had a way of putting people down to make herself look larger than life. It was her MO and nobody liked it, but it was what Willa had to put up with to be with an esteemed publishing house. You had to be at the top to get into that club, and it wasn't easy at first. But, once you made it, life was pretty good.

She had to face the fact that, while she didn't like Susan Crandall or her tactics, Susan had worked damned hard to write that last book, the one that wasn't a rip-off of one of hers. This time she had ripped someone else off and look what happened: she won the award. That is, if she even knew where she was at the time. Poor girl. Really got into the sauce before the big moment instead of waiting to celebrate. Wouldn't it have been awful if the "big secret" of who had won the darned thing hadn't been right? God knows what Susan would have done.

The headache was mercifully continuing to fade. Food had helped with that. She now poured herself a glass of ginger ale and sipped it slowly. It was truly the best soda to ease the pain. When she was little, when she would get sick, her mother always poured her a glass of ginger ale and then tucked her into bed. She would read to her until she fell asleep. She was safe then and surrounded by unconditional love. Willa wondered if she would ever have that again.

The memories flooded back. Once you open that window, it's too hard to keep them at bay.

It was snowing and she watched as the flakes danced down to her window. Snuggled in bed with the warmth of a radiator next to her, she slipped her feet over to the comforting heat. She wished she felt better because, if she did, she'd be outside joining the ballet of snowflakes, sledding or, better yet, skating on the pond out back of her house. She would pretend to be the skating queen in the land she ruled.

All these wonderful thoughts washed over her now. She remembered that her mother was always there, writing her books at home so she could be with her only child. Willa closed her eyes and could still recall the sound of the typewriter clacking away. She was always there then and she's still with me now. I know it to be true. She sends me messages when I least expect it. I don't see Daddy as much. Where has he gone?

One stupid decision can cause a lifetime of pain. If that man had not passed that car. But he did, Willa. He did.

The memory faded and she was lying there, shaking. Lately the past seemed to come to her too often. Maybe her parents were trying to get a message to her. She would always talk to them as if they were in the room with her. It helped.

"If you could give me a clue here, it would be greatly appreciated."

She wondered what they would do in her predicament. Surely being the creative people they were, they could help her get her rhythm back. Her father's weekly comic strip, *Welcome to My World*, was all about fixing troubles people got into. She could use a little of that right now. He had so many fans, and, when he died, they almost went into revolt when someone else kept writing it.

It was still so painful to think of them gone. It had been years now and, yet, it never goes away. Hell, she had to move on, but how to do it was the question. The more she thought about it, the worse the blank in her head got. So maybe the answer was to go off somewhere and relax for a couple of days. Who knows?

Deep into her thoughts, she almost didn't hear the phone ringing. She hated to be interrupted. Looking at her caller ID, she really hated to be interrupted. "This is just what I need," she said out loud. "Time to face the music and take this call whether I like it or not. Hello, Kit."

"Sweetie, so good to reach you. I was worried about you yesterday. I looked for you and saw you had left in quite a hurry."

Her stomach was turning again. She really didn't like this lady.

"Yes, Gwen and I decided to take off. We stayed to see Susan's triumphant performance and then left."

"Yes, well, Susan apparently had gotten into some vodka thing and she was nearly unconscious by the time she made it to the podium."

"She did look like she was definitely having a problem. Poor girl, but she did win the award."

Kit must have heard the sarcasm in Willa's voice but decided to take a different tack with her. "Anyway, Susan got her award and she deserved it this year. You will be right back there getting another one next year. You know you can't win them all, Willa."

"Thanks for reminding me of that."

"Well, anyway, Willa, down to the business at hand. I've been waiting to see your new ideas and a few pages from your next novel. You are behind and we can't have that, can we?"

"We certainly can't, but, truthfully I don't have anything for you right now." There it was, out in the open. The long pause that followed told her everything. Kit was pissed.

"Kit? Did you hear me?"

"I did indeed and I can't believe what I heard. You have nothing? Not one page written?"

"Not one page, or even an idea."

"What's wrong, Willa? Are you ill?"

"Not exactly. It's something else."

While Kit gathered her thoughts, Willa glanced down at the newspaper on the table in front of her, scanning down the sideline shorts of the articles inside. One of them caught her eye. She furiously read the teaser. Kit was still not speaking.

This story interested her for some reason. Maybe it was the young girl's picture. She wasn't sure.

Finally Kit decided to talk. "Willa, are you still there? Don't you have anything else to say to me about this? I mean, we do have a contract, you know."

"Yes, I know, but, to be honest, Kit, I'm a bit tied up at the minute, and don't mean to run on you, but I think I may have something for you soon. I'll get back to you in a few days. Next week at the latest. Promise."

"Willa, you're brushing me off and I don't like it one bit."

"Sorry, Kit. I don't mean to be this way, but I really am in a rush and I will get back to you. Have I ever done anything to disappoint you in the past? I won't this time either. You have to go with me on this."

"Okay, Willa. You have always come through for us here, so I'll let up . . . for now. I do have Susan's new book to get out so I guess that will keep me tied up for a while, but don't take too long. You know our legal department doesn't like to have to deal with sticky matters, and neither do I."

"I hope that isn't a threat, Kit. I deserve better from you."

"Of course you do, dearest. Talk to me soon and get writing."

Willa didn't even bother to say good-bye. What was the use? The beautiful old battle-ax would just have blown her off anyway. *I tell you, the bitches are out in force. One would think it was Halloween coming up and not Thanksgiving. Oh well, Kit will leave me alone for a little while so I won some time. Now about this article. Let me see.*

Willa reread the summary on the front page and then turned inside to read the expanded piece:

ISLAND WOMAN TO SPEAK ON WATERMEN'S CHALLENGES

After reading the article, Willa went to her computer and began to research some of what this young college woman was talking about concerning the challenges facing this huge industry. She would be speaking in front of a congressional committee day after tomorrow. Well, there was only one person she knew who could get her into that hearing: her dearest friend in town, Prue Harding. She picked up the phone and made the call. Thank heavens Prue was in the office.

"Hi, Prue. I have a favor to ask of you."

"Hi to you, too, Willa. What's wrong? You don't sound like yourself."

"Well, let's just say I had the worst day of my life yesterday and I didn't win the award and I have lost my mind."

"All that in one day? You're out of sorts then. What's up?"

"What's up is I need to get into that hearing day after tomorrow that your gorgeous boss is chairing. The one on commercial fishing."

"No can do, Willa. It's a full house now. Seems a lot of congressmen are involved with this issue, so it's hot."

"Hot or not, I have to get in there. You can do this; I know you can."

"You know I would do almost anything, within reason, for you, but this isn't one of those that I can do."

"I can't take no on this, Prue. It's important, and, besides, your boss does like me a little."

"Willa, I wouldn't take a chance introduction to the congressman and leap to the idea he's interested in you."

"Why not? He's interested in every single female in D.C. No offense to you."

"No offense taken. Why is this so important to you anyway?"

"I know we haven't seen a lot of one another lately. Both of us have been busy, but I've been going through something really bad."

"What? Are you ill? I'm so sorry."

"Nothing like that, but an illness of another kind. Don't tell anyone, but I have writer's block, and I've never had it before. I can't even write a sentence that makes any sense."

"Oh my, that is bad. I've heard all writers get it at some point. This is your time, I guess. But still, what does that have to do with this hearing?"

"I don't know, but it does. I've been searching for something that hits me and this young gal's comments rang in my heart. There's something about this. I will only know when I hear her."

"Well, you know I could get fired for being the one to get you in there and then have you write something."

"You'll do it then? And you won't get fired. I don't think there's a love story in commercial fishing."

"I tell you, it's standing room only."

"Then I'll stand. Please?"

16

Prue didn't answer for a minute and then said, "I'll try. That's all I can do. If he says no the first time, I won't ask him again."

"Fair enough and get back to me right away. Thanks, you're a doll, Prue. If you get me in, drinks are on me at The Willard."

"I'll take that and raise you one. Dinner, too."

"Done. Just don't ask any friends to join us."

CHAPTER 4

Nellie was living up to her name: she was nervous. The kind of nervous you get when you know each and every word that comes out of your mouth is going to count. People will only listen if what you're telling them matters to them. That's the whole nut in this city of shameless peddlers. Washington was full of nothing other than folks looking out for themselves and no one else. You scratch my back and I'll scratch yours: that's the way of it.

To someone like Nellie and her kind of people, it was hard to conceive of folks behaving that way and not caring one whit about the rest of the world. It was all about what was in it for them. She had to make them care. No fooling around. This wasn't rocket science but it was an urgent plea on behalf of men who do their job and yet were finding it increasingly difficult to do so. They can't understand the power people, but know they are the folks who control what they love to do. There had to be a coming together of the minds, no matter how hard it was for either side.

She was down to the last day and still hadn't decided on the exact attack. There was only one person she could rely on to tell her how to do it: her mother. She always had solid advice, and, the fact was, her mother understood better than most what she was up against. Her mother had tried once to make the political types understand. It hadn't worked.

Nellie was a water child. Raised on it, surrounded by it, and in love with it, the water was her entire being and the reason she went to college to learn more about it. Now, out of all the students studying the Bay waters, she had been chosen to give this presentation. She was at the top of her

18

class and worked almost full time for a major research company called Global Waters Enterprises.

She needed to connect right now and calling home was like being out there on the island. Or, what some called, the end of the world. She dialed home, and, when she heard that special voice, she was out of heart, as they say on the island.

"Hey there, Nellie, how ye comin'?"

"Pretty well, Mama, but I sure can use your advice right now."

"Let her out. We'll get ye fixed straight away."

"You know I am going to speak tomorrow in front of a whole lot of important people. I don't want to mess it up. If I say anything wrong, it could go badly."

"You won't, Nellie. You know your stuff; now say your piece. The folks over here and elsewhere on the water have their hands full with just fishin', but with all these rules and laws comin' all the time, they can't see the need of it. We have to have some letup or we won't be fishin' anymore. Ye have to tell them that."

Nellie smiled. She would advise them, but, if she ever said it the way her mama just said it, they would get up and walk out of the room, scratching their heads that a crazy person had just tried to speak to them. It was the way folks on the island put things and her mama wasn't going to change at this point in her life. It was an interesting language, spoken mainly by the old-timers. Part Old English, part Eastern Shore, and part southern, it was a wonder anyone understood them. But she didn't have it so strong. And, when she had gone off to college, she had really tried to fit in. But, when she went back home, it was a different story. Old ways die hard.

She'd had a roommate from New Jersey and they had used to laugh about their accents. The roommate said everything with a "w" in it and couldn't change that now. Nellie just tried harder and she was determined not to make any slips during this hearing.

She teased her mama a little. "Well, I'll tell them, but not quite like you would,"

Frances laughed and knew exactly what her daughter was talking about, so didn't take offense.

"I won't ever change neither. You're ready for this, ain't ye?"

"I thought I was but then my mind plays tricks on me and tells me I'm not ready at all."

"I've always known that to be the sure-tell sign that ye *are* ready. Go with it and just think of us back home when you're speaking. They're folks just like us, really. They have to eat—and remind them that if they don't lighten up some and listen to us, they aren't going to eat their beloved Chesapeake blue crabs. That should count for something."

"I'm not sure. These are sophisticated people and they don't understand our ways or what we really do or how we live. Not sure they ever want to understand us. It's kind of the situation where they go out to eat in their fancy restaurants but they don't want to think how their food got to that plate."

Frances Ruth loved and missed her daughter so much. She could tell Nellie was in a pickle or she wouldn't have called. She had to calm her down just as she used to do when her daughter would come down sick at school and had to come home.

Those were the times all the mothers grieved so that their children had to go off on boats across the water to get to school. If something happened or they got sick, they had to get a boat to bring them back. Frances had had to do that many times. The folks on the island did have friends in the town where the boats pulled in, and so, when things happened, they had their own safety nets. But sometimes it didn't work, and they had to send a boat to get them, or the children would have to wait in school until a boat could get there. It was a tough life, but it was their life.

"Sophisticated or not, they love to eat crabs and oysters, so there has to be a way we can all get along out there on the water. If they would just ask us to help them, but they think we're fools. Our people have been working these waters forever and there isn't one waterman who couldn't tell you where every cut is and where the crabs are runnin' or the oyster beds are the best. They know it because they've been raised on it. Tell them that, Nellie."

"Maybe you should be the one telling them."

"I've done that, thanks to some good people over there who do care, but now things are different. Seems they don't want to listen and prefer to let this industry die off in favor of foreign markets or government-raised oysters. The plain fact is that it may be cheaper but it's not as good for the folks. Money talks today and ye just can't get people to listen."

"You always know how to spin me up, don't you, Mama? Here I have this fancy education that you and Dad worked so hard to give me, and yet you say it plain and simple and could probably get further with your common sense than I ever can."

"Don't know about that, Nellie. From what I can see, common sense doesn't run wild over there."

Nellie laughed and said, "You're the best. How's Daddy? I miss him so much. I miss seeing him come home after a day on the water and telling us how it was out there. He's such an old salt."

"A stubborn old salt. I about had to hog-tie him this morning to get him to put on a heavier coat. Weather was getting a bit chilly and it began breezin' up. Darned if he wasn't going to listen to me, but then he decided what was best for him."

"You two love each other so much. You both like to growl at one another every day. I think that's how you communicate. No sweet, sloppy stuff for you two. Give him a great big bear hug from me."

"I will do that. Do ye feel better now?"

"Yes, ma'am. Thanks. When this is over, I'm coming home for a good visit. I miss the island and its ways. We just live different from others."

"Yes, we do. It would be nice to have you here for a while, Nellie. Denny keeps askin' for ye."

"He's a sweetheart. You tell him I'll drop by when I get home. His mama makes the best corn chowder, and, just thinking about it, my mouth is watering."

"Be careful, Nellie Ann. I love ye, girl. Bye now."

Nellie sat still for a minute after the call with her mama. She suddenly was awash with homesickness. It wasn't the first time. She felt this way a lot, but she'd always known she had to leave. It was one of the most important things her parents had talked about since she could remember—that she had to get an education, even though that meant leaving the island.

This was a bit different though. She wished her mother were going with her to this hearing. She was so proud of her mama, who had spent her life fighting for the rights of the watermen. And their wives, who spent their lives devoted to their men and the crabs and oysters they brought back each day in their season. Her mother was respected as a woman who told it like it was, and because, when she said it, there was little left to say. Years had gone by, however, and now it needed to be said again before they lost their culture forever. Now it was Frances's daughter who would say the words and hope they stuck and trust that someone, somewhere, would believe and help them and all the commercial fishermen throughout the country. She had to make them understand that this was a real problem that loomed every year.

Nellie couldn't stop the tears rolling down her cheeks as she thought about the daunting task ahead of her. She had to make the case.

And then there was the island—her island—and how she loved it. She would go home for the holiday. She did miss it so much and, at this very moment, she very much missed Denny.

CHAPTER 5

Prue definitely felt awkward asking her boss for this favor, even if it was for Willa. It wasn't the end of the world, but she never liked calling in favors. In D.C., favors were what got you places and you only used them for people other than yourself when you had to. But, when Willa asked for something, it was never frivolous, so she took the shot.

The two young women were tight. Guess you could say best friends. Wasn't hard to understand why. They were both similar in personality and professional drive. They'd met at the same Starbucks when Prue first got to town and was looking for a place to live.

Prue had a job with the handsome and famous bachelor congressman, Charles Armistead Lee. He didn't need much of an introduction; his name said it all. But she was no shrinking violet either. She was the direct descendant of a former president—Warren G. Harding—so they both had a lot of political history behind them. And they were both stubborn as all get out.

When Prue first began her job as special assistant to Lee, many gossiped that they might be having something more than a job in common, but that couldn't be further from the truth. Prue was a woman on a mission and Lee's office was just a stepping-stone to what she really wanted,

When Willa offered to have her stay as a roommate for a while, Prue jumped at the opportunity. She knew who Willa was, loved her novels, and they got along really well. So this was a great way to begin working in D.C.

Willa had been left a good deal of money when her parents were killed, and she'd put it to good work when she'd rented a swanky apartment not far from downtown Washington and the White House. The apartment was very large and afforded them both the space they needed to keep out of each other's hair. It worked beautifully for five months, but then Prue needed to be alone and so did Willa. It was a great place and Willa was a peach to let her stay, but it was time for her to make the next move in her independence.

Prue was keenly aware of the congressman's reputation with women, and, no matter what, she was going to keep this job—and keep away from him. It couldn't ever happen if she wanted really to take her place in Washington one day. She wanted a clean record, something hard to find in the ultimate sin city.

Prue went into her office and set things up for the day, praying the congressman would be in a good mood so she could ask him for the favor. She was in luck because, when he walked in, she could see he was in a very good mood. Must have been a spectacular date the night before. Time to strike while the iron was hot.

"Good morning, Prue. Ready to get started today? I have a lot of notes I want transcribed for that hearing tomorrow. This is going to be an interesting session and I want it to run without a hitch. I want to get this issue resolved going forward."

"I'm ready, Charles." He was less formal with his staff in his office than in public, so the congressman didn't mind being called by his first name when there weren't visitors in the office.

"Good. After you get those papers ready, I've made reservations for lunch, unless you have other plans."

"Lunch? It's just after breakfast."

"I know, but I'm going to take you to a place that needed reservations so I made them. You are free, aren't you?"

"I hope you're not taking me for granted," she teased.

"Good, then it's settled. I'll let you know when I'm ready. Oh, and bring a pad so you can take some notes down while we eat."

"Ah, just what I want to do over lunch. Work. Okay, where are we going? If I may ask?"

"A great new place called Yitzi's. A great delicatessen. Unbelievable food. By the way, this Evans girl looks interesting. Her mother is kind of infamous around here, you know. Apparently she spoke before a committee a ways back and got people all riled up. I hope her daughter isn't like her because I don't intend for that to happen under my watch. These watermen and their families are a rough people and stubborn as mules."

Charles stopped in midsentence and looked at Prue. "Are you listening to me?"

"Oh, yes, I'm listening. The watermen are stubborn as mules. Isn't that what you said?"

"Come on, I've been rattling on. But something is on your mind, so you better say whatever it is."

"Well, as usual you can see right through me and I do have something to ask you, but it can wait."

"No, no, it can't. Ask away and let's get it out and dealt with."

She did love his mild southern drawl. It made him even sexier, if that was possible. No wonder the women flocked to him. "Okay, here goes, but think about it before you say no."

"That's not a good way to start out, Prue."

"I know. Well, anyway, my friend Willa Carpenter—you met her one time?—well, she called me and she wants to go to the hearing tomorrow. I told her it was already standing room only and—"

"Tell her yes. I know we're tight on space, but let her come. She's that famous writer friend of yours."

"Yes, that's her."

"I don't need to worry, do I? You know this subject is important to me and to many powerful people here in Washington. Don't need anything interfering in what I'm trying to do."

She had to think fast or she wasn't going to see Willa in that room tomorrow.

"She's interested in the topic. She read the article in the paper yesterday. I really don't know why but I asked her the same questions you are asking me and she said she just wanted to see this young woman and hear what she had to say. You know writers don't often make sense, Charles. They take a lot of time to create characters. Maybe Helen Evans fits someone she is writing about."

"I'll trust you on this, Prue. You're damn good at your job so you understand the consequences. Where did I meet your friend anyway? As I recall, she's beautiful."

"Very, and you liked her, best I can remember."

"No trouble, Prue. Promise?"

"Promise. And thank you. You really aren't like what they say you are," she teased again.

"What do they say?"

"You know your reputation, Charles. I hear you're one cool customer."

"Yep, that's me. We'll leave in a little while."

As Charles walked back to his office, Prue picked up her phone and called Willa. When she answered, she was short and to the point. "Mission accomplished. Be on your best behavior tomorrow and I'll meet you at the Scotch Bar at The Willard at six o'clock tomorrow evening."

Willa shouted, "You go, girl! Six o'clock it is and I'll be sure to bring a sack full of cash. Thanks! You're the best!"

CHAPTER 6

When someone on the island said they were "going off," they meant they were going to the mainland. It was one of the many expressions that had become part of the lexicon of the people of James Island. When strangers go to the island, it takes them awhile to understand much of what's being said, but, sooner or later, they get enough of it to get by. If they aren't there long enough to do that, which many of them aren't, they just think it's quaint.

The Old English has been with them for generations, dating back to Captain John Smith and his sailors, who ventured out to discover new lands up and down the Atlantic coast and, especially, up and throughout the Chesapeake.

At one time, many islands existed in the Chesapeake, but, today, only two are left still inhabited by this rich and colorful culture. It's also a fact that other island cultures in the southern coastal parts still speak in that same dialect. Some are relatives through marriage down through the years. Some of the families from North Carolina all the way up and into the Chesapeake are related by blood and bound together by their work on the water. Most all are watermen who fish crabs and oysters.

Today Frances was going off to "grub up," another way of saying food shopping, no easy chore when you live on an island. Today's trip would be doubly tough as the holidays were coming and there was a whole lot of food to buy for the special dinners.

"How ye comin', Cap'n Tuck?"

"Morning, Frances. Ye goin' over to get your food for the holidays?"

"Sure am. Don't want to do this but once before the holidays come."

It was only seven thirty in the morning and the boat was ready to leave. Everything got started early on the island. Soon a whole lot of other women showed up to do the same thing as Frances.

"Hey, Frances, how are ye? Haven't seen ye around for a spell. You okay?"

"Sure am, thank ye, Bess. I've been busy what with all the holidays comin'."

"Know what ye mean. It's a mess, isn't it?"

Frances laughed as Cap'n Tuck loosened the ropes and got ready to leave. They all knew another boat wasn't going off for the mainland until the afternoon, so you couldn't be late and miss this one. That's the schedule and you fit your life around it. Besides, their men had already left before the sun came up to head out on the water.

"Hey, Frances, tell me about Miss Nellie. How's she comin' over there?"

"She's doing real good and makes both Jimmy and me so proud. She's going to speak before a congress committee tomorrow. I know she's all tied up about it, but she'll get it done. She's one smart girl."

"You and Jimmy aren't too proud of her, are ye?"

"Not too. She's coming home for Thanksgiving, and I am so thrilled, I don't know what to do."

"Is she going to stop by and see our Denny? He's sweet on her, Frances."

"Those two have been something since they were children, but, sweet or not, he's a waterman and I don't know if Nellie is set on living that life anymore. She grew up with it and she sees how hard it is on a family and all of us."

"True enough, but it's in her blood. You can't get rid of your roots, you know. Break Denny's heart, though, if she didn't come on back to the island."

"I'm not going to tell her any of this, Bess, and ye best not either. Our kids have to work things out for themselves. If it's meant to be, it'll be without our fussin' about it."

"You're right, but, just the same, it would be nice."

Frances laughed with her good friend and said, "Good heaven knows what kind of children they would have if they decided to take up with one another with all our blood running through those poor children. They'd be hellions for sure."

"Probably so, but they'd be so happy."

To change the subject, Frances gathered all her bags and freezer totes and got ready to dock up.

"Do you have a lot to get, Frances?"

"What do ye think? We always have a lot to get. Your island store does all it can, but we can't afford to forget anything. It's a long and expensive trip to the big store if we do."

"That's for sure. I'm so glad my Floyd can still run the store, but it can't do all we need."

"Watch yer step, ladies. The water's rough today and the boat's a-rockin'."

"Like we haven't done this forever, Tuck. What do ye take us for, a bunch of fools who don't know how the water gets when it breezes up?"

Tipping his cap, he said, "Just warning ye, Miss Frances."

Smiling at him, Frances said, "Know ye are. I'll be sure to get the fixings for my sweet potato pie so ye can come around soon and have ye a piece."

"Yours is the best, no doubt about it, Miss Frances. Where did that recipe come from anyway?"

"Don't know. It's older than dirt and I suspect it's come from a way back. Handed down through the generations of folks who came here afore time."

"You might be right about that. I won't forget you made that invitation. That pie of yours wins every time when they have that church bake-off."

"Ye are a mess, Tuck. I'll see you this afternoon. I'm sure we women will weigh yer boat down with all the food we'll be hauling."

"This boat can take it. She's built with the finest white oak around. It's mine as long as I live, and then I want to be buried in the marsh with her."

"Good luck on that. Ye know we aren't supposed to do that anymore, and, besides, your son might have different thoughts."

"I know that but I still have my dreams. She'll go to my son for sure and he'll make good use of her."

As Frances handed him the fare for the trip, she smiled and says, "See ye on the turnaround, Tuck. Thanks for the ride."

Tuck finished tying up his boat as he watched to make sure all the women were safe and on their way. Some of them had family who live in Somerville who would come and get them. They'd moved over to make more money than they could on the water. That was happening more and more lately.

The Tucker family had always run the transportation boat. Twice a day and charters in the summer—it was how they made a living. They were good, decent folk and people relied on them for everything that came and went from James Island, including the mail.

James Island was really a group of four islands, three of which were connected to each other by bridges. Tuckerton—which Frances and Jimmy Evans, among others, called home—was the only one carved out eons ago in a way that made it accessible just by boat. In the beginning, the Tucker family had lived out there by themselves. However, as their family had grown, others also came out to join them. It may seem just a small piece of land to most who visit there, but the people were firmly planted in their traditions and culture, and clannish until they grew to trust you. Trust is an important thing on the island because they all depend on one another for everything.

Today, many Tuckers lived there still and most were waterman, but this part of the Tucker family had always been the mainstay of how one got off and got back on the island. They knew these waters as well as anybody, and they knew boats. Everyone had one, most used for crabbing in the late spring and fall and oystering in winter. It's their lives out there and they darned well have to respect it. When a boat is in trouble, she'll tell you and you best listen or else trouble is to be found

Times were changing out here and Ray Tucker knew all about it. People had left Tuckerton to find work on the mainland; the young people no longer wanted to make a living on the water because they couldn't make near the money they could off island. So, even though it killed them to leave, they had to. Nothing stays the same but, out on James Island, it mostly had. Until now. Yes, Cap'n Tuck had seen and heard it all, and most of it brought a notion of what was to come. And it made him and the others so sad.

Well, I better get a move on here. Have to do my own errands and be back in time to help the women with their food parcels and make sure the kids are all accounted for and on board after their day at school. Yes, I'll hear it all on the way back. Nice that some things never change.

CHAPTER 7

This was going to be a day like no other for Nellie Ann Evans. She'd spent the entire evening before going over a dozen key points she wanted to make at this hearing. She knew she had to be brief because that's what she had been told. Besides, her mother had always taught her that people who go on forever don't know anything and those who say it in a few words know everything.

However, this still wasn't going to be easy, so she decided to do something she'd done all the way through school whenever she'd had to stand up and make a presentation: she tied a rubber band around one of her fingers. Then, whenever she started to wander in her remarks, she would tighten it. Even though she would have the luxury of sitting at a desk for this presentation, she knew this would work. Glad she'd remembered to think of it.

Now for the right outfit. Appearance was important, but, for her, this wasn't so easy. She wasn't one to be fancy, the result of a practical mother and a lack of money. On the island, no one had tons of dollars to throw around, especially if it had been a bad year on the water. Then everyone had to tighten up to make it through until the next fishing season started with its hope for a better catch. However, she had to present well on all fronts and she knew first impressions went a long way. She also knew what the outside world thought of folks even from across the Bay, let alone the islanders. Washington was a town full of elites and smugness ruled, especially when they thought you were less educated than they were. Foolish notions, but that's what ran this place.

A classic camel-colored turtleneck with a slimming black skirt would do perfectly for this occasion. The camel favored her reddish brown hair and the black made her look more slender than she was. She wasn't heavy at all, but she did have a big frame, and so she had learned to work with that. Most Eastern Shore and islander women were built that same way. It was their heritage and in the genes. They were built for the work they did on the farms and beside their husbands in the crabbing shanties. This was an agricultural world, not the world of stuffy folks who had easier physical lives.

"There, that looks good," she said out loud, a pleased smile on her face. "I'm ready to go."

With her briefcase in hand, she slid into the old vehicle she loved: a used Chevy truck. It had been bought with money she'd earned picking crabs the summers leading up to college. It had belonged to a waterman who got a new one. He had taken care of it as if it were a child. Probably had been to him, and now she took care of it the same way. Maybe she wasn't going to arrive in D.C. in a classy upscale car, but what she had to say was heartfelt and that's all that mattered. And she was prepared to do it.

Time to go. Today was not the day to be late.

Willa was up early preparing for the day ahead. She felt happier about going to this hearing than anything she had done for the past few months. She hoped it would go well for the young speaker and prove fruitful for her, too. She had stayed up late into the night researching commercial fishing in this country. Apparently there were many issues facing this industry and the men and women who go out on the water to bring the catches to market. The challenges were many, and, at the moment, some of them seemed a bit too heavy to allow the industry to survive. This was definitely a complicated issue.

She wondered about Helen Evans. She must have real brass to take on the establishment. And she must be fairly brilliant to be chosen to come before a congressional committee. The short newspaper article said she came from an island. Well, that's one you don't hear every day. Wonder if she is savvy on how the games are played in this city. Oh well, this was sure going to be interesting.

The first order of business was to get to the coffee pot. Couldn't do anything without her morning joe. Second, a hot shower. Couldn't do much without that either.

Willa carried the hot cup of coffee into the bathroom, turned on the shower, and hopped in. Her shower was equipped with a huge shelf attached to the tile to hold many items for her enjoyment, one of which was a water-resistant radio. She had to hear the news of the day so she could begin with a twisted stomach. Then she switched off the infighting of the esteemed Congress and turned on music.

Now she was rocking. A little Adele wakes up the sleepiest of heads. Yes, that was better now. "Rumour Has It" sure hit the nail on the head today, because rumor had it she was going to get her head together and she would bet it was going to start at this hearing. And that the very attractive congressman was going to pay attention to her, even if it's just a little. Yep, rumor had it that he was without a gal now, so who knew what the possibilities were on that score? Fact is that a lot of things were going to happen today and Willa couldn't wait. Her hope was that, by day's end, she could say this had been a really, really good day.

The shower was such a good place to think about things. If she were to write a period novel, she might cast Prue as the woman in love with the handsome, dashing southern congressman who was a direct descendant of that famous and romantic character, General Robert E. Lee. And Prue wasn't a slouch either, as, a direct descendant of the late president, Warren G. Harding. True, he'd had a dubious presidency due to the Teapot Dome scandal, but, of late, historians were seeing him in a different light. He'd been the first leader to recognize women's rights and the civil rights of recently freed slaves. Ah, yes, there was a lot there to work with, if only she could get it together in her head.

Quit it, Willa, and get going. What you are going to do is listen to this young woman and figure out if there's something interesting about an island girl who comes to the city to fight for her people. Promising, to be sure.

She couldn't be late today; Capitol Hill hearings didn't wait for anyone.

Fortunately, her entire wardrobe was one that any woman would envy. All classic lines that never went out of style. Swooping her long, blonde hair on top of her head, she pulled on a Donna Karan white blouse and paired it with a Donna Karan black pantsuit. Who didn't love Donna Karan?

One last quick glance in the mirror and Willa said, "Yep, you look just fine. Now it's time to get back in the game."

Nellie arrived at the room thirty minutes before the hearing was to begin. She was still a basket of nerves but wasn't going to let anyone else know that. She kept telling herself she was given this chance for a reason and that reason was to help her people. In fact, to help all the people who lived and worked on the water all around the country's coastal areas. There was no question this was a daunting task, but she could handle it.

She had to, because this might be the only chance someone like her would be allowed to speak. Most of the time the speakers were EPA people or other organizational bureaucrats who were interested in other, more political things for the Bay rather than the fishermen and how they made their living.

A woman approached her. She was older, seemed a bit stiff and a lot stuffy, and had obviously been involved with these sessions for years.

"Good morning. I take it you're Helen Evans? I'm Nancy Bean, the secretary for this hearing today." Nellie immediately got the impression this woman was looking down her nose at her. It evoked thoughts of the stodgy professor at school who had once spoken about the British royalty and told them the way one was to address the Queen was "ma'am as in ham." That description fit Ms. Bean to a T.

"Yes. I am, ma'am, and it's nice to meet you. I go by the name Nellie."

"Oh, how quaint. Okay then, Nellie it is." She pointed to the table at the front of the room. "You can sit over there. It should give you enough room for all your papers and resource items."

Nellie didn't appreciate her attitude at all but decided to be what she called southern polite. "Thank you, ma'am."

Nancy got the message loud and clear. She pointed again. "Nellie"—she said the name as if it were going to soil her fingers—"you can hand any of your visual presentation materials to that man over there. He collects them first and makes sure of the order you want them in. That is, of course," she added, "if you even have any."

"Yes, I do have a few. Is the hearing running on time?"

The older woman stared at her. "Why, yes, dear, my hearings always do."

Again that attitude thing from her. *Be on guard, Nellie. These folks are all wound tight and could snap at any second. To them, you're a country bumpkin.*

"Thank you, Nancy." With that Nellie held her head high and made sure she gave the woman the look that said, I can handle you, this hearing, and anything else you care to throw at me. "I think I'll get on with my preparations."

Score one for the bumpkin.

Nellie went off to get set up, totally unaware of Willa sitting in the back of the room watching the entire exchange with the older woman. If only she could have known how impressed Willa Carpenter was with the way she had handled herself, it would have given her the confidence she needed.

Willa removed a pad and pencil from the worn-out briefcase that had been on so many writing expeditions, she couldn't even remember them all. It had been the last gift from her father, on her eighteenth birthday. He had given it to her and said, "Happy birthday, sweetheart. Use this for all the things you will write." She'd been astonished that he had known that her secret passion was writing. She'd thought she had hidden that from them. Parents: they seemed to know everything. If only they had lived to see that that was true.

Willa was still steamed about her tape recorder. They'd taken it and told her she could pick it up on her way out. Security was tough in this town. Not like the days when she was a little girl and would come to see the White House and Capitol, walking through the halls with hardly anyone noticing that she and her family were there. Yes, the whole town was pretty buttoned up now, since 9/11 had changed everything forever in this country. We were determined never to have something like that happen again. So her recorder was a small price to pay, she guessed, but, still, it was hard to really grasp the tones of voices when you were writing it down and not recording it for later use, too. Oh well, she was in this hearing at any rate and that was due to Prue. She'd promised her there would be no problems. And that meant for Willa to behave. No small order.

Sitting in the back of a room was a good place if you wanted to notice everything, which was the whole point for her. The only one not there yet seemed to be the ringmaster of this circus. She had attended other hearings and they were always the same—one person leading the discussion and then all the others talking longer than they should just to make their points. It really was boring, but maybe today it wouldn't be. This young presenter was so different; she looked young and fresh and a little naïve. That fact bothered Willa. This was a blood sport to them, and they loved playing it as long as they weren't the people with the blood on them at the end of the game.

Finally the door at the front of the room, behind the committee seating, opened and out walked Mr. Stud. He was something to behold. A debonair dresser, he made quite the appearance. *Stop it, Willa. This is business. Well, a girl can look, can't she?*

He shook all the right hands and smiled to the other members of the committee. Then he walked over to greet Helen Evans and have a brief word or two with her. He had a gentle manner and handled the nervous girl with great aplomb. He was good at what he did. Impressive.

Suddenly he looked up and seemed to catch Willa staring right at him. A look of recognition crossed his face as he left the speaker's side and began walking straight toward . . . *me. Good Lord, here we go. My heart is jumping around like a schoolgirl's would be. What's wrong with you, Willa? Calm. Down. Remember—behave.*

Extending his hand, he reached out to Willa. "So we meet again, Miss . . . Carpenter, I believe?"

He really could take a girl's breath away. *Say something, you idiot; don't just sit here.* She rose to her feet and, all of a sudden, everything in her briefcase fell out all over the floor. *Great move, Willa. This should impress him.*

"Hello, Congressman Lee."

He just stood there, smiling with those perfect teeth of his.

Willa added, "Thank you for allowing me to come today. I really appreciate it."

"It's your girlfriend you should thank. She wouldn't take no for an answer."

"That's my Prue. But, really, thank you."

"My pleasure. Perhaps one of these times we meet, we can do it over a cup of coffee."

Did he really just say that? Was he intimating a date?

Willa flashed her best smile. The one that took them in. "I don't see why not."

"I really have to get this hearing going or that woman sitting over there will kill me. Nice to see you today."

As he walked away, he pointed to the woman who had been speaking to Helen before. She seemed to command everyone's attention. Must be highly respected. And, by the way, did he really say he'd like to have a cup of coffee? Can't wait to tell Prue that one tonight over cocktails.

When the congressman found his way to his seat—while Willa was picking up everything that had fallen out of her briefcase—he called the hearing to order.

Show time.

During the opening statement, Willa began writing down Helen's physical attributes. She was really quite a remarkable-looking young woman. She had auburn hair of medium length. Willa couldn't see her eyes but guessed them to be brown. She had a solid and large frame. Came from the work she did on the water, no doubt.

She had seen fishermen before; she'd grown up on water, too. Mystic, Connecticut, was one of those special towns on what was considered part of the New England coast. It wasn't Maine or Massachusetts, but it still had the look of those small towns up there. The Connecticut lobstermen had this same look of wholesomeness and good clean air. Helen was very much from this kind of stock.

After Charles had finished his statement, Helen was introduced. When it was time for her opening statement, she quickly said that, although her birth name was Helen, everyone knew her as Nellie. Saying that seemed to calm her down sufficiently to walk into the fire. The only odd thing was that she had a rubber band on one of her fingers. It must be a fetish for good luck, Willa thought. Then Nellie Evans began to speak.

> I am pleased and honored to be with you this morning to talk about a subject that is near and dear to all our hearts. Whether you are from a big city or live along our coasts, the one thing all people love is to eat the wonderful variety of fish and seafood that is brought in every day from the oceans and the bays along the coastlines of this great nation.
>
> I hope today will begin a serious conversation that will lead to a better understanding of the commercial fishermen and the industry they support. Each and every one of them risk their lives every day to go out on the waters and bring their bounty back to your tables. You and I may be from different walks of life but we have much in common as one nation and one people. If we cannot sit down and discuss these differences and some of the issues that are bothering us, we will never see eye to eye on the very thing that is so important to so many of us.
>
> As we seek to open this topic which has been discussed before without resolve by many, let us promise that, this time, we will seek to try to dig deeper so we can have a positive outcome.

For the next hour and a half, Nellie Evans spoke on behalf of the water community, addressing the way-too-many regulations being handed out to the watermen of the Chesapeake and fishermen in all states. Some were good, but many were over the top and hurting the watermen. They were born to fish, not fill out paper work and do things that seemed unnatural to them.

And so it went, back and forth, with the panel asking questions they already knew the answers to and Nellie responding in plain English they really didn't want to hear. The battle lines were drawn. Environmental speakers wouldn't give an inch, fiercely defending their positions no matter what Nellie said in response. At one point, things got really heated until Congressman Lee toned it down.

Nellie stood her ground, and, for someone who was a novice at this, she certainly had a command of the issues that left the panelists hunting for words. Finally, they came to a standstill and so the hearing came to an end. No blood had been drawn, but no one could walk away without having a lot to think about.

Willa sat there stunned at the breadth of knowledge and the grit of this young girl. She was someone to be reckoned with, especially as she passionately told stories of her times out on the water with her father and and the hours they had spent bringing in the crabs or, in the wintertime,oysters. She definitely knew her stuff and was very determined. Willa loved that in her. But it was her personal testimony that drew her to Nellie like a moth to the flame. Nellie spoke about her home with such love and conviction. There was something more about her and her people that Willa had to know. It was time to meet her and try to speak to her out of the glare of this place.

Nellie was packing up her material as Willa approached.

"Excuse me, Miss Evans. I am Willa Carpenter and I wonder if you would be able to speak to me in private?"

Nellie looked up suddenly and, with a look of utter amazement, said, "I know you. I read your books, I think. Are you *that* Willa Carpenter?"

Willa smiled. "Guess I can't hide anywhere, can I?"

"You most certainly cannot. Your books have been my companion on many occasions. Sure, I would love to talk with you. Where do you want to go?"

There was such a young-girl quality about this Nellie that was so refreshing. "How about we walk out of here together and let me pick something up that is being held for me, then grab a cup of coffee right down the hill at the art museum snack shop? I don't know about you, but I don't feel quite ready yet for lunch."

"That would be great. I'm ready; let's go."

Willa felt something shifting around inside. She was beginning a new chapter in her life. Where it would lead was anyone's guess, but this felt right.

The special blend coffee tasted wonderful and was much appreciated after the hearing. Nellie ordered tea; obviously that was her drink of choice to settle the nerves.

"Would you mind if I turned on my recorder, Nellie? It helps me remember the important stuff."

"Well, I don't know if anything important is going to be said right now. I think I'm all out of important for today."

"I hear you. That certainly was your baptism by fire. First time, huh?"

"First and last, I think. I said what had to be said but it didn't go near far enough. Needs something if there ever is another time. I don't feel it was impassioned enough."

"Believe me, it was plenty impassioned." Willa stopped for a sip of coffee and looked around. "This museum is really nice. I haven't been here in a long time."

"I haven't ever been here. The only museum I have gone to here is the one on American history. I love it there but always wonder why there isn't anything about watermen or the life and times of the fishing industry. It's been with us since we came here."

"First of all, let me get this straight. You call your fishermen 'watermen' and not fishermen. I don't understand that."

"Yes, I know. Most people don't know what a waterman is. They are the men who go out and harvest crabs, oysters, and fish in the Bay. They don't go out in the ocean. They stay to the brackish waters of the Bay, the rivers, and the cuts in the marsh. They also trap muskrats in the wintertime. They make some powerful good eating."

Willa began to turn green at the very thought of eating a rodent. "Good God, tell me they don't do that."

"Why, yes, and they're considered a delicacy to folks back home. Watermen all over the country eat 'em."

"You know something, Nellie? Your speech changes when you talk about your home."

Nellie laughed. "I suppose it does. I roll straight back into it when I talk or think of home."

"It sounds like it's kind of from the past. I like it even if I don't understand all of it. You miss it a lot, don't you?"

"Sometimes it hurts how much I miss it, but I got my education and that was as important to me as it was my parents."

"I know your parents must be so proud. Are you one of the few young people who went away to get an education?"

"That's a polite way of asking if most of the people on the island are educated or *just* watermen."

OMG. Willa knew she had hurt the girl's feelings. "No, Nellie, that's not what I meant at all. I just wondered how many of the young people left the island to go on with their pursuit of higher education. I certainly didn't mean to imply that the islanders were ignorant. I get the distinct feeling it's quite the opposite. There are way too many people with degrees down their sleeves who can't find their way out of a paper bag."

Nellie giggled at that one. "Let me tell you this, Willa. I have been over here at the University of Maryland for four years. This year I got real lucky to get into one of the marine research centers associated with the college. That was a real shock to me. I mean, you have to be at the top of your class to do that, and I was, but it was still no small achievement on my part.

"Having said that, I need you to know that most of the people I am working with are really smart, but they have nothing on the people where I come from. The islanders have something in short supply in the outside world and that's common sense. They have natural instincts that come from living on an island and being surrounded by water. In one sense, you grow up fast to the ways of nature and how it can tell you things and how it can hurt you. In another, you grow up a lot slower to the ways of the world. And is that so bad?"

Willa took in every word and watched how Nellie expressed herself. There was such a genuine and honest quality to her. She was a complicated woman and yet, at the same time, so simple.

"I get it, Nellie. I really do. City folks live differently from country folks, but that's not a bad thing, nor does it make one better than the other. They're just different. And I, for one, can't even imagine a life lived surrounded by water."

"It's a whole different world out there. I'm glad I'm going home day after tomorrow for Thanksgiving and that this presentation is behind me now. I need to touch base with my reality, and that lies out on the beautiful water of the Chesapeake."

A broad smile crossed Willa's face. There was so much to learn about these people and how they lived and how they spoke. "I envy you, Nellie. You have a home and you have family and you love both with all your heart. It's truly special."

Nellie caught the tone in Willa's voice that said sad. What could she have said to bring this on? "You have a home and a family. Where is it, Willa? I mean, didn't you say you came from Mystic, Connecticut?"

Small puddles formed in Willa's eyes as she turned the recorder off. Now it was Nellie who felt as if she had said something wrong. "I'm so sorry, Willa. I didn't mean to pry."

"You're not prying. I asked you questions and you have every right to ask me some. I'm thirty-plus years old and have written eight best-selling novels. I really have the world by the tail and a future that's very bright, but I don't have half of what you have . . . anymore."

Willa stopped for a big breath, and then went on. "I lived in Connecticut, so you see I grew up by the sea, too, and I used to watch the men go out in their small boats. They were mostly lobstermen but they all have a kindred spirit, don't they?

"I didn't pay too much attention to them when I was young. It was just a way of life there and kids don't pay close attention to detail. It's their home and they take it all for granted. Your talking about your island and how much you love it brought back memories. It's okay, though; it's good to have memories."

Nellie wasn't sure if she should ask anything more. She could tell she was on tender ground with all this talk of family and home. And yet she had a feeling that, despite all Willa Carpenter's fame, something was bothering her that went deep.

But Willa kept talking. "You asked me a question and I want to answer it all for you. My parents were killed in a car accident when I was eighteen. It was a rough time for me. and. as you see by my emotions, you never really get over that. But I had a wonderful and caring aunt and uncle who took me in and saw to it that I went to college and was able to fulfill my dream of one day being like my mother: a writer."

Nellie felt so awful. She wanted to say so much and yet her natural instinct told her not to say much at all.

"That's so sad, Willa, but you have really made a something of yourself. Your parents would be so proud of you if they were still here. Your books aren't just romance novels; they take us readers places and make us feel emotions we never thought we had. That counts for so much. In a way, Willa, you remind me a lot of my mother. While she would tell you that she's just a plain old island woman, she has inner strength beyond anything I've ever seen—until I met you. Who knows? Maybe your parents are closer to you than you know."

"You have no idea how close you are to being right on that score, Nellie. I feel as if my mother is always guiding me. And about your mother? I hear she is one strong-minded lady, and I so respect that, when someone has something they are passionate about. Heard she caused quite a stir when she came here once upon a time."

"Yes, she did. She's a force of nature! Nobody is like Frances Ruth Evans. My daddy is a mild-mannered and quiet man whom I adore, but my mom is where I go when I need advice. She is wise beyond wise. I think she's been here before, to tell you the truth."

"Some people are like that. They're old souls and seem to come into this world just knowing things. Even though my parents aren't here, I feel them around me all the time. Did you know that my father wrote and illustrated cartoons for the newspapers?"

"No, I didn't, Willa. You sure have some powerfully artistic genes swimming around in you."

"Never heard it put like that before, but you're right. We both have strong genes."

Nellie glanced down at her watch and let out a gasp. "Will you look at what time it is? Speaking about my mother, I remembered I have to call her or she'll shoot me."

Willa looked at the wall clock and couldn't believe the two of them had been talking for nearly an hour and a half. "Good heavens, I have to go, too. Thank you so much for your time, Nellie." She stood to leave.

"Wait, Willa, I have an idea. Don't laugh at me, but I want you to come on out to the island for Thanksgiving. I mean it. The only way you're going to understand everything is by seeing it and living it for a few days."

Willa sat back on her chair and let a breath out. "Oh, I can't do that, Nellie."

"Why? Do you have somewhere else to go?"

"Well, yes, sort of. I mean . . . ."

"Then I won't take no for answer. I'll tell Mama tonight that we are having a guest. She'll freak out when I tell her who it is. She loves your books, too, but Daddy doesn't know she reads romances."

"Stop, Nellie, I really can't do this. I can't just impose on your family."

Nellie sat back and looked at Willa for a minute. "You don't want to come?"

"Oh, no, it's not that at all. I would just feel a bit strange, you know. I wouldn't know anyone."

"You know me, and, if you know me, you already know everyone. Trust me on this, Willa. Come and stay with us. Let us show you our island. Of course it would take far longer than a couple of days for you to understand everything, but it's a start. Besides, then you'll know if there's something out there you want to write about."

Willa didn't have any more excuses. She was beaten. "Okay. I'll do it. But how do I do it?"

"Give me your e-mail and I'll send you directions. It's easy really. Oh, I am so excited! You're going to have the time of your life."

Willa wasn't sure about that, but it would be the most unique thing she had ever done. Oh no, she thought. How would she ever explain this to Prue? And thinking of Prue reminded her she had to get going.

Willa dug into her briefcase, then handed her card to Nellie."I've lost my mind, but I guess I'm up for this adventure.

"You won't want to come back, Willa. I promise you that."

To say good-bye, they hugged each other.. Willa wondered, how do these things happen in life? One minute a stranger, the next a friend.

"It's been wonderful, Nellie. Thank you so much for talking with me, and now here we are friends. Funny how that works."

"Life is full of great surprises if we are open to them. See you day after tomorrow, Willa."

It was the beginning of drive time as she made her way home and the streets were jammed up, but that was D.C. starting at this hour of the day. Overcoming one's angst about it was one of the first lessons you had to learn. It came with living in a big city.

Suddenly Willa wondered, did I make the wrong turn back there by saying I would go out to this island with this young girl I really know nothing about?

The oddest feeling came over her and she started speaking to her parents. "Are you two up to your old mischief, rearranging my life? I've got to trust you on this one because I sure am a little scared to do this. For first-offs, you know I'm terrified of the water. I guess I sort of left that out of the conversation with this new friend of mine, but she would have been so disappointed. And, if you two are at work here, then you want me to go, right?

"Okay, okay, I get it. I'm going, Mom and Dad. How I'll manage the boat is another story. You'll have to help me on that one. I'll take the Bonine and pray like hell that I make it."

She edged forward with the rest of the traffic in her lane. "Miss you, too. Hang with me, won't you? Your baby girl down here has lost her mind and can't seem to find it."

CHAPTER 8

You know there are just some people who can't be on time, and Willa was one of them. No use yelling at herself for it; it was in her nature. Prue, on the other hand, was fanatical about being on time—even early—but she knew all about Willa and accepted it, as friends do.

After teatime with Nellie, Willa had gone straight home and begun reading on the topic at hand. There was so much to learn, and it was clearly going to take a long time to get the gist of what was really going on. But now it was time to lighten up. As it was, she was late, and Prue's nails would be tapping away on the counter at the Scotch Bar inside The Willard. That little habit took more than friendship to accept.

Willa's cell went off the minute she stepped out the door. She knew who was calling.

"Willa, you better not still be home."

"Well, not exactly, sweetie."

"How not exactly are you?"

"Oh, I would say ten minutes, give or take."

"You better have a good story, Willa girl. I'm ordering you an extra-smooth cosmo as we speak."

"Have I told you lately that I love you?"

"Yeah, yeah, yeah. Get here soon, but just be careful."

"Relax. By the time I arrive, you'll have every guy at the bar drooling over you. Save one for me."

"Good-bye, Willa." Prue ended the conversation with the look of someone who couldn't quite put her finger on something going on with her friend—but determined, tonight, to squeeze it out of her.

By the time Willa walked through the majestic doors of The Willard Hotel, she was out of breath and ready for that drink. Walking into the Scotch Bar, Washington's hottest little place for political and celeb types, she nodded her head. Yep, the girlfriend had men all around her. She couldn't blame them. Prue was a raven-haired beauty with that perfect milk white skin. A stunner.

When Prue saw her, she waved her over.

Willa said, "Well, I see you took my advice."

Turning slightly, Prue picked up Willa's cosmo off the bar. "I think this will help you right out."

"Sure will," Willa said, taking the tasty libation from Prue's cold fingers. After a sip, Willa purred. "Now this is wonderful."

The guys laughed and one of them apparently decided he liked this lady.

"Hi there. What was your name?"

"Willa. What's yours?"

"Ted. You know you look awfully familiar to me, and what is a 'Willa'?"

I don't believe this guy. The "look awfully familiar" line went out with Granny's drawers.

"Well, first answer is, a Willa is a Wilhelmina. And, second, you may recognize me if you visit Barnes & Noble or other bookstores often."

The scruffy, sandy-haired guy looked confused. *Geesh, where are the rough-and-tumble guys who used to hang out here?*

"I get it now; I know where I've seen you. You write those girlie books."

Oh, God, he didn't say that, did he?

Before Willa could sock him in the face, Prue dug her fingers into Willa's arm, said good-bye to the lot of them, and steered Willa over to the table she had reserved.

"Was the look on my face that telling, Prue?"

"Yep. They really were nice guys though."

"Nice if we were in high school maybe. What do they do in this town?"

"Well, one of them is a page in the Senate and I didn't have time to hear about the rest of the roosters."

"Cocks, more like it."

"Willa! You really don't like men very much, do you?"

"Not men like them, I don't. Ye gods, Prue."

"I hear you looked pretty nice today."

"And where did you hear that?"

"Where do you think? My boss, that's where."

"Oh. Him," Willa said teasingly. "He did come all the way to the back of the room to say hello. I thought that was special."

"I think he's taken with you, Willa."

"Don't get your hopes up, Miss Matchmaker. I'm way too busy right now."

"You can't tell me you would turn him away if he landed on your doorstep one night."

Willa gave a devilish kind of smile and replied, "Well, I might take him in for a while. You know, it's that rescue instinct of mine."

"You're bad, Willa. But I do think he's attracted to you. Maybe going forward, huh?"

"Well, right now, going forward with anything would be nice."

Prue looked at her friend seriously. "What's eating at you anyway? I mean you've really been out of it lately."

"I know and I'm sorry, Prue. You shouldn't have to pay the price when your girlfriend loses her mind."

"What do you mean?"

"Writer's block. It hit when I was trying to come up with a new novel. Nothing. I mean absolutely a blank wall."

"This isn't good. Whatcha going to do about that?"

"Take a break away for a while."

"Well, that usually helps everyone. I'll see to it we all leave you alone when you come out for Thanksgiving."

"I'm not coming, Prue." Willa held up her hands in defense. "Please don't be mad at me. I'm going to an island."

"An island? Which one?"

"All right, Prue, I'm going out to James Island."

"Start talking to me, Willa, before my temper blows up."

The waiter served another round while Willa mustered up the courage to explain to her friend about this change of plans. Then he asked if they wanted another round served before they ordered. Prue took over.

"We'll order now. Ready, Willa?"

Willa looked at the young, handsome server and said, "Bring me a petite filet, rare. Nothing else."

Prue shot her a quizzical look.

"I need something rare and manly."

"Then you should have gone for the big strip."

Willa looked back up at the server and said, "She's right. Bring me the largest strip you have with the moo still in 'em."

The waiter didn't answer, just wrote it down. Prue's order was a whole lot easier: a Caesar salad with grilled chicken. He shot away from the table as if he were on fire.

"Okay, Willa. Why James Island?"

"I got an invitation from that sweet young presenter this afternoon."

Prue leaned back in her chair and said, "Oh, this is going to be good."

"Yes, it is actually. I went up to her after the hearing and we got to talking and one thing led to another and before I knew it, she asked me to go out there for Thanksgiving."

"Mother and Father will be so disappointed, but, if it's something you feel you must do, then go. How are you going to handle your fear of water, Willa? Island are surrounded by them, and you have to get there by boat."

"I know that and haven't dealt with the water thing, but I have to go. Something is propelling me out there. I won't know anything about that culture if I don't go."

Prue stopped for a minute, then said, "Why do you want to know anything about that culture? You were that taken with it from hearing her talk?"

"Yes, I was, and there might be something out there that will jog my mind and get me to writing something—"

"Hold on a minute, Willa. You promised me you wouldn't do anything like you're thinking."

"I know that, Prue, and I won't hurt you. At first I thought it was all about the fishing and the issues. But it's not. There's something so much bigger out there. I know it. That's what I have to hunt down."

"You could get me fired, damn it, Willa."

"You're not going to get fired, Prue. Don't get all spun up."

"It's not your job on the line, and you know I can't have any slipups."

"It's okay. Really it is, Prue."

Prue trusted her friend, but things happen. "I'm going to miss you terribly over the holiday."

Willa touched Prue's hand. "I'm going to miss you, too. I adore your parents, but tell them I'll come out another time. Ohio isn't that far, you know. We can take a long weekend."

"Oh, all right. I'll bring you back a whole cooler of leftovers."

"I'd like that. Your family has the best side dishes, especially that vegetable pudding thing."

"You mean the corn casserole?"

"That's the one. Really, Prue, everything comes along in our lives for a reason, and meeting and talking with Nellie Evans was one of those things. I know it. I don't know what I'm headed into, but it's out there."

Dinner arrived, and, between sipping drinks and eating, not much else was said. At the end of the meal, Willa gasped for air. "That was the best steak ever, and the moo is now mooing in my stomach. I'm stuffed."

"It was quite a chunk of beef, I'll say that, Willa. And you ate it all."

Willa looked down at the empty plate. "Bad girl, Willa." She chuckled, then said, "I have to shove off, Prue. Remember, this one's on me; I don't welsh on anybody."

Prue smiled. "I have to get going, too. I have some last-minute things to clear up tomorrow before I leave. Be careful, love, and I want a full report when you return."

"You're on, and tell Mr. Handsome to call me after the holidays."

"Think you're interested, too."

"Not really, but he did say we should go out for coffee and you know I never turn down a Starbucks."

"You're impossible, Willa, but I love you. Thanks for dinner."

CHAPTER 9

The sun wasn't up as Willa walked to the kitchen to get a cup of hot tea. Again, she was scolding herself for the one too many drinks she had enjoyed the night before. Why don't we ever learn?

She took the tea and plopped on the sofa in her living room. She really loved this place. It was elegant without screaming ostentatious. It was one of those ritzy addresses within walking distance to everything, including her beloved Willard Hotel. It was big enough to have company but not too big that it overwhelmed her. Yes, it was perfect.

Her building was a mix of interesting people and she loved that, too. Many nights she would go down to the lobby and keep the night doorman, Harold, company. She learned about everyone in the building and what went on. He loved the company and she loved the stories. He came on at six o'clock and didn't go home until after midnight. He had worked for the FBI, always on the inside, at headquarters, and, after many years, retired in good standing. But when his wife died, it had broken his heart, and, after moping around for a long time, he decided to get a job to make his nights go by faster. Harold was a special man, and he made her feel safe in many ways. She could tell she made him feel pretty special, too.

The healing effects of the tea were kicking in now and she was coming back to life. Was she crazy going to a place she'd never been before with a girl she doesn't really know? Why did she say yes? She should have just gone home with Prue like she always did. But, then again, she liked this girl immediately, and there was something about Nellie's innocent approach to life that intrigued her. She wanted to meet her mother. Boy, she has to be some lady! Raised on an island and yet courageous enough to stand on equal footing with the politicians. Wow! That's something. Talk about spunk. Easy to see where Nellie got her logical mind from. It would be okay. It was going to be an inspiring weekend. Holidays were always the worst, so going to this island was just what she needed.

Willa said aloud, "Something's out there for me, isn't it?" She stopped, then started up again. "Oh, I really have to stop this running dialogue with myself! Do I do this because it's my way of feeling like my parents are still here? Willa, stop this. You have to start writing again. That's how you escape. Face up to it once and for all: they're not coming back. Now go to that island."

Nellie had said to meet her at the dock and she couldn't miss it because you just went straight on the main road and, if you didn't stop, you'd go right into the water.

However, before finding Somerville and any dock, Willa had to go over a big bridge, and not your average, run-of-the-mill big bridge, because people spoke about it with frantic terms like "ye gods" and "hope I can do it." Like it or not, she had no choice, and, if there was something over on that island that could help her jog back her literary being, she was going over that bridge with bells on.

Just as her confidence was running on high, she made a slight turn in the road and there it was: the behemoth of the Chesapeake, staring her right in the face. Maybe this wasn't a good idea after all. Her hands began to sweat and that old black magic started to work its way straight through her body. *Good God, I can't do this. I know I can't do this. Help!*

Inching her way to the tollbooth due to a traffic backup was not exactly what she needed right now.

Think, dear girl. You just have to do this and then you're good to go. Think about what makes you feel good and free and then it won't be so bad.

She made it through the tollbooth. Now there was no way out; she had to go forward. Gulls were swooping and careening above the bridge. She loved them. *Concentrate on the gulls, Willa.* They were birds with attitude and she liked that. Reminded her of herself. "Okay, birds, lead the way over."

And they did. They did indeed. She opened the windows and let the air flow through the car, which also made her feel ever so much better. And then she popped in some Adele and shouted, "Let 'er rip."

She drove like a bat out of hell thanks to now unimpeded traffic flow, and, as she looked out on the Chesapeake, she felt herself drawn to it in a strange way. It was speaking to her with an overwhelming feeling of . . . yes, inclusion. It said she was wanted over here. It kept moving her forward without fear until she was off the bridge and onto the Eastern Shore. It was wonderful, and, as each bend in the road came, she was being hurled into another world. She felt free and at peace. Nothing was beyond her reach.

What had happened to her? Did some spell befall her on the way across? Maybe. Or maybe her mom and dad really were still around and looking down on her. Whatever, she was grateful for the help. She was really feeling so free and wonderful and then she remembered: she had to make a phone call. That changed her entire mood, but she had to make it.

"Hi, Kit," Willa said, trying to sound happy when the diva answered her phone. Didn't she ever leave her office? Her joy was definitely over.

"Why, Willa, how lovely to hear from you. Where are you? I can hear birds squawking. Are you on a beach?"

"Not exactly. I'm on the Eastern Shore."

"Should I even ask?"

"You can, but I'm not sure you'll like it or understand it."

"Willa, what's going on with you? You're avoiding me like the plague and there can be only one reason for that. You don't have a book and you haven't even started one. Am I on the right track?"

Willa pulled to the side of the road to talk to Kit. She didn't need a ticket to start off the holiday, that was for sure. Speaking with Kit was bad enough. But she had to be open and honest with her and let the chips fall where they may, like it or not.

"Yes, Kit, you are. I have nothing to give you and may not for a while."

There was a decidedly pregnant pause at the other end of the phone. Kit was not amused.

Finally breaking the silence, Kit said, "Let's stop playing games, shall we? What's going on, Willa? You told me you were working on a book. Were you lying to me?"

"I wasn't exactly lying. I was onto something and just wasn't in the mood to share it at the moment. Besides, I have a far more serious problem going on right now. I have writer's block, Kit. I am totally jammed up. It's never happened before and nothing is coming right now." There. She'd said it.

Kit didn't miss a beat. "That's terrible, Willa. Why didn't you tell me right off? Every writer gets it sooner or later. You've been banging out novels for years and your brain clearly is in retreat. It actually can make you insane."

Well, that wasn't exactly what Willa had wanted to hear, but it wasn't the screaming and yelling she had thought would happen.

"I'm sorry, Kit. I just couldn't admit this to anyone. I've been trying everything but nothing has worked, so I'm going away for the holiday weekend. I think it may help."

"Smart move, Willa. I think it's exactly what's called for. I tell you what: don't worry about anything. It will come back, and, when it does, your next book will be as successful as the others. Have a good time and be in touch soon."

With that Kit hung up. Nothing more, nothing less. She was gone. Willa sat there, stunned. The woman had all the answers and fancy footwork, didn't she? In one breath, she's spewing fire like the dragon she is, and then, in the next, she is being syrupy sweet. Go figure. Willa sure couldn't, and, at this point, especially couldn't allow her to interfere with whatever was going on with her. She's a fabulous publisher, but she can cut through you like a knife in hot butter. Willa didn't need any more pressure and Kit had picked up on that.

Willa took a deep breath and pulled back out on to the highway. Kit was either being clever, or she meant it. Didn't matter; Willa was back on her way. Putting the windows up as she now felt a bit chilled, she shouted out, "I still don't like you, Kit Winthrop, and, when I find my story, we will talk again. This time on *my* terms."

CHAPTER 10

Thank heavens for GPS. No matter what people say, you gotta have it when you don't have a clue where you're going and you're the only one in the car.

Willa didn't know why she hadn't thought more about this trip. If you go to a land where the Bay is on one side and the ocean on the other, wouldn't it stand to reason that there would be a whole lot of bridges, rivers, streams, and marshland? Didn't matter now, though, because she was doing this and nothing was going to stop her now. Nothing could be any bigger, any taller, or more daunting than what she had already crossed a while back. Good girl!

Two-and-a-half hours later, a sign greeted her: Welcome to Somerville.

"Well, I'll be damned. I made it."

Willa hadn't even finished mumbling those words when she saw the water to her right. Her GPS said to keep heading straight but she had to see this.

She made a right turn and pulled over at a small playground. She jumped out, camera ready. The first thing she noticed was the slight smell of earth. It was wonderful. Or perhaps she was smelling the marsh grasses as they lapped up the water from the Bay. Walking a bit farther, she started snapping away and got a few impressive shots of the marsh going out to the water. "This is beautiful," she said, standing there taking it all in. She had a feeling something much bigger was waiting for her. And that she'd better get on now or Nellie would give up on her and she'd miss the boat.

She drove down Somerville's main street, taking it all in, noticing that there had been a vibrant community here once upon a time, but now it was what she would call quaint. Old buildings with stories behind their bricks and shingles . . . shipbuilding yard with hundreds of wire traps of some kind . . . she was in another world. And, although she felt slightly intimidated by it, there was also a calmness inside her and she sort of felt akin to it all. She didn't know why—but then she didn't know why she had agreed to any of this in the first place.

The dock was straight ahead of her and she heard the last direction from the aggravating voice on her GPS: "Now continue straight for a quarter mile and you will be at your destination."

There was Nellie, waving to her. Eureka!

"Hey, Willa. I thought you might have chickened out."

Willa jumped out of her car, and walked up the steps onto the dock to greet her new friend.

"Hi, Nellie. I thought about it, but I wouldn't want your mom to get mad because she made so much food and her guest didn't show up."

Nellie laughed, then said, "You can't leave your car here; there's no long-term or overnight parking. But don't worry. You and I are going to drive over to my Aunt Rita's house and park it there. "

"Oh! It's not an imposition?"

"Not at all, When folks come over to see us, we always use Auntie's house to park the cars."

"Oh, okay."

Nellie hopped in Willa's car and they drove a few blocks east of the docks and pulled around the side of an old, clapboard home. It didn't look so well taken care of on the outside, and Willa wasn't exactly comfortable leaving her fairly new car there.

"Are you sure, Nellie?"

"Come on, Willa. Once you meet Aunt Rita, you won't have any questions at all."

Willa followed Nellie up the creaky steps and knocked on the front door. It opened and there stood Aunt Rita.

"Why, you come on in, honey. I have some food for ye to take over. And this must be the famous Willa Carpenter you said was going over for the holiday."

Willa extended her hand and said, "Nice to meet you."

"I have read one of your books and loved it. You sure know all about love and you're so young. Away ahead of yourself, aren't ye?"

Willa picked up on the 'ye.' She knew that the folks here had their own way of saying things. "Thank you, I'm glad you enjoyed the book. Which one was it?"

"*The Lady in Waiting.* I always wanted to read another one, but I was lucky to read that one. I don't have much time for reading."

"Well, that was one of my favorites, too."

"I sure am honored to have ye here. Now you'll park your car out back. No one will bother it, and please make yourself comfortable. I have to get those pies for you-all to take over. Tell your mom, Nellie, that I'll be over tomorrow on the early boat, and I'll help her get the food out."

"I sure will, Aunt Rita. What kind of cake did you make?"

"Ye know I always make my favorite lemon one, and your mama will make the one everyone in these parts shouts about. Have to say she makes the best sweet potato pie."

Nellie looked at Willa and said, "I'm getting hungry with all this talk of cakes and pie."

So was Willa. In fact, with the smells in that house, she could have eaten a whole pie right then.

"Come on to the kitchen then. I'll cut you a slice of another one I made. Chocolate. That'll keep you on the way over. Now, Nellie, do ye have everything you need?"

"Sure do, Aunt Rita. Thanks so much. I've really missed being home."

Rita looked at her and said, "Your mama and daddy have missed you something terrible, but don't go a-telling them I told you that."

Willa enjoyed watching Nellie and her aunt. She loved her aunt, too, but it wasn't like what she was seeing here. She and her aunt weren't nearly as informal. He aunt was a wonderful woman, but she didn't show much emotion.

"Hadn't we better be getting back to the boat?"

"You bet, Willa. Once Aunt Rita gets everything all packed, we will take off. Cap'n Tuck doesn't wait for nobody . . . I mean, anybody." Nellie held her hand up to her mouth and looked apologetic. "I fall right back into it when I get home. Old ways, you know."

Willa smiled and said, "I know how that goes. When I go back to Connecticut, they have their own sayings, too, and dialects are easy to come and go for us all. It's a kind of nice way of feeling that you really can go home again."

"What a nice way of putting that, Willa. That's why you're such a good writer. I envy you that. I know words in a technical sense, but your talent is rearranging words in a poetic kind of prose. Even when your characters get mad at one another!"

"That's hilarious, Nellie. I have to remember that. By the way, what kind of cake is that? I've never seen one with such skinny layers."

Aunt Rita held her lemon cake up and stated proudly, "This here is a James Island Cake and I bake the best lemon one anywhere around here, if I do say so myself."

Tasting a piece of the chocolate James Island Cake, Willa purred like a kitten, then said, "Where on earth did you get this recipe?"

"Oh, Willa, this is an old recipe. No one really knows where it came from. It's our Maryland state dessert and we eat 'em up. They're really out of this world, aren't they?"

"Well, I can tell you, ladies, I can't ever remember eating one better. Can I learn how to do this?"

"We'll have ye here one day and ye can make one for yerself. It's not hard, once you get the hang of it."

Nellie looked up at the old clock on the kitchen wall. "We have to go. Cap'n Tuck will surely leave us if we don't get a move on."

Willa didn't want to leave. The outside of the house certainly didn't tell the story of the inside—spanking clean, comfortable, simple, and filled with love. "Thank you. You are an interesting woman, Aunt Rita."

"I'll bet I am to you, city girl. But, ye know, we have our ways down here. Been like that forever. I used to live on the island, but, when my Donny took sick, I had to come over here to live. After he passed, I stayed here and began baking cakes for extra money. I miss it out there, though. Yer gonna fall in love, you know?"

Willa raised an eyebrow, but Aunt Rita continued. "Bet ye do. It's a kind of love ye can't explain to anyone. They either have it or they don't. Ye have it, I can tell. Now, you pull yer car to the back and get yer things. Then we'll take off for the dock in my old clunker out there."

As Willa walked out of the old woman's house, her eyes scanned her surroundings one more time. She wanted a mental picture for a future description. She didn't want to forget a thing.

Especially that slice of cake. That was truly love at first bite.

CHAPTER 11

To say fear was gripping her would be an understatement. Willa was sitting on a boat piloted by a "Cap'n" who spoke as if he was from a foreign land and filled with people she didn't know who all understood him because they spoke the same language. And Willa, trying desperately to look calm and cool. Not happening. Water had always frightened her. There was a reason.

Her parents had owned a vacation home in Bar Harbor, Maine. Every summer they had made the trek—packing, hauling, carting—but without ever seeming to mind. Her mother had always called it their "creative" time, when she had taken her time to sort life out and decide what came next. Her dad was still working because you couldn't tell the *New York Times* you're going away and expect all your fans to put your comic strip on hold. It just didn't happen that way. But he had a lovely, small studio in the garage and she remembered how she loved to go and sit and hang out there with him when he was beginning his doodles, as he called them.

One day, she had gone down to the small private stretch of beach below their house. It was very hot, and Willa remembered wanting to go into the water to cool off. When you're young, you don't pay attention to signs of danger, and she wasn't going to wait for her mother to come down. She would be along shortly. A huge mistake.

Willa had put her towel down on the sand and waded out in the shallow waves. This wasn't new to her; it was just that, this time, she was alone. She had kept going until, before she knew it, she was out too far and the waves were coming in too strong.

Suddenly, one crashed in on her and pulled her little nine-year-old body under. She remembered feeling trapped and flailing her arms, trying to get back to the top. Instead, she kept being drawn farther down.

Her mother was on the path down when she saw Willa go under. She yelled to Willa's father but knew she couldn't wait for him. She had to go in and get her daughter. She dove in and under the waves. It was a miracle; Willa's limp, small body was thrown against her and she grabbed her up and back to the beach.

Willa could still hear her parents crying for joy on that beach. And she had never gone near or in the water again.

This boat ride was a huge event for her. That's how she knew there were forces beyond her leading her out to this island.

"Are you all right, Willa? You look a little, well, a little scared. Today's not bad. The water's calm. You ought to go across when it's not."

"I'll take your word for it, Nellie. You're all used to it and grew up having to do this, but this girl is not very seaworthy."

"Takes time, but you'll come around."

"How long is the ride?"

Nellie reached down to take hold of her hand for a minute and said, "Not all that long."

Willa smiled. "By the way, Nellie, I have a favor to ask of you. While I'm on the island, I just want to be Willa, not a celebrity."

Nellie nodded her head and said, "Suit yourself, but that won't be easy to do."

"Why?"

"Because I did have to tell my mother who was coming with me, and she let out a whoop-de-doo. She knows who you are. A lot of the women out here read your books, Willa, so that favor isn't really going to be doable."

"Then, at least, let's try to tone it down a bit?"

"Why? People here will be excited to meet you. I mean it's not like there are hordes of people out there. You shouldn't feel like you're on display or anything. It's a tiny island, Willa."

"Just how small is this island, Nellie?"

"Well, it's down to about seventy now; once there were two hundred.

In the summer we do get a lot of visitors. Tourists, you know, who come to see what this place is all about."

"Really? Where do they come from?"

"You'd be amazed, Willa. They come from all over the country and some from foreign countries, too. Believe it or not, there's a lot written about these two remaining islands. Out of an entire chain of islands, there are only two inhabited ones left. One here in Maryland and the other in Virginia."

"What happened to the rest?"

"They sank back into the water or the people left. One completely sank last year, matter of fact. It's all a matter of time. The water takes back land every year, a little at a time. And then, when a big storm hits, a little more can go. It's a cat-and-mouse game and has been over thousands of years."

Willa hadn't really ever thought about that before. Islands to her meant Caribbean, sun, playing in the winter—not anything like this. But, now that she was being forced to think about it, there was a lot to this living out in the middle of nowhere.

"Doesn't that scare the heck out of all of you? I mean a big storm, and you're in the middle of it?"

Nellie laughed and so did some of the other women who had been listening to the conversation. One couldn't keep from saying something. "Nope, we're not afraid. The land gives you plenty of warning before it quits on ye."

Willa was amazed at how they all looked at life.

"Hey, look, Willa. There she is. Land ho!"

Willa turned in the direction Nellie was pointing. All this talk had made the time fly by. *My that Nellie is a sly one. She knew all along how to get my mind off what I feared so greatly.*

"I can see it all now, Nellie. You really are surrounded by the Bay. It's amazing."

As Captain Tuck finagled the boat through the last of a narrow channel he called the "thorofer" to come into the dock, Willa was suddenly acutely aware of the diesel engine of the boat chugging away to maneuver its way so smoothly on the water. It had a distinct sound and she found it astonishingly reassuring. All her senses were heightened by this new adventure she was on.

Nellie slightly nudged Willa as she pointed across the water. "That's the main part of James Island over there. Do you see the small bridge? That connects this piece of land and that one. They have cars over there."

Willa thought that was an odd thing to say, but she didn't respond. Didn't they have cars everywhere?

As they moved through the narrow channel, Willa saw the small town of Tuckerton. She tried quickly to describe it to herself so she could write it all down later. "It's a neat place."

"You just wait, Willa Carpenter. You haven't seen anything yet."

Just then, a cormorant flew over the water not far from the boat. Willa gasped with delight as it swooped onto a bobbling buoy. Then she noticed the bird seemed to be looking straight at her.

"Well, hello there, lovely seabird," Willa said, a smile on her face.

"Aren't they wonderful?"

Willa stared at it for a moment as they passed by. "All sea- and shorebirds are wonderful. I love the adorable painted-faced puffins that nest on the huge banks along the Maine coastline. I would sit for hours watching them. In fact, my dad used them a lot in the summertime editions of his comic strip."

"That's great," Nellie replied. "I've seen puffins, actually. My parents have friends up around there who fish and live in another water community on the Maine coast. There aren't many of us left anymore. That's what makes these islands so special down here."

"This really is something, and it's so beautiful, Nellie. You were a lucky girl to grow up in such a place."

"You haven't seen anything yet, Willa. You're going to fall in love."

Willa didn't answer because there was something else going on inside her at that moment, something she couldn't explain. Perhaps an awakening was going on. She didn't know, but, whatever it was, it evoked familiar feelings.

As the captian began the final turn to "dock up," she saw people waiting for them—in golf carts. Huh?

Nellie was waving her hands in excitement, looking more like a young schoolgirl than a young woman who had just stood toe-to-toe with the big dogs in a congressional hearing. "Come on, Willa. There's Mama down at the end of the dock. Isn't she something?"

Willa really had no idea what to expect. Her first glance saw a woman who could have been anyone's mother filled with excitement to see her daughter return home. However, the little she did know about this woman included the fact that she had also been to Washington to speak years before, so she had to be someone of strong convictions and with a mind of her own. Willa was definitely excited to meet Frances Evans.

Nellie reached over and gathered her bags. Willa followed her cue and did the same. The boat was now firmly docked and she found herself saying a silent, quick prayer of thanks for making it across the water . . . safe and sound. *And let's not forget Cap'n Tuck. Thank you, God, for him, too.*

As they waited their turn to get off the boat, Nellie nudged Willa and whispered, "The trip is twenty dollars, one way."

"Oh, I wondered about that, Nellie. Thanks." Willa reached into her backpack and before Cap'n Tuck gave her a hand up, she slipped a twenty-dollar bill into his hand. "Thanks for a great ride. See you on the way back?"

With a proud, wide smile, he said, "Sure will, ma'am. Have a good holiday now."

Willa returned the smile to this man of few words who spoke volumes with his actions and mannerisms. While a bit aloof, he certainly made his passengers feel safe and welcome.

So far, so good, in this great adventure of mine. I'm certain it's going to be like no other I have ever been on before. and I look forward to every minute of it. If nothing literary comes of it, then so be it. But I just have this feeling.

CHAPTER 12

Willa was more than a bit nonplussed. *Nice going, Nellie. I'm back stuck in the throng while you're rushing to the arms of your mom. A little help here might be nice. Ah, a small break in the action to my right. Better take it quick. For a small dock, it sure does get busy when ole Cap'n Tuck pulls in. Now just be careful, girl, that you don't trip and fall into the water. Would be just my luck. Wouldn't that be a nice way to introduce myself to this island, not to mention my hostess for the weekend? Yeah, wouldn't be real cool. Keep moving.*

"See our weekend guest has her hands full trying to get down the dock, Nellie."

"Oh heavens, Mama. I was in such a hurry to see you, I forgot about Willa." Nellie turned around to see Willa, looking a little worse for wear, but smiling and heading straight toward them.

"I'm so sorry, Willa. I got a little too excited to see my mother." Nellie took her mother's hand and said, "And, speaking of my mother, I would like you to meet her. Willa, this is Miss Frances Evans."

Willa dropped her bag and extended her hand. "Nice to meet you, Mrs. Evans."

"Now stop right there, girl. I'm Frances, do ye hear?

First impression: honest and straightforward. Willa blushed and said, "I hear, and thank you so much for allowing me to join you and your family over this special holiday. I just hope I'm not intruding."

"Ye must be kidding. Ye couldn't intrude if ye tried. Holidays are all about family and friends and, being yer so famous and all, we are the ones who are just so darned happy to have ye. Now come on and let's get a move on here. I want to show you around this here home of ours before we go on to the house." With that, Frances jumped into her golf cart and the girls packed their bags onto the back and joined her in the cart.

Second impression: warm and friendly.

"So this is how you get around," Willa commented. "No cars, just golf carts. How neat."

"Ye know, Willa, everyone here in our small town of Tuckerton knows yer comin'. Things have a way of getting around here."

Not exactly what she'd wanted, but she knew it was a big deal of sorts so would go with the flow. "Well, I hope I don't disappoint you all."

"Can't do that. Too many of the women have read yer books, including me. You have a big fan club over here."

And when she wrote books, had she ever thought of women living on islands reading them? Nope. *Make a mental note of that, Willa.*

As Frances drove down one narrow blacktop path that connected to another, Willa tried to take it all in. The homes were lovely. Some small, but some much larger than she would ever have expected. How do they do it, she wondered. Everything has to come over on boats. It was truly amazing.

Nellie hadn't said a word. She was watching her mother and hanging on her every word with sheer delight. The love between them was real and profoundly deep. Willa found herself very jealous of what they had. She'd had that, too, and then it was gone in an instant. Her mother would have loved this out here. She would have seen the romance in it, and she would have said it had passion. To her, passion was what moved you forward.

"How ye comin' back there, Willa? Nellie and I are reacquainting up here. Maybe ye should have sat up here with Nellie pullin' up the rear."

Frances seemed to enjoy everything in life. She was a great study in happiness and real joy.

"I'm doing just fine, Mis . . . I mean, Frances."

"Now yer comin' on to it." Miss Frances was the perfect mother type. She gave you the sense she could take anyone in and make them believe she was their mother. Willa loved the way she spoke. It was magical to her ears though she didn't know why. There was a quality of honesty to it, and it was so refreshing.

Nellie turned and sat sideways so she could see Willa better. "See, you're getting the hang of our way of speaking. I can tell you kind of like it."

Laughing, Willa said, "Yes, I guess I do at that. Your mother is an honest and direct woman and I like that. It's not like D.C. where everything said has fifteen meanings."

"They call that doublespeak, don't they, Willa?"

Looking out at the water that surrounded them, she answered, "They should call it lying."

Frances laughed out loud and yelled, "Ye sure got that right."

Nellie looked happy. "So what do you think of it so far?"

"So far, so good."

Frances interrupted to say, "See that ugly-looking place over there? It's the dump."

"Dump?"

"Yes. Where we take all our garbage, and, on a hot day like we get in the summer, ye don't want to stay long there."

Willa hadn't thought of that. There weren't any garbage trucks out here. She had to remember that everything happened by boat. So hard to conceive of when most people take cars, trains, taxis, and buses for granted. The water was their highway and the boats were what traveled that highway for everything.

"I have so much to learn over here."

"It'll come to ye. We live an entirely different life over here, but it grows on ye, if ye let it."

"I must say it's so odd not seeing cars. I see every home and building has golf carts in the yards."

"'Twarn't no need of cars here. What would we do with them? There are a few small trucks but that's about it for them."

Did she really say "'twarn't"? They really do speak the old language.

Nellie saw the look on Willa's face and whispered, "You'll get used to it."

Willa placed her hand on Nellie's arm and said, "You sure worked hard to lose your native language,"

Frances piped up. "Wouldn't do her any good at all if she spoke like this over there. I remember how hard it was when I went over to speak, but I decided that this is how I come and I'm not changin' for anyone. It's different for our college girl here. I want her society-presentable, not like her mama and daddy."

"Stop it, Mama. Ye are the best." Nellie laughed. "See, I can fall right back into it."

They had almost circled the island with Frances pointing this out and that out and so much Willa couldn't take it all in. Didn't matter, because she knew she would be walking this place many times before the weekend was over.

Pulling the cart up in front of a store, Frances yelled, "The tour stops here for a minute. There's nowhere better to get to know us than this here general store. Its owner is Floyd Bradshaw and his people come from way back."

The sign that welcomed both visitors and islanders said, BRADSHAW'S GENERAL STORE, HOME OF THE BEST CRABS IN THE WORLD. As Nellie got out, she whispered to Willa, "You are about to return to the past. Hold on."

Willa could only guess what she meant. Everything here was a return to the past in some way or other, but she found herself enjoying it immensely. Bradshaw's, no doubt, was sure to be something special.

Walking through the doors, Willa realized she might as as well have had a sign around her neck that read, "I am the new stranger in town. Be nice to me or you'll end up in one of my future books." Four old men's faces greeted her, their old worn-out farm hats perched on their heads. She froze in place.

Two of them tipped their hats to her as they all said in unison, "Howdy, ma'am."

Say something, you idiot. Standing here looking like a statue isn't going to work. Spit it back at 'em. "Howdy to you, too." They loved it. These fellows seemed to be the sentinels of the store. If you could get their approval, she figured you were in.

Frances and Nellie had gone over to the counter that ran the entire back wall. Refrigerated cases below the counter held food, so much of it that she was instantly starving. There were deli meats, cheeses, salads, and desserts. She wanted to dive in and never come out.

"Come on over here, Willa. Let me introduce ye to this old feller here." Willa stepped past the men and walked over, knowing every eye in that store was on her.

"This here is Floyd Bradshaw. Floyd? Floyd, meet Willa Carpenter. She's a famous writer. Heck, you wouldn't know about her, but yer Bess would. She writes romance books."

"How d'ye do, Miss Carpenter. I don't know much about those girlie novels, but, if ye are a friend of Miss Frances, then yer a friend of mine."

"Pleased, Mr. Bradshaw."

Frances leaned over and said, "Just call him Floyd. Mr. Bradshaw isn't here; he run off with Miss Frances, my mother."

Willa just looked at Nellie's mother.

"I'm just kiddin' with ye, Willa. By the way, where did ye come by that name? It's real pritty."

"Why, thank you. It's really Wilhelmina, but I liked Willa better as a kid, so I stuck with it."

"I agree with ye there. Wilhelmina is a long handle for a little one." She paused to look around. "So this here is our store. We get what we can here, but, for the rest of the things, we have to go to the mainland. Rita, my sister—you met her—she brings some things over when she comes round to visit us. She'll be here tomorrow."

Willa nodded and said, "I liked her. I look forward to seeing her again."

The store owner spoke. "And did ye taste any of her cakes?"

"Why, yes, I did, Floyd. Never tasted anything quite like them before."

"And you won't neither," Frances said. "My sister makes the best anywhere around. You know they're the state cake. We fought hard to get that to be."

"Well, you should be very proud of that, Frances. They're absolutely wonderful."

"Come on now. Time to get you girls to the house. I have a mess of things to do yet for the holiday." Frances looked around to find Nellie and saw her across the store talking intently to a young man.

"Look at those two, will ye? That's Denny, Floyd and Bess's son—and Nellie's heartthrob."

Willa smiled at the way Nellie and her boyfriend were looking at one another. "Think it's best we don't disturb them right now?"

Frances turned to leave and said, "See ye, Floyd. Have Bess come around to meet Willa and tell her to bring one of her books. I'm sure Willa will sign it for her." Then she yelled over to Nellie. "Time to go."

As Nellie walked back over, Denny headed out the door.

Floyd looked at Willa and said, "Would you? I mean she would about die to have that happen. Oh, here, before ye go, take these along and have 'em later."

She looked at the package he handed over the counter and said," I don't know what's in here, but thank you."

Nellie poked her and said, "Floyd just handed you our gift to the world: crab cakes. All lump, mind you. Not all flaked up with fillers."

Willa looked up at Floyd and smiled. "I will enjoy every bite of these. Again, thanks."

Nellie tagged Willa's arm and said, "Race you to the cart. Mama is waiting on us."

As she left the marvelous store, she knew she would be back many times over the weekend to visit this Floyd. His store had made quite an impression on her, and, yes, she was back to a past you could only read about these days. And here it was, right in front of her.

Nellie giggled her fool head off watching her climb back into the cart. Frances was already to take off, and, as soon as she got into her seat, they jerked away. And then Willa heard it: a sound vaguely familiar, but not one she could quite put her finger on.

"What's that sound, Nellie? I think I've heard it before, but it's not coming to mind."

"Those are our resident peacocks."

"Peacocks? How do peacocks get out here? Are there any other zoo animals on the island?"

Frances laughed out loud. "Girl, we have peacocks and dogs and cats. No zoo animals. 'Ceptin' maybe a lion or two," she teased. "That's about it, but those peacocks are special. Cap'n Tuck's family brought a mess of them some years back but only two survived. Maybe the others got into the dump fer too long."

Willa's whole body was shaking, she was laughing so hard. This woman belonged on a stage. "Well, thank heavens it's only a lion or two," she joked. "Otherwise, I wouldn't sleep a wink."

Frances was clearly having fun. "I like this girl, Nellie. She's good for ye and I know ye are good fer her."

Willa leaned forward and said, "I'll second that."

CHAPTER 13

Prudence Harding wasn't getting out of D.C. anytime soon if she didn't get all the paper work done. Congressman Lee's commercial fishing hearing was her source of angst right now, and she still had an hour or so of work to do until she could wind it up, file it, and head to the airport. She was mired in the muck and had to get out.

At the same time, she couldn't help wondering how Willa was making out on her all-water extravaganza. Prue couldn't believe she was doing this when she was terrified of water. Sure to be some good stories when she got back. She envied Willa's life as a writer. Had she been better at the abstract, she might have given it a try, but she knew her destiny was to be in the only world she had ever known: politics.

With her concentration on the ABCs of the file cabinet, she didn't hear Charles walk in.

"Hey, Prue."

Startled beyond belief, she jumped so hard, she hit her head against the cabinet.

"That wasn't funny, Charles. I hurt my head."

He stood there laughing. "I'm sorry, Prue. I really didn't mean to scare you."

"Yes, you did." She added, "What are you doing here anyway? I thought you'd left."

"I had some things to do and couldn't leave before now. Had to come by and pick some stuff up and take it home with me."

"The congressman going to work over the holiday? Heavens! What's this world coming to?"

"Yes, I am. It's reading I want to do, and I want to talk over some of it with my father. He's so good at seeing all the different sides to an issue."

"It's not easy coming from a political family, is it, Charles? We kids suffer the elders."

"Yeah, you're right about that, but they know. Still, times have changed so much. I miss the old smoke-filled rooms and the bargaining that went on. Seemed a better way than this mess today."

"My, aren't we waxing philosophical?"

"I hear it's going to snow," he said, changing the subject.

"Yes, and I better get out of here soon. The traffic is always bad, but, when the weathermen forecast snow, even if it's flurries, the drivers get nuts." Prue checked her watch. "I have to get out to the airport. If I don't get home, my mother will skin me alive. Thanksgiving is her favorite holiday, and she's upset as it is with Willa not joining us. She loves to have her come."

"Where's the gorgeous writer going? To her boyfriend's house?"

"I'm going to forget you said that. Besides, Willa doesn't have time for a boyfriend."

"Sure, Prue. I'll bet she has plenty of them."

Prue was annoyed with his insinuations about her best friend. "Stop it, Charles. She isn't that type of woman and we shouldn't be talking about this. Your private life is private and so is Willa's."

"I'm sorry, Prue. I didn't realize you were so touchy about her. She is a stunning woman and I can't believe she doesn't have a special man."

"You aren't going to get a peep out of me regarding Willa. Now, if you don't mind, Charles, I have to get these papers from your fish hearing in the file so I can catch my plane."

Charles pulled back, apparently sorry he had gone that far. And he looked as if he were mad at himself for being obvious. "Okay, you're right. Not another word about our writer."

"She told me you asked her for coffee sometime," Prue said, laughing.

"Now who's teasing? Yes, I did, and let's drop it."

"Okay with me."

The congressman looked thoughtful. "You should have heard that young girl, Nellie Evans. She was something. Impassioned is the word I would use. You have to admire that."

"I heard she was very good. Willa really liked her."

"I hope Willa doesn't think she's going to write anything about this hearing, Prue."

"I don't think so, Charles. She writes romance novels."

"I don't know; writers have a nose for things and this subject has been kicked around for a long time. Big money is behind this. It's politics at its ugliest. People are going to get hurt."

"She's just curious, Charles. It's a very different culture and Willa's attracted to that. She uses all kinds of interesting things for background."

"Funny thing about curiosity. It killed the cat, you know."

"So I've heard, but Willa isn't a cat. This girl seemed to hit a spark inside her."

"I don't know why, but something tells me Willa is looking for something and it better not be in my business, Prue."

"It'll be all right. She's going to learn a lot this holiday." Prue turned to the window and looked out in the direction of the Bay. "She's going over there, to that island for Thanksgiving, Charles. Nellie invited her."

"How in God's name did that happen?"

"She and Nellie spoke after the hearing. I told you Willa connected with her. They talked for a while and then Nellie invited her to visit her family for Thanksgiving."

Charles exploded. "I told you she was meddling, and now we don't know what's going to happen. I tell you, Prue, I don't care who your relatives are; if this goes south, I'll blame you."

Prue had a pretty good temper, too, and she didn't care for what he was saying to her right now.

"That's not even a veiled threat. Listen to me, Congressman Lee: I don't care who your relatives were either, and if—and I don't think it's going to happen—but if Willa finds something over there and wants to write about it, I'll back her to the moon."

This was clearly not what either of them wanted, and Charles backed away first.

"You're right, Prue, and I shouldn't be saying any of this. Let's see how it goes. For all we know, she might find out something that could help us."

"That's true. I'm sorry, Charles. Let's both quit this and get out of here. Have a wonderful holiday in Charlottesville."

"You be safe going to Ohio. Enjoy your family." He smiled. Then, before he walked away, he turned and said, "Prue? Do you think your best friend would ever go out with a pompous lug like me?"

Prue chuckled and said, "You never know. Now get going before the snows starts falling."

CHAPTER 14

From Bradshaw's store onward, Frances pointed out so many places on the island to Willa, they were all beginning to run together. She was becoming very hungry and a lot tired, and obviously enough that Nellie said, "Mama, we really have to get on over to the house. I know you want to show Willa everything, but she's pretty worn out right now."

"Yer right, Nellie." Frances turned a little and said, "I've run ye all over and you'd think ye were leaving tomorrow. I'm sure you're hungry and here I go on rattling away."

Willa smiled at her. "I am kind of starving, and smelling these crab cakes isn't helping."

"Know what ye mean about that. Floyd makes them pritty good, but he can't hold a candle to mine or my Jimmy's. Actually, all the folks out here know magical things to do with the crabs." Then, laughing, she added, "Ye might say the crabs and us are married to one another."

What a wonderful way to put it, thought Willa. "You might say that, Frances. From what I've seen, crabs are everything here."

"Got that right, Willa. It's a love story really, and marriage is what describes it best. Sometimes good, sometimes bad, but we always stick it out."

Her logic was amazing. For a woman who only went through high school, she was extraordinary. Nellie was right about her mother. She's wonderfully different and refreshingly honest.

The golf cart pulled up next to the house. They were home, or, at least, Nellie and Frances were home. Willa was just a guest.

"Looks great, Mama. I see Daddy fixed the roof."

"Finally!" Frances laughed. "Ye know how hard it is for me to get that man to fix anything around this house."

"That's not quite fair, Mama. He's always out on the water."

"Still and all, Nellie, I can't do it all."

Willa listened to the easy banter between them. While the words were differently put, it was very much the same as the conversations she had used to have with her mother.

"Come on, Willa, let's go in and get some lunch."

"From your lips to God's ears."

"What a great expression," Frances said. "I'm sorry I've kept ye captive all this time."

"Don't apologize, Frances. You're proud of your island, and, from what I've seen so far, I understand."

"It's kind of romantic, if ye ask me."

"Well, I see everything in the world as romantic."

"Maybe ye will write about us folks out here one day." Laughing again, she said, "We're so romantic, don't ye know?"

"Mama, leave Willa alone. She's starving right now, so let's take care of that first. Then you two can conspire about romance and the island."

Opening the door to the kitchen, Frances led the way. Willa noticed she didn't use a key and that struck her as odd. Who doesn't lock their doors?

"Give me those crab cakes Floyd gave ye. I'll heat 'em up and rustle up some lunch for us all. Nellie, take Willa around and get her settled in."

"Come on, Nellie. I want you to feel right at home here."

"I'm sure I will."

The house was a home, and there is a difference. The living room had comfortable rocking loungers and a sofa that had obviously been used, but didn't look worn out. Pictures were on every wall. Jimmy and Frances's room was full of their wedding pictures and a slew of baby pictures of their darling Helen, who had only really ever been called Nellie. Apparently Helen was a grandmother's name and it was with honor that she was named after her. But they preferred Nellie, a common nickname. However, there was some Helen in Nellie. Names fit the people who wear them, Willa thought, and there was a transcendent quality about this girl that

Willa related to on many levels. Nellie thought deeply about things, and, when she loved, she did it with all her heart.

"Come on, Willa. Let's go upstairs and you can unpack your things and maybe then you'll feel more like you're family."

"That sounds good."

There were two rooms upstairs, divided by a lounge area with a TV and two more of the loungers that called to Willa and said, "Hey, come sit and stay awhile."

"You take that room. It's our guest room, or maybe it should be called our all-around-everything-dump-it-here room."

Willa walked in and looked around. There were beds under each of the sloping ceilings and a table in the middle. Very comfortable looking. It didn't take long to get set up, or to feel as if this were home. But, right now, all she wanted was to eat something.

Frances yelled, "Lunch is on the table."

Willa walked down the stairs into the kitchen and sat down. She couldn't believe all the food in front of her. Frances put a crab cake on her plate and said, "Give 'er a taste and tell me that isn't the best thing you've ever eaten." The pressure was on, but, when Willa took a bite, it wasn't even a contest.

"OMG! These crab cakes are fabulous, Frances."

"Told you Floyd did a good job, but mine are better. Now here's one of Floyd's."

Willa bit in and chewed. Then she looked up and said, "Honestly? Yours are a bit better."

Nellie giggled and said, "Are you sure you're not a politician? Hey, Mama, have any slaw to go with these crabs?"

"Always have slaw at the ready. Learned that from when I was a little girl."

While almost inhaling the crab cakes, Willa found time to look around the open kitchen with the table in the middle. A more formal dining room adjoined it in an all-in-one-room setting, separated only by carpet in the dining room area. This was indeed the center of the home, which told Willa that food wasn't the only thing that went on in here. This was the center of their life together.

Old art projects still hung on the refrigerator. How old must they be by now? More pictures lined the walls, and awards that thanked Frances for her service to this and that. But what meant the most to Willa were all the cookbooks on a homemade shelf next to the stove.

"I love your cookbook collection."

"Oh, those old things. I should clean 'em out but can't bring myself to do that. I've had 'em forever and some have been passed down through time. I couldn't part with them. One day they will be in Nellie's kitchen."

Nellie smiled at her mother. "I think I've read them all a hundred times."

"You like to cook, Nellie?" Willa asked.

"You bet I do. When I'm not doing something for this project of mine, or studying, I'm cooking in my tiny-as-Tinkerbell kitchen."

"That's descriptive, Nellie." Looking at both of them, she asked, "What are your favorite recipes?"

Nellie went first and said, "Hands down for me would have to be Stewed Jimmies."

"Okay, what are jimmies?"

Frances burst out laughing, "They're boy hard crabs."

"Oh. Then if boy crabs have a name, what are the girl crabs named?"

"Sooks," Nellie said.

"Now, why didn't I know that? Everyone knows crabs have names."

"It's just what they are, Willa. Has been like that since the beginning of time."

"And for your favorite recipe, Frances?"

"That's not easy. I love it all. Food and me are fast friends. Guess of them all, I would have to say I love the sweet potato pies. You'll get to eat some tomorrow."

She could almost taste it already. "I have to say, I haven't ever had one of those."

Nellie's eyes lit up. "You're gonna love Thanksgiving here on the island. You'll eat 'til you pop. It goes on forever. All day."

Willa smiled gently. "I just hope I don't die."

CHAPTER 15

Prue finally got all the files straightened up; she was free to take off. Stopping first at her apartment on Dupont Circle to grab her already packed suitcase, she hailed a cab and went on to Dulles to catch the flight to her family home outside Cincinnati.

She was so ready to get out of D.C. She was still a little upset over the confrontation she'd had with Charles. She wasn't expecting him to ask so much about Willa, nor was she expecting him to go crazy over where Willa had gone for the holiday.

Yes, she was ready to go home.

The Harding family home was quite a place. By all standards, it was a mansion, and one befitting the heirs of a former president. It was set on a high knoll in Indian Hills, a classy Cincinnati suburb. The drive home from the airport was always exciting for Prue. She was close to her family and being with them as much as she could these days was important to her. Thanksgiving was her favorite of all the holidays, and the only thing that would make things a little less than perfect this year would be Willa's absence. But she knew Willa was stressed over her writing and she hoped going out to that island would help her relax and get her creative juices flowing again.

While Prue sat waiting for her father to pick her up at the airport, the conversation with Charles replayed itself again and again. Why did it matter so much? Willa knew the rules of the game and she would never do anything to put Prue in jeopardy.

Charles was really spun up about this. He loved the Chesapeake and cared about what happened to it, but he was going way overboard about this. He was almost an expert on that body of water and what they had to do to try to preserve it, and knew it was going to take time. He had studied marine science and was well respected on the subject. So what was with him?

There would be many meetings on this before the legislation was done, and Willa had seen but a small measure of what the issues were. The mighty Chesapeake affected many people, not just those who worked on it, but also those who lived around it, including in other states besides Maryland and Virginia. It was a life-force, not to mention the largest estuary in the country. What went on out there affected millions of people, so it was definitely going to take time and a whole lot of money.

Willa wrote love stories, not political ones, so what had him all riled up? Or could it be . . . *oh, there's Daddy. Thank God, he's come to rescue me from this ongoing conversation in my head.*

As she threw her arms around him, Chester Harding—Chet to his friends—hugged his little girl.

"My God, you're a sight for sore eyes, love."

"You too, Dad. I'm so glad to see you."

"Why, Prudence, you sound a little down. Come on now. The car is just outside in the ramp. Let's get out of here."

Chester Harding was a big, distinguished-looking man, and there was a distinct resemblance between him and his daughter, except his black hair was graying at the temples while hers was a deep indigo. The Hardings were a good-looking family with great genes, and Chester had done his part in passing them all on to his only daughter. She was what some would call a "stunner." She had also inherited his stubbornness, but she saw that as a plus because she was on her way to the top in Washington, even if Charles Lee didn't know that quite yet. Her father did, and he was going to use every contact he had from his days as a major "bundler" for his party to help. He knew how the game was played better than most, and he wasn't going to let anyone or anything keep his daughter from her dreams. It was said about Chester Harding that he was more than a man—he was a force to be reckoned with.

Once in the car and on the expressway, Chester turned to his daughter and remarked, "You look tired, Prudence."

"You know, Dad, you and Mom are the only ones anywhere who call me by my birth name. It's nice to hear it once in a while, even if I think you're speaking of someone else."

"You never really liked your name, you know, but your mother insisted on calling you by your baptized name, so blame her."

Prue smiled lovingly at him. "I know, and it wouldn't be the same if either one of you called me Prue at this point."

"It was your grandmother's name and she insisted." He looked at her and smiled warmly. "She was a very determined lady. Just like her granddaughter."

"I'll take that as a compliment, Dad." Prue chuckled, then turned serious. "How is Mom doing these days? I know it's hard on you, and I should be back here helping her and you."

"No, you should not. We've been through this, Prudence. There's nothing you can do for her that I don't. She's doing as well as can be expected and we all take one day at a time. That's how we get through it."

Prue saw the shadow cross her father's face when he spoke about her mother. She had breast cancer and had it beaten for five years, and now it was back. But she was a stubborn woman, too, and was determined that, if she could win once, she'd do it again. Prue knew the odds weren't in her favor, but every day was a new day in medicine and its advances against cancer.

Prue gently touched his arm. "Is she holding up okay?"

"She's pretty good so far, honey. She has good days and bad ones. We count the good days and celebrate each and every one of them. We have a glass of champagne and I bring her a rose. That's our miracle time together."

"You love her so much, Daddy. That's what keeps her going."

He turned quickly to look at his lovely daughter. "You know, dear heart of mine, I have loved that lady since the first time I took her out dancing. It was moonlight and kismet."

"Daddy, that's so romantic. Willa would love this story. Right up her alley."

"I'll miss having Willa here. Where did you say she went off to?"

"She went to an island in the Chesapeake, and, if I'm not careful, it could turn into something ugly for me."

His tone changed immediately. "What do you mean?"

"Well, I asked Charles if she could sit in on one of his congressional hearings. She had read an article in the paper about it and was interested. He agreed quite eagerly, but then, when I told him she wouldn't be coming home with me this holiday, and he asked where she went, he blew his stack."

"Why would he do that? Is he personally involved with her?"

"They'd make a great pair, but, no, they're not. He thinks she's going to write something that will sabotage his whole effort on behalf of the Chesapeake in Congress, and he really gave it to me right before he left this afternoon. Told me he would hold me accountable if she messed with this."

"Well, girl, keep an eye open for any trouble. Willa knows her way around the block, you know. I've always been glad the two of you teamed up as friends. How's her career going. Any new books?"

"That's one of the reasons she went over to that island. After she heard this young woman speak at the hearing, she spoke with her for a while, and, low and behold, the girl asked her over there for the holiday. And she said yes. She's having some personal problems, too, and so she thought getting far away would be good for her. She said she has writer's block."

"Ouch. That's cruel. I hear that's a bitch when it hits. Can take awhile to get back on line. I once had a great young man who wrote the best political articles; then he came down with it. Took him almost two months to get his juices flowing again, and, by that time, I had another person doing his job. I felt bad for him. I really liked him, but, in the business of politics, time is everything."

"That's awful. He must have been really upset."

"He was and I felt like a dog, but that's the way it goes."

Prue watched her father as he told that story and saw how hard he really could be when it came to business. She had heard that Chet Harding could be a prick, but he was her father, and that's all that mattered.

Prue smiled and changed the subject. "When I see Willa, I'll tell her she'll have to come on out and listen to your true-life love story. She will love that and maybe use it in a one of her best sellers. She really loves you two and thinks of you as her parents now."

"That had to be rough on her. She was young when that accident happened. I know your mother and I really love her, and we'll miss her being at the table."

"You know, Dad, there's something deeper that goes on with her sometimes. I can't put my finger on it, but, reading her books, I see it. She hasn't made peace with it all yet. She was so close with them. Being an only child, like me, she was the center of their universe, and, even though her aunt and uncle took her in after the accident; life changed forever for Willa. I hope one day she can figure it all out."

"I do, too, Prue. Well, here we are. Home at last."

As they swung through the gates and up the long driveway, Prue got so excited to be home. "Oh, Dad, it's so good to be home. I see you finally had the gates painted. They look great."

Clearing his throat at her obvious though gentle reproach about his tardiness at taking care of home duties, he laughed and said, "Well, yes. I knew if I didn't, there would be hell to pay from my little girl and we can't have that. Welcome home, sweetheart."

Some trips go smoothly and some do not. For Charles, this trip wasn't going well at all. It had begun snowing way earlier than the meteorologists had predicted, and so the drive down Route 29 and into Albemarle County wasn't the pleasant one he always looked forward to.

Charlottesville was one of those special towns in Virginia where history met the mountains and formed near perfection. He loved this area and this town. Which was growing way too fast into city status. It seemed everyone wanted to "move South" these days.

His branch of the Lee family had moved here some time ago and it was where he had been raised. Along with the Lee family home, Charles had his own historic home. He'd purchased it shortly before his election to Congress and had gone to great pains to restore the stately residence as it had been during its glory days. It sat in the hills and he enjoyed the quiet walks he took up the mountain not far away. From the top, he could see Thomas Jefferson's home, Monticello. He would sit for an hour or more at a time, wondering what Jefferson would think if he were to come back today.

Being a Lee was no small thing in the state of Virginia, or in the whole South for that matter. Charles belonged to the same quiet southern societies that the Lees had belonged to since they had come to this country. In colonial times, they'd been part of the gentry, in the same league with the Washingtons and Jeffersons. He was thus part of the American tapestry, and, while times had changed, he had never lost his admiration for his family history or what they had been a part of in the forming of this great state and nation.

Talking out loud to himself was routine for Charles. He had done it forever because it helped him organize his thoughts. It drove Prue and the rest of his staff crazy, but he was their boss, so, whatever he did was never questioned. Right now, the topic rolling around in his head was the holiday and, perhaps, a certain someone.

"Why is Willa Carpenter really on that island? She is up to something. It's never enough for a writer; they have to pry and peel the onion until they find something. Their curiosity always leads them to put things into words and then those words become books. Prue was doing her close and beautiful friend a favor, but it could be trouble.

"I have to be careful in Washington. No one is your true friend. No one. Remember that, Charles. Trouble comes in beautiful packaging. But this one seems different to me. I've been in her company only twice and yet she's living in my head. Mother would be glad if I settled down, but I like my single life. My work is too important to me to have to take the time for a wife and then children. There's so much I want to accomplish for this country, and, so far, I haven't had any trouble dating any woman I want. But still . . . .

"Stop it, Charles. Go home, call Mother, and then take yourself outside for a nice long walk in the quiet of the softly falling snow."

CHAPTER 16

Looking over at the small clock on the table next to her, Willa shot up straight. "Oh, no," she groaned. "This can't be. They probably think I'm awful, sleeping in like this." With that, she threw on her sweatpants and hooded sweatshirt and padded down the hallway to the bathroom to at least comb her hair before she went downstairs.

Frances was the first to spot Willa coming down the stairs and into the kitchen.

"Well, look what the cat dragged in, Nellie."

Nellie turned to see her new friend slowly walking toward her. "Good morning, Willa. We didn't want to disturb you. I hope we didn't."

"You should have, Nellie. I can't believe it's nine o'clock already."

Frances said, "You were worn out, Willa. If ye haven't done this before, it can be a bit overwhelming to come on out on a boat and then get dragged all over."

"I loved it, Frances. I just don't think I knew how tired I really was. I think it was the anxiety of being on the boat. I'm scared witless of the water."

"Well, ye are up now, so what can I get ye for breakfast?"

"Really, coffee is all I have in the morning, but let me get it. From the looks of things on your counters, you've been up all night baking and cooking."

"I'll hear none of it. You sit. Here's your coffee. Now enjoy."

"Can I help at all? I mean I've never seen so much food."

"Willa, I'm out of heart this morning having you two girls here with Jimmy and me."

"'Out of heart'?" she mumbled.

Nellie leaned over and said, "She means she's happy."

"Oh, I see. 'Out of heart' means happy?"

"Yes. You're going to hear a lot of that today." Nellie laughed. "Just stay close and I'll interpret."

"I think that's a great idea, Nellie. Don't leave me for a moment. I think I could get into trouble fast here."

All of a sudden, the side door opened and in walked Jimmy, carrying a bushel basket with a top on it.

"Where do you want 'em, Franny?"

Willa knew this was going to be good.

"Ye put 'em right there for now, Jimmy, and sit down and I'll get ye some coffee."

After serving her husband, Frances sat down next to Willa, and she realized she already felt like family.

"Looky down at that basket, Willa. Jimmy brought us a mess of crabs who will be in a pot pritty soon. They think they can escape. Listen to them. They're a lively bunch."

Jimmy took a sip of his coffee and smacked his lips. "Sure is good coffee, Franny." Then he looked over at Willa and said, "I hear you're a writer."

"Sometimes," she answered, looking straight back into the man's blue eyes. He was the epitome of a fisherman. Or waterman, as they were called down here. He looked no different from the men who trapped lobsters back in Mystic Seaport. He was tall, with gray hair and strong arms and hands. His skin was deeply creased and weathered, but what stood out most was a gleam in his eyes that said how much he loved his family and the life he had chosen to live.

"How ye like it here so far? Has Franny dragged ye all over up and down?"

Willa smiled. "She has, but I like everything so far. Living on an island is so different from anything I have ever known."

"Wait 'til you see the dinner Mother will be dishin' up fer the holiday."

It seemed all fishermen and their families shared the same talk, only with different accents and words; still and all, they were of the same tribe.

Willa took a sip of coffee while beaming a little, thinking of how happy she was at this moment. She felt completely free. Then she looked at Frances and said, "That's why I'm not eating a thing beforehand."

Jimmy was clearly a direct-speaking man. Willa could tell he had no time for the frivolous talk of women. He was studying her face, but she couldn't make out what was on his mind. He was hard to read. Much harder than her father, who would have been cracking a joke or two at this point. How different their worlds were, and yet they were both good men, simply born to different kinds of people with different dreams.

"When are ye fixin' to feed us, Franny, so I know what to do with those crabs?"

"Daddy, open the box up and show Willa what you brought us."

"Okay, girlie."

Willa wasn't exactly sure about this. Crabs weren't something she knew about. But she did know about lobsters, so how bad could this be?

Jimmy took the lid off and it was pandemonium from the start. The crabs were moving like a thousand worms in a bucket, all begging to get out. They must have sensed what was coming for them on this day. They *were* the feast and they knew it.

Just then, some of them made a go for it and went over the top. Frances and Jimmy ran to catch them as Frances yelled back to Nellie to shut the others back up.

"Ye old fool. I'll have crabs into everything," Frances shouted.

Willa started giggling; she couldn't help it. Soon everything went to hell in a handbasket. It was as if the free crabs had called to the others for backup. Within moments, the box had tipped over and they were doing a full-court press to charge at full speed anywhere other than that kitchen. They were running for their lives.

Nellie took one look at Willa and she began giggling, too, but she also clearly knew what this could mean. They could have crabs all over the house, and, when they died, the smell wouldn't be funny at all.

Frances called out, "I'll go this way, Jimmy. Nellie, you go over there and we'll head 'em off and get them back into that derned box."

Willa sat and watched, her sides splitting. She couldn't remember when she had laughed so hard. In the end, after some fancy footwork, the crabs lost their valiant battle and back in the box they were.

The victors sat around that worn but loved kitchen table and laughed for a half hour until Nellie finally said, "Willa, get dressed. I want to show you more of the island, especially where they pick the crabs down at the Co-op."

At this point, Willa figured she wouldn't even ask. She would just go with the flow.

Willa was thinking to herself. *If I told anyone back in D.C. I was headed to a crab-picking co-op, they would stare at me as if I had lost my mind. Well, maybe I have at that.*

Nellie couldn't wait to take her over there. She said it was a short walk. Actually, the whole of Tuckerton was a short walk.

"What are ye thinking, Willa? I can see a thousand questions running through your head. Ask them."

"Well, first off, I loved your daddy. He seems a gentle giant, not unlike the fishermen back on the coast of Connecticut."

"All watermen have a bond, no matter where they live. It's what they do that nobody else understands, that makes them stick close together. My daddy isn't unique compared to others here, but he's unique to me. He never says what he doesn't mean and he takes action on it. My mother, too. When she speaks, it's clear what she means."

"She must have been a hit in D.C. Nobody there speaks what they mean. It's all 'spin.' Which is another word for lie. It's easy to see why people all over this country are getting so restless with the folks in that city. Nothing ever changes—except, when they talk, we lose our money."

"My mother was brave to go there. She wasn't afraid of them, and, while I was very nervous, I'm not afraid of them either."

"Watch out, Nellie. They can mess with you. My best friend has a top job with one of them. You met him the other day. It's too early for me to figure out what way the wind blows for him."

"You mean Congressman Lee? Your best friend works for him?"

"How do you think I got into that hearing?" Willa grinned. "But look what came of it!"

Nellie smiled. "Yes, I'm so glad we met. And, I believe that, for some reason we don't know yet, our meeting and our friendship are going to do something."

"I know what you mean, but we have to be careful. My friend could lose her job if I write about anything that has to do with those hearings the congressman chairs, and I couldn't stand knowing I did that to her."

Nellie looked at her with understanding. Then she smiled again and said, "Well, Willa, we're here. It's the only crab-picking cooperative left. This is where the women pick the meat out of the crabs legally so they can sell it to the open markets and restaurants."

"Go on."

Nellie walked through the door as Willa followed, listening to every word. "They ship the picked crab meat by boat over to the mainland and then it goes off to various restaurants and markets up in Philadelphia and New York City."

A woman sat at a long table, picking crabs, and, when she saw Nellie, she smiled and said, "Why, Nellie Evans, you're home."

"Morning, Miss Ida. See you're still pickin'. About at the end of the run though."

"We were lucky this year. We were all able to get crabs right up until the end and they're still here yet. They haven't taken off down the Bay. I should be over at the shanty helping Wilbur but he told me to come on over here and leave him be for a while. Ye know how men are."

"I sure do, Miss Ida. This is a friend of mine who's visiting for the holiday. This is Willa Carpenter. Have you ever read any of her books?"

Willa poked Nellie. "I thought we had a bargain that I was off duty this weekend."

"Can't help it. Sorry, Willa."

"Why yes, I have. I read one a year ago. It was good. You wrote that?"

"Yes, I did." Willa smiled gratefully. "Hope you liked the way it turned out."

"I've read a few of your books, but that one—*Misty Evening*—sure had some twists. But it ended right."

"That was one of my favorites, too. It was a real old-fashioned love

91

story." Willa walked closer to the table. "How long have you picked crabs, Miss Ida?"

"All my life. Look at my hands and that'll tell ye something." Ida held her worn, weathered, nicked-up hands toward Willa. "Ye don't make a whole lot of money doing this to have pritty hands like yours. It's not like what ye do, but it's our way. Wouldn't know anything else to do."

Willa looked at Nellie. "Do most of the women here pick crabs?"

"They used to, in season, but things aren't what they were, so some went off to find work over on the mainland. Things are changing so fast here now."

"Ye can say that again, Nellie. I hear you spoke about us over there in D.C. How'd that go? I'll bet they couldn't have cared less about us folks."

"Well, that's not all true, but they sure didn't go out of their way to ask a lot of questions. Maybe I'm just too young and they think I don't know anything. Mama got further than I did."

"She sure was proud of ye. She talked to everyone about your being there. Don't tell her this, but she was as nervous as a schoolgirl the day ye were speaking."

"She wasn't the only one," Nellie said. "Now it's a wait-and-see game, Miss Ida. Nothing changes overnight with those people."

"Well, it isn't going to change much anytime soon neither, Nellie. They got it in their brains to keep on at us out here, and they think they're doing us good. Too many rules and regulations coming all the time. Our men can't keep up, and all they want to do is crab and oyster. Now what's wrong with that? Ye don't need a thousand rules to do that."

"Next time I'm sending you, Miss Ida." Nellie laughed. "Well, we have to get going. I want to show Willa some other places before Mama serves up every dish in her cookbooks. Stop by later. I know she'd love to see you."

"Give Miss Frances my best and enjoy your visit, Miss Willa. I can't believe I met a celebrity."

After they made it outside, Willa said, "I'm no celebrity and I'm here as a plain old visitor."

"They will remember this forever, Willa. Let the women have some fun."

"Okay, you're right. Where to next?"

"I want to swing by Bradshaw's for a minute and then we'll head back on home. Mama likes to start fairly early and then we eat all day. You'll see."

"You wouldn't be stopping by Bradshaw's to see if that handsome Denny is there, would you?"

"Am I that transparent?"

"Yep."

Luck was with Nellie. Denny was running the store for the few hours it was open on the holiday.

Willa got to spend her time with the old men, still sitting on the same chairs that no doubt had held them for eons. But this time was different when she walked in and sat down. They opened up and out popped the most wonderful stories filled with wit and wisdom from the waterman's world. She was enjoying herself immensely when Nellie turned around and abruptly said, "Time to go, Willa."

She looked at Denny's face and it appeared he was moonstruck. It didn't take a tree full of owls to know that boy had it bad for Miss Nellie. *Did I, Willa Carpenter, just say* Miss Nellie? *They're gaining on me.*

"Come on, Willa. We have to go."

I said my good-byes and waved over to Denny, who looked sad to see them—more accurately, Nellie—walk out the door.

"Why did you leave so fast, Nellie?"

"Because I couldn't stand there like an idiot, just talking to him like that."

"I don't know why not. That boy has it bad for you, Nellie."

"I know that, but I don't know how I really feel about him. I'm in a different place with my life right now, and I don't know if I can ever come back here to live. And he would die off the island and water."

"Ah, a romantic conundrum."

Nellie eyes rolled and she stared at Willa as if she had two heads. "A what?"

"Look it up."

"It doesn't sound good, Willa."

"Look it up."

"We better hurry. We still have to help Mama with the cooking and then you won't believe your eyes. You're about to eat a feast. I mean a real feast, like they did way back when."

Now it was Willa's eyes that rolled, thinking of what was to come. "I can't wait."

By the time they had stopped briefly by the church, the mainstay of the island, and the graveyard—an education in and of itself—they made it back just in time to help Frances finish her holiday duties.

A half hour later Frances announced, "It looks great, girls. Now go get ready for dinner. Daddy's outside with them derned crabs. They won't be going overboard no more."

Willa looked at Nellie and knew the crabs had met their fate.

Showered and dressed simply for dinner in slacks and a knit top, Willa went downstairs and found a few extra people had come by to join in. She had a feeling that's the way this day was going to go. Before she knew it, she was sitting at the table, now expanded to seat twelve.

After they had all introduced othemselves, Frances sat down and it was time to give thanks. Apparently this was Jimmy's duty, and he executed it perfectly, thanking the good Lord for all the bounty that was now spread on every counter, every shelf, and every serving piece in the house. As they prayed, Willa kept her eyes discreetly open as Mr. Jimmy Evans offered up a prayer fit for angels. It had been too long since she had enjoyed that moment with her parents, but she felt they were right there with her.

"Now that the good Lord has been thanked, let's eat." Frances smiled. "Nellie, you help Willa with this."

Nellie took her by the arm and she stood up. "I'll follow your lead. Where do we start?"

"I'll help you. Just ask if ye don't know what it is."

As Willa looked around at the dishes, she could tell those naughty crabs had been spread around to almost every recipe in the book. They had sure paid for their momentary victory, and she could hear their spirits crying as they were stewed, breaded, fried, and broiled. She didn't see one solitary piece of turkey.

"Do you folks eat turkey?" Willa asked timidly.

"Sure we do, but the crab dishes always come first, and over there are the oysters. They're so good. Mama makes them the best around. The turkey will make an appearance in a little bit."

"Good heavens, Nellie. I don't know if I can do all this. What's that dish over there?"

"That's the best. Mama's recipe for Chesapeake Rockfish Imperial. You'll love it."

"I've never heard of rockfish."

"It's strictly a Maryland fish, and it's not easy to get anymore. Restrictions on fishing it have made it a real treat."

Willa looked around and really wondered if she could do this all day, as these folks seemed to do. How could she eat the turkey and all the fixings after this? *Stuff it, girl; stuff it.*

By the time Jimmy walked inside with the fried turkey, she was ready to evacuate her stomach, but smiled on. It smelled so good and she would have to have a taste, wouldn't she?

Fried turkey was catching on everywhere, but every holiday she had heard of more fires because of fools who didn't follow directions, so it wasn't something she had ever wanted to pursue on her own. But she was glad she tried this ole tom. He tasted like nothing she had ever had before. Willa wasn't talking anymore. She was gobbling.

A little later came the final test: did she have the courage to eat dessert? She stared them all down, knowing she was definitely going to have some major stomach problems.

"Why, Franny girl, ye've outdone yerself. Sweet potato pie, applesauce pie, yer famous pumpkin pie, and yer James Island fig cake. What do ye think of all this, Miss Willa?"

She couldn't tell Jimmy the truth. As it was, her stomach was blown up as big as a hot air balloon, and her greatest fear was that flatulence was not company-presentable at this holiday table. What could she say?

Nellie apparently saw her difficulty and came to the rescue. "I think Willa and I are going to do the 'push-back' for now, Daddy. It's a lot of food all at once and we can't kill our guest."

Frances let out a whoop and began laughing. "Ye liked it all, didn't ye, Willa? Well, get up and take a walk and it'll still be here when ye get back."

She managed to eke out a smile, hoping the food wouldn't ooze back up into her mouth. All she could get out was, "Yes, thank you." She couldn't get out of the room fast enough. When she got to the bathroom, she was somewhere between heaven and hell. She felt like the goose as it was getting stuffed so folks could enjoy foie gras. *I will never eat that again. I promise you, goose. I know how you feel.*

She realized it had been the best and worst dinner she had ever had. The food was the best part but dealing with the pain of overfeeding was definitely the worst. She persuaded Nellie not to walk with her. She needed to do this alone and Nellie needed to be immersed with her own people.

Willa walked out the door and down narrow lanes new to her. She headed straight to the water on one side of Tuckerton. She had seen it out of one of the windows in the house, and it was calling to her.

When she reached it, she saw the magic of this place. The old shacks—no doubt for the crabs and the watermen—were weathered and looked frail, as if they had been there a million years. She looked back at all the homes, so lovely and holding the collective history of all the generations that had come here, and those still here.

She felt a spark light up in her soul. One that hadn't been there before. She was being given a gift, and all she had to do was reach out for it. But something was holding her back. She wasn't ready for the gift yet, but, standing on that old dock, she knew for certain this wasn't going to be her last trip over here.

She was connecting to something much bigger than herself. She felt the presence of her parents in a comforting way. The way it used to be. She didn't want ever to let go, but, as in all things, she knew the time would come when she would have no choice. She would have to leave and go home, or at least, the home she lived in now. But something was out here, and she would find it no matter how long it took.

CHAPTER 17

"The boat's rocking, Nellie. Make it stop."

"It's not slick cam. Or 'calm' as you would say. I'm sorry, Willa, but, when it's like this, you just have to hold on. Cap'n Tuck knows how to handle it."

"I'm going to drown, just like when I was a child and the wave pulled me under. Help me, Nellie."

Not until the sound of her cell phone woke her up did Willa realize she was having a horrible nightmare. She shook her head to break the scene from her mind, then leaned over and answered her phone.

"Hello?"

"Willa? It's Prue. You sound sort of odd."

"Yes, it's me, and, yes, I sound odd. I was asleep and having a really awful nightmare."

"Then I guess I'm not sorry I woke you up. What were you dreaming about? Congressman Lee?"

"Funny, Prue. I was dreaming I was on that damned boat and I was drowning."

"Wow! That isn't so funny. Anyway, just called to see if you want to go out and grab a hot dog at that neat little place, Yitzi's Delicatessen?"

"Would like to see you, Prue, but I don't really feel like going out right now. Maybe dinner, after you get through with work?"

"I'm not at work. I took an extra day off. It always takes me that long to get back into Washington mode. How about if I stop and get Chinese and a bottle of white wine? Then you don't have to go out and we can settle in for a long talk."

Willa said, "Now you're singing my tune. I'm dying for a glass of wine. They don't drink on the island. They frown on it, so no wine with the turkey, crabs, or eight million other dishes I stuffed down."

"They don't drink? Not even wine? I suppose they're religious over there."

"I think you're on to it now, Prue. But what they miss in drinking some wine, they more than make up for with food. I have never seen nor eaten so much. It's a wonder I didn't sink on my way back, so best pick up a pint of steamed vegetables for me. No rice; that might do me in all together."

"Go take a shower and I'll be there in an hour."

"Now we're a poet, are we?"

Willa hung up and realized how badly that dream was bothering her. She was still afraid of so many things. When would that go away? Ever?

She looked up at the ceiling and said out loud, "Why can't you take these doubts away from me, Mom? Why did you and Daddy have to leave so soon? I need you more now than when I was little. That island holds something for me. I felt it, but have no idea what was calling to me from the water. Still nothing comes to mind for me to write. And yet, it's out there. I know it. That answer isn't going to please Kit Winthrop. And poor Susan Crandall; she has no one to steal from. A sad state of affairs for sure."

While Prue opened the Chinese cartons, Willa poured the wine, but she obviously wasn't paying attention. Prue stood there staring at the wine overflowing the glass, then yelled, "Hey, Earth to Willa. I only brought one bottle. You can stop pouring now."

Willa jerked back to life. "Oh, sorry, Prue. I'll take this one and you pour what you want. Here."

"What's wrong with you? I'm the one who tends to get lost in my thoughts, but never you."

"I think I'm going through some kind of phase lately. First I can't focus and now I feel this overwhelming confusion all the time. Can I be losing it altogether?"

Prue gave Willa a strange look and then responded, "I know what you mean."

They stood there staring at one another for a minute. Prue clearly didn't like this; she was uncomfortable. An immensely private and controlled young woman, she rarely showed her vulnerability to anyone, even her best friend. Willa was so opposite and often tended to the very dramatic, but, in this case, Willa was obviously having a hard time.

Finally, Prue laughed, then said, "So, the island was fun. Did you learn anything over there, Willa?"

Willa was glad Prue had switched the mood and very happy to tell Prue about her experience.

"Dear God, Prue, I learned so much but there's so much more to learn. I've decided to go back again, but not until I read up on that place and the whole Eastern Shore. The folks are different and a bit clannish, but they are undergoing huge changes and may not exist in the same way if the winds over here don't change." She paused, then said, "It's a wonderful place, but there's a certain sadness that surrounds it. I can't explain it, but I could get lost in the sheer innocence of it for a very long time."

"Sounds deliciously mysterious and I know, Willa, you're going to write a romance that uses that as a backdrop. The folks there will love it. It's one of the things people love about your books. They're set in real places people can relate to, and the people who do live in those places love to read how you weave your stories through them. You give readers a place to dwell in, and, when the story is over, they're sorry to leave."

"You know, Prue, no one has ever told me—in those exact, beautiful words—what you have just described. I'm going to write that down and give it to my PR people. Really quite lovely."

"It's true, Willa. You're a master of love."

"Well, let's not go that far. Maybe because I can't seem to fall in love in my real life, I write about it so well from my subconscious. Now, tell me what's eating at you? You seem to want to keep talking about me, romance, and the island."

"Can't fool you, can I? Well, there is something—or a few somethings—I need to talk about with you."

Willa laughed. "As long as we have wine, I'm all ears."

"I don't know if I should tell you this or let nature take its course, but here goes. I was cleaning things up in the office and thought everyone had left for the holiday. All had, except for Charles, which really surprised me."

"That's really weird. Most of the superstars skip out way early to get started on their holiday. We wouldn't want to have them overworked or anything, would we?"

"I'm being kind of serious about this, Willa."

"Yes, I see that. Sorry. Go on, Prue."

"Anyway, we got talking and that's when he asked me . . . ."

"The plots thickens, but I fear not in a good way, Prue. What the heck did he ask you? Or are you going to drag this out?"

"Wait, hold on, Willa. We were talking about nothing really, but he was sort of nervous. He was so odd, and then he asked if you were going home with me this year like you usually do."

"Snooping? The suave and debonair stud of them all was snooping?"

"When I told him you weren't going home with me this year, he asked outright where you were."

"You didn't tell him, did you? I mean these politicians smell trouble from a million miles away."

"I had no choice, Willa. I had to tell him. Did you want me to lie to my boss?"

"They lie to us on a daily basis, but they call it 'spin.'"

"Willa? You're talking about a profession I love."

"That's interesting, I never thought of politics as a profession. Weren't politicians originally meant to go to Washington to represent the people's wishes and then go home?"

Prue shot her a dirty look. "You know it doesn't work that way anymore."

"'Tis a shame, but please let's not quibble about things we aren't going to change. So what else did he say as he was asking for my life history?"

"That's a bit over the top, don't you think, Willa? At any rate, when I told him, he lost it. He got really mad. I was shocked."

"Gee, I wonder why? I told you, they can smell trouble a million miles away."

"He said he had done both of us a favor by allowing you to come to that hearing and this is what happened. Then he added that he would hold me personally responsible if you wrote about anything that related to that session."

Willa started biting her lip. She was a bit speechless and a bit mad. Well, more than a bit.

"If he thinks he can tell me where I can and can't go and what I can and can't write, he has another think coming. And to hold you responsible? That's beyond the pale. If he has something to say, he can say it to my face."

Prue had never seen Willa react like this. "I shouldn't have told you."

"I'm glad you did. That man is asking for me to call him right now and tell him where he can go."

"You wouldn't, Willa. I need to keep this job, at least for a little while longer."

Willa saw she was upsetting Prue. "I'm sorry. I don't ever want to hurt you. It's just he has no business in my business."

"You know what I think, Willa? I think you like him a little and maybe he likes you a little, too."

"Now who's playing the romance writer? I wouldn't like him if he was the last man on earth, and especially now.

"This is always how it starts: a sandbox fight."

"A sandbox fight? Is that what you call someone who wants to know where I go and what I do?"

"Yes," Prue answered quietly. "It's a sandbox fight."

"Being you know so much about this, how does the story end?"

"Only the two people in the sandbox know that, Willa."

"Seriously, Prue, don't say anything more about me to the good congressman. I don't want you to hang for this. I know you have an agenda in D.C. Well, who doesn't? But you don't need to have your best friend being the one to ruin it."

"It's going to be all right, Willa. I'm a big girl from a tough family so I can handle what comes. I just got nervous when I saw his emotions, but, really, I think he's taken with you."

"Prue, you and I are close, and you know I have demons that hang out with me. I have to work through them and that's going to take time. And time right now is tight for me because I miss and need my writing.

A serious relationship can't now be, and may never be, for me. What I do know is that, when I left the island, I felt so alone again. There's something out there and it seems to call me."

"I know you've had a tough time, Willa, but that's what makes you who you are, and it's that sad side of you that helps you write the stories you do. You're in touch with so many emotions."

"Yeah, too many of them. They seem to pop up just when you don't expect them and then they take over. It's hard and I have to learn how to control them."

"That will come when you meet someone who makes you want to control them. Right now, you need to write, but please be careful. These folks over here take things real personal; you know that."

Willa smiled. She really loved Prue for so many reasons and her deep understanding of the human condition was uncanny for someone only thirty-three years old. But wasn't she the same way? Hadn't life given her the insights to see into others' souls and be able to touch them?

"You know something, Prue? You and I are two peas in a pod. We come from families that taught us to be what we are today. Yes, we're young in years maybe, but old in time. You'll make a fine politician one day when you're ready, and your father will be there to make this happen. He was in this game and he knows how to play it. That's something special most don't have. It's in your genes."

"And you, Willa, look at your genes. You are already a famous writer. You've achieved so much and you're only a little older than I. We're two amazing ladies, but please be careful. Even Charles doesn't understand how bad things can get. He's getting better at it, but there are some old dogs in this fight concerning the Bay, and they're not going to lie down and let someone walk away with what they want."

"Thanks for the warning, Prue. You help Charles then, and try to protect him, and I'll try to steer clear of trouble."

"Thanks, Willa. This is going to get interesting. I want to be a good politician one day. I don't want people to be sorry they sent me to represent them because I failed at the job."

"You won't. You're learning now what not to do, and that's a valuable lesson."

Prue leaned over the coffee table and picked up the fortune cookies. "Want to start with dessert first?"

"Hell, why not? But mine always says, 'learn Chinese.'"

Prue broke out laughing. "They all say that. Read the other side, Willa."

Willa was teasing Prue; she wanted to see her beautiful smile. "You mean the side that says I will find my love on an island?"

"You never know, Willa. You never know."

CHAPTER 18

"Well, what did you think of my new friend, Mama?"

"She seems to be a nice young lady, Nellie, and it was certainly something to have a famous writer here with us in our humble home for Thanksgiving. I hope she was comfortable enough. Why did she run off so soon?"

"I think she wanted to stop eating! And to think about all she had seen. I saw her face on the way across. She kept looking back at the island, and seemed so deep in thought. There was a wistful expression on her face, as if she were remembering something else, perhaps from another time."

"She is certainly a quiet one, but then no one ever gets a chance to talk around the likes of me and the other folks on the island. I probably talked her ear off too much."

"I don't think so, Mama. She hung on your every word, and she told me she had never eaten so many dishes made with crabs. I told her she should come back in the summer when crabs are in their prime and we're all out in the sheds or on the water."

"What did she say to that, Nellie?"

"She said she just might."

"Then don't tell her about the greenheads and how they can run a person straight into the Bay to escape 'em. I mean, we do have some pests out here, but those greenhead flies are the worst."

"No, that wouldn't be a good way to have her come back at all. Their bites and stings are nasty. Think I can save that fact until we see if she's going to return to the island."

"What's on her mind to do, Nellie? Is she looking for something over here? I mean I know anyone would be taken by ye, but ye have only met, and then she accepted your very hospitable invitation for the holiday, but that girl is looking for something far more than friendship."

"I suppose, but aren't we all? She's really interested in what's going on inside the crabbing and oystering industry around the Bay. She took a whole lot of notes when I was speaking."

"Ah, this is the first chance we've had to talk about that, Nellie. How do you think you did? I know how hard it is to do that."

"Mama, not to put too fine a point on it, but I don't know how you had the nerve to sit in front of them and talk. That's a tough crowd over there, and, way back when you went, it had to be terrifying."

Frances laughed wholeheartedly at her daughter. "The talking was the easy part, but the sittin' still was a whole other matter. Those people just like to sit and do little else. They're used to doing that for a living. I am not and so that was the hard part."

Smiling lovingly at her mother, Nellie said, "I don't think I'll be doing it again. Congressman Lee is a good young congressman. And he certainly is handsome; I hear he's a bachelor. Anyway, he seems kind of nervous to push this thing too far. I think he wanted to hear from one of us, a younger generation islander. He wanted to hear certain things that he can use to satisfy some of them and yet not get in the way of those who really want us off the water."

"At the rate they're regulatin' and not caring what we really think on the situation, they'll have their way sooner than they know."

Nellie stared out to the Bay, "It's so beautiful out here, and all over the Bay. The men have been going out forever, Mama, and they know things that bureaucrats could never imagine to understand."

"We all know that, Nellie, but they aren't of a mind to listen. Oh, they tell us they care, but their actions speak louder than words."

"Mama? Would you ever have another go at it? I mean would you return over there to really fight this issue?"

Frances kept on looking out to the water with Nellie sitting by her side. She slid her hand through Nellie's and said, "I don't know, love. It's a tough thing to know when you're licked or if there's something more you can do to help stop time from closing in on you."

"That's so well put, Mama. You could do it, you know. They still remember you, and some asked for you and how you're doing. You told them straight and plain, and, believe it or not, some people admire those who stand up to the winds of such drastic change."

"Maybe, but some despise those who stand in their way or try to reason with them. The bureaucrats have their own agenda and no one is going to spoil it. At least not for now."

"But now is now and tomorrow may be too late for us out here and all those who still fish around the Bay."

"That may be true, Nellie, but there are many fishermen and their families going through this. All around the coastlines of America, we're all the same, doing the same and wanting the same for our folks. We want to continue to bring in our fish and crabs and seafood and feed this great country, but the regulations are killing us. We can't keep up with it. We fish; we don't do paper work. If we could get them to understand that, we could have a place to start, but, as long as they keep on pressing us more and more, it won't be long before we're done."

"What happens then, Mama?"

"That's to be seen. Now, let's go eat some leftovers and laugh a bit."

"Sounds good to me. I don't think Willa will eat for a week. She's not used to our ways, especially eating."

"Worldly women always have one eye on their waistlines while we island women have our eyes on the table. It's how it is and has been and, as long as we're here, it's how it will be."

"You go on, Mama. I want to stop in at Bradshaw's. Do you need anything?"

"Heavens no, but smile nice and be sure to say hello to Denny for me."

"Mama! I'm going to go to see Mr. Floyd."

"Sure you are, Helen Ann. Well, tell Mr. Floyd that Miss Willa loved his crab cakes and thank him again for such a kindness."

"Helen Ann. You don't call me that except when you're getting at me, Mama."

"Aha, Helen, that's exactly right. Why don't you come clean and just admit you have a spark for Denny? He's sure got it for ye."

"Well, let's let it be for now and see how it all turns out. I have to go back day after tomorrow, so no use to get all bothered about it now."

"You'll break that boy's heart, Nellie. He means to have you as his wife."

"Well, we'll just see about that, won't we? Maybe Congressman Lee will take a shine to me, although I don't think it's me he's thinking twice about."

"He'd never get better, but you're a realistic girl. I taught ye that. Ye have to stay with your own or it just doesn't work out."

"I suppose that's something else you're right about, Mama."

CHAPTER 19

"Do you really have to go back so soon, Charlie?"

"Yes I do, Verinnia. I had a really good time with y'all, but, when duty calls, you know how that goes."

Reaching up to give her brother a big hug, Verinnia whispered, "I finally accepted Thomas's proposal, Charlie."

"About time. You've made that poor boy wait forever. Have you told Mom and Dad?"

"Not yet. I was waiting to tell you first. He'll make a wonderful brother-in-law."

"Where's the ring? I hope he did it right."

"Oh, Charlie, I just told him I would marry him. I don't think he was prepared for me to say yes, after all the times I told him to come back another time. If a ring is coming, I might suspect it would be at Christmas."

Charles stood back and looked at his little sister. He beamed proudly. They were as close as brother and sister could be. And she was about the only one, other than their parents, who could get away with calling him Charlie now that he had joined the long line of Lees of Virginia in the U.S. Congress.

"Well, Miss Verinnia, I won't miss that occasion. Thomas could use some support after your abuse all these years." Hugging her again, he said, "I'm so happy for you two. So you'll be Mrs. Thomas Hibbons one day soon. It has a ring to it: Verinnia Hibbons."

"It does at that. He's such a romantic and he says my name makes him wild."

Wincing a bit, Charles said, "Too much information, Sister. Well, he is from a good Virginia line and that counts in this family."

"He loves me, of course, but he also loves being a part of the long line of Lees. That counts more than everything in this state. Aren't we lucky, Charlie?"

"We are at that. Hey, kid, I have to go. I'll be back at Christmas to see that big rock you're going to get."

Verinnia smiled. "Don't miss it. I'll count every minute until I see you again. Behave, big brother."

Charles snickered at her and said, "I have to, don't I?"

With one last hug, Charles got into his Tahoe and drove out the long winding driveway of the family home. He wasn't even off the property before he was missing his family, his childhood home, and his genteel way of life in the heart of Thomas Jefferson country.

"Damn," he said out loud, as he got on Route 64 and headed west. "Time off is always so short. I'm going to miss them. But there is much to do ahead of me and I have to make my move fast to make sure there are no messes to clean up. I'm going to find out what Willa Carpenter is up to. And we are going to have our first date, whether she knows it or not."

Prue had left a couple of hours earlier and Willa was knee deep into research about James Island and the other island on the Virginia side of the Chesapeake. She couldn't believe how many islands had been out there before time either sank them or people deserted them. At one time, you couldn't go very far without running into another one, and most of them had had vibrant communities, centered on Methodism and a strict Christian life, but all revolving around the water and crabs and oysters. Now the future of the remaining ones was uncertain, not only because of nature but because of too much interference by people who didn't know or understand their way of life.

Eyes tired, Willa took a break and padded to the kitchen to pour a cup of tea. She was feeling as if something was beginning to gel in her mind, but not clearly enough to put any words down on paper.

The ringing of the phone was annoyance enough, but, when she looked at the caller ID, she felt death would have been preferable. Still, not answering wasn't an option.

"Why, Willa dahling, you're back. I was hoping you would be. How was your little trip away? Did it help?"

"Hello, Kit. My Thanksgiving was good; I hope yours was, too." A voice from the dead would have been livlier. This woman was really getting on her nerves.

"Anything new to report to me, Willa?"

"Not really," Willa nervously replied.

The expected pause came and Willa really wanted to get off the phone fast.

"I don't know what to say to you, Willa. I mean you're way behind and we do have a contract. Is anything forthcoming?"

Oh boy, I'm stuck now. Wait 'til she hears this answer. "Another trip I think, Kit."

This time the pause seemed endless, but Willa could hear her fuming all the way from her office.

"All right, then. We have to cut the mustard here and quit dancing around."

Here it comes. Hold on, girl.

"I am going to call our lawyers and have them take a long look and see what can be done about this. While I sympathize with your 'problem,' I can't go on any longer without something from you that has a story line. Susan is coming along nicely and I just took a new, young writer aboard, so I have to move on. You're one of the best, Willa, but it's business with me."

It didn't take Willa one nanosecond to fire back.

"Well, go right ahead, Kit. The situation is what it is, and, although I hate that overused expression, I can't help that my mind is taking a holiday. Frankly, I don't appreciate your ingratitude for the years I've pumped the best sellers out for Kitwin Publishing. And to think I'm only in my thirties. What do you want from writers? A book popping off their fingers every few months? It's impossible, and so go get your lawyers and I'll talk to mine."

She heard the snort over the phone. "Well, I never. Really, Willa, this matter has gone too far. I would gladly have sent you anywhere to work on this. You know there are ways to get past the block, but, if you would prefer not to write with us anymore, then you should say so."

"I didn't say that, Kit, but you throw Susan Crandall up at me all the time, and, if you would take a minute to remember, *I'm* the number one-producing gal; she's not and may not ever be, if she keeps on stealing other writers' story lines. Why don't you talk to your lawyers about that? I've said my piece now, and that's all I have to say. If you want me to stay, I will, but only under the condition I move at my own speed."

Kit hesitated a moment, apparently thinking better of their argument. "I think we should both cool off. I'll back off, Willa, but not forever."

"Then we have an agreement for now. Enjoy the holidays, Kit. I'll think about what you've said and see what can be done."

As Kit was beginning to say good-bye, Willa hung up. She couldn't stomach one more word.

Why doesn't Kit leave her alone? Something is beginning to break loose, and, given time, it will all come into focus. In the meantime she was going to prove to Kit that Susan Crandall was a nitwit unlikely ever to go anywhere permanently.

As Willa picked up the phone, she could hardly contain herself.

"Susan Crandall residence."

"May I please speak to Susan? This is Willa Carpenter. Thank you."

She has a maid as an answering service? Makes me want to yak.

"Willa, what a pleasant surprise."

Yeah, right. "Hi, Susan. I hope you had a nice holiday. Why I called was to let you know that I'm taking a sabbatical from writing for a short while and that Kit tells me wonderful things about your new upcoming book. I just want you to know that I may not be continuing on with romance books, but I wish you all the luck in the world."

"What's going on, Willa? I mean, you're the absolute queen of romance right now."

"Well, I had a story line but it didn't gel and something else came along."

"Oh. What was the story line? Maybe we can collaborate. I would love that."

I'll just bet you would. Willa told her the story line, not believing it was this easy. Susan lapped it up like a cat and warm milk. She took the bait, without question. What an idiot.

"Well, I think it isn't your best, Willa, so good idea to let it drop. But thanks for calling. That means the world to me. Good luck on your new ventures. I can't wait to hear all about it."

"Oh, you'll be the first to hear, Susan. I know we'll keep in touch. Bye."

Willa stomped around her apartment. "That fool. That absolute fool, and Kit thinks she is Miss La-De-Da. Well, wait until Susan calls her with my idea and Kit sits back in stunned silence as she remembers that that story line was my first book. Yeah, that'll learn ya, Susan. Sound like ole Frances now, don't I? I'm missing her already."

CHAPTER 20

"Why I agreed to accept this date, is beyond me. Now what to wear." As Willa pawed through her clothes, she tried to figure out where this date with Charles Lee had come from. Thin air? I doubt it, she thought. "This is nice. Black always works, and this dress is flirty without yelling sex. God forbid! He's the last man—"

The phone rang. It was Prue, interrupting Willa's self-conversation.

"Hi, girlfriend. What's up?"

"What's up with you, Willa? Let's start with the fact you didn't tell me you were going out with my boss. Then we'll move on to *why* you didn't tell me."

"Hold on, Prue. I didn't tell you because, at first, I thought it was a wrong number or a joke."

"Hold on, Willa. You can come up with a better one than that."

"But it's true. I didn't recognize the number on the caller ID, and then, the second time he called, the phone was all staticy. By the time I realized it really was Charles, he was saying, 'Well, is that okay?' I said yes. I mean you don't say no to a United States congressman, do you?"

"That's a real stretch, Willa."

"It's the truth. He said to meet him at The Willard at seven tonight."

"I know that because it's on his calendar. I wonder what's up with this?"

"I won't know unless I meet with him, will I? I'll tell you everything. You know that."

"Well, all right. I guess I'm at a loss."

"Join the club."

"What are you wearing?"

"My black Dolce & Gabbana."

"You are not! Get out of here. Are you?"

"Sure am. If I'm going to meet with the high and mighty, I better look like one myself."

"You already are the high and mighty, remember? Honestly, your modesty boggles my mind."

"Then stay boggled and let me get dressed, or I'm going to be late and that is a no-no, no matter who you think you are."

"Yes, he does like punctuality. Try not to mess this up, Willa. Maybe he just wants to get to know you."

"Fat chance. In this town, there are no get-to-know-you dinners at The Willard."

"Guess you're right, but be careful. He's looking for something, and he is the most charming of them all."

"Maybe you ought to be in a black dress and going out with Prince Charming."

"Wouldn't work because he's my boss, and we know my rules on that topic. Besides, I don't own a Dolce & Gabanna."

"Maybe you should piss off on your rules, Prue."

"Never. Just let me know. And behave."

"The minute I get home, to the last statement? Maybe."

She hung up and turned again to her wardrobe. *Now where was I? Oh, the little black number. This one should be perfect. A last look, and, yes, the blonde looks very fine tonight.* "And now here's to you, Charles Lee."

Charles wondered if he were doing the right thing, but he had to find out where this gal was coming from. It was insurance, and he needed every edge in this most touchy situation. Lobbyists were wolves nipping at your heels all the time, and, when they had big money to back them up, it was really hard to hold the balance and stay clean.

Pacing in the foyer next to the Scotch Bar, Charles looked down at his watch. Seven fifteen. Well, that was strike one. He decided that, if she didn't get there within the next two minutes, he was walking on her. No woman was worth the wait. Then he saw her come through the door. Was it his imagination, or was she even more beautiful than he remembered?

Willa saw him and flashed a smile. Trying to walk gracefully, her heel caught on the edge of the carpet and she almost tripped over the thick Persian area rug. Recovering quickly, she said, "I'm so sorry, Charles. The cabdriver was into telling me about the city and I couldn't make him go any faster."

The annoyance he'd felt a few minutes ago evaporated immediately. She was gorgeous and he wasn't used to feeling a bit . . . well . . . as if lightning had struck him.

"That's okay, Willa. I have to admit I'm a stickler for being on time, but I do understand the plight of the person taking a cab. They can be pretty bad, I hear."

"Guess that would be one reason to be a congressman. You get a driver and don't have to resort to the way we peons live."

"Ouch! Was that a put-down?"

"Maybe, but a teasing one. Am I forgiven?"

"Only if we can go in and eat. I'm getting kind of hungry."

"Lead the way, Congressman."

The Scotch Bar sees its share of politicians and celebrities, but, when the two of them walked in, it caused a bit of a stir. Willa didn't like to admit she was well known, but she was. And Charles Lee's striking looks always attracted at least a casual stare from women, so, when they entered, the room was immediately abuzz.

"Here's your table, Congressman. I hope it's to your liking."

With a brilliant smile, Charles said, "It certainly is, Christopher."

Willa said, "You know Christopher? He's the best."

"That's why I know him."

Oh, he's not too conceited. Two yuks.

"What do you want to drink, Willa?"

Christopher was hovering, ready to take their order.

"I'll have my usual, Christopher."

"Ah, yes, Miss Carpenter. A cosmopolitan."

"And will you have your favorite, Congressman?"

"Yes, a Glenlivet. Then we'll order."

The dinner went quite well for a while. The meal was excellent. And then Charles made his move.

"I hear you went over to one of the islands for the holiday. How did that go? Do you know people over there?"

Willa took the measure of him and knew he was on a fishing expedition. He knew damned well she didn't know anyone over there. However, she could lie.

"No, I don't know anyone over there, or, I should say, I don't know anyone well from over there."

She had to admit he looked even cuter when he was biting his lip. *Huh, same habit as me when he's thinking of the right words to say. I saw him do that in the hearing. I remember writing that one down under "Description: Charles Lee."*

"I see. Well, who do you not know well over there?"

Willa leaned in close and said, "Charles, why don't you just tell me what's on your mind? I'm no fool, and, if you remember, I write stories about people who manipulate other people."

"I guess you do at that. I'm sorry." Then he blurted out, "Willa, I have to be completely open with you. I asked you to dinner to find out if your intentions are honorable on this commercial fishing subject."

"Well, I see you're capable of getting down to business, and at least now you're being honest." Willa stopped, then started again. "I don't know, Charles. That's all I can say. You must know I struck up a conversation with your speaker, Nellie Evans. We hit it off, and, in a somewhat bizarre set of circumstances, she asked me over to the island for the holiday. I usually go home to Prue's folks, but I wanted to learn more about this place and the people."

"And what did you learn, Willa?"

"I learned that there are always two sides to everything."

Charles sat back. He realized she got even prettier when her dander was up, but knew he had to get her to take a back seat on this one.

"When Prue asked me if you could come to that hearing, I said yes because you were her friend, and, also, because I wanted to meet you again. Am I getting too honest now?"

"No. Maybe. I don't know. Go on." Not her best use of words ever, but he was making her uncomfortable by being so brutally honest. She didn't expect such frankness from a politician.

"Well, it's true. You're an interesting woman, Willa, and I would like you to promise me something."

"Keep talking. I'm listening, Congressman."

"I want you to promise me you won't write anything about this that I don't know about first. Can you do that? I know you're going to get a story out of this. I can smell it. That's what politicians really do for a living, you know. They are wise to what's coming down, and, if they think it's trouble, it's their job to head it off."

"While you're being so open, Charles, tell me why this is so touchy. What's going on? We are all Americans and we all want what's best for one another. These people just want to fish, and, from what little I've seen, you folks here are making their lives hell with rules and regulations."

"You see, you can't help yourself. It's in you to find a story. You're as bad as the press."

"The press doesn't write about these things very much, Charles. You know that. They're in the tank for the government, not the people, unless it hits their interests."

"Wow, you're really upset about this."

"I haven't even begun to dig."

Charles said nothing for a minute, staring at her with an intensity that made Willa begin to sweat.

She said, "Look, I don't know what I'm going to find, but I know there's a whole lot swirling around in those waters out there. I will promise you this. If I find a story, I will come to you first about it. I can't say I'll shelve it, but I can promise you, you'll be the first to know."

"That's all I'm asking, Willa." Then with that Pepsodent-perfect smile, he added, "But we both know Prue will really be the first to know."

Willa realized he had had her at hello. She'd been hooked on him the first time out in the pond. Charles Lee could undoubtedly talk the pants off of a woman in a heartbeat, but she was determined to stay focused.

"You're on to me, Charles."

"Yes, I am. And one other thing while we're at it. When we're in private, you can call me Charlie."

CHAPTER 21

Standing at the kitchen sink, sipping her morning tea, Willa still couldn't get her mind off the charismatic and oh so charming Congressman Charles Lee. Charlie, her ass. Wake up, girl, smell the coffee. He's up to something and wants it badly enough to play her like a piano. *If he thinks he can get me to drop this island thing because he turns on that smile, he's wrong. He's going to learn that it takes more than two cosmos and a steak dinner to get Willa Carpenter to fold. Seriously! I need to talk to Prue. Where is my cell?*

Prue wasn't having an easy day either. With one day left before she had to return to the office, she had thrown everything from her closet onto the floor. Now the chore was to decide what to keep and what to get rid of. The challenge this year was not to get rid of all the pieces she always wanted back after her purge.

"Come on, Prue. Answer. Hello?"

"Hi, Willa. I'm not really in a friendly mood right now. What's up?"

"What's up? My dinner with Charles last night. Or should I say, 'Charlie.'"

"OMG! That's right. I completely forgot. I'm so involved here, waging war with my closet. How did it go?"

"Go? Well, it went all right. The man is so pompous, arrogant, self-absorbed . . . ."

"Oh boy, he really got to you."

"Got to me? Oh yes, the charm offensive was oozing all over the place. But we did have a great dinner; the food and service is always so good."

Prue burst out laughing. "He really laid it on, did he? He's good at that."

"Laid it on? I wouldn't say he had to go too far for that. He was as direct as a bulldozer coming straight at me. He told me to lay low with this island thing and he made it quite clear he wants me to mind my own business. I should keep on writing romances while he conquers the world."

"You really liked him, didn't you?"

"Hell, yes, I liked him. He has spunk to come at me that way."

"To tell you to mind your own business? Wow! That is spunk. Poor man. Doesn't realize what he's done, does he?"

"I can tell you this. When men start to complain like this, there's a reason, and that reason is now going to be my business."

"Willa, please don't. I can lose my job over this."

"No, you won't; I promise. You aren't going to get hurt in this war."

"Oh, we're at war status now, are we?"

"You bet. And do you want me to tell you the most maddening part of this all? He told me that when we're in private, I can call him Charlie!"

"I don't believe that. No one here calls him Charlie. The only ones I know who can are his parents and his beloved sister."

"Really? No one on the Hill calls him Charlie? Well, to be honest, he doesn't fit the 'Charlie' moniker."

"That's not exactly true. He can be a real good ole boy sometimes, especially when he's talking to his buddies back home."

"Do they call him Charlie?"

"Maybe over the phone, but, when they call and I answer, it's always Charles."

"Well, whatever people call him, he's going to be 'Asshole" in my book if he continues to tell me what to do."

"Awakened a sleeping tiger, has he?"

"A tigress, Prue. By the way, need any help sorting those clothes? I'm in the perfect mood."

"Nope. This is my cross to bear and this closet thing has to be all done by tomorrow when I head back to the mill."

"Oops, gotta go, another call is coming in. I don't recognize the number, but maybe it's 'Charlie' from an undisclosed location."

"Go on and catch you later. Maybe we can have dinner at Yitzi's Deli?"

"Maybe."

The call wasn't from Charlie; it was from Frances Evans.

"Good morning, Willa. Bet ye weren't expecting me to call ye."

"You're right about that. How are you? Is everything all right?"

"Fine, fine—really. Nellie's gone down to Bradshaw's and I got to thinking and wondered if ye had a good time out here."

"I had a wonderful time. I really had to get back, though, Frances, and I knew you and Nellie had a lot of catching up to do. There's nothing like alone time with your daughter."

"We've not stopped talking since. Jimmy just shakes his head and goes on about his business. He knows how much I miss Nellie when she's gone."

"I know you do. She's really a very wonderful young gal with a lot of promise."

"That's what I want to talk to ye about, but not right now. She'll be leaving tomorrow and on her way back over. She's got a ton on her mind. I was wondering if ye could keep an eye out on her for me."

"Well, where she lives isn't exactly around the corner, but, yes, I can make that promise. I'll call her and I'll be sure to go out to see her before Christmas comes."

"I'd appreciate that and so would her daddy. She's all we got."

Willa heard both the love and concern in Frances's voice. She remembered her mother had felt the same way and would have given anything to have someone watching out for her little girl.

"No problem. I'll be glad to do it."

"I also wanted to ask ye back for Christmas if you can come. We would love to have you."

"That's so lovely, Frances, but I've already made plans to go to my aunt's home. I haven't seen her in a while, and, at Christmas, family should be together. But there is something I would like to ask of you."

"Name it."

"I would like to take you up on your offer to visit out there after the holidays. I saw your island, but I didn't see it the way I want to see it."

"I think I know what you're talking about." Frances paused, then said,

"I tell you what. Why don't ye wait until the winter is passed—if ye can wait that long—and then come the beginning of April? That's when the men start getting ready for the crabs. Oystering will be at an end and the crabs will soon start swimming up the Bay if the weather gets warm."

"Actually, I'd like to come a few times. I know that's awfully nervy of me, but I have to see this all for myself."

"I understand, Willa. That's fine with us, but let me talk with my sister, Rita, over to Somerville, and see if ye can spend a few days with her. I'll come over and take ye around and show ye what used to be, so you'll have a better picture of all of it down here. It's pritty much the same all around the fishing towns, but at least you can get a better idea of it all."

"You know, that would be really good. Could we set that up for after Christmas?"

"You bet. Let me get back to ye after I talk to Rita, and we'll set it all up."

"Thank you so much, Frances. There's something about it over there. I can't put my finger on it, but it's definitely something powerful that affects me."

"It's called love, honey. The Bay has that effect on some people, and, even though you're an outlander, you may have roots over here ye don't even know about."

After they said good-bye, Frances's last words hung in the air for Willa. "Ye might have roots over here ye don't even know about." *I wonder.*

CHAPTER 22

Willa shot into the shower right after her call from Frances. She was feeling something she hadn't felt for a long time: creative. Her mind was going in a million directions and she was getting ideas as if a thousand points of light were going off all at once. She knew just the place to go for that extra nudge to help it along—the Library of Congress.

While she was heading there, Charles Lee was making a phone call.

One of his family's close friends, Nelson Beauchamp, was the head of the BWC—the Baywaters Commission—which was heavily involved and invested in the work of the house committee on the Chesapeake Bay. Nelson lived along the Bay in a sprawling mansion and was a source of much money for Charles's campaign. A huge presence and a powerful man, he had turned his organization into one of the most powerful lobbies in D.C.

"Hi, Nelson. It's Charles Lee. How's life treating you?"

"Pretty well, Charles. What's up with you?"

"I didn't get a chance to speak with you after the hearing last week and wondered what you thought of Miss Nellie Evans."

"Nothing. That's what I thought. Nothing. She's got a lot of information and she bears a strong message from the water community, but they're going to have to comply with the rules or they are going to find themselves in a heap of trouble, whether they like it or not."

"She was persuasive, Nelson. I could see the looks on the faces of the others on the panel. She brings grievances that are real. I understand their side, too."

"Most of the people on that committee aren't worth their spit, son, and you know that. So this Nellie what's-her-name is just fulfilling your obligation and their sense of fair play. Now, listen here, Charles, your job is to hold these dogs at bay. My organization is the king of that water and you know it. We aim to clean it up and keep it that way. And we aim to have these watermen comply with all the regulations. It doesn't matter if they like them or not. It's the law."

"They don't see it like that, Nelson. They see this as a way of taking their fishing rights away."

"Tough! It's the world they live in now. Hell, we don't like all the regulations either, but we can't do a thing about it, and a lot of those rules are for the best for both the oyster beds and the crab populations."

"Well, we'll have to see how this works out. Just wanted to warn you off on something. There was a woman sitting in on our hearing—Willa Carpenter—and she's a writer."

"I've heard the name. She's not only a famous writer, but I see her in the society section of the paper once in a while. She's a real beauty. How did I miss seeing her?"

"Think she was keeping a pretty low profile. Anyway, I had dinner with her the other night and she seems to be taken with these folks across the Bay. Even went over there for Thanksgiving. I just want you to know, I think she's going to write about us."

"You don't say. Doesn't she write fiction stories that women read?"

"Yes, she does, but she might try her hand at a new kind of story. It's just a hunch I have."

"Well, Charles, use that Lee family charm and I won't worry. There's not been a woman yet who couldn't be persuaded to change her mind about something when you turn that on."

Charles snickered. "I'm not so sure with this gal. She's a hellcat."

"Keep an eye on her. Let me know if you hear anything. In the meantime, have fun with her."

"I will, Nelson. Say, when are we going out to shoot skeet? It's been awhile."

"Soon. Thanks for the call. Now, you remember, if you need anything, you just give ole Nelson a call. Money is no object, son. Say hi to your daddy for me."

"Thanks, I will."

The Library of Congress is a most impressive place. The building reveals its own story. With stained-glass windows and high-domed ceiling, one feels dwarfed in its majesty. But, among the books, one feels one's place. Established by an act of Congress in 1800 and restocked with Thomas Jefferson's books after the Capitol (where it was then housed) was burned by the British in 1814, this library was meant to be a place where people could come and study and spend time around literature. When Willa was there, she was immersed in her element.

She had asked to look at all manner of books on the Chesapeake and its history. For hours she sat reading and taking notes. She was falling in love with this huge body of water that gives life to so much of the natural world. There was magic in the Bay and all the waters that ran into her.

This is incredible. I had no idea. She didn't think many people did. The Bay *was* the early history of the area and the nation. John Smith explored up and down and through these waters. She had to admit, as a child, she had never paid much attention to all the things the guide was telling her group when they had visited Williamsburg, Virginia. She'd been too busy looking at her colonial clothes. What do kids care about oyster shells used as roads and in yards? And even less where they came from. Now it was all coming together. It's too bad that real learning is wasted on the young because it isn't until much later in life that you ask the questions that count.

So here she was, learning about all this. What next? She could feel the block lifting because all she wanted to do was write. But what was she going to write? Willa whispered, "Help me out, Mom. What would you do?"

Yeah, like she's going to tell me. Willa, you're in this alone and you have to figure it out.

"I'm sorry to interrupt you, Miss Carpenter, but it's almost time to close, and I have to get these books back to their home."

"Oh, I'm so sorry. I've been so into what I'm reading that I forgot about the time. Give me a moment to write some of these titles down, and then I'll pop them over to your desk."

"Of course. And may I add, it's such a pleasure to have you here. I love your books. Are you working on a new one? About the Chesapeake? It certainly does lend itself to romance."

"Can't tell yet. You never know where one thing might lead to another. And thank you for being a fan."

"I have read all your books and look forward to a new one. Take your time. I'm not leaving for a while yet. It's been a particularly busy day in here."

"It's good to see how many people still love the hardbound books."

"I know what you mean. Some day I'm sure most will be digital, and young people won't know how wonderful it is to feel a book, turn a page, and smell the paper."

"It's easy to see why you're a librarian."

The woman walked off as Willa finished up. Then she dropped the books back at the desk and took out her phone to call Prue about this Yitzi's place.

Well, Yitzi's Deli certainly was something. Way out and wild. Eclectic artwork and collectibles plastered all over the piercingly bright yellow walls. There was an unmistakable Yiddish theme going on. Old-world music in the background brought it all together. Willa loved it.

"This your first time here, Prue? I thought maybe you had lunched here with Mr. Perfect Smile."

"As a matter of fact, I have. Isn't it wonderful? It's the neatest place going in town today, and the food is fabulous. Let's see: bagels, blintzes, matzahs, hot corned beef, spaghetti, goulash with spaetzle. What's spaetzle?"

"It's like a Hungarian noodle, I think," Willa said. "That must make them international."

"I don't know about that, Willa. The last time I was in New York

City, I noticed that some of the kosher delis were going vegan. Is that international fare?"

"You're kidding, right, Prue?" Willa chuckled.

"What looks good to you?"

Willa decided to have a little fun with Prue. "I think I'll go with the shiksa soup and a roast beef on rye. Does that come close to being kosher? I need all the help I can get."

"Shiksa soup? What's that? I don't see it on the menu."

"It's not exactly called that. That's my name for it, Prue. It's what I call kosher split pea soup. If I get really lucky, the chef today threw in the ham bone."

"You're impossible, Willa. Please try to behave when the server gets here. What's got into you anyway? You're so impish tonight. Got ole Charlie on your mind?"

Rolling her eyes, Willa answered, "Definitely not, but I do have something wonderful to tell you."

"What? Should we have gone to the Scotch Bar and celebrated?"

"No, I think Yitzi's Deli is the perfect place for this announcement. My writer's block is leaving town. I'm actually beginning to go back to thinking like a writer and story lines are flying all around in my head."

"Ah, an early Christmas present, Willa. This is wonderful news. What brought it back, do you think?"

"A combination of things. Getting away to that island was really good for me, and then I think the kicker was getting so fired up at Charles Lee. I was really pissed at him, Prue. I think that jolted my brain back into place."

"They say opposites attract."

"What are you talking about, girlfriend? He's not even on my radar, and he's about as opposite from me as they get. It could never work."

"If you say so, Willa, but, on that happy announcement news, let's toast to your good fortune and seal it with this Dr. Brown's Cream Soda." Prue held the humble can high and declared with a dramatic tone, "To Willa Carpenter and her creative mind. Long may she write all the stories we love to read."

They tapped their cans together as Willa smiled devilishly. "Mazel tov!"

CHAPTER 23

Three taps on the kitchen door and Mabel Corbin walked into Frances's kitchen.

"I wondered when your ugly mug was going to show up."

"Nice to see you too, Rita. Are ye still here? I thought you'd be off first thing."

"Why rush? It's the holiday and even I deserve a break."

"True enough. How was your holiday? I'll bet Frances was as happy as a pea on the vine seeing her Nellie. Nellie looks good. I saw her just now heading over to Bradshaw's."

"Mabel, you know what I think? I think—"

"What is it you think?" Frances said as she walked into the kitchen.

"I'm not talking behind Nellie's back or anything. I would say it to her face if'n she was here. I think she's a bit smitten with Denny."

Frances shot her sister a mocking look and said, "Ye don't say, Rita. Where've ye been all this time?"

"Well, I don't like to go around makin' accusations or nothin', but those two belong together like jimmies and sooks. Made for one another and no schoolin' is going to change that."

"Think ye have it all figured out, do ye? Well, Nellie may have a spark for Denny, but she has a lot more to do before settling in. And where would they live? Nellie is a city girl now."

Mabel said, "If you don't mind me getting into this here conversation, Nellie will come back here. It's home."

Frances poured a cup of the fresh coffee Rita had been making before Mabel arrived. "I don't know about that anymore, Mabel."

An astonished look crossed Mabel's face. "Ye can never leave yer home, Frances. It's in her blood. Being over there for a while doesn't change that."

"She has dreams and I want her to fulfill them so she doesn't ever feel cheated."

"Frances, dreams like Nellie's can be accomplished right from here, with her people."

"Well, you two old hens have it all figured out, don't ye? Life isn't that simple."

"Come on now, Frances, tell me ye wouldn't die to have Nellie back here."

"I won't ever tell her that, Rita. It would make her feel pressured and she would never forgive me."

Hoping to change the subject, Mabel lifted the lid of the glass dessert plate and helped herself to a slice of crumb cake. "This sure looks good. You bake it, Rita?"

"No, she did not, Mabel. I did. Jimmy's been callin' for it for a time now, so I decided it being a holiday and all, to bake it for him. Ye know I try to watch that man's weight because he can't seem to do it fer himself."

"And it seems to me, the more ye fuss at him, Frances, the more he eats out on that boat."

Frances laughed. "Yeah, I know. We go on like that. Been doin' it fer years."

Rita smiled at her sister. She missed her husband so much. They'd been a pair just like Frances and Jimmy. Now he was gone and her heart could still barely stand it.

Seeing the look on Rita's face, Frances got up and walked over to the counter. "Come on, Rita, let's make us some cookies. Nellie can take them back over when she leaves tomorrow. She loves your cookies."

Rita walked to her sister and hugged her gently. "Ye always know how to make me feel better."

"Yer my sister. Don't ye think I know when you're blue?"

"Cookies sound perfect."

Mabel said with enthusiasm, "I agree!"

Nellie didn't see Denny when she walked into the store and she felt her heart sink a little.

"Morning, Nellie. If'n you're looking for Denny, he went out early this morning. He changed his mind and decided to go out and bring back some fresh oysters."

"Oh, I see. Well, Mr. Floyd, I really came for some flour. Mama said she's a bit short."

Floyd had never known Miss Frances to be short on anything come the holidays, so he suspected maybe Mama had been playing cupid. "Okay then. Help yourself and stay a spell. We haven't talked for a while. Tell me how your big day went over there in Washington. Do ye think anyone listened?"

At his question, all the old men sitting across the room turned and waited for her reply.

"Well, Mr. Floyd, you can never tell what politicians hear and what they don't, but I gave it my best. But, as you see, something really good came out of it, with Miss Willa Carpenter and I becoming friends."

"I should think so. Is she going to write about us?"

"I don't know. She seems to be searching for something to write about, and we would be as good as anything. She needs to find that first, I think, before she can do any writing."

"Well, Miss Nellie, you've always been one to know about people. Yer daddy calls it 'perception.' Don't know if it is or not, or maybe what all that word means, but you do have a feeling about folks."

"Daddy reads all the time and comes up with these words, Mr. Floyd. People would be downright amazed if they knew what kind of books he reads. He loves to read the classics."

One of the "store sitters," as Nellie called them, spoke up. "Classics? Jimmy Evans? Go on now, girl."

"Oh yes, Mr. Dan. He loves to read about the travels and adventures of Homer. Why, sometimes I think that's who he thinks he is when he's out on that water."

"Ye never know. Mebee ole Homer's come back through Jimmy. Salt water isn't all that flows in his veins, I reckon."

"Well, you can go on and tease him some, but he's a really smart man, just like all of you. You just don't go on about it. Why, at the drop of a hat, you-all can spout any verse from the Bible. People out there today don't know anything about the Bible. They say they can't understand it, so why bother. That's just an excuse, I think. Would be something if God didn't listen to us and our crazy way of talking."

Wesley Ames chimed in. "That's what Floyd was saying to ye, Miss Nellie. Ye knows about people."

"I try, Mr Wesley. I try. But for the life of me, I wish someone could tell me how to read those folks over in Washington. They really do speak another language."

"They don't know anything, Miss Nellie. They think we're dumber than dirt over here, but could they go out and last five minutes on that Bay?"

"No, no, they couldn't, Mr. Dan. I don't think they understand what you all go through to bring them their crabs and oysters."

"And they don't want to, neither. All they want to do is tell us what we can and can't do. Doesn't matter a lick to them who they're hurtin'."

"I hope that isn't completely true, Mr. Wesley. I hope there's at least one congressman who will really care about what becomes of us all out here."

"Sweet girl, that would be a miracle. They keep on dumping more and more on us. We old men here are all done for our years, but what's the future?"

"That's the big question right now, isn't it? We have to hope we can make our case."

Just then, Denny walked through the door and Nellie's face turned the color of cherry pie.

"Hi, Nellie. What's going on? It feels like a funeral or something."

Nellie smiled up at him and answered, "Kind of something like that, you might say."

Denny was completely puzzled. "What?"

"Never mind, Denny. Walk me back home."

Denny didn't waste a minute. "Let's go."

CHAPTER 24

Christmas was over. It was time to get going. Willa loved being with her aunt and uncle for the holiday, but it was always a struggle. The memories were still there, far too palpable, and that would never change. No matter how hard they all tried to dance around it, there was no denying the eight-hundred-pound gorilla in the house.

Framed comic strips of her father's work and lighted book covers of her mother's most famous novels were showcased all over the house. How could she possibly escape their ghosts? She had once spoken to her aunt about it, but she'd said it was how she coped with her sister's death; it made her feel as if Jenny were there with her.

Willa understood, but, still and all, it was a pain inside her every time she visited. And every time she visited, the dreams came, and, with them, the scene in the hospital the night her parents died, and also her feeling of drowning. She loved them so much, but she could only visit once a year. That time was over now and she was ready to move forward.

Frances had told Willa that, anytime she wanted to visit, she should give her a call so she could make sure clean sheets were on the bed. Willa called right after she returned to Washington because she was ready to get started with her writing again and knew being on the island would be just the right place to give her the peace she needed to get back in the game.

Arriving at the dock, Cap'n Tuck smiled and said, "Back again, are ye?"

Willa found she missed that funny dialect more than she had expected to. "Yes, I am. Are you ready to take me across?"

131

"Will be. Ye get settled on the boat and we'll be shovin' off directly."

Willa took a deep breath. This time she was on her own. *You've done this before. It's what Nellie called "slick cam" today and no wind. Take notes and try to enjoy it.*

With the chugging sound of the engine and the untying of the ropes, off they went. She was heading straight back to the magic of the island, only, this time, she really had to release herself and listen to what it was saying to her. This time, she was going to capture what was calling to her out there.

"How were yer holidays?"

"Good. How were yours?"

"Aw, ye know, too much eatin' again and too much fussin'. My grandkids come over and stayed with me and my wife. They sure make ye laugh."

Willa smiled back at him. "Glad to hear you had a nice time. Remind me, please, Tuck, how long is it to get out to Tuckerton?"

"Not more an a half hour. Ye'll know when we come through the thorofer."

This time she knew what he meant. How about that?

As the diesel engine sang its song, Willa looked out to the water. She wasn't afraid a bit, and felt as if she were seeing it all for the first time. However, she still remembered Nellie trying to calm her down by talking her over; now she was on her own. Baby steps, she thought.

She had a thousand questions but didn't want to drive Cap'n Tuck crazy. But just one wouldn't hurt, would it?

"What do you all do when a storm comes?"

He looked at her and smiled. "Hide."

"No, I'm being serious. What do you do?"

"We all know when they're comin'. We live by our radios. That's how we know what to expect. When the bad ones come, some go off. Some stay, but it's always a nail-biter. It's our homes and we have to protect 'em best we can."

"Did you ever go off."

"Once. I knew it was going to rip into us out here, so I went to Somerville. Glad I did 'cause, when I come back, almost every building on the island had some piece of it that needed fixin'."

"Did some stay out?"

"Yep, and they're still fussin' about it."

"How about the women? Do they always leave?"

"Why, no, ma'am. They're tougher than us men. Ye ask them; they'll tell ye."

That tickled Willa. She should have known that answer after she'd spoken to some of the ladies on her first trip out. They were a tough bunch.

Coming through the thorofer, as Cap'n Tuck called it, Willa was again transferred to another time and place. It was as if you entered a fog bank, and, coming out the other side, found yourself in a place you thought you had been to before, even if you never had. It was comfortable and peaceful. The emotions ran strong through Willa. There was definitely something about this island that was pulling her.

"Where's Miss Frances? She's usually out there, waiting."

"I told her I wanted to do this on my own this time. I didn't want to bother her, and, besides, I wanted to make myself remember where places were on the island."

"Makes sense, I s'pose."

Willa was stupefied at how one man could say so few words and yet make himself known.

This time, Willa wanted to go straight to the post office to speak to the women who made it their daily ritual to gather there and talk. The men had the store; the women had the post office. Seemed fair.

"Do ye need any help, Miss Willa?"

"I packed light, so, no, I don't. Thanks."

"Well, how long will ye be out here?"

She was pretty sure if she answered this, her answer would reach the post office before she did.

"I'm not sure." A safe answer.

"Well, you know how this works. If'n you're goin' over, you be here at 7:15 in the morning."

"Gotcha. Thanks." *See, Willa girl, you can do this one or two word thing.*

Not fifty or so feet from the end of the dock was a map of the island. Let's you know quickly that you can't much get lost in a place this small. Rubbing her chin with her hand, Willa studied it. She hadn't had time to do this the last time because she was in a golf cart being rocketed all over the island.

"Amazing," she said softly. This was the neatest thing she'd ever seen. Why didn't more towns do this? Such a simple thing, but so helpful. *Okay, I am here . . . and so the post office is to my left up this path. Got it.*

Gathered in the post office were four of the most interesting looking women Willa had ever seen. All looked as if they could have been sisters. Maybe they were. That in itself told a story.

As she walked in, she knew she was going to get the once-over, but, hey, she was on their turf now.

"Good morning.. Mind if I sit for a minute?"

"Suit yerself."

Well, it was a start. Thank God there'd been an empty chair. Otherwise, she didn't know what she'd have said that wouldn't make her stick out like the tourist she was. Then she remembered the magic name.

"I'm staying at Frances Evans's house. I thought I would come over here first, though."

"We remember who you are. The famous writer."

"Well, I guess you could say that. I do write books."

"Most of us have read one or two. After ye were here, we went over and got a few more."

"Did you like them?" Boy, she felt as if she were asking a loaded question.

One of the women leaned over really close and whispered, "They're a bit . . . racy, if ye know what I mean." Then, in a more normal voice, she added, "But, yes, I liked the story. Kept it hid so my husband didn't see it. though."

"What would he have said if he had seen you reading it?"

She answered, "He probably would've been scared to come home for a week."

All the woman burst out laughing. Willa felt more at ease now. They were teasing her.

"Maybe they would have liked what you read."

"Maybe."

They didn't use too many words either, she realized.

"Would you mind if I asked you a few questions?"

"'Spect not. Ask away."

"How do you women feel about what's happening to your way of life?"

A woman who identified herself as Lilly answered. "We try not to dwell on it much. 'Twon't do us no good anyway. Every month seems there's something else the government tells us to do in regards to our fishing. The men can't do it all. Not that those folks are being mean or anything. They just don't understand us at all. When the crabs run and we catch a good lick, we can't be doing paper work. It's that simple."

"Is that the biggest complaint?"

"Well, some, but they also want to control us, and, if'n they never been out on the water and netted crabs or brought in oysters, how do they know what it's all about? For them it's about control, and it's not just the government folks neither."

"Then who else?"

Suddenly the women seemed too nervous to speak. They were afraid, but of whom?

"Okay, I understand."

"No, you don't. We don't mean no disrespect, but there's others who say they care, but they don't. They're in this fer themselves."

"Politics," I said, "It's a dirty business."

"Dirty is one thing, but, if they don't quit it, we won't be on the water much longer. Guess that's what they want."

"Would you talk with them?"

Another woman seemed to be holding back, and, yet, she definitely was the alpha female of the group. She said, "Miss Carpenter, my name is Louise. We've tried to go that route. It's not that easy. Everyone who comes out here thinks we're dumb old island people. That we fish and so how can we possibly know what's good for ourselves? We aren't educated like they are, and they use that against us. We've tried, but we gave up."

"So. how's this working for you now?"

Another said, "I'm Tess, and I'll answer this question. We're at a standoff with them right now. They watch us from the air, on the docks, everywhere. For all we know, you could be one of them, coming out here to get information for them, sorry to say."

Willa realized she needed to be careful. "I'm not, but what I am is someone who has taken an interest in your culture. It's beautiful and you are what America is all about."

"America . . . or what it used to be."

"People are trying to find a way through this, you know."

The fourth woman behind the postal desk, obviously the postmistress for this tiny outpost, said, "Fishing is all we do. If we stir up trouble, it doesn't help. I'm sorry, but there's the beginning and end of it."

"I see," Willa said softly. "It would be a shame to see all this disappear over time."

"It already is. Our young folks can't make a living out here, so they go to the mainland to get work. It'll pass unnoticed once we're all gone."

"That can't happen," Willa said strongly.

"Nice to see you again, Miss Carpenter. Have a good day to you now."

She was being dismissed, plain and simple. When they didn't want to talk, they didn't want to talk.

Getting up and walking out of there was tough, but she now understood the picture more clearly. These people were fighting for their very existence.

As she walked away, she turned in the opposite direction of Miss Frances's house. She felt depleted. She had come here wanting to understand, and now she did. Within the first hour on her own, she had found out what was going on with herself, and out here, and she couldn't do anything to change it. Maybe there was no way to stop what's coming. A new day would take its place.

She walked for another hour before she found her way to the house that was fast becoming her home. When Willa walked in the door, Frances was sitting quietly in the living room, reading.

"Wondered if you had fallen in the water."

"I stopped at the post office and then walked around," she answered as she plopped into the other recliner. Rubbing its worn and smooth corduroy with her hands, Willa let out a soft sigh.

"What's bothering ye, girl? I felt it from the first minute I met ye."

"Nothing. Something. Everything."

"Well, it can't be all that bad. Something and nothing we can fix, but everything might take awhile."

Her logic was perfect. And her comfort so desperately appreciated, Willa felt she could stay here forever.

CHAPTER 25

Kit was downright worried about Willa. She had never seen her act like this, and, though she was a very tough businesswoman, she adored Willa. The young girl was as talented as they come, more so even than her mother, Jennifer, had been

Willa had become the daughter Kit had never had, but she tried hard not to show that. If she did, it might have destroyed what Willa had. She had seen every writer she'd signed to Kitwin Publishing come down with writer's block at some point in their careers, but what Willa was going through was something more than that. And she wasn't sure Willa was aware of that.

Willa was too close to the situation, but what Kit saw was a complex combination of someone trying to write when something deep down inside was digging at her. If Willa could unearth that, she would spring back better than ever. While there were contractual concerns, Kit would go to the ends of the earth to help that girl find her way back.

However, in the meantime, she had to deal with Susan Crandall, whose ego was spinning out of control. One award and a couple of really hot-selling novels had created a monster, but she was making money for the house. How do you tell someone like that that they're average and they have to do better?

Susan was thinking of how she could go about reframing Willa's suggestions for a story line when her phone rang.

"Good morning, Susan. We have to talk."

The tone was set and even slightly vague Susan got the message. "Hi, Kit."

"I know you're about done with this new book, and we are all waiting breathlessly for it, but I want to know if there is another one coming after this?"

"Funny you should call. I was going to get in touch with you. I have this really great idea for a book."

"Great. Let's hear it."

Susan began to roll out the concept. With each descriptive word and character, Kit became more and more horrified. This story was way too familiar.

When Susan finished, Kit sat quietly on the other end of the phone, her mind racing a million miles an hour.

Susan finally asked, "Well, what do you think?"

"Where did you come up with this story line, Susan?"

"I don't know; it just came to me, like all my plots do."

"Really? Say, have you talked to Willa recently?" Kit asked innocently.

"That's the oddest thing, Kit. You must have mental telepathy! I did speak to Willa the other day. She called out of the blue to say hi and how are you and the next thing I know we got to talking and she told me she was going away again for a while."

Kit couldn't believe it. Willa had deliberately set Susan up. That Dartmouth mind had outwitted her nemesis hands down. Willa had known Susan would come to her with that proposal and would look like the fool she was; then she would believe Susan needed to be stopped from her endless "borrowing" of Willa's original thoughts.

"Susan, did Willa actually give you that book plot?"

Susan knew she had been so busted. She didn't know what to say. Finally, she stammered, "Well, she did say that she had thought of writing a book with a similar theme, but then she said it wasn't working for her." Defensively, she added, "She told me to try it out!"

"Willa actually gave you a book plot, Susan, and you didn't think something was up?"

"I did, at first, but then when she said she wasn't going to use it, I thought why shouldn't I use it? It's good. I mean it's really good."

"Yes, it is, Susan. It's too good to be true. My dear, you've been had by someone who is way beyond you. That story was Willa's second book. A book, I might add, you probably never read. And she played you like a fiddle."

Kit sighed. "She's been complaining to me about your writing for years. How you take her books, use the underlying subject, change things around, and end the story a bit differently. Writers—not good ones mind you—do that all the time. When a hugely successful book comes out on something, like a dog for an example, people swoon over it. The original gets the lion's share, but there's still a lot more out there to grab. Then the industry has a spate of doggie stories. With you, it's romance, Willa's romance. You mix in some fantasy or sci-fi and you produce 'chic lit' that the readers really like. They don't care if your books are similar to someone else's. So, I have accepted it all this time, but it has to end, Susan.

"This latest book of yours is really so much better than your others. You stepped out this time. Can't you see? You have talent on your own. You don't have to steal Willa's work and change it around. Do your own writing and stop being afraid."

The silence on the other end of the phone was palpable. "Do you have anything else to say to me, Susan?"

Susan had to say something. She couldn't leave it like this, which was, by all accounts, a mess.

"Yes, yes. I do, Kit. You and Willa are right. I've been terrified to go on a limb and Willa is so good that I borrowed a bit and I'm so sorry. Willa must hate me and I don't blame her. I adore Willa and she never really gave me the time of day. I want to be her friend, and, when she called, I guess I thought maybe she really cared. I see she's just pissed at me."

"Hold it right there, Susan. You had this coming for a long time. You're damned right you can't use this plot line, but you can use your brain and go in other directions with your writing. Which I strongly suggest you start thinking about."

"I said I'm sorry, Kit. I really am. I don't know what else I can do."

Kit knew, if she didn't salvage this conversation, she would soon have two writers down and out and that would be bad for the company.

So Kit joked, "I'll tell you what, Susan. Try writing *Cinderella*, but make her a bitch and Prince Charming a serial killer."

The flood of laughter told her all might be well after all.

"That's really funny, Kit, and I think that would sell. But it was your idea and so I can't use it, can I?"

"Well, I don't think so, but do you see what I'm saying to you?"

"Yes, I do. As painful as this conversation has been, Kit, I guess I deserved it and I guess I deserved to get put in my place by Willa, too. I hope she's on to something really good. She's such a good writer. I do envy her."

"Everyone does, Susan. But, if you start writing your own work, she will be the first one to sincerely appreciate it. I know her deep down and I know that's all she wants from you."

"Okay, enough said, all right? I get the message. Now, the book I'm doing now is just about done. I'll send it over in the next few days."

"I can't wait. I know it's going to do well for us. Let's never have to have this discussion again. It's too painful for both of us."

"You got that right."

Kit felt as if she needed a shower after she hung up. This business was rough, and, when you had to call out a writer, you knew the creative evisceration that was happening to them. It was dangerous. You had to check every word or you could ruin them completely. But some of the realities of the game had to be brought to bear.

Kit was a tough woman, but even she didn't like to do what she had just done. One thing was certain: she never wanted to have to do this to Willa.

CHAPTER 26

It was time for Willa and Charles to meet and get to the bottom of what was really going on. She had now made two visits to the island and spoken to almost all sixty of its residents, and it was obvious there was a great deal more to this whole situation than anyone understood.

When Charles came on the phone, Willa had to admit to herself she enjoyed hearing his voice.

"Well, good morning, Willa. To what do I owe this call?"

"Hello, Charles. I don't mean to bother you, but I was wondering if you could spare any time today. Maybe lunch?"

"Well, first of all, I believe it's Charlie to you, and, second, I'm looking at today's calendar and it's pretty busy. How long do we want to make this lunch?"

There was a devilish tone to his question and any other time she would play. But not this time.

"If you can do lunch, then I think we can wrap it all up in an hour. Does that work?"

"I can move some things around and make it work. Where do we want to go?"

"How about Yitzi's Deli?"

"I've been there; excellent choice. Should I wear some armor?"

"Why do you say that?"

"Just something in your voice. Meet at noon?"

"Okay, noon is good, Charles. Or Charlie. You really aren't a Charlie to me, you know."

"Whatever makes you comfortable, Willa. I'll have Prue reserve a table."
Oh, boy. Prue will be all over me now about Charles and me.

Just what she was up to was Charles's first thought when they hung up. Well, whatever it was, he would find out in a couple of hours. He was definitely interested in this girl, so, if Yitzi's Deli was the place, then that would do. He leaned over, pushed his call button, and said, "Prue, could you please make a lunch reservation at Yitzi's? For two, at noon."

"Of course, Charles. Who is the other party?"

"Your girlfriend, Willa. Thanks."

He could be so adorable, Prue thought. No wonder every single female in D.C. was after him. She would be, too, if she didn't have other plans. And considering what she and her father had talked about when she was home, she would have to make some decisions soon about leaving this office for the next step in her career. The family business always came first for the Hardings, no matter what.

He was late—unlike him. He was Mr. Punctuality, so apparently he really was having to make an effort to squeeze in this lunch. That meant they would have to get down to business quickly.

The server came around again and, just as Willa was about to order her drink, there he was.

Taking off his navy overcoat, the sandy blond Adonis flashed his smile and said, "I'm sorry, Willa."

"Hi, Charles. As long as you're here, you may as well tell the server what you want to drink."

"Black coffee for me, thanks."

Settling into the chrome chair with the bright red leather seat, he said, "I moved everything around so we could have more time. I thought if you wanted to, we could hop into my car and take a drive along the Potomac after lunch."

What was going on with him? First he was jammed and now he wants to go for a leisurely drive?

"Well, that sounds delightful but I don't want to keep you. I know how busy you are."

"Done then. We'll eat and take off."

"Would you like to choose what I'm eating, too?"

Chuckling, he crinkled his face. "No, that you can do for yourself."

The server returned with his coffee and her Dr. Pepper. "Are you ready to order?"

"Absolutely. I'll have the roast beef on a hard roll. I want the rarest roast beef you have, and the lady will have the turkey on rye with lettuce, no mayo. That should do it."

When the server had left, Willa bit her lip, which she had a habit of doing. She could tell he enjoyed getting to her. "Well, that sure was what I wanted. How did you know?"

"All women eat lighter fare. That's how they stay so thin."

Willa leaned across the table. "Well, Charlie, I'm not all women and I would have loved a raw hamburger."

He leaned over to her now. "Well, that wouldn't have been good for you."

"Do I care what you think? Can I change my order?"

"Nope, too late. You'll love the turkey."

The little exchange clearly made it "game on" between them. Willa loved a challenge and hadn't had one in a long time.

The last man who'd done that to her had been a man she loved. They were in college and he was about the most wonderful person she had ever known outside her parents. And then it ended. He turned out not to be the most wonderful when he jilted her for her best friend at the time. Her heart had broken. But he'd had the same, strong way about him that Charles did. She hoped this man wasn't the same kind of snake. But he was a politician, so her inner alarm bell went off. That turkey sandwich better be the best one she had ever tasted.

"Now, what is it you wanted to talk to me about, Willa?"

"Direct and to the point, aren't you?"

"I guess that's a result of my profession. If you don't come out and say it, all kinds of bad things happen."

"See your point. Well, I don't exactly know what I want to ask you, but I can begin."

"Go for it."

"Well, I know you weren't happy about me going over to James Island, and I want you to know that I'm not going to make trouble for you or Prue, but I am going to write about the island." She paused thoughtfully. "It's like nowhere I've ever been before. It's going back in time, and to a time when we all felt comfortable in and memories were made. The people are honest and refreshing and I don't want to see their lives or their culture vanish. Their story is deeply human and all they want to do is love their families. And fish. This shouldn't be a political tug of war."

"I thought romance was your thing."

"This is a romance, Charles. It's a love story of a people, their way of life, and how deeply rooted we all are with them. They are originals."

"Willa, I don't want to be sorry I let you into that hearing. Prue doesn't want to be sorry she did you a favor. There are sensitive issues in this."

"You know, Charles, sensitive is a code word in this town for 'I don't want to talk about this; it's a hot potato.'"

"You know this town well, I see."

"Yes, I do, and one of the things that really ticks people off outside the beltway is when politicians use the word 'sensitive.'"

"You're right. I can't argue with you. But, for years, the Chesapeake Bay waters have been in decline. Many organizations, including the state and federal government, are trying to bring the Bay back. The runoffs from the north of the Bay are killing it. The farmers are killing it. And the watermen are killing it. It's a mess, and no one has all the answers, but we're trying to make headway out there before it's too late."

"What if it's already too late? What if you can't save it? What about that?"

"Don't even say that. It's the lifeline of this entire coast and the largest estuary in the country. That Bay holds our collective history of the beginning of this country. It's more than water; it's who we are and where we came from."

Willa could see this man got it. He saw what its worth was and he had that magical thing Frances also had: passion. He was in love with this body of water. You could hear it in his words.

"So why wouldn't you want to raise awareness of the wonder of this body of water and give me your blessing to write their story?"

"Aha, see, there *is* a book. I knew there would be. Writers can't help themselves."

"Not yet, but it's coming. I can feel it."

"There have been dozens of books about the Chesapeake. What makes you think that yours will make a difference?"

"It will, and it will because I will put a human face on this. If you listen only to the rich and powerful, you miss the essence of what you just said to me. You have real feelings for this water. Don't let those would make money off it and the land that runs along it, take the narrative. You have to lead here, Charlie. It's what people expect you to do, and, if nothing else happens, you owe that to those who sent you here to make a difference and not become what they hate so much—another political hack."

"You're right, Willa. I do care and care deeply. That Bay means a lot to more people than you know. But what, exactly, are you asking me to do? If you want my approval for a book, I can't give that outright, because you're going to do this anyway. So what is it you want me to do?"

Willa took a deep breath. "Come out there with me. Meet these people and talk with them. They are the America of 'once was.' They know what's coming and they can't do a thing about it. They're fishermen, for God's sake. They don't know politics and they don't want to know politics. All they know is that they get up before the sun even thinks about getting up. They go to their boats and they go out on dangerous waters to bring in the crabs, oysters, rockfish. The fish we all love. Talk to them, Charlie. Hear what they tell you before you make decisions they don't have a hand in. That's not America. That's not how we do things. Or should I say, how we used to do things. Help them keep their culture."

"Okay, Willa. I get it. I get the message. Let me think about it. I don't think it's a bad idea to do what you're asking, but I'll have to think about it."

"What's to think about?"

"It could make it worse if I go out there. But, you're right. I should see it up close and personal, and speak to these people myself. Another time I also need to go to the other island—the one on the Virginia side—because

I hear they're having problems, too. But not this trip; this trip would be for James Island. If I decide to go."

"You can't make it worse. If you speak face-to-face with these folks, they'll see you care."

"Let me think about it. There are some powerful people who don't share your romantic ideas about the watermen and their culture. They want to bring the oyster beds back and produce the oysters by using their own methods. It's complicated and money is involved in this."

"Isn't there always? This can be worked out if both sides are equally involved."

"I said I'll think about it, Willa. That's a start."

CHAPTER 27

Nellie was crying her heart out. She'd already been back in her apartment for a few days, but it was finally hitting her. She always felt sad to leave, but, this time, it was hitting her bad. Now, in the privacy of her own surroundings, she couldn't stop the flood of tears that were telling her she was making a huge mistake with her life.

She was completely confused about everything. She thought she had known what she wanted and how to go about getting it, but now, nothing was making sense to her. Maybe it was just the holidays. They do that to everyone, don't they? They make us yearn to be young again and conjure up all the memories that go with the turkey and the mistletoe. Or was it Denny who was bothering her? Why did he have to look so good and make such a fuss over her?

She needed help but couldn't call her mama, who would be half mad and half glad. That wasn't going to help her. She had to make up her mind which world she wanted to live in. She had valuable work here to accomplish, and she had to remember that island people don't cry. They cope.

But there were so few of them left now. Of all her friends, only Denny and his best friend, Ike—or Hot Dog, as everyone called him—were left. The rest had all moved off the island to seek their education or jobs. But hadn't she done the same thing? So why now were all the doubts coming?

She blew her nose and wiped her eyes, and then started laughing as she thought back to when Hot Dog had gotten his nickname. It had been the Fourth of July, and he and Denny were seven years old. They'd been jumping off the dock into the Bay, a favorite pastime, when Hot Dog had gotten powerful hungry. He had run off with a few of the other kids following behind. When he'd reached his house, the backyard barbecue was going full blast and his daddy was grilling hot dogs. When Ike said he could eat a dozen, the kids bet him he couldn't eat more than three. He took the bet, and, when he shoveled the twelfth hot dog into his mouth— just before running off to the bathroom—he'd earned the nickname that had followed him the rest of his life. No doubt, when that boy died, "Hot Dog" would be right under his real name on that cemetery stone.

All the boys had nicknames. No one thought that was different or anything of note. They just did. It was an Eastern Shore thing. There were plenty of men walking around with names like Hambone, Slim (who weighed three hundred pounds), Sonny, and Junior. Splitter? He'd split the most logs one holiday and his daddy had been so proud of him. All manner of names had popped up over the years. It wasn't easy to earn your nickname, and most had consequences. Ike, for example, had spent two whole days throwing up those hot dogs.

Nellie missed the island ways. The kids of today would never know the sheer freedom she had experienced walking anywhere, at any time of the day or night, with no fear. Everyone on the island knew everyone and the adults watched out for the kids. If the kids did something wrong, it didn't matter which adult saw it; they yelled at them just the same. The island was a community in which everyone belonged to everyone while being run in an orderly manner: the way things used to be all over this country. Common sense prevailed, but now came the chaos created by government sticking its nose into everything. Plain old common sense is what makes life work.

Take the water, for instance. Water safety is taught from the time a baby can crawl because, when you're raised with water surrounding you, you had better know its ways and what to look for when it gets angry.

Nellie remembered back to when a particularly bad hurricane had come onto the island. Some folks had left before it hit but Mama wouldn't leave. She was staying put with her home. Daddy had been mad at her, but understood, and didn't say a word. They had hunkered down in the kitchen for the duration, Daddy listening to every word on the shortwave radio and she and Mama playing card games.

It had been bad. The wind had come up so hard, they could hear the shingles tearing off the roof and the wooden shutters banging against the house. They'd had candles burning and their generator had given them enough power to cook some soup. They'd been scared, but no one had said anything out loud about it.

The Bay had been angry that night, but, when the storm passed and everyone had come home, they had all gathered in the church and given thanks to the good Lord for helping them out and not bringing too much hardship.

Nellie closed her eyes. She could still hear her Mama leading everyone in singing their favorite hymn, "'Til the Storm Passes By." They sing it to this day over the blessing of the boats before the men go off, but that night had brought such special meaning to all of them on the island.

"That's what I miss," Nellie shouted. "I miss all that goodness everywhere around me. People don't lie, cheat, or make up things that suit them best. And here I am trying to get city people, politicians at that, to understand something so foreign to them that they can't even imagine a world like that. I'm so torn. I don't belong over here. I belong over there, with my people. They're my blood. And, I hate to admit out loud that I love Denny, but I'm sure I do. He couldn't survive if he tried to live over here and I'm not sure I can either. We're both cut from the same cloth."

That's when she thought of an answer: Willa. She could talk to Willa. She wrote about things like this so she must understand what Nellie was going through. Mama would want to help, but she was really not the one she needed right now. Mama would just tell her to come home, but she needed to thrash this out. She needed someone who could see the whole picture and there was only one person she knew who fit that bill. Willa.

Willa had been shocked when she got the call. She'd had no idea she meant so much to Nellie. Their fledgling friendship was so new. Granted, some things are like that, and, for Willa, life always seemed to hold great surprises. So, when Nellie had called a few days after Willa's lunch and drive with Charlie, she'd accepted the surprise gratefully.

"Hi, Nellie. How are you doing?"

"Not so good, Willa."

"Are you sick? How can I help?"

"I guess you could say I am sick, but not in the way you mean. I'm homesick."

"Oh, now that's hard to cure, but not impossible. A guy named Denny doesn't have anything to do with this, does he?"

"Denny, Mama, Daddy, Floyd—all of them out there. I hear you had a nice visit with Mama."

"We did indeed. Your mother knows how make guests feel so welcome."

"She's good at that. I'm much quieter than Mama. She says it like it is. That's why I think . . . ."

"Think what, Nellie?"

"Well, I think Mama should get involved again in the politics of these issues with the island. She may not have the formal education but she is the best spokesperson I ever heard. She has a way about her. She is the perfect example of an island woman. She lives the passion she feels."

Willa heard the angst in Nellie's voice. She had come to her for advice. She remembered the favor Frances had asked of her; now she had to take care of her daughter. She knew she had to be careful, however, because she had the feeling she might be an idol to this young woman. That was always a burden one had to take seriously.

"I'm very flattered, Nellie, that you would talk to me, but are you sure your mother or Denny might not give you better advice?"

" I certainly cannot talk with Denny. All he wants is for me to come back home. And Mama won't make that call for me. She knows, if she influences me, it won't last."

"Again, she's a wise lady. What do you really, deep down, want to do?"

"Do you ever truly know that, Willa? Aren't you searching for something, too? I watched you when we were on the island. You were feeling something you have felt before, but can't quite reach out and touch again. If you don't mind me saying so, my personal opinion is that the island calls to you in some personal way and you are going to have to deal with that and listen. Well, right now, it's calling to me."

"I see you've inherited your mother's wise ways. It's true; I won't deny it, Nellie. There's a message out there for me but I'm not ready to receive it. But you, dear friend, have a different calling from that island—one that can't be denied or forgotten. It's your home. It's where your roots are and it's in your blood. Some people can leave without looking back, but, with others, it's more like a calling to be out there."

A silence fell between them for a while, and, when they spoke again, they both skirted around any deep issues. There was no need for that anymore. They were helping each other in a way that was profound. Two young women from opposite ends of the world had been oddly pulled together at this moment for a reason. That's how it seemed to work in life. You meet the people you're supposed to meet and they touch you in a way you might never have imagined. Through Nellie, Willa had met Frances, and Frances had come to be so special to Willa. Almost a mother.

"I'm going to go back to Tuckerton, Nellie . . . with Congressman Lee."

Nellie gasped. "You are? How did this come about?"

"It's kind of a long and winding story that doesn't matter right now, but I met him for lunch the other day and we spoke about the Bay and life along its shores. I asked him to go, to see for himself and speak to the folks."

"And he said yes, just like that? Wow, Willa. You are something."

"I don't know about that, but he agreed to go. Do you want to go out with us? I know your mother would love that."

"I would love to go, but this trip is for you two. You've been back over and know the territory now. People know who you are, so . . . so, good luck. I can't believe it."

"He thought you were quite a young woman, Nellie."

"That's important, but I'm not the one who needs to be involved in this issue. It's you, Willa, and Mama. I realized that when I was there for Christmas. Mama still has the desire to do something to help everyone work together. My opinion is Frances Evans needs to be called back into action."

"Well, maybe. But don't put yourself down, Nellie. You're a special gal, and I don't know what's ahead for you, on the island or off, but something is ahead for you."

"Maybe we'll both find what we're looking for, Willa."

"Maybe so."

CHAPTER 28

Willa looked like death warmed over. As a writer, she stayed up many nights into the wee hours, which made it a grueling chore to be awake and ready to go anywhere by zero-dark-thirty.

As Willa sipped her morning tea, shaking off the night boogums, she thought about Prue's call, setting this trip up for her and Charles. Her girlfriend was really giving her the business about this trip over to the island. She had really laid it on, and, the truth was, there was nothing going on between them. Why did Prue think there was?

Both she and Charles had a mission. Willa knew what hers was and would figure out what Charles's game was on this trip. She was glad he had accepted her invitation to go over because it was the only way Willa could get him to understand the human side and what was at stake for the people there. Willa was in no way looking for any personal relationship. She had too much to do right now.

Dressed with ten minutes to spare, Willa took a last look around to see if she had forgotten anything. Ah, the tape recorder. A writer can never leave home without that. Glancing in the mirror by the front door, Willa made a funny face and said out loud, "Perfect."

"Well. it makes me feel good anyway," she said as she walked out the door.

Harold, her favorite doorman, was working this morning. When he saw her face as she exited the elevator, he said, "OMG! It's a ghost walking toward me."

"Funny, Harold. Say, aren't you supposed to be my late-night date?"

"I switched with James. He had an emergency. What the heck are you doing up so early? Does it have something to do with the good-looking man I just told to park over there?"

Willa peered out the front door and said, "Oh, no!" just as Charles waved to her.

"Can I help you, Willa?"

"No, thanks, Harold. Two small bags don't need a couple of people to get them to the car." Smiling good-bye, Willa scooted out the door and over to the big Chevy Tahoe Charles was leaning against. "I thought I had done it. I thought I was on time, even a little before."

He laughed and took her two bags. "I am a stickler for being on time, but, I have to say, you did just fine."

"Thank the stars. I don't want to start out on bad footing."

After climbing into the behemoth of a vehicle, Charles smiled as he handed Willa a cup of hot tea. "See? I noticed the other day at lunch."

"How really sweet of you. I sure need this. The eyelids, you know. They don't work too well at this hour."

"We're off, mademoiselle. This drive really is a pretty one, and it will give us a lot of time to get to know one another better."

"I'll agree with you on that. From the time you go over that bridge, it all changes. It's a different land. And it changes again when you go over to James Island."

"It's a great place, the Eastern Shore. It's the playland of D.C. and Maryland, but we Virginians favor our Virginia Beach."

"I've never been down there. And I hear the Outer Banks of North Carolina are also wonderful."

"Yes, they are, but, all in all, I'm a mountain boy. I see you like the water."

"Might say that. I was raised in Mystic, Connecticut, so the sea is in my blood. My parents had a summer home on the coast of Maine. Bar Harbor. We went there every summer for a month. My mother would write and my father would do his comic strip while I would go on adventures."

"What adventures did you find?"

"Neat ones. I loved to walk down to the harbor in the early morning and watch the lobstermen go out."

"No wonder you have taken such an interest in the fishing industry along the Chesapeake. So, are you going to write about it?" Charles's question appeared innocent, but it also seemed to Willa that he was doing some fishing of his own.

"To be honest with you, I don't know. It would make a wonderful setting for a romance, but there's so much more to it." She changed the subject."Have you ever been over to the other island, Charles?"

"No, and I need to go, especially since that one's in Virginia. I'm sure after this trip, it will spur me to go to the other one, too."

"How can you head a committee on this subject when you haven't come over here to visit the towns involved and the islands?"

"Just trust me. I can. You know, there are many issues involved with this. As I told you, the water cleanup is one and the oyster beds are another, and the runoff problems from development and farms have a hand in this as well. It's so many things all contributing to the problem."

Now it was Willa who wanted to be careful not to tip her hand. "I know that, Charles. But, at the same time, what happens to the economies of the states that depend on the seafood? What happens when the watermen can't afford to do it anymore? I can't for the life of me figure out why people haven't thought about that."

"I hear you, Willa, and that's why the government is trying to raise its own oysters and why so much emphasis is on cleaning up the Bay. It's complicated."

"It wouldn't be nearly that complicated if you all worked together, but, from what I can tell, that isn't the case,"

"And that's a two-way street. Getting everyone to the table is the toughest battle."

Willa looked over at him and noticed the seriousness in his eyes. Deep down, he did care more than most politicians who seemed usually to brush lightly over things and never really solve the problem. Charles, at least, was willing to take this time off and go over there.

"I'm impressed, Congressman. You seem a bit more involved than most."

"Willa, I care about this, and it's on many levels I care. One is historical, as we've talked about. I'm a Lee and, in Virginia, that means something. We have a long line going back to the beginning of the country. We're not known to be decorations on the cake, but men who take a stand—with their women right next to them. I may be a bit young, but I'm not afraid to do battle with people who are in the game for themselves. We are where we are because we've earned the people's respect. Or, at least, that's what I've been taught."

"Again, impressive, Charles. You must be a party of one up there on the Hill."

"You'd be surprised. There are more than you might expect. It's when they stay too long that the real corruption seeps in. We weren't meant to stay in Washington forever, but it's hard to leave with all that money floating around."

"And power. Let's not forget the aphrodisiac of the profession."

Charles turned and looked at Willa. "Are you sure you write romance and not political novels? Your grasp is astounding."

"Romance, and that's all. I find politicians boring characters. Most are too in love with themselves to be in love with anyone else."

"Ouch. Do I resemble that comment?"

"I don't know you well enough yet, but I'll let you know. I like men who are full of surprises."

"I'll remember that. However, on the opposite side of the playing field, I don't like women who are full of surprises. Usually those surprises spell trouble."

"I'll make sure to remember that statement."

They looked at each other. There was no mistake that they had each understood exactly what the other had just said.

The time flew, and it seemed they had just left D.C. when they arrived in Somerville. They were early, and starved. So they went up the main street and saw a local place called Virgil's.

"Looks a little run-down, doesn't it, Willa?"

"Nellie mentioned this place to me. She said they have great hamburgers."

"These kinds of places usually do. That sounds good about now."

Willa actually knew more about this place than she let on. Virgil's was a watermen's place and, she thought, a good place to begin their journey.

Walking through the door took guts for two sophisticated folks from D.C., but, having accomplished that feat, they went straight over to one of the spanking white booths along the side. Willa couldn't look at Charles's face. She knew what he was thinking.

As Willa was reading the short menu on the table, a young, pretty girl came over to take their order.

"Well," Charles said, "I think I'll go with the cheeseburger with fries and a Coke."

"The All-American, huh?" Willa said. Then she smiled at the waitress and said, "I'll have the same thing, thank you."

"Copycat. I see we're both going with all-American fare."

"Think that's the safe thing to do, don't you?"

"Yes, I do."

Willa's eyes scanned the room. Old men sat talking to one another as they had probably done for decades. That weathered look made it obvious they had been watermen. She assumed the younger men were still out on the Bay bringing in the catch from the day.

Willa leaned across the table." They're so interesting-looking, aren't they? You know by looking at them that their lives have been in the sun and that hard work has been their companion."

"That's rather a poetic way of describing them, but, yes, you're right on the mark. These men have worked hard all their lives. I see the same thing with the coal miners and the farmers. These are productive men."

"Their wives work right next to them. Their lives are hard, too, but there's a simple joy about it all."

The food arrived and Willa about inhaled it. Charles wasn't too far behind.

"This was really good," Charles commented.

"Yes, it was. Maybe not quite as good as Yitzi's Deli, but not bad."

"Not nearly as expensive either. I kind of like this place. Reminds me of what all the old mom-and-pop restaurants used to be like."

"Makes you homesick, doesn't it, Congressman?"

"Shhh, I don't want to start a riot in here, Willa. You never know these days who's friend or foe."

After lunch, Willa asked some of the men how things were going. They gave her an earful, but Charles wanted to learn more. They finally told both visitors to go on over to the watermen's marina a little west of town. They told them to see the oyster shells just sitting there, all piled up.

When Charles asked about it, one old man said, "Just go on over, and, when you see it, think of how those shells could be used to make more oysters, but they won't let us put 'em back in the water. They don't know what they're doing over there in Washington and the capital of this state. And they don't ask us neither."

The tone of this man's voice said all that needed to be said. He was done talking. Willa and Charles walked out, got in the car, and followed the directions to see what the men had been talking about.

They found the shells. Millions of them, piled so high you wondered how they didn't topple over. Willa grabbed her camera and started taking pictures.

She said, "I don't understand this. Why don't they let the men dump them back in the Bay?"

Charles didn't answer but stood staring in disbelief. He had heard about this, about how the EPA and state weren't allowing this anymore. This was the result of a new idea: raising oysters in government-run beds. So far, it hadn't been the success they were hoping for.

"This isn't right, Charles. I don't know why, but it doesn't look right."

"Come on, Willa. We'll miss the boat."

"Looks to me like someone already has."

CHAPTER 29

Cap'n Tuck was surprised to see Willa appear on the dock.

"Hey, yer back so soon?"

"Yes, I am. Aren't you the lucky one?"

"Brought a friend with ye this time, I see."

"Yessir. This is Charles Lee, and he's come to see the island."

"Will ye be going back later this afternoon?"

"Yes, we will."

Willa led Charles to a seat on the boat. "Looks like slick cam today, Cap'n."

Charles stared straight up at her. "Slick what?"

"Slick cam. It means the water's as smooth as glass. I told you they speak differently over here."

"You can say that again. I caught the 'ye,' too."

"Old English."

"I just hope it's not catching."

The engine started up and they were off.

Cap'n Tuck proceeded to talk on his shortwave and Charles and Willa looked out on the water. The salt air was refreshing, and cold. But they were dressed for the occasion in winter coats and gloves. Willa pulled her coat tighter. The mid-March weather was pretty, but it was still chilly out here on the water.

"How long does it take to get to the island?" Charles asked.

"It's not a long ride. Maybe thirty minutes."

"I thought longer. I don't know why."

Charles watched the oyster boats coming back into the marina with their catches of the day. "This is neat, Willa. Seeing it up close and personal sure beats a committee hearing, listening to someone describing all this."

"From what I know, oystering is almost over, and then the men start to get their crab pots ready to go out so they can drop 'em down when it's time."

"Boy, you really have been studying up on all this."

"Not as much studying, Charles, as talking with Frances Evans, Nellie's mother. I can't wait for you to meet her."

"I'm looking forward to that. I have heard some interesting stories about her. I've heard that she isn't a formally educated woman, but she probably knows more about this topic than anyone."

"Well, maybe not more than the men who actually go out on the water, but Frances is a walking encyclopedia on all things crabs and oysters. I guess you could add rockfish to that, too."

"Is there a restaurant on the island?"

A woman sitting near Charles heard the question, and almost burst out laughing.

"Not exactly. Floyd's General Store is the closest thing to fine dining they have out there. Why do you ask that anyway? Didn't Virgil's fix you up until dinner?"

"Not really. And the cheeseburger was a bit greasy."

"It's the grease in the cheeseburger. Are you okay, Charles?"

"I think so. Can't say for sure right now."

Time passed quickly, and soon they were passing through the thoroughfare, the cormorants and gulls welcoming them. "Isn't it beautiful?" Willa asked.

"It does have a certain charm, I'll say that."

Cap'n Tuck began slowing down the boat as they made the wide turn into the dock. Willa leaned in close to Charles and said, "He charges twenty dollars each way."

"You're expecting me to pay?" he teased. "I thought you asked me out here."

Willa gave him a look and he knew what that look meant. He pulled out his wallet and smiled at her. "Don't worry; I have us this way. We'll argue about going home later."

"You are a peach, Charles."

"Whatever happened to you calling me Charlie?"

"I didn't like it so much. You're a through-and-through Charles to me."

"Well, I know what you mean. My sister's called me Charlie since we were kids. My parents do too, sometimes. But most of the time, it's Charles."

Frances came zooming up in her golf cart just as the two of them disembarked. "There she is. Let's go, Charles."

Charles followed Willa slowly. He was watching several women hauling their grocery bags to waiting golf carts. "Willa, there are no cars."

"I know. It took me awhile to catch on to that, too. There aren't any roads either. Just dirt or blacktop paths. No need for cars out here. Everything moves by water. It's an island."

Charles looked as if he was beginning to understand a few things, and one of them was that these people were tough.

Frances made her acquaintance with Charles and the three of them took off in the golf cart.

"It's nice of you to take time out for us today, Frances."

"Don't need to thank me. It's my pleasure to show ye my island."

Charles smiled, and Frances said immediately, "We talk funny, don't we? Well, it's a combination of Eastern Shore, waterman, and Old English. We just can't seem to cast it off, so you'll have to forgive us out here."

Charles, sitting next to Frances, said, "I like it. I don't always catch what you're saying, but I like it. It's part of your tradition."

"Ye might say that. Say, how did my little girl Nellie do in front of all ye important folks?"

"She did fine. I hear you've been over there once or twice yourself."

"Indeed I have, Congressman."

"Please, call me Charles."

"I was honored to do it, Charles. I love my people and I love our way of life. But it's passing fast."

"I want to speak to you about that."

"Well, no better place to do that than around my kitchen table. We'll go there right after I give ye the Cook's tour of our island here. Our first stop is our big post office."

When Charles saw the post office—the size of a pea—he laughed.

Frances said, "You'll get used to us. We say things backward, so, instead of saying tiny post office, we say big post office. Don't know why we do that, but it's been our way forever."

Willa suggested, "Why don't you tell him about Grandma Shady, Frances?"

"Well, Charles, when I went over to speak to those folks in D.C. a number of years ago, people here were amazed I was doing that, and, when they saw me all dressed up with lipstick and all, and my hair fixed pritty, they called me Grandma Shady. I laughed until I thought I would die. Ye see, Grandma Shady is our way of saying a fast lady, and, being I'm not that, it became a joke. Oh, I didn't care at all. They can call me anything they like in fun, just as long as I'm doing something good for other people."

Frances started getting out of the golf cart. "Well, let's go in, and don't mind the ladies. Their bark is worse than their bite."

Charles had the look of a deer caught in headlights as he walked in. Seeing the four women sitting in a circle and talking didn't improve that feeling. Then one of them spoke.

"What you got here, Frances? We know the famous author, but now who's come to look at us?"

"Is that any way to say hello to a congressman, Dora?"

The women sat up straight and became quiet.

"This here is Congressman Lee from Virginia, and he is taking a closer look at our lives out here and over on the mainland. He's the man who Nellie spoke in front of over in Washington."

You could've heard a pin drop in that little old post office. Frances finally said, "I can't believe ye don't have something to say to this nice man after he come all this way."

Dora went first. "Nice to have ye here. Are ye related to Robert E. Lee, being you're from Virginia and all?"

Frances gasped and said, "Dora, now ye know better than to be draggin' that all up."

Charles grinned and said, "As a matter of fact, I am, ma'am. Sounds to me there's a story to be told."

163

Frances threw up her arms. "Well, go on now, Miss Dora. Ye brought it up, so you have to finish it."

Willa dragged a few folding chairs up to squeeze into the circle. She was now fascinated about what this was going to be about.

"Well, as the story goes—and don't quote me—but when Robert E. Lee was a young man and courting Miss Custis, her daddy owned all these islands and sent Master Robert out to survey four of them. Ye did know he was a surveyor, I suspect."

Charles, immersed in the tale, nodded.

"Well, after he was done with the job he was sent to do, he then ran off a bunch of the men who were running these islands 'cause they were scoundrels and drunkards, and the Lee family was quite religious, you know. When he arrived back to Virginia and made a full report to Mr. Custis, he told him exactly what he thought of these islands, which wasn't very much. Hear tell he said the island was too derned buggy and full of rascals."

Charles howled and said, "Miss Dora, I have heard a lot of family stories, but this one takes the cake. Rascals and buggy, huh?"

Dora was now in full command of the post office stage. "Derned right, and we still don't drink on the island, and we don't much appreciate any rascals comin' out here."

"That's wonderful," Charles smiled. "I will make sure to tell that one to my father. He'll love it."

The door opened to Cap'n Tuck, bringing in the mail. "Anything to go out, Florence?"

"Here, take these. And I'll take the prescriptions from ye."

Charles and Willa looked at one another, puzzled.

Frances said, "Ye see, we call our medicines in over to the mainland, and then they get them ready and bring them to the dock. When they come in here, we log them in and then deliver them."

Charles whispered to Willa, "I would never have thought about that."

Frances heard him and said, "There's a lot we have to do that you can't imagine. Our kids go by boat to school 'cause they shut our school down here a few years back 'cause there weren't many young ones left out here. Now ye see how we get our drugs and groceries. It's not a life for crybabies out on the water. We have to think everything out in advance."

Willa was taking notes while Frances spoke. Charles was clearly stunned by what all the people had to do to live out in the middle of the Chesapeake.

"Now you've got me wondering about a whole bunch of things."

"Well, come on then, and I'll show it to you before these ladies keep you all day and you miss your boat back."

Willa laughed. "We wouldn't want to do that now, would we, Charles?"

CHAPTER 30

Charles was full of questions. Frances was full of answers. Willa couldn't keep up.

Sitting in the kitchen, Charles had one more question before he and Willa had to get back to the dock.

"I can't thank you enough for taking all this time with us today, Frances. You've exceeded your reputation. But there is one more thing I need to ask."

"Go on, Congressman."

"Would you consider coming to Washington and speaking and working on this challenge with me? You have so much knowledge that it would prove very helpful."

"I appreciate your saying that, and I love my people and the water and the life I've been blessed to live, but I've done that before and Nellie just did it, and it seems to me that the bureaucrats aren't going to listen. Neither are the folks on the Baywaters Commission. They're the rascals that have really given us fits."

Charles said, "I don't understand. Aren't they supposed to be helping you?"

"You'd think that would be the case, wouldn't ye? I was involved with them a time back and so were a lot of the watermen or their wives until we learned they were more interested in their land and their power. A lot of them own land up and down the Chesapeake and they aim to keep it all to themselves. They don't like the watermen very much. I know it's hard to understand, but it's the way of things. We've tried—believe me, we've tried—to tell them things. They don't want to hear it. They think we're uneducated because we're fishermen."

"That seems so odd, Frances. But can I get you to think about it? You have passion and a fire in your belly for this."

"Ye know what passion and fire amount to?" Frances said. "They amount to dreams, and dreams can become nightmares."

Charles stood up and grabbed his coat. "Just think about it. I need to have you on my side."

Frances laughed and said, "A Lee? And you need the help of an old woman? Go on now."

Willa hugged Frances tightly. "Think about what Charles has asked you, Frances. Please?"

"What about Nellie? I don't want to interfere with what she's doing over there. My time's come and past. She's so smart."

Willa remembered her conversation with Nellie and how torn the young girl was about her life right now. She had a gut feeling Nellie didn't have quite the fire and passion her mother did. Leaning close to Frances, she said quietly, "It might surprise you if you asked Nellie about this."

Frances let go and looked into Willa's eyes. "Okay, I will talk to her. And, while we're at it, how about you? Has the island answered your questions?"

Willa blushed. "I think I'm getting close. Good-bye, Frances, and thanks so much. See you on the other side of the Bay."

Charles seconded Willa's statement and they left.

Walking down the path, Willa pointed out men playing a game of horseshoes in a backyard. "When's the last time you saw that?"

"Not long ago, actually. My dad and I go out and play horseshoes when we have something political to discuss."

"Really? Must be a southern thing. I haven't seen that game played for years."

Charles teased, "Damn Yankees."

"That's good, real good, Charles. How to win friends and influence enemies today, huh?"

"You bet. That's what we pols do best. Hey, how about we go back to that general store before we leave and grab a sandwich to eat on the way back?"

"Can't get enough, huh? Don't blame you. Boy, I'm tired. It's been a long day."

"That's right, I got you up at . . . what time did you say?"

"Zero-dark-thirty. Please don't remind me. It's a miracle I'm still on my feet."

The boat ride back was peaceful. Willa was peaceful. Charles was anything but peaceful.

"Do you think she'll do it, Charles?"

"I don't know. What do you think? You know her better."

"My guess is she will."

"How about Nellie?"

"Nellie is in love, Charles, and when that happens, all bets go out the window."

"Sounds like you know all about that, huh, Willa?"

"Maybe. But that's something I don't talk about."

"Did you get hurt? When people don't want to talk about it, that's usually what's happened."

Willa bit down on her lip in a gesture not everyone, including Charles, knew meant: keep your distance.

He said, "I can see you did, but time heals all wounds. Don't you know that?"

"You're so sure of yourself, aren't you? Well, time doesn't heal *all* wounds."

"It does if you let it."

"Well, Mr. Know-It-All, time doesn't heal the pain of losing your parents when you're young."

When he saw Willa's face, Charles was sorry he had ever started the conversation. Quietly, he reached over to move the hair blowing across her face. "I'm sorry. I shouldn't have said anything. I didn't mean to hurt you."

"I'm sure you didn't, but my hurt isn't over a man. It's from a loss no one can replace."

Charles put an arm around her. "I understand, Willa. I didn't lose a parent but I lost a brother. I have my dear sister Verinnia, but she can't take the place of my brother."

Willa turned and looked into his eyes. "The pain is awful, isn't it?"

"Yes, but we have to go on. Prue tells me your parents were both famous. Is that right?"

"So now it comes out. You and Prue talk about me, do you? Yes, my parents were very famous in the creative world. My mother was a best-selling writer and my father was a well-known comic strip writer and illustrator."

"That's pretty awesome. It's not easy to come from a famous line, is it?"

Willa smiled sadly at him, but then her humor kicked in. "You should know that well, being a relative of the famous surveyor Robert E. Lee."

Charles broke out laughing. "You sure know how to turn things around, Willa."

"I like to laugh with you, Charles. It's easy and natural. So, while we're enjoying the moment, how about a bologna sandwich?"

"Absolutely."

After one bite, Willa said, "It's something how good this bologna sandwich and Coke can taste, isn't it?"

"It's the simple things in life that are the best, Willa." And with that, Charles reached over and took Willa's hand.

CHAPTER 31

Was it her imagination or could she really have begun falling for someone over a bologna sandwich? Only time would tell, but, right now, something even more wondrous was going on in her life: the veil of blankness that had covered her brain was finally lifting and she was actually writing.

Yes, words were spilling out all over the screen. And the best part was, they made sense! She had to seize the moment and keep forging ahead because she was afraid it might be a dream and all go away when she woke up.

But she wasn't dreaming because her cell phone was going off. *Oh boy, here we go. She's going to want to know everything.*

"Good morning, Willa. I just got into work and Charles isn't in yet, so wanted to get the scoop before he walks in. How was the trip?"

"Are you talking about the trip, or are you going to go somewhere else with this conversation?"

"Touchy. That's a reveal right there."

"It astounds me how you can go from one day away to . . . to something's going on between us."

"Dish, girlfriend. No woman on this planet can spend a day with Charles Lee and come back home the same."

"Well, you've got something there, but I think he's the one who's changed."

"Really, Willa, what went on over on that island?"

"Nothing you're thinking. We went over there, he talked to so many people, and I think he may have seen some things he hadn't before."

"What are you talking about?"

"I think Congressman Charles got up close and personal and it scared him. Why? Because now he is going to have to make a decision."

"You're talking about his committee work while I'm talking about the two of you."

"Prue, there is no two of us right now. He saw what's happening to the watermen both on the mainland and out on the Bay. He heard them and he heard some things that had never been said before and I think that makes him vulnerable. And no politician likes to be vulnerable."

"Does that apply to writers, too?"

"You just won't give this up, will you, Prue? Yes, he's nice, charming, interesting . . . ."

"Everything a girl wants, right, Willa?"

"If I were writing him into one of my romance books, yes, the girl would end up with this Prince Charming. But that's not what I'm doing right now."

"Willa? Stop the presses. Is that clacking on a keyboard I hear while we're talking?"

"My, what good ears you have, Grandma. Yes, and today I'm celebrating the fact that, when I put hands to keyboard, I'm in heaven again."

"Oh, Willa, this is incredibly good news, and I'm so happy for you. It must have been this trip with Charles. Don't you see? He's the one."

"Honestly, Prue, we're not having this conversation. Do you hear me? And what I'm writing is nothing like my romance novels."

"Then what are you writing?"

"A love story, but not the kind I usually do. This is a real, honest-to-goodness story of the love of the fishermen for their fish and their families and their way of life."

"I knew it would come back to you. This will be another best seller, Willa. When you're done, women all over the world will be in love with these people."

"I think it's been percolating since Thanksgiving. However, there's still something deep down that's bothering me, and I have to get to that and dig it out and get rid of it. It's one of those things that's coming close to the surface but it's not ready to show itself."

"Try not to think about it, Willa, and it will come to you. I'm just so excited for you. This has been a really bad patch. This does call for a celebration. Drinks at the Scotch Bar at six?"

"There is one thing I am concerned about, and that's that this might boomerang back on you. I don't want to put you in the middle of any of this, Prue."

"We'll take it one step at a time, Willa."

"I promise I'll let you know as this goes along. Oh, and please go easy on Charles today. I hear he fell head over heels this weekend."

"And you didn't, of course. See you at six, Willa."

Just as Prue was considering calling out the troops to find Charles, he walked through the door. A dozen calls in the "must answer" pile were already waiting for him. Was it her imagination, or was he walking a bit lighter and was that smile of his a bit brighter?

Dying to ask about the trip, but knowing that wasn't a good idea, Prue smiled and said, "Glad you're all right. I was beginning to get a little worried. Here are your messages and you'll note the ones that have to be returned soon."

"Thanks, Prue, and if you're wondering about the trip with your girlfriend, it was very informative. As a matter of fact, so informative that I want to review the minutes of that last commercial fishing hearing."

"Okay, I'll get the minutes right away, Charles. Anything else?"

Charles knew what she was driving at, but this wasn't the time for that conversation. As he looked down at the "must call" list, he saw that Senator Reynold Richardson had tried to get hold of him and an ASAP was attached to the note. That meant something was up and Rennie, as he was known, wasn't a man to be kept waiting

Senator Richardson was a very powerful man, with the clout to make or break you in Washington. And he wasn't a particularly great friend of the independent fisherman's problems. Why he felt like that, no one seemed to know.

Moments later Prue brought the file and a freshly brewed cup of coffee.

He said thank you as he picked up the phone and called Rennie on his private line.

"Hey there, Charlie. How are things going?"

"Just got in this morning, Rennie, how are ye . . ."—Charles stopped himself just in time and then continued— "you?" Guess that dialect had stuck with him more than he had wanted to admit even to himself.

"I'm okay, I guess, but I'm concerned." The word "concerned" always meant trouble in politic-speak.

"What's got you concerned this morning?"

"I don't see any progress being made on putting more pressure on those rascals out on the Bay. I heard about that young girl and that she wasn't near as good as her mother, but she got some of the committee set to thinking about these issues. I know they're a salty group of people, but they have to comply with all the rules."

For the first time, Charles realized that he cared, but not about what the politicians and lobbyists thought. This time it was the people. "You know, Rennie, they have a tough life and all they want to do is fish and make a living."

"We know that, Charlie, but you know there's a whole lot of money being put down for our own people now. We're building the aquifer centers and the water is improving. And, once we get the oyster farms going and successful, we won't need to have all those men out there on the water. The government will control it."

"The aquifers are a ways from working completely, Rennie, and, in the meantime, the regulations and constant new fees are killing off an entire population's livelihood."

"They're dying off anyway, Charlie. In less than ten years, there won't be near enough of them to produce what we can. It's business, plain and simple. And why, may I ask, are you so interested in these folks all of a sudden? You know how we want to play this, son."

Charles spoke carefully. "Rennie, you know I've always cared about this. You know that. It's just that it's my job to look at the situation from all sides. There aren't easy answers to hard situations."

"Being a committee head isn't easy either, Charlie. If you go soft on this, I can make sure that committee has a new chair."

"Are you threatening me, Rennie? All I said is that we have to be careful with this and not throw the baby out with the bath water."

"Now, listen here, son. If we can't get those stubborn bastards to do what they're supposed to, we'll take them out all together."

Charles had had it with the threats, and, if the senator called him "son" one more time, he thought he would jump through the phone and hit him.

"I don't like your implications, Rennie. I don't like them at all. Four hundred years of history is out there on that Bay, and, business or not, those people deserve better than what they're getting."

"Hogwash. Listen to me, Charles. I've known your family since I was a young man. I know your daddy and he's a good man and understands how things get done around here. Maybe you ought to have a talk about all this with him. He might straighten you around. Something's happened to you. I don't know what, but you know I'll find out. Just get back on the path, son. Now I've said all it is I have to say."

Rennie hung up. Charles sat stunned . . . and fuming. He muttered to himself, "That old mule isn't going to get his way on this. I'm going to fight back. If I lose the next election, so be it. Whether she likes or not, it's time for Miss Frances to come to Washington."

CHAPTER 32

Words kept coming and Willa kept putting them down. This wasn't at all the kind of book she was used to writing, but it was one that had to be written. However, she knew this one might truly cost her Kitwin Publishing. Kit Winthrop had been good to her word and left her alone to work through this period, but, when she heard what was being written, it might be too much for her this time. No matter what happened, she had to talk with Kit, She owed her that much.

Kit had just left a lunch meeting with Susan Crandall when Willa's call came. After talking with Susan for a couple of hours, this would be a most welcome conversation. "Hello, Willa dahling."

"Hi, Kit. Do you have a minute?"

"I have two. Just let me get into my car here and then I'm all yours. There, I'm in. What's up?"

"Well, first of all, I'm back to the world of storytelling."

"That's fabulous, dear. I told you, it comes and goes through a career. So, now what?"

"Well, I have begun a book."

"Music to my ears. What's this juicy tale about?"

"That's the problem, Kit. This one isn't going to be a juicy romance." She hesitated, then thought, to hell with it. "It's going to be about the watermen's lives and, in specific, about the people and the battle they're facing now."

Dead silence came from the other end of the phone. Willa braced herself for the scream that would come next.

That didn't happen. But what did shocked the socks off her. "Before I say anything, tell me more about this."

Kit was interested. *So, go on, Willa, and make this good. You've got one shot.*

"Well, it centers mostly on an island in the Chesapeake, but it could be about any of the people who fish for a living. And there are other inhabited islands all over the world where people's lives revolve around the fishing industry, so the appeal is international."

Willa kept going as Kit listened. Finally Kit spoke. "I actually like it. I think it's plucky and maybe it's right for you. Your readers are loyal and they love you. Just one question. Can you make it a love story?"

A sigh of relief quietly released itself from Willa's body. She had come through without any scars. A good sign.

"I assume you mean a love story between people."

"Isn't that what love stories are, Willa?"

"Not this one. This *is* a love story, but it's the love a people have for the water and what comes from it."

"Can't you extend that a little, dear? I mean these people fall in love, don't they?"

"Yes, they do. Would that make you happy, Kit?"

"You know it would. And it would make your readers happy as well."

"We both know that characters talk to the writer, so I guess I could try to make one fall in love. My call on that one. Who knows how they will like it."

"You know, Willa, sometimes I think you're a little crazy—but there's nothing wrong with crazy."

Willa laughed. "Thank you. I happen to like crazy and I happen to like being able to sit down and have words fall out of my mind again."

"I am thrilled for you, for me, and for all of us. Keep in touch as you progress and don't forget the romance angle. It makes money, sweetie. Glad you're back, Willa." She added, "I was about at the end of my rope with Susan. And, by the way, that was a nasty little trick you pulled on her."

Willa chuckled. "Don't tell me she didn't deserve it. That girl is out of control. It was the award that sent her over the edge."

"As I recall, Willa dahling, it was the booze that done her in."

"Thanks. I needed that, Kit. I'll be in touch and I'll remember what you said."

Willa was still chuckling over the Susan Crandall remark Kit had made when her phone rang. "Damn it! I'm never going to get back to work today." However, the voice she heard when she picked up was one she didn't mind talking with at all.

"Good morning, Willa. How are you?"

She definitely was feeling something for the man at the other end of the line.

"I'm good, thank you. I didn't have to be up at zero-dark-thirty today."

She heard him laugh. She knew he liked that expression and it made her happy to make him happy. What was going on here?

"Willa, I have a problem and really need to talk it through with you, but would prefer not to do that over the phone. How about lunch? I can make it a late lunch, around two o'clock, if that works better for you."

She was surprised and happy and confused all at once, but she wasn't going to miss this chance to see him. That she knew outright. "Two would work for me today. Where?"

"Where else? Yitzi's fine delicatessen, of course."

"I'm becoming a regular. I hear something in your voice. Is everything okay?"

"It's complicated. We'll talk later, and thanks for saying yes on such short notice."

"No problem."

As she ended the conversation, she felt very content. Was she coming down with something? Not hardly. Or was she succumbing to that disease that seemed to affect all women who entered the web of Congressman Charles Lee?

"Be careful, Wilhelmina. You have to be sure what's real and what isn't."

No mistaking that voice in her head. It was her mother's.

177

The weather had turned warm in Washington, normal for early spring. While the rest of the country was still facing snowstorms, the cherry blossoms were about to be born. It was a magical time in the city when this happened. Only downsides were all the traffic and the all the tourists.

Willa wore a classic French sailor's long-sleeved tee shirt with a pair of very upscale jeans. She had the perfect figure for that style. Long, lean legs, along with her rather long blonde hair swept up on top of her head, made for a striking look. Finishing it off was a bright red scarf around her neck.

Well, not fancy-schmancy, but enough to get his attention. *I could be on the cover of* Vogue *with this outfit. Not that you are too conceited, Willa dear. Come to think about it, I have been on the cover of* Vogue *after my fifth best seller,* Love's Desire. *If I finish this project, it sure won't have a title like that. Get going, Willa. You'll be late and we know what Charlie thinks of that.*

This time it wasn't Willa who was late; it was the good congressman. She had a table—no easy feat—and when he walked in, she stood and waved to him. He looked a bit weary.

"Don't even say it, Willa. I know I'm late."

"Not to put too fine a point on that, isn't it you who lectures people on that sort of thing?"

"Go on; have your fun. It's been a hellish day, that's all I can say."

Do not go any further. Willa, He's on a short string.

"Care to share, Charles, or are we at the 'it's five o'clock somewhere' stage?"

"I think the latter."

When the server came, Willa ordered a cup of tea and Charles promptly ordered a beer.

"I see, she commented. Going to be a serious conversation."

"Willa, I need you to help me. I need you to talk Frances Evans into coming to Washington. I will set the date for the hearing, but I have to have her speak. Nellie can't do this. She's too young, and, this time, the committee would tear her to pieces."

"Mind telling me what this is all about? Or should I take a stab at it?"

"I'll tell you but we have to keep a tight lid on this. Understand?"

"Understand." She did that zipping-her-lips-thing with her fingers. Charles seemed slightly amused.

Charles proceeded to tell Willa everything about the call from Rennie Richardson and about the other things swirling around the topic of fishing in the Chesapeake. He explained the condition of the Bay and how cleaning it up looked to be an ongoing issue—one that could possibly take decades to fix. If it could be fixed at all.

"I see, Charles. Everything truly is political, isn't it?"

"Yes, it is, Willa. This issue is a juggernaut, and it's why there are never any real solutions, just bandaids until the big boys can get enough power to come down on the watermen. Now they have it. They've amassed millions of dollars and there are real heavyweights involved and Rennie Richardson is the top one."

"What do you want from me? You want me to get Miss Frances to come over here and get into this muck? Seems almost cruel, doesn't it? I won't do that to her. I really care about that woman."

Charles stared at her and then said, desperately, "I need her, Willa. She is exactly what is needed to bring this battle to the fore. I'm not like these men and this may cost me my next election, but I don't care. I have loved the Chesapeake since I was a child. I fished that body of water with my grandfather and we loved those times together. Frances can do this, I know she can. She's made of passion and steel, and those two put together are invincible."

Willa said, "It seems you sure have gotten yourself in a stew over this all of a sudden. You should have gone over there a long time ago."

"Yes, I should have. I relied on information from others: others who were most likely paid well to feed me what the other side wanted me to know. I should have known better, but I have always hoped there were moments of clarity in this situation."

"What was the turning point for you over there?"

Charles hesitated for a moment and then beamed his wonderful smile. "It all changed, Willa, when I found out that the Lee family had a relationship to that land. That makes this personal for me."

"Oh, my gosh, you're right. I all but forgot that fact, except that it was an old tale, you know."

"Still and all. Will you ask Frances?"

"Under these new circumstances, I have no choice but to ask her. So, yes, I will, Charles."

In the middle of the busy, noisy enclave that was Yitzi's Deli, he slid his hand over hers. Her insides were already jumping around like a pea on a griddle when he said, "You know something, Willa? When this is all over, I want to see more of you. If you're okay with that?"

CHAPTER 33

Nellie was now the one who needed to make a decision. She lacked just a few classes in order to graduate, but her involvement with Global Waters was extremely important. She loved her research job and, especially now, had to continue the projects she was working on. But she missed home so much, she was seriously thinking of going back.

Of course, Denny had everything to do with this. She was in love with him.

Her job had been perfect from the moment she landed it. She got to study marine issues in the Chesapeake waters, and, having grown up on the Bay waters, she was well suited for the position. But it didn't feel right to her anymore. Getting the information together and then out to the public in an unbiased fashion was always an uphill struggle. The research was being driven by political money, and that always corrupted things to some extent.

While Nellie was trying not to make a mistake with her life, Willa was trying to figure out exactly what she should write. On top of that, she knew she could no longer deny her attraction to Charles. The electricity was there, and, when that happened, there was little one could do to stop it.

However, she was a terror when she started a new book, so, if she was to do this, she had to keep her feelings under wraps for now. And Charles was beyond busy, too. She knew it was going to be up to her to keep this under control. She remembered what new love was like. It made a person crazy and it took root in one's mind as well as heart, a driving force that couldn't be stopped. She had to be careful; she had to be the one to put the brakes on as hard as necessary.

Right now, she had to take things in order, and at the top of the list was getting Frances to come to Washington. Charles needed her because, with Miss Frances behind him, he was convinced they could get people to be reasonable and resolve some of the more pressing issues. Willa knew, though, that she wasn't the one to ask her: it was going to have to be Nellie. Frances needed to hear it from Nellie to know she wasn't overstepping her daughter.

Just as Willa was picking up her cell, a call came through. She couldn't believe the power of telepathy.

"Hello, Willa. I have to talk with you. I need you to help me make a decision."

"This is really amazing, Nellie. I was just about to call you. I need to speak with you, too. Where and when?"

"How about dinner tonight?"

"I'm supposed to be having drinks with my friend Prue at The Willard, but I could push that a little later."

"You girls sure have fancy happy hours. That would be great if you can change things around."

"How about I meet you in Georgetown at The Tombs? Can we do it around five o'clock?"

"I should be able to do that. Thanks so much, Willa. By the way, what did you want to talk to me about?"

"We'll discuss everything when I see you. Be safe, Nellie."

Willa was waiting with a hot cup of tea when Nellie arrived. She had been very lucky to get one of their premiere booths, always in high demand. The Tombs was a Georgetown tradition.

"Hi, Willa. Hope you haven't been waiting long. Traffic is a bear this time of the day."

"I think you did really well, all things considered. In fact, I would say you're early."

After ordering, Nellie got right to it, explaining to Willa what was bothering her and asking her advice. After all, hadn't Willa told her to call if she needed something?

"So, what do you think, Willa? Am I crazy to trade a successful life over here for love over there?"

"Is anyone crazy to throw love aside for what is perceived to be success? Success is a life lived happy."

Nellie spent a minute chewing on what Willa had said. "You know, you're right. I hadn't thought of it that way."

"You know, Nellie, I admire you so much, and so do many other people. You had the courage to leave the island in the first place and go out and live in an entirely different world. Now you've done that, so you know what's out here and can have the satisfaction of knowing you did it. And, when you went home for the holidays, your mind was on coming back here to live and work, right? But one glance at Denny told you something very different. You knew immediately where you belonged."

"Mama and Daddy sacrificed so much for me and I don't want them ever to be disappointed."

"The only disappointment a mother and father will ever have is to know their child isn't truly happy. I don't think they would mind at all if they had you near them, happily married to Denny, and they could be a part of the lives of their grandchildren."

"You know, Willa, you have the voice of reason and you're exactly right. You write what you feel and, now knowing you, I can see there is a great depth to you." She paused, then looked straight at Willa. "But there's a great sadness in you, too. Is there something I can do to make it go away?"

"I just wish I had a family to share my joys with, that's all, Nellie. Don't waste this precious time before it's too late. I would give anything if I could have had more time with my parents."

Nellie reached over and squeezed Willa's hand. "Thank you so much, dear friend. Who would ever have thought that my giving a talk would have an outcome like this?"

Willa realized that two people had now held her hand with hopefulness.

"You're right, Nellie. Who would have thought? But now I need something from you."

"Anything, Willa."

"Well, given this conversation, it appears it may have worked itself out already, but I need you to tell your mother that Congressman Lee needs her to come to Washington. She needs to come and speak from her heart—as she always does. It's nothing about you; it's simply that Frances Evans has a quality about her that transcends the everyday. People know when she says something that she means it with all her heart, and they can see her purity of purpose. This group will be tough, but your mother has a way of making the complex simple."

"Okay, Willa, I can do that. After speaking with you, my mind is made up now so there's nothing stopping Mama from coming over here and having her say. She can handle it, Willa. Believe me, she can handle it. When do you want me to talk to her?"

Willa's eyes danced teasingly as she answered, "Yesterday?"

On the ride back home, Nellie practiced what she would tell her mother, but the bigger issue was what she was going to tell Denny. He hadn't actually asked her to marry him; it had always been unspoken between them, but, if she went back home, she was sure it wouldn't be long before he made it official.

There was something else on Nellie's mind that she hadn't discussed with Willa, a family thing that might make it impossible for her mother to leave home. Her daddy had looked so tired lately and both she and her mother were worried about him. He was getting older now and was out on that water every day in rain, wind, sun, and anything else weather could throw at you out there. It takes a toll and he was paying for it now. If he got sick, how would they afford to help him? The watermen didn't have benefits or pensions. They went out on their own and prayed their catch was good. If she did go back home, she was going to have to figure out a way to make money and that wouldn't be easy. She had to do that before she left here and have it all settled so she could go in peace.

Willa wasn't home five minutes before calling Charles. When he came on the phone, she said, "We're in."

"We're in what, Willa? With you that could mean a lot of things."

"Oh ye of little faith. I just had dinner with Nellie and she's going to ask Frances. It turns out she's going back to the island to live, but that's on the qt right now."

"Boy, they're right. When you want something done, ask a busy person."

"Exactly. And now this would be the place you would say thank you, Charles Lee."

"How about drinks tomorrow night?"

"OMG!"

"What's wrong, Willa? I would think you would love to have drinks on me."

"It's not that, Charles. What time is it?"

"Seven o'clock, why?"

"I'm supposed to be in the Scotch Bar having drinks with Prue right now. Oh, I am in trouble."

"Call and tell her you'll be late. And that it's my fault."

Willa's eyes rolled. She couldn't tell Prue exactly that. For sure, she'd never hear the end of it.

"Okay. I have to make tracks. Yes, I'll have drinks with you tomorrow night. Call me. Bye."

Willa was off the phone so fast Charles didn't know what had hit him. But did he ever with this girl?

CHAPTER 34

It was still before dawn when Frances sat down to her kitchen table. She had listened to the weather radio, and, when she heard there were gale warnings out, she had told Jimmy to sleep in some. Now, while a fresh pot of coffee perked, she prayed.

There seemed to be a lot to say to the good Lord this morning. Nellie's call the night before had everything to do with that. Jimmy had gone off to bed when the call came. Frances was used to that because that was the time of day Nellie was free finally to sit down and relax. While most calls were the usual mother/daughter chatter, last night's had shocked Frances and that wasn't easily done.

Ye see, I don't want my Nellie to ever be unhappy that she's making this big decision, and I don't want to be unhappy if I make the wrong one neither. I've been in that nest of bees before and it's a mess. Politicians, as you know too well, Lord, are a whole different critter. They're out for themselves and not for those who elected them to speak on their behalf. I guess I have to trust in Ye and leave it there. 'Tain't nothing I can do to change what Yer will is anyway, so I just want to tell Ye, I'm so happy Nellie's coming home. Denny will be happy Nellie's coming home, and I know, when I tell Jimmy, he'll be bustin' inside with happiness. So, thank you, Lord, and have Ye a good day.

Frances had said her piece for the day.

Just as she got up to pour a cup of the heavenly smelling coffee, Jimmy made his appearance in the kitchen.

"Morning, husband. Sit on down now and I'll get ye a cup of coffee.

There's some things we have to talk about, but I want to get some of this octane in ye before we start."

"Okay, Franny."

As Jimmy sipped away, Frances made a couple of eggs and some dry toast for them both. She always made sure her family ate in the morning.

Jimmy leaned back and rubbed his rather robust stomach, covered this morning by an old, worn, white tee shirt that had been bleached so many times, its smell was unmistakably Clorox. "What's itchin' at ye, Franny girl?"

Placing the plate down in front of him, she said, "Eat this while I tell ye."

"Get on with it now. Bad weather or not, I have to go on down to the shanty in a little while."

"Okay. Here's the gist. Ye know Nellie called last night and we got to talkin' and I could tell this wasn't just a callin'-home-to-Mama call. Well, she went on and told me that she was leaving her job and has decided to come home. She was working on how she could do that and still make money over here, but she's comin' home. Isn't that something, Jimmy?"

Jimmy's face was awash with emotion. He wasn't one to show it, but, this time, he couldn't help himself. "This is good news, Franny. I miss my little girl and never wanted to tell her how much."

"She knows that, Jimmy. And she misses us—*all* of us—the same way."

"Know Denny will be bustin'."

"They'll be married for sure one day. Now, there's more."

Jimmy knew that tone. "Tell me now, Franny."

"Well, it seems I may, if it's okay with you, be going back to Washington."

Jimmy's face went from sheer joy to displeasure, even though he tried to keep it to himself.

"Now don't go gettin' all fussed up about it, but it seems that nice congressman who came over here with Willa wants me to talk to those rascals over there. So, what do you really think, Jimmy?"

Jimmy rubbed his chin with his big right hand. "Will it pleasure ye to do it?"

"I think so. It's time we're heard from, Jimmy. It can't do us any worse than what's already happening. If they aim to make it so hard for us to crab and oyster anymore, then we have to stand up now, before it's over and done with. We're almost to that point now."

"Ye have the words, girl, so go use 'em. Just remember, people 'round here won't all be standin' and cheerin' if ye do this. Last time, some got pritty mad about it and blamed ye for some of the rules they placed on us."

"They came around after time, Jimmy. Besides, I think this time might be different. There are a lot of people out there who need to know what's happening to us. We all belong to one another, and, if one piece of us goes, so does the rest."

"I see your heart is in this, Frances Evans. When do ye leave?"

"I don't know. I don't even know if that fine Charles Lee knows yet, but I suspect I'll hear from him when he wants me."

"Can you believe that old scudder Floyd will be our in-law one day, Franny?"

"Jimmy Evans, have you heard half of what I've said to ye?"

"Yes, darlin'. But still, Floyd and us? Would make our girl happy, though. Denny is a good boy and he's a great waterman, even though he's only twenty-nine."

"What's that got to do with it? That boy's been out on the water since he was knee high."

"You're right, but there was a time I thought he'd leave the water, too. 'Tain't easy no more out there. Does Nellie have an idea of how she can make money?"

"She'll find it. She's so smart, Jimmy. We sure did that right."

Jimmy smiled back at his wife in the way that said, I know. "Well, if yer done yabbin' at me, I have to go on out. The *Miss Nellie Frances* is in need of some work. Good day to do it."

"Are ye crazy? You'll get sick."

"No, I won't. I can fix the part that's broke inside the shanty. I'll turn the heater on."

Frances rolled her eyes and said, "Go on, then. I'll bring yer lunch out to ye. I'm cookin' up a mess of chicken this morning."

"And maybe one of yer sweet potato pies? That sure would round it off."

"Oh, all right, old man. I can make ye a sweet potato pie, but, after the holidays, ye have had your share already. You'll have to watch it."

"That sounds fine, Franny." He walked over to his wife and gave her a tight hug. "My little girl is comin' home and my big girl is goin' to Washington. Life sure is something."

It had to be love. No matter how Prue had tried to maneuver around her dear girlfriend, it ended up the same: a girlish giggle and no definitive answer. She was totally frustrated, but one thing was certain—Willa wasn't ready to give up anything about her boss. Secretly, Prue hoped this would turn into something because she had always thought they were perfect for one another, but she knew she had to leave it alone and let it happen with no outside interference.

"Morning, Prue. Are we ready to work?"

"Seems an odd question as I'm sitting behind my desk and you're the one just walking in."

"I can always count on you to keep me straight. Nice to know who the boss is, huh?"

"Just so you don't forget that . . . Congressman."

Charles handed her a list of people to call. "I want to set a date for another hearing. Make it middle of next month and please list as the guest speaker, Frances Evans."

"Nellie's mother? *That* Frances Evans? The one who almost set this place ablaze last time she spoke?"

"One and the same."

"How do you know she'll do it, and won't that undermine what her daughter is doing?"

Charles leaned over Prue's desk and said, "No. Now before you go on and keep me from my other work today, Miss Harding, let me explain. Nellie is going back to her island to live and be happily ever after with Denny. And her mother, who will help us move along these endless discussions, is coming over here and will address the issues of the people over there. Is all this clear?"

Prue sat in stunned silence. Why hadn't Willa told her this last night? What's going on with all this and why couldn't she know? She stared back at him while deciding what to say and then, before she could retrieve them, the words came out of her mouth. "Are you falling for Willa?"

Charles looked shocked by the question, as she gasped and covered her mouth. "What did you just say? Or shouldn't we repeat that, Prudence?"

She didn't know whether it was the direct look or him calling her Prudence that gave her the idea he was pissed.

"You do know we don't discuss our personal relationships inside this office, don't you?"

Prue nodded her head. She also made the quick decision she wasn't going to act like some simp. "Yes, I do, Charles, but she is my closest friend and I don't want her hurt."

Clearly she was in "game on" mode. "Okay, Prue, you're right. She's your friend and now she's mine. What comes of our friendship is anyone's guess. She's a neat lady, but, right now, we're working on this fishing thing, and, together, we have a good shot at putting some serious issues on the table."

"You're right, Charles. I'm sorry for saying that. I had no business—"

"Look, Prue, sometimes it's hard not to talk about our personal lives in here, but we just can't. I've always respected your discretion with this subject, so, please, let's just forget anything was said and leave it at that."

"That's fine with me, Charles, but if you ever decide to change that rule, I'm here. Willa is a very unusual woman and I'm so lucky to have met her and now have her as such a good friend. I want her to be happy."

Charles said, "I do, too. I think she's found something here, though, and I'm very grateful to her for helping me. This is going to get rocky and make some folks very upset. Hope you can stand the heat."

"Looking forward to it."

"I can see why you and Willa are friends. You both have grit. And you both drive me nuts."

CHAPTER 35

Nellie decided not to go into her office. It was just too awful outside with the rain pounding down, and she needed to think. She called in and told them she would be working from home this morning.

It was then that the light bulb went on in her head. If she was so important to the research projects she did for Global Waters Enterprises that they allowed her to work at home sometimes, they might let her continue her work on the island. If she got the projects done, what difference would it make *where* they were done?

Made sense to her; now she had to have it make sense to the powers-that-be at GWE. She immediately called her boss and asked for a meeting later that day. When she agreed, it seemed like a sign she was one step closer to going home.

While Nellie pored over dozens of papers in her apartment, Denny was trying to get work done in the pouring rain on the island. When days like this hit in early spring, they called them "soakers," an appropriate name because there was nothing that wasn't soaking. The rain was coming down in sheets sideways across the four islands that made up James Island. Tuckerton—the smallest and the farthest west— got it first when it was blowing in from Baltimore.

Cap'n Tuck was out already and heading his boat on over to the mainland. The kids had to get to school and the mail had to go through, regardless of the weather. In a hurricane, they didn't go, but everything else was just part of living on an island.

There wouldn't be any fishing today. The winds were strong and forecast to go on all day, so other work had to be done when it hit like this. For Denny, it was time to start fixing up his crab pots and repairing any damage to the shedding troughs. Working on the boat itself was something you had to do in better weather, and those days would come soon enough.

He loved this old shanty. It had always belonged to his family. Each generation had taken pride in keeping it up, and, as the years went along, added to it. He had seen what some people were doing to deserted shanties over in Somerville. Outsiders were buying them up from the families and making them into small gazebos along the shore. They called them "quaint," and used them for having cocktails at sunset and dabbling their feet in the water while saying, "Isn't this sweet?"

The watermen didn't take too kindly to that. It was one more piece of their culture leaving them. One of the old-timers who had raised Cain about what was happening was a fiery old waterman named Dickie Short. He'd been something else and had brought a lot of attention to the area before he passed on. However, his old shanty went to the young man who had come there as a reporter to help him get the message out. The reporter ended up staying, got married, and began teaching people about the water culture of the Chesapeake. He fixed that shanty up and still used it when he went out crabbing.

The Bradshaws' shanty wasn't so small anymore. Over the years they had turned the front part into a small office with a couple of chairs and a heater. The closest thing to it might be those icehouses in Minnesota.

But the shanty was all things crab and oyster. An old set of oyster tongs was still in there, propped up against the corner. They didn't hand-tong for oysters anymore, but they would never get rid of the old tools. They'd been in the family since forever, so they were a treasure.

Through a door in the back wall, you went into the shedding room where the troughs lined the sides. Pipes ran under and along them to carry the water up from the marina and then circulate it through the troughs for the crabs. They swam in there until they began to shed. Then, when they did, they were taken and iced up for the market. They were known first as "busters" when they cracked their shells; then, when the shell began to break off, they were called "peelers."

Soft-shell crabs brought a nice price in season, but it was hard work. So everything had to be fixed and ready to go by crab season, now coming up soon. That meant having some days like this were really a blessing for the watermen. They could use the extra time.

While checking over his pots, Denny was thinking about Nellie. He wondered what she was doing. He missed her so badly and seeing her over the holidays had just made him miss her more. When she had told him she was leaving to go to college fours years back, he remembered the pain; it had never really gone away. But he also knew that his mama was right when she'd told him, "Ye got to let someone go sometimes to make them know how much they should come back."

How he hoped she would, because, of all the people in the world, he knew she wouldn't ever be happy until she did.

By afternoon, the rain had let up a little and Nellie was ready to go. Her course was set and now she had to make this happen. Then she would call over to Denny and tell him.

He had been her friend all her life. They had gone Bay jumping in the summertime as children, and she would tease him and make believe she was drowning and watch him swim out to save her. Children raised on islands made their own fun. It might be hokey to city kids, but, to them, it was the freest and most wonderful life a child could ever have. After all, what city kid gets to drive all over an island in a golf cart and pull up on the shore and watch the sun set? They could sit and watch the gulls swoop and soar, sentinels of who was coming to their island. Kids just grew up knowing the natural world, and with an appreciation for it. They felt a need to care for it because they were all a part of this water world.

Cindy Ellison was a wonderful lady to work for and with. She was intelligent and had been a good mentor for Nellie. Now Nellie hoped she was compassionate, too.

"Come on in, Nellie. Hideous day, isn't it?"

Nellie sat down on the comfortable chair in front of her desk. Cindy wasn't a small woman, but not what you would call hefty either. She did know how to make the most of her full figure, however, and was very attractive in a city-chic way. Nellie was a big-boned girl herself, and, although she dressed well, no one would ever say she was petite. It simply wasn't in her genes.

"Now, what's this all about, Nellie? You and I haven't had a long conversation for a while so we're overdue."

Nellie was nervous but determined. No backing out. Her mind was made up. "Well, Cindy. I've come to talk to you about my future here at GWE. I love my work, but I realized when I spoke in Washington a few months ago, how much I missed the island and living on it."

Cindy's brow furrowed. She had been around long enough to know what was coming next. "Go on, Nellie."

"Well, I've been thinking . . . well, wondering if I could continue my work but do it from the island and send it over online? And, if needed, I could come in sometimes if there was an important meeting or something."

Cindy's expression didn't change much at first, and then a smile crossed her face. Nellie wasn't sure if that was good or bad.

"Well, Nellie, I don't really know the answer to that question. We've never had this asked of us before. I mean people do work at home a good deal, but you're talking about working from an island way out there."

As she pointed out the window, Nellie knew, if she didn't come up with something fast, this idea would sink in the water she loved.

"I understand that, but wasn't it because of the fact I came from the island that you-all wanted me in the first place? Now, my work would go on, but just from a home a wee bit farther away than the other employees' homes."

"I see you have this all figured out."

"I hope so, Cindy, because, mostly, I want to go back home. I love what I do and I want to do as much research as I can to give people an idea of what happens in this beautiful Chesapeake. But can't I do that from the island?"

"In this day of technology, I don't see why you couldn't, but that doesn't mean top management won't nix the idea. Let me ask them and get back to you."

"I don't mean to be a problem to you, but how fast do you think you could do that?"

Cindy laughed. "In that much of a hurry, are you?"

"Yes."

"Well, I suppose in that case we could have an answer to you by the end of the day. Let me see what I can do."

"That's really great, Cindy. I have a bunch of work on my desk to do anyway, so I'll be here. Waiting."

"Yes, Nellie. I get the message. But if the answer is no, will you still leave and go back home?"

Without hesitation, Nellie said, "Yes. I will."

CHAPTER 36

When Senator Richardson got the memo about the hearing, he went ballistic. "I thought I made myself clear to that pup who was running this show. Damn you, Charles," shouted Rennie. "I'll show him who he's dealing with."

He buzzed his secretary. "Miss Purdy, tell them over to Congressman Charlie Lee's office that I'll be there in twenty minutes and I don't expect to be kept waiting."

Miss Lila Purdy did as she was told. She always did. She had been Senator Richardson's secretary since he had come to the Hill. And she once had been his lover, too, but that had been a long time ago now. She wanted to leave, but he wouldn't hear a word of it. He had told her she could stay forever if she liked, or until he was no longer around. So she stayed.

Rennie paced around like a wildcat, cussing up a storm. He wasn't to be taken lightly and he'd thought Charlie Lee knew that. Suddenly his door opened.

"Yes, Lila. What is it? I'm as mad as a hatter this morning. Did you call them over to Lee's office and tell them I'm coming over?"

"Of course I did, and his gal over there said, 'Come right along.'"

"She's a good gal and a pretty one. I don't know how she puts up with the likes of that young man. I thought he'd listen to me, but he went right ahead and called for another hearing."

"Prue Harding is pretty, but I don't think she'll be staying with him for long."

"What do you mean, Lila?"

"Some gals come to work and that's all. Some, like Prue, have other agendas."

"Well, whatever. I better be going. I just can't believe he's doing this."

"What exactly is he doing that has you so fired up?"

"He's bringing that golderned woman back here, that's what he's doing. Frances Evans."

He didn't have to go any further; Lila knew now why he was so upset.

"Talk it out, Rennie. Don't make things worse with your temper."

Rennie picked up his trademark wide-brimmed straw hat and walked over to her. "You always calm me down, Lila. I don't know how you've stayed with the likes of me all these years."

A smile on her face, she answered, "Neither do I. Now go on. Play nice."

Prue knew what was going to happen in a few minutes. The senator was going to walk in and all hell would break loose. She knew the congressman had sunk his teeth into this issue of the watermen, and, once that happened, young or not, he wasn't going to let go.

Charles walked out of his office and said teasingly, "How much more time do I have to live?"

"Not much. You better gird your loins. The lion is entering the cub's den."

"Well, we'll see how this ends up, won't we?"

Just as Charles returned to his office, in walked the senator. Prue began saying, "Good morning, Senator—" But he walked past her and straight back to Charles's office. He closed the door behind him.

Charles stood up and extended his hand. "Rennie, how are you?"

Rennie reluctantly shook his hand and answered, " Not well, son. I got your memo and thought we better speak immediately about this."

"Sit down, Rennie. I knew you might be a little upset, but I've made up my mind. We have to get to the bottom of all this and go in a different direction."

"And you think that ornery woman will help us do that? You know how hot this issue is, and bringing her back to plead the case for the poor old waterman is just going to make it worse."

"I don't think so, Rennie. I went over there and I spoke personally to a lot of these men and women. They need help and they aren't getting it."

"And I should care, why?"

"Because you're a senator, aren't you? And aren't you on this committee? And aren't we trying to come to grips with *all* the issues? Not just those in the interest of the Baywaters Commission and the lobbyists and fat cats who live along the shores? I mean, damn it, Rennie, these folks have been out there on that Bay for a very long time, and we don't give a whit about them. Don't you think that matters?"

"What's happened to you, Charlie? Have you talked this over with your father?"

"What's he got to do with this? I know you two go back a long way, but that doesn't affect this issue. The government has to lighten up on these men."

"Why? Their time is over, Charlie. It's a new day."

"Spoken by an old man. No disrespect meant, Rennie."

"You know how this game is played over here, and, if you go poking about in this, I can't protect you."

"Then don't try. I can make my case on my own."

"It appears to me you can't. Isn't that the reason you're bringing that old woman back over here? Her daughter wasn't up to the task, but Frances Evans is. You may not have been here when she spoke last time, but I was. It tore everyone up."

"Apparently not enough."

"I see you aren't going to undo this. So be it, then. You're on your own, son. I won't help you."

"I understand that. I just want to do right by those crabbers and oystermen. That's all."

Rennie got up. As he turned to leave, he said, "We'll see."

After Rennie left, Prue came into Charles's office. "Are you still breathing?"

"Yes, I am. The old coot. He thinks because he and my father went to school together a long time ago, he can push me around. He can't. This is important and I don't want to screw it up. There's a whole lot at stake."

"And maybe more for the Bay, huh?"

"We need to work hard on this, Prue. If this hearing doesn't break through, I'm afraid nothing will."

"It will, Charles. Your heart is in this one. I've never seen you like this before. It will."

"Then let's get to work. I want to get more information on the history of James Island. I want as much as you can get."

Prue left. She hadn't received an answer to her question, but she knew his not answering had been an answer in itself.

She also knew she could help him in regards to Rennie Richardson. But that she would keep to herself. For now.

It was late afternoon and Nellie was going crazy waiting. Finally, Cindy tapped on her door and walked in.

"Nellie, I have an answer for you and it's yes. Now you have to make a plan for us and then you can make a plan for you. By the way, this wasn't easy, but you are very respected upstairs."

Nellie grinned from ear to ear. "Thank you so much, Cindy. This will work, I know it will. And thank you for telling me what they think up in the big offices."

Cindy couldn't help but be happy for this young gal. She was a good worker and she didn't doubt for a minute that they would never be disappointed with their decision. After all, how many other people were going to come and ask to work from home . . . on an island?

"When do you think you'll be leaving us here?"

"As soon as I can make all the necessary arrangements. Maybe two weeks, a little more. Is that okay?"

"That's fine. If I can help with anything, let me know."

Cindy Ellison closed the door and Nellie picked up the phone and called Denny. She hadn't felt this good or free for a long time.

"Hello?"

"Denny? I'm coming home. And this time it's for good."

He didn't heard another word after that. No matter how hard the rain was still coming down outside, in his heart and in his shanty, the sun was shining.

CHAPTER 37

Nellie had left the island to get an education and spread her wings, but what she'd learned was that her wings would end up taking her back home. Tuckerton was a hard place to leave behind forever. Now she knew that those who had left and not returned, had to feel a sadness deep down inside them that would never leave.

Now that her decision was made and plans were in place, she called Willa and thanked her for everything. She noticed during their conversation that Willa didn't seem to be surprised at all that she was returning home. Willa wished her well, told her she would return to the island herself one day soon, and said she hoped their friendship would continue. Nellie had assured her it would.

When the day came, Nellie slipped out her apartment door, took a final look around at the city digs that had been her home, and, before closing the door behind her, said good-bye. Next step: drive to Somerville, where she would leave her car with Aunt Rita and then catch the boat across to home, to Mama and Daddy—and Denny.

When she had told her parents what day she would be back, she told them not to say a word to anyone, especially Denny. She wanted to surprise him. They promised, and that was a pledge.

Nellie was a basket of nerves all the way home.. Most of her things were on the boat; the rest would be shipped home, which meant it went into Somerville first and then onto the boat to get across. Nothing was ever easy.

She was so relieved she had worked it all out with GWE and she could go on working with them. She loved what she was doing and felt it helped all watermen on the Bay. And it was going to provide the money she would need. She hadn't told Denny yet about the job. She would save that because he was old-fashioned about the way a husband was to work while the woman took care of the home, and it was going to take up considerable time to help him understand. But she had that all figured out. He would adjust to it after awhile. Marriage was full of that, wasn't it?

The boat docked on time, but Nellie knew time wouldn't really play a major role in her life anymore. Here, one lived by the earth's clock of sunrises and sunsets. They were all you had to know.

She and Frances hugged so hard on that dock, she knew for sure she had made the right decision. She didn't want to miss any more time with those she loved.

"Oh, Mama, am I really doing this? Am I really home for good now?"

"You bet your daddy and me aren't gonna let ye go again. And I suspect neither will Denny. He's been driving me crazy to know when ye are coming home. Thank goodness that stops today."

Giggling a little, Nellie said, "He sure is going to be surprised, isn't he? He's probably working away getting ready for the crabs."

"They all are. Ye know what this time of the year is like. Too bad ye missed the blessing of the boats. We had a good crowd."

"Well, there will be plenty more."

"I hope so," Frances said wistfully.

"You're nervous about speaking, aren't you, Mama?"

"Why wouldn't I be? These folks are all fired up to get us off the water, and I'm older now than I was years ago. And not half as ornery."

Nellie smiled and put an arm around her mother. "Older has nothing to do with it. You still are a force to be reckoned with, and, as far as not being as ornery—well that's debatable."

"Maybe so, but still and all . . . ."

Frances pulled the golf cart up to the side of the house and said with a whoop, "You're home, Nellie girl!"

"I can't believe I'm home to stay. Sure feels good."

"Well, it'll only be your home until that Denny gets around to asking ye to marry him."

"Yeah, but that could take awhile, Mama. Now let me get my things in the house and then go directly over to his shanty. Won't he be surprised?"

"He'll jump right out of his skin, girl."

Denny was busy getting ready for crab season, now only a few days away. His boat had been blessed along with the others in a very special ceremony.

The Blessing of the Boats dated back as long as anyone could remember. Prayers were offered up, hymns sung, and a whole lot of good eating went down at the firehall in Tuckerton. Floyd Bradshaw and his wife, Bess, had cooked up most of the food, but others had brought James Island Cakes, along with a dozen other island specialties. Frances baked and took her sweet potato pie and cooked a whole bunch of Rockfish Imperial. Everyone loved that dish.

With all that good food and the Lord's blessing, it was now time to get down to the business of crabbing. If it was a good year, they would make money enough to pay their bills with cash. They didn't like to use credit cards. And, hopefully, there would be enough to get them through until winter and the oyster season began.

All the water communities around the Chesapeake moved to their own rhythm, one they all felt a kinship with. There were also watermen on the North Carolina coast doing the same things and making the same preparations for the crabs that would start stirring down there a little earlier than those in the Bay. The families down there had some of the same last names as the James Islanders and those who lived on the other island, the one in the Virginia waters. Many of the families had married other island families down through the generations, so they really were a true family and spoke with the same dialect, another strong bond between them.

With this being such a busy time, Frances was having second thoughts about leaving and going to Washington, but she had given her word she would. Nellie kept talking to her about going over and how important it was. Jimmy always went to bed when they started. He wasn't much for "woman talk," as he called it.

It was nearing the day Frances would be leaving, when, one early morning after her prayers, Jimmy came in the kitchen, sat down as always, but Frances didn't get up to get him coffee. She stayed seated. Something wasn't right, so he sat there until she began to talk. It was the way of the couple, and, after all their years together, they just knew what the other was thinking. Finally, Frances broke the silence.

"I don't want to go and leave ye here to do all the work, Jimmy. It's not right. I should have told them I couldn't come until after the season gets on a bit."

"You can't do that, Frances. City folks don't understand us folks, so they set the hearing at their convenience, not ours."

"But I've always been with you during crabbin' season."

"Nellie will be here. Don't you worry none."

"I have to do this right, Jimmy, or else they'll do us in for sure."

"The whole world isn't on your shoulders, Franny. They've been on us for years and now the handwriting is on the wall for us watermen. They don't care."

"You're right, but we can't let it go down without a fight."

"Well, Miss Willa got that congressman to come over. He talked to a whole bunch of us and we told him how things were. And he listened."

"Willa has been great and she's been a good friend to our Nellie. I like her a lot and I hope she comes back out here one day soon. I'll ask her when I'm over there."

"You're staying with her, aren't you?"

"She didn't give me a choice. Yes, I'm staying with her."

"Well, that seems fair and all, after she came and stayed with us."

"Yes, Jimmy, I know that must have been something for a gal like her."

Jimmy got up and poured his own coffee and a cup for his Franny.

"Why, thank you, Jimmy."

Smiling at her, his eyes danced with mischief as he said, "Don't you go getting spoiled or nothin'. I only do this once every forty years or so."

Frances smiled, but then turned serious again. "Why do those men over there in Washington think we are so dumb? We may talk different but we have the same feelings, same loves—"

"Whoa, girl. We don't exactly have the same of anything. They are politicians and all they think of is themselves. That makes them a whole different animal from us. We work by our hands and we don't ask for anything from anyone. They wouldn't last a minute doing that. We're different; that's all there is to it. That's why they think we're dumb. We don't take it from others."

"I suppose you're right, Jimmy, but there have to be a few others like Congressman Lee."

"Mebbe so, but not many. Besides, I heard that story about Robert E. Lee and his supposed relationship to these islands. Do you suppose Willa's congressman feels a family tie?"

"I can only hope so. I was thinking that may have been what got his attention. The high-and-mighty Lees being associated with this here place might have scared him, too. At the very least, it shows him how far back we go. Now, if we could only find one of the committee members I am going to speak to that went back to Cap'n John Smith, we might stand a chance."

Jimmy looked over at his wife and said quietly, "Feel better, Franny?"

"Yes, I do. If ye say it's okay with you to go, then I'll go with a clear head and full heart."

"You go get 'em, Franny girl. Just come back to me alive."

Crab season had come to the waters of the Chesapeake. The crabs had started swimming up the coast a few weeks earlier, and now they had come all the way up the Bay, all stopping at their own particular spots. The men left way before the sun was up to go out, put their pots down, and claim the same waters their families had crabbed for generations. They all knew the water like the backs of their hands. The season had begun.

And today Frances Evans was leaving for Washington. She and Jimmy had said their good-byes the night before, and now Nellie was left to get her mama down to the dock with her luggage for the long visit in D.C.

"Mama, now stop your fussing and let's get going. Cap'n Tuck will surely leave without ye."

Frances climbed in the golf cart and turned to her daughter. "He wouldn't dare leave without me; he knows I'll be to the dock on time. And was that a 'ye' I heard from your mouth?"

"Just comes back naturally."

"Sounds kind of nice. I'm so glad you're home, Nellie. How's Denny doin'?"

"He's been like all the men, busier than they know what to do. Denny thinks it's going to be a good lick this year."

"I hope so. We can use a good run with the crabs. The women are all ready to pick over to the Co-op. They'll make good money if there are a lot of crabs."

"What would everyone do without you, Mama? I mean, you have fought for so many things, but I think the Co-op must surely be your best."

"I gave it all I had and it didn't look too good for a while. But then it happened. The women need a place to pick crabs legally, and I remember when there were so many women picking you could hardly move in that place. But now so many women have gone off the island or got too old to do it, and so that's coming to an end, too, one of these days."

"But you're going to tell them our story and then tell them what's happening now. If anyone can get them to listen, you will."

Frances patted her daughter on the leg. "Thanks, sweetheart. Ye look after your daddy now."

Nellie carried her mother's bag to the boat and kissed her. "Behave now, Mama, and give 'em hell."

Cap'n Tuck was smiling at Frances as she came toward the boat. Everyone on the island knew where she was going and they were so very proud of her. The ones nervous about all the attention didn't matter. This had to be told.

Tuck helped Frances onto the boat. "Well, if it ain't Grandma Shady all dressed up and going to the big city."

"Oh, Tuck, hush now, and don't ye call me Grandma Shady 'cause I ain't no shady lady at all."

"Haven't seen ye wear makeup in years, Miss Frances. Can tell you're heading out to be one of the city people."

"Maybe you should just steer the derned boat and leave the talkin' to me."

As the boat pulled away from the dock, into the channel and toward the open water of the Bay, Frances looked out and saw some of the workboats dropping their pots, watermen doing what they'd done forever. She thought of Jimmy, out in another area of the Bay, and she knew he'd be thinking of her, too, as she went out on her mission.

Tears formed in her eyes as she got farther and farther away from the island. Even though she went over to the mainland all the time, this was different. She was heading into stormy waters— though she wouldn't be on water at all. Nevertheless, this storm would be harder to ride out than any other she'd been in. In this storm, she would be fighting for the survival of her people and a way of life.

CHAPTER 38

Frances had been up most of the night before, pacing the floor. She always got this way before speaking to a group, something she did quite frequently. She considered it a great privilege to talk to outsiders about the life she loved so much, and it was especially important to her to emphasize the role of the waterman's wife. It was very much a team effort, a fact not many people understood. When the men were gone up the Bay, which happened several times during the year, it was up to the women to take over and run the families and take care of problems back home.

But this speech would be before no ordinary group, simply interested in the way of life on the Bay. This was going to be in front of some very influential leaders in this country, as well as agency people who held great sway with those leaders.

She had packed two bags: one for her clothes and one for the recipes, stories, poems, and props she thought helpful in speaking. Not that any of them would care about the recipes, but she wanted them along anyway to give to Willa because she had asked for some of them.

The other things were good for demonstration purposes. She was always surprised at how few folks knew much about the early life on the Bay, and she wondered why there wasn't an exhibit in the American history museum in Washington about the Chesapeake and its part in early American history. Whether the men and women of a sophisticated Washington would think her presentation provincial and discount it out of pocket was irrelevant to her. She had done this every time she spoke about the subject and always found it received well by those who heard her.

As the ferry continued on its way, she and Tuck talked some, and then she talked to the kids going over for school on the mainland. It was never easy for the children, but, as the population dwindled, so did the number of kids who had to make the trek over and back every day. At the rate the island was going, with so many leaving to live in Somerville or other mainland communities, one day there would be no children taking the boat in the morning.

Tuck smiled, then said to Frances, "They're a good group. I fuss at 'em a mite, but I think we have the best kids anywhere."

"It's how we raise 'em, Tuck, and the freedom they have over there on the island. They have to make good decisions from early on, and they know every adult has their eyes on them. That helps keep them in line. We live in a different world from over there."

"And glad I am that we do."

They continued to chug along out on the Bay. The sun on the gorgeous spring day was up by now and shining brightly on all four islands that made up James Asland. A great gray heron waded in the shallows, looking for its morning quarry, as gulls circled over the boat, swooping down to touch their wing tips to the water. Frances loved the gulls. They were birds with attitude and reminded her of herself. They loved life and were well suited to the water world, and, no matter the difficulties, they always survived.

Thirty minutes later, they pulled into the dock at the Somerville marina. On time; another good trip over. Frances paid Tuck the fare, picked up her bags, and got into her sister's car to continue her journey.

"Morning, Rita. How ye comin'?"

"Just fine, Frances. How about you?"

"All right so far. Thanks for taking me to Salisbury. I appreciate it. I see ye were up early this morning getting your cakes baked."

"Yes, indeed. I have an order for fifteen of them up to a Salisbury shop. That will bring in some badly needed money. I'm expanding my market up there a little at a time, so things are looking up."

"I'm glad for ye, sister. It's tough these days. Why, look at the prices of everything. They go up every day now, and it's hard to make ends meet."

"I been thinking about selling the house and moving over to the island, but nobody is buying a house like mine anymore. It's too old and needs too much work, so it's better I stay put for now."

"Do ye need Jimmy to come on over and help ye fix some things?"

"I already asked him and he said he'd be over in a couple of weeks. He wanted to get crabbing underway first."

"I feel awful that I'm leavin' Jimmy now when he needs me, Rita. But he said it was okay and that what I was doing was important and that he had Nellie around to help him while I'm away."

"He's right. He'll do fine, Frances. He's a resourceful man."

Frances said, "Resourceful or not, he's a man and they always need help." Both women laughed.

Rita arrived at the Salisbury airport in time for her sister to catch her flight. Even that was hard these days. One had to fly up to Philadelphia to get another flight back down to D.C. Gone were the days of the Baltimore commuter, but Rita couldn't drive her all the way over, so Frances didn't have a choice. It was okay, though. It would give her time to adjust her thoughts for the hearing the next day.

"Thank you, Rita. Ye are a good sister. I'll call ye to let ye know about the return trip."

Rita hugged her sister. "Ye take care and don't go lettin' those big shots make you feel anything but good, because that's what ye are."

"I appreciate that, Rita. Have a safe trip home now, ye hear?"

With that, Frances disappeared into the small terminal as Rita watched. They were very close sisters and that was a real blessing. So many siblings didn't get along, and, while they didn't always agree, they never let the small things get in their way.

Willa was waiting inside the terminal at National. The plane was on time and that was a miracle itself. Seemed these short flights could get off schedule in a hurry, due mostly to the weather coming off the Bay or the Potomac River, bodies of water that played havoc especially at the change of seasons. Willa really missed Miss Frances, though she hadn't realized how much until she had spoken with her. She was thrilled she'd be having her as an apartment guest.

Frances had become her surrogate mother, even more so than her aunt. While they were from different worlds, she felt a strong bond with Miss Frances that she didn't have with her own aunt. Hard to explain, but it was there. She *almost* filled the void, though Willa knew no one would really ever do that. Even though it had been over ten years since her parents had left this earth, Willa still felt their presence within her. She wondered if it would be that way forever.

Frances came through the security gate, and, upon seeing Willa, smiled a smile as big as the whole outdoors. As they embraced, she said, "Hey there, girl, how ye comin'?"

"Perfectly fine now, seeing your face." The truth was, Willa adored this old woman, with her pleasant face and ample but fit body. Frances was the essence of friendship and love.

"An ugly one at that, huh? Well, let's get my luggage and get out of here."

"Absolutely. I'm taking you to lunch at a really neat place."

"Where? Now wouldn't ye think I knew all the restaurants in town to ask ye such a question."

"It's a deli I have recently discovered, and it has the best food. You'll love Yitzi's."

"I would love any place you took me, Willa." Then she squeezed Willa's arm and said, "I've missed ye, girl."

"I've missed you, too, Miss Frances."

Willa hailed a cab and they were off.

By now, Willa was on a first-name basis with the man at the door at Yitzi's Deli. He smiled and said, "You made it in good time, Willa. I have your booth waiting."

As they walked to the booth, Frances said, "Well, whooee, look at who's Grandma Shady now."

Knowing what that expression meant, Willa burst out laughing. "I doubt that. You're the one who fits that title because no one else has your style."

When Frances opened the menu, she said, "How is anyone supposed to make a decision with all these choices?"

"Just take your finger and point. They're all good."

Frances did just that when the server came, and picked a blueberry blintz, though she had no clue what it was. When Willa told her, she said, "Kinda like our crepes with a mess of blueberries on top. Sure sounds good."

"Yep, kinda right on, Frances. Now tell me how you're doing for tomorrow's hearing."

"Well, I'm not sure yet. I'll let you know when I'm done."

"Good attitude, but is there anything I can do to help you? Charles—or should I say, Congressman Lee—wanted to meet us but he's tied up getting ready for tomorrow, as you can imagine."

"I can imagine. I thought about this and nothing else for the past few weeks, and I decided to tell it the only way I can: straight out. At my age, I can't change and why would I want to? I know what's going on here, and it's only gotten worse over the years, so to tell of our troubles is the only thing I know."

The food arrived, and, when Frances saw the blueberry blintzes, her eyes got huge. "Now, do ye think I can eat all this?"

"Bet you can."

As they ate, they talked of the island and Willa felt that tug at her heart again. It was there no matter how much she said it wasn't. She said, "When I get my work to the point where I can leave, I want to go back over there."

"Now's the time. The crabs are coming into the Bay, so it's a good time to see what we do."

"And eat some more of Mr. Floyd's crab cakes."

"Oh, that man would have ye think they're the best. You've tasted mine and ye know they're better."

Willa laughed and said, "I'm not stepping into that controversy."

Lunch was over and all seemed well. Time to get Frances unpacked and settled in. She had promised that, although she was speaking only one day, she would stay another day or two so Willa could take her to see some of the sights.

While Frances had seen most of them through the years, she had promised, sensing that this young woman needed her to be with her, and, if walking around some monuments helped her, then that was what she would do. But then she had to get back to Jimmy and her island.

CHAPTER 39

Willa and Frances spent the rest of their day together going over things for the hearing the next day. By bedtime, Frances was ready to go. Charles had called to say he was looking forward to seeing Frances again the next morning and to thank her for making this important effort.

The sun wasn't up yet but Frances was. She got her coffee going and then sat down at Willa's antique wooden kitchen table to do what she did every morning: say her prayers. Willa heard her and padded quietly down the carpeted hall, stopping to listen to the sounds of a soft and devoted voice in prayer, sounds that took her back to another time when she had been a young girl.

Closing her eyes, she saw the small white church on the coast of Maine where her parents and their neighbors from the small town were doing the exact thing Frances was doing now. Nostalgia washed over her. She hugged herself softly, rocking, as if she and Frances were praying together. It had been a long time since Willa had prayed like this. Too long.

When Frances was done, Willa hesitated a moment, not to be too obvious about the fact she had been standing there, and then she joined her dear, dear friend.

"Good morning, Frances. I heard you talking to someone and didn't want to interrupt."

"That someone is my best friend and constant companion. I was speaking to God, dear."

Willa smiled and put on water for a cup of tea. "I see you found everything."

"Yes, I did. I hope you don't mind me knocking about in your kitchen."

"Not at all. I want you to feel like this is your home. Isn't that what you told me when I was in yours?"

"So I did." Frances smiled. "Shows I liked you from the start."

"Are you sure you're up to doing this, Frances?"

"As ready as I'll ever be. I know our people like the back of my hand, and being the wife of a waterman is like having a waterman here to tell his own story this morning. Same thing. We're interchangeable parts."

"That's a good way of putting it. While my tea is steeping, I'm going to take a shower."

"I took mine last night so I didn't have to take too much time this morning. I'll be ready to go when you are."

After Willa left, Frances got up from the table. She was a bit nervous, although you wouldn't have known it to look at her. She was always the picture of confidence, but, right now, she needed to look put together, so she went to her bathroom, looked in the mirror, and said, "Here goes." With that she pulled out a small makeup case she had brought from home. It was for special occasions and this was certainly that. She leaned in to the mirror with a grin on her face and whispered, "Here's to Grandma Shady."

When they were both ready, they nodded their approval at one another as Willa called down to get a cab. She was surprised to hear Harold's voice. He must have been pinch hitting for someone again to make some extra on the side.

Within minutes, they were downstairs, then in a taxi and on their way.

There seemed to be more hustle-bustle to this hearing than the one before. And certainly far more people attending. Prue was there and Willa and Frances waved to her as they took their seats in the back row. Today, Frances was deliberately set to appear last; Charles was going to take every advantage for this that he could. He knew how powerfully Frances could speak, and so last was where he wanted her.

Willa noticed how perfect Prue looked officiating at her duties and how in her element she was. Prue was born for this town, no doubt about that. And then she spotted Charles, also doing what he did so well: greeting people and shaking hands.

She also noticed a vaguely familiar man who she couldn't place outright. He was walking up to Charles with a stern look on his face. Who was he? She kept trying to remember. He was a much older man, very distinguished, and he obviously had something to say to Charles. Charles's look changed when he saw him approaching.

Then Willa remembered. She had seen him many times in *Washington Post* articles. He was none other than the powerful senator from Virginia, Rennie Richardson. But why that look in Charles's eyes? *Whoa, girl, you're getting so you can read his looks.*

"Well, good morning, Senator Richardson. Nice to have you at the hearing."

Both of them were putting on a show for the press with their smiles and political posturing.

The senator leaned in to Charles and quietly said, "You can cut that crap out, Charles. I'm here to watch this and get everything firsthand. I am counting on you, son, to do the right thing and throw in with our team on this matter." He then took Charles's hand as a flash went off.

"Morning, fellas." Rennie smiled to the press.

Charles stepped back after the photo op and answered, "I'm going to be fair and listen to everyone who is speaking today." Then, spotting Willa and Frances in the back of the room, he smiled at Rennie and said, "Excuse me, Rennie, I see our favorite speaker has arrived."

Rennie wasn't amused. He watched as Charles walked to the back row and began speaking to the one woman he knew could upset the entire applecart. He respected the old woman's spunk, but there was no way some country island woman was going to outwit him.

Frances saw the senator looking at her and smiled at him. She remembered how fiery he had been the last time they'd met, but, today, nothing was going to stand in her way. She was on a mission.

Charles gave Frances a warm hug and said, "So good to see you, Miss Frances." Then he looked at Willa and his smile deepened. "Good morning, Willa. Glad you're here."

Willa returned his smile and answered, "I wouldn't have missed it for the world." Both of them appeared to enjoy the gentle message that seemed to be moving between them.

When everyone had been seated, Charles called the hearing to order. After a few opening remarks, he called the first speaker.

One by one, the speakers talked about the conditions of the Bay, plans to continue cleaning the water, the aquifers and how they were working, and the project to renew the oyster beds.

Frances paid close attention to them all. Some she thought had good points, and, if given the chance, she knew the watermen could really help them improve on what they were doing. Some of the speakers just made her mad. They were so disapproving of the watermen that there could be no talking to them about sharing information. Mostly, they were bureaucrats or others who seemed to have another agenda all together—an agenda she knew too well. They wanted the Bay for themselves and their pleasure boating.

Then it was her turn up at bat. If anyone wanted to know what going to the gallows felt like, Frances would be able to tell them. The props she had brought seemed all wrong now. They weren't going to work, she realized as she gathered them together and then took her seat at the table in front. She sipped some water, cleared her throat, and looked at the notes she had brought with her.

She wasn't going to use them. She was going to speak from her heart, and no notes were needed for that. She took a deep breath and looked up at the congressman, whose look said he was worried she wasn't going to say anything. She smiled at him and began.

Good morning. I had the privilege of coming before this committee once before, many years ago. Although many of the members and the chairman have changed, it would seem the issues have not. So, I've been asked to return with an update on the many concerns that come from the watermen—the commercial fisherman of the waters of the Chesapeake Bay. I am sure 'tis the hope of all of us—some directly affected and other individuals and organizations and politicians also involved—to finally put a working plan in motion that will have a good effect on all of us, and one we will truly take to heart.

For the sake of time, I have put together a packet about issues affecting the water communities not just on the Bay, but all over America. We are a community of people with local issues, but we all share in the difficulties facing us and our industry today. As ye will note, I use bullet points to provide a clear picture.

I will, however, take a few minutes, to go deeper into some of the main problems, and then into solutions that will go a long way to making this work for us all.

With that, Frances asked that a short video be shown. It had been shot a year ago on James Island and at many of the marinas up and down the Bay, but also included photos of their neighbors to the south on the North Carolina coast, some from the Gulf Coast, and Pacific and New England fishermen. Together, it provided a large view of the entire industry but with a very specific focus on the crabbing and oystering of the Chesapeake.

The video ran only ten minutes, and there wasn't a sound heard during its presentation. It vividly showed the decline of fishing in and around the Bay over the past two decades, highlighted by interviews with some of the old men who had spent their lives on the water, and by their explanations of what they thought had happened to make it change. There were old pictures of the small sailboats—skipjacks—of years gone by, gathering in the oysters, and new ones showing how few were left today.

The video told the story, and, when it was over, not a word was spoken. Frances had definitely scored a home run with this prop.

Willa knew Prue had to have had a hand in this to get it set up. She wondered if Charles had known about it. She glanced at him quickly, and, from the look on his face, he was surprised, too, but pleased. This had been a stroke of sheer genius.

When the lights came back on, Frances continued.

That film pritty much says it all. We work from morning until night. The wives of the watermen are just as involved as their men. In the crabbing season, we work sometimes twenty-four hours checking the peelers for the soft crabs ye love so much.

We are losing our culture both on the water and, just as importantly, from the pages of American history. From the time people existed here— either native, explorers, or people who wanted to live a free life here on these shores—the fish of the Chesapeake waters have fed them. It is who we are and what we do and it's all passing now.

The water is a bit cleaner now than it was decades ago, but not near clean enough. Two sides blaming the other doesn't work to get this job done. It isn't this one's or that one's fault; it's a collective issue, if ye will, and blaming the other has just gotten us where we are today.

So now, how can we try to save what's here? It's not certain that the commercial fisherman can survive. The heavy fees and regulations placed on the watermen are making it near impossible to make a living. And, if that doesn't do it, this Clean Waters Act will. Our young ones know this and most don't want to go out and work for long hours, little money, no health care, and no benefits, to barely make ends meet. Not many would do this work, but it's in our blood and it's been in our blood for over four hundred years.

I have given ye a short list of suggestions going forward. A moratorium on the fees and regulations just has to happen if we are to make it at all. Ye who are lawmakers and organizations can do this. Ye can bring laws to the floor to help us get relief.

The second concern is the paper work that is asked for. When it's crabbing season, the men are just too busy to answer all kinds of questions on a paper. They have all they can do to keep up with the daily duties both out on the water and when they get back. That could be looked into.

We suggest that we be asked to be a part of the solution to the oyster bed decline on a regular basis. Our older men who don't go out on the water anymore could be a part of that team. I'm sure ye remember old Dickie Short. Well, before he died, he tried to help some and he tried to get a stop to all the development that was hurting the water in the Bay. Ye didn't much listen to him, and so then the blame got put on the farmers and watermen, but ye know that there's a whole lot more to this than that. Yes, some have really tried and succeeded to some extent in what they're doing, but so much more has to be done, if it can be corrected at all.

So I've said what I came here to say. Maybe I haven't said it in the most eloquent of ways, but it's from my heart. It's what we know and what we live. If ye let us show ye how we keep our beds clean down in the lower Bay without using fancy methods that spend millions of dollars with no sure answers to if it will work or not, we can make a difference. And, maybe, if we can make more money, our young people will want to do this.

One last thing I would like to add. Being a waterman is a calling like being a doctor or a preacher. Ye have to want it so bad, ye can't live without it. Not all people who grow up with it want to do it, but, when they see what's happening now, the seeds can't grow in them at all. Help us to put that spirit back in our heritage and let us hope that the culture and traditions of the Chesapeake watermen will be around for as long as there are crabs and oysters.

I thank ye all for this time and opportunity.

There wasn't a sound in the room, and then one man in the back stood up and began to clap. Frances looked up and a smile broke loose on her face. It was Tug Alston, who'd been just a cub reporter when he he had come to Somerville a few years back now. He had met that old waterman, Dickie Short, and, after Dickie's death, Tug had stayed on and threw his life into trying to make a difference. He married Dickie's grandniece, and, together, they had written about the life of being on the water. Pretty Lindy Alston also now painted it. Tug clapped and clapped, and soon the entire room was clapping for Miss Frances. Only one did not: Rennie Richardson. But the day had been a success.

The hearing was adjourned.

As Frances gathered her materials, Senator Richardson walked up to her. "I have to hand it to you, Island Woman. You had them eating out of your hands."

She smiled. "Maybe. Maybe not. But how can you dispute what I said here today?"

"I can't really, Frances, and I want you to know that you're a woman of courage and one who doesn't give up. I don't either, but maybe there's something to what you said. We'll see. One senator can't change the whole Environmental Protection Agency, but maybe we can start somewhere. I'm getting old and maybe it's time for me to think about retiring. I just wanted to tell you that you did well today. How about that, Miss Frances?"

"I don't believe my ears, Senator. But it's a start. We have to start somewhere, and, if ye truly mean it, it would go a long way to a new beginning."

"Well, there's a whole lot to this issue, and some of it isn't for conversation here. I have to tell you, though, in our older years we sometimes get romantic notions and that's good. Shows we can still dream, but the politics of today isn't so romantic. Matter of fact, it's quite the opposite. The winds that are blowing today don't want to remember what once was. They want to make their own present history according to their visions and dreams."

"Isn't very good though, is it, Senator? History is history, and, when you wipe it away, you change it forever."

"Truer words were never spoken, Miss Frances. All I can do is say I won't block anything you're trying to do and I'll talk to Charles. He's a good young man and he serves this committee well. He has spunk, and I respect spunk, but he'll have a rough time going forward."

"Well, he can handle it. Seems like we had spunk in our youth, too, but I'm beginning to feel a little tired and a lot older, too."

Rennie took her hand and said, "Good to see you, Frances." She returned his handshake genuinely, but, as he walked away, she just knew that old dog couldn't learn a new trick.

CHAPTER 40

Charles made sure he caught Willa before she and Frances left the building and asked them to join him for dinner. Willa smiled, as she thought what a nice thing it was for him to do. Both said it would be lovely. He'd had to dash but would let them know where later on.

Prue had left the hearing immediately. She needed to make a phone call before she saw Charles back at his office. When she was in a private setting, she dialed home. Her father answered. "Hi, Dad. I need to ask you a few questions."

"Is everything okay, Prudence? You sound sort of odd."

"Everything is fine, Dad. I just need to pick your brain a little. I need to know if you might have any information on Senator Rennielas Richardson."

"Whoa, girl, he's big stuff in D.C. circles. What's this all about?"

"Well, he's been making veiled threats to Charles concerning a committee Charles heads, and I wondered how deep he is in with the folks invested in the commercial fishing industry on the Chesapeake."

"Prue, what's going on? I thought you were just Lee's office assistant and all-around right hand, but now you're asking me things that go way beyond that. It's not smart to mess in where you don't belong."

"Dad, I've been thinking about a whole lot of things lately, which we'll discuss at another time. I know this is a delicate issue, but, if my instincts are right, Rennie Richardson is up to his ears in something. And you taught me it's always good to hold an ace in your hand. This is important and I need to know."

"You sure have learned your lessons well, my dear. Since I still have some friends there from my days as a lobbyist, I should be able to round up some information on Rennie. I do know he's pretty tight with a lot of them, and I do know they give heavily to his war chest. He's got a huge one, so I would suspect he's got plenty of things he would rather keep under the radar."

"Thanks, Dad. I appreciate it."

"While I've got you, honey, I spoke to some of the folks inside the party and they keep asking when another Harding is going to enter politics. Given that any thought lately?"

"As a matter of fact, I have. I think it may be time for me to get serious about Congress. What do you think about that?"

"You've always been my ambitious girl, Prue, and I knew this day would come. You keep thinking about it and I'll start to pave the way."

"Thanks again, Dad. Let me know what you find out. My gut tells me it's going to be a long list of stuff. No one stays in power in this town without a lot of dirty laundry."

"It's the game and how it's played. I'll get back to you. Are you sure you're ready for this game?"

"I will be soon enough."

That night, Charles took Willa, Prue, and Miss Frances out to dinner at a small bistro in Georgetown that he liked a lot and that gave him excellent service. After they sat down, Charles ordered a bottle of champagne. Frances raised an eye, so he added an iced tea for her.

"Well, ladies, I think it's been a great day. I think we have a better-than-average shot at moving some of your suggestions forward, Frances, and I want to thank you. Without you and your passion, I think we were dead in the water."

"Well now, don't go dying in any water on my account." Frances laughed. "But I do have something to tell you. Its a wonderful surprise."

As the champagne was being poured, Charles leaned across the table toward Frances and said, "Holding back on us, are you? Please go ahead and surprise us all you want."

"When the hearing was over and everyone was breaking up, I had a visitor come to speak with me. It about shocked me to death. It was that old, crusty blowhard, Rennie Richardson. Now he and I go back to the last hearing years ago when he was still a congressman and the head of a committee then that talked about the condition of the Bay water and the impact of commercial fishing on the Bay. Anyway, he said he really appreciated what I said. I tell you, I just stood there like a rock waiting for him to pick me up and throw me through the wall."

Charles was clearly surprised, too, and wondering what the sly old fox was really up to. "You mean he was buttering you up before he ate you?"

"Maybe, but maybe not. We were pritty good enemies way back then, but he seemed to be sort of mellowed now. He could have been lying to me, but he said he thought some of the ideas I brought forward might work. He did remind me that some have been tried and failed, but there's always a new group of people at the table."

"He was probably referring to me. He's let me know recently that he's pretty steamed at me, so I still don't trust him, Miss Frances."

Willa chimed in, "He looked to me to be putting you on, Frances. I know you want to believe the best in people, but that man is trouble."

"You may be right but we have to begin to trust one another if we're ever going to get anywhere. Our situation is desperate, so we'll take what we can get."

Prue had kept quiet long enough. "I have a few things to add to this discussion, but first I think we should make a toast."

Charles agreed and said, "Of course we should. I'm sorry, ladies." He poured the bubbly and held up his glass. "To good friends and victories." They all drank, then Charles said, "Now, Prue, what's on your mind?"

"I'm not surprised Rennie went over to Frances. As a matter of fact, I was waiting for him to do that."

"How's that?" Willa asked.

"Last time Rennie was in our office, he was in a foul mood, and, as I recall, he was actually intimidating you."

"He tried," Charles responded.

"That made me very mad. Here you are, trying to help the Bay and clean up the water and find a decent way for both sides to come together to work on serious issues, and this man, this senator, was hustling you like a two-bit hood. I was furious. When I saw him talking to Frances, I knew he was never going to stop; he can't help himself. So I made a call and found out some things about Senator Richardson."

Willa sat there stone silent. She couldn't wait to hear the rest of this.

Charles said, "Who did you call?"

"I called my father."

"Sweet Jesus, I can't believe you brought in the big guns for this. I can handle this myself, you know."

"Charles, I know you can, But Rennie Richardson isn't a nice man and you're trying so hard to get something good done for people who deserve it."

"Well, now that you've done it, let us know what you found out."

Willa sat there thinking how upset Prue had been at her for writing a book about the island and the challenges, and then here she'd gone out to bring down Armageddon.

"Well, it turns out, to no one's surprise, that Richardson has quite a money trail."

Frances was totally confused now and said, "How would your father know about any of this?"

"Oh, sorry, Miss Frances. My father was a high-powered lobbyist in D.C."

Charles said, "Go on, Prue."

"Well, it turns out that Richardson has been taking money from a lot of organizations, but the one that's really pumping it in is none other than the Baywaters Commission."

"Why that son of a—"

"Charles, don't," Willa begged.

"It's all right, Willa," Frances broke in. "I've heard it all before."

Charles said, "And I can only guess why they're so helpful to his cause. My guess is someone on their board has a great deal to gain if they can get the government to take charge of something they can profit from on the Bay."

Prue shot him a thumbs-up and said, "Bingo, Charles, and that person would be their board chair."

"And what projects is he interested in?"

"The plants being built for restoring the oyster beds. He owns a huge construction company."

"Well, isn't that cozy?" Charles growled. "This town make me sick sometimes. It could do so much good but it always turns out to be about the money."

Frances sat there for a moment, then piped up. "Makes you appreciate living on an island."

Chalres smiled at Prue and said, "Well, he isn't going to win this time. I'll see to that and make sure Senator Richardson never says another word about what goes on in the Bay again. As a matter of fact, I think the good senator is about to retire."

"Good move, Charles," Prue added.

"You're something, Congressman Lee," Willa remarked. "I'll have to keep an eye on you."

"Thank you, Prue. I know I may have been a little angry with you at first, but I do appreciate your loyalty to me and I will handle this from here, okay?"

"It's perfectly okay."

As they all continued their dinner, Prue watched her boss. She was happy she had done what she did. She had truly been a help to him. She would miss him. And soon she would tell him why.

It had been a long day to be sure, and, after the gooey dessert was finished and the check paid, Charles said good-night. He so wanted to kiss Willa, but this was neither the time or place. There would be other nights.

Prue said good-night also, but as Willa and Frances hailed a cab, they didn't seem to be ready for the day to end.

"How about a cup of tea when we get back?"

"That would be great, Willa. I do love a cup of tea before bedtime."

It didn't take long to get the tea started, and, while it was steeping, the two of them got into comfortable clothes.

"Now this feels better, doesn't it, Willa? I can't stand to stay dressed up for too long, and danged if I didn't want to get all that makeup off. I don't know how you women do it."

Willa laughed. "I guess when you grow up with it, you would feel naked without it."

Sipping her tea, Frances was getting up the courage to tell Willa something.

"What is it, Frances? I can tell you want to say something to me, so just do it."

"Okay, Willa, but please don't be mad with me. I have to go home. You've been so kind to let me stay with you, but my job here is done and I have another one yet to do back on the island. It's crabbin' time and Jimmy needs me back there."

"Nellie's there, and surely they wouldn't mind you staying another day. I want to take you around."

"Honey, I've seen all the monuments here and been to the museums. I don't need to shop—I have all I need—and, right now, what I need to do is go home."

Willa knew there was no stopping her. "Well, then it's settled, but we'll have to change your flight."

"I already did that. I didn't want you to have to go to any trouble on my account. You've been so wonderful to me already."

"No more than you've been to me. You're really something, you know that, Miss Frances Evans?"

"Go on now, Willa. I'm honored you would even know someone like me."

Her comment really threw Willa, and her brows furrowed at the thought of this great and courageous woman telling her that *she* was honored.

"I think you've got that turned around. Frances, you are one of the most outstanding women I've ever known."

"I don't know about that, but I'm real happy things turned out the way they did. Now I can go back home and tell the men that, if they give some, these folks over here will, too. Maybe we can take two of the most stubborn groups in the world and get them to calm down a bit so as everyone makes out."

"If that's your goal, you'll do it. I've learned one thing and that's not ever to get in your way when you're on a mission. Now, what time does that plane take off?"

"I've already ordered a cab. I don't want to take up any more of your time. You have things to do, Willa, and the only question I have for you is when are ye coming back to the island?"

"Can't stand not to have me underfoot, eh? Well, I'll tell you what. When I get my thoughts together and the book underway, I'll let you know I'm 'going over.' Tuckerton will be as good a place on this earth as I can think of to write, and to see everyone. When's a good time with you folks? I know that this time of the year gets a little crazy."

"Well, if ye can wait until the fall, things calm down some, and yet ye can still see what's going on."

"Whatever you say, Mama Evans."

That took Frances by surprise as few things did. She had already sized Willa up and knew the girl had something digging at her down deep, and now, her saying this was a real gesture of how much she needed to be connected to an older woman who cared about her. She knew Willa had lost her parents and always figured that one day Willa herself would tell her when she was ready. Today was that day. In her own way, with one word, she had said it all.

Frances smiled lovingly at the beautiful woman standing in front of her. "Mama. That's nice."

Willa was shocked herself. She never said things like that but, this time, it slipped out. And it was the right time. Was it another message from her mother? She liked to think it was.

Willa turned quickly, walked down the hallway to her bedroom, and closed her door. She leaned against it as the tears dripped down her face. She hadn't quite bargained for her emotions to spill out the way they did. She was always in control and only summoned them up when she wanted them, not in this unexpected way.

What was happening to her? First, her mind had gone on a vacation, and, then, in the blink of an eye, she'd been hurled into another world where people live as they did years ago—where trust, honor, and love were the ways they still lived their lives. Miss Frances was the epitome of all things decent, and yet she was willing, for the sake of her entire way of life, to come to a place that holds no honor for the just of this world.

And then there was Charles Lee, who had come onstage to confuse her and make her feel emotions she had tried to forget. Emotions that scared her to death. She felt as if she were running, but where to?

Then the quiet voice that had come to her since she'd been left alone at eighteen, whispered in her heart. "Be patient, my angel. Time will tell you all."

CHAPTER 41

Willa simply insisted on taking Frances to the airport herself. There would be no cab and no argument. After a tearful good-bye at the airport, that mission was accomplished. Now, Willa had another chore to do on this beautiful spring day, and one that might not go as well. She couldn't put it off any longer, so she pulled into a small park and got on with it. The saying "go big or go home" rang in her ears.

Nervously biting her cheek, she waited to hear the voice on the other end of the call. When she heard, "Hello, dahling," her moment had arrived.

"Hi, Kit. We need to talk. Do you have time now?"

"Always for you, dahling."

Damn! Kit pulled out the "dahlings" like they were Tootsie Rolls.

"Here's the book idea, and this one isn't going to be what you had hoped for. It's not a sappy romance. I'm breaking loose for a change. It's going to be a contemporary fictional story about politics and what the hell is going on these days. What do you think?"

"I think you've lost your mind, Willa. Your readers won't like it. I don't like it."

"Well, to the point, Kit, I do and I'm going to write it. I could always throw a love interest in it, but that's not the message."

Willa could hear Kit tapping her long, perfectly manicured fingernails on her desk and knew she was in for the fight of her life.

"I know you've always liked to weave a message into your subplot, but it's been one that wasn't too strong and usually played to the love theme.

But what you're suggesting isn't you. I just don't see anything going for it, Willa. You're a talented romance writer, as your mother was, and now you would write a book totally out of your genre? How can you?"

"When a story comes along that you think has merit and has the dynamics, you have to write it. Surely my readers would love to see that the author grows, too. I have written eight best sellers that were formula writing and it's time for a different approach."

"Most times that doesn't work."

"Hogwash. You know damned well top writers switch it up now and again. What are you so afraid of anyway? The book will sell if we market it the right way. You know that. You can sell books thirteen ways to China, Kit, and, if you do it right, people buy 'em. We both know this. PR and buzz sell books."

"Maybe. What is this story that has you so spun out of control?"

Here was the moment of truth, Willa thought. Searching for the right word, the only one she could think of was, "Fish."

Kit tapped on her phone, making a horrible sound in Willa's ear. "I think my phone isn't working right. I thought I heard you say 'fish'?"

Willa was now indeed in a basket of bees.

"What's going on, Willa? You said fish, didn't you? I don't think there would be any way to sell that book."

"You might be surprised, Kit. Everyone eats fish, and, if the fish they love are dwindling in numbers because the men who go out and get them can't afford to do that anymore and are disappearing, people will read this book."

"Dear God, you aren't suggesting that you would write a nonfiction?"

"Not at all. It would be a fiction . . . just with a message."

"I don't know what you're doing," Kit said in an annoyed voice. "But write fifty pages, let me see them, and I'll tell you if we can work with it or not."

The words were out of Willa's mouth before she could bring them back. "Actually, Kit, I'm going to write this story with or without you. We've always worked well together, but, lately, I think it may be time for you and I to part ways and for you to concentrate on Susan Crandall's writing. You know, ride that wave until someone else comes along to knock her off her perch. I'm changing in ways I never thought I could, and maybe you

229

as my publisher might have to change, too. My days of telling stories of betrayal, lust, and happy endings are boring me to tears. I need to write a different book."

"You're going to look for another publisher, after all I've done for you and with you?"

"Maybe I am, Kit. Maybe it's time."

Willa could tell Kit was in shock. *She* had always been the one to say when things were over. No writer in her right mind would ever walk away from the deals, and the care, that Kit had given Willa. Clearly, she was none too happy with this.

"I might remind you, Willa, you're under contract with us for one more book and that one has to be a romance, not some wild-eyed story about fish."

"I will honor that, Kit, but in time. I know I have a contract, but the time limit is two years and I'm only in year one right now, so I have time."

Kit didn't want Willa to walk. Not only was she a best-selling author who brought a lot of money into the firm, but she really loved this young woman. She had been with her from the start, and, although it had begun as taking care of Jennifer Carpenter's daughter, Willa was brilliant and turned out to be as good or better than her mother. She had to try to keep her.

"There may be a way to work through this, Willa. You go ahead and start your outline on this new project that seems to possess you right now, and I'll do some thinking. Maybe you could find a way to weave a love story through this fish tale and then we would all go home happy. I can sell that."

"Yes, you could, and I will think this through, too, Kit. No guarantees, but we've been together a long time and you've stood with me through some pretty rough patches. I haven't forgotten that."

"You're a really special and gifted talent, Willa Carpenter. Your mother and father would be beyond proud of how you're turning out. You're young and you have so much ahead of you. Maybe even your own real-life romance if you wouldn't work all the time."

Willa knew Kit was right. Her life had been all about writing. She had buried herself in it, mostly so there weren't any lonely times when she could think too much, miss too much. But now something was stirring inside her. Maybe it was maturity, but she had always had that, as the child of two parents who had taught her independence. Maybe they'd had a feeling that perfection here on earth couldn't last forever and they needed to prepare their only child. Whatever it was, she had stepped away now and was taking the first move toward a different life, whatever that might be.

"You know, Kit, you might have something there. Maybe, after this book, I'll rest for a while."

Kit's sigh sounded like relief. "Think and write, dear, and maybe this story will lead you to places you haven't been before."

As Willa hung up, she had the greatest desire to be back on the island. She wanted to be surrounded by the very thing that once had scared her so very much: water. The same water that nurtured a culture and gave those special people life. She wanted to walk the small paths, listen to the peacocks call to one another, and spend time communing with all the spirits of days gone by.

But, most of all, she wanted to face her demons and be at peace.

Charles had his own agenda. He was going to get to the bottom of the issues surrounding the Chesapeake Bay and one of them concerned Rennie Richardson. Then he was going to put a real plan into action. He wanted to prove to both sides that this could be done. Then he wanted to ask Willa out on a real date. He had to know if she had any of the real feelings toward him that he had about her.

After Willa had spoken with Kit, there had been no time to waste. She began laying out an outline for the book she would begin to write very soon, telling the story of a people becoming a vanishing culture. A people so dedicated to their life that they would do anything to hang on to it. The prognosis was doubtful and time was running out for them, but, if they could only hold on a little longer, maybe life would stand still for a moment more and they could go on.

When the phone rang, Willa was deep in thought. When she answered, she found herself surprisingly confused. It was Charles and she didn't quite feel as thrilled about that as she would have before. Was she too involved in the new project? Was she trying not to get hurt by a man who seemed to have a different woman on his arm each week? Or was this just bad timing? What was going on with her?

"Willa? It's Charles. Are you okay? You sound a little . . . distant."

"Hi, Charles. No, I'm not distant; you caught me in the middle of something."

Charles could feel the ice over the phone. Could he have been so mistaken about her?

"Bad time to talk?"

"Kind of, but you called, so you must have something on your mind. What's up?"

To heck with it. He had called, so why not go forward? "Well, I was thinking about you and wanted to tell you how good it was for all of us to be together the other night. Actually, it was a good day all around. I am hopeful we will make it work this time. I don't know where Rennie Richardson is coming from, and, given Prue's revelations, I think I'll hear from him again soon. He's not done with us, I'm afraid."

"You're probably right, Charles. He's a powerful man and powerful men don't give up easy . . . if at all."

"Willa, I know you're busy now, but we all have to take a break at some point. I was wondering if you would like to join me for dinner?"

"If you're asking about dinner tonight, I can't. I've just started this project and I want to keep on it and get the outline done so I can start writing the entire story."

"Oh, okay. I truly understand. Your readers are probably getting anxious to read another one of your books."

Willa laughed lightly and then asked, "I take it you're not one of them, and your reading trends to the more male-oriented stories?"

He heard the lighter tone and responded, "You could say that. Things like issue-papers on water, issue-papers on how to clean the water, and then there's that really wild best seller: *How to Avoid Murder in a Washington Hearing.*"

"That's good, Charles. I can't wait to read that one. I tell you what.

When I get this outline done, I'll call you. I want to go out to the island. Maybe you'd like to come? Frances and Nellie would love it."

Charles knew all couldn't be totally lost if she was asking him to join her out there. "We'll talk when you're ready, Willa. Good luck with the project. You'll have to tell me about it when we see each other."

"I will and thanks for calling, Charles. I'll be in touch soon."

CHAPTER 42

Everyone has doubts. No matter how sure we are when we make a decision, there will come a time when that small voice inside us will question if we are really sure.

Nellie got her father his coffee and packed his food, then watched him walk out the back door and head over to the marina for his day out on the water. She had other plans for this early morning. She wanted to walk over to a favorite, quiet place she had gone to all her life. An old shanty no one had used for years, it was still in pretty good shape, even considering the wear of time. She had put a few folding chairs in it for such occasions. It was where she escaped to think about things.

The sun wouldn't be up for a while yet and that's just what she wanted. Sunrises on the island were as beautiful as the sunsets. And they meant there was another day to explore, work, be with the people you had known all your life. But, this morning, she wanted to sit quietly and restore her faith that she truly had made the right decision.

The door creaked a little from age and use, as she opened it. So did the floorboards, not quite as steady as they once had been, but steady enough. She looked around. It was so quiet in here.

The only sound you heard was the small workboats' engines puffing away, taking their crews out on the open waters to begin the routine of checking and bringing up the crab pots. That sound was something every single person out on the water knew by heart—with you from birth, the same ebb and flow each day. The boats chugged out to do their work and then chugged back in.

Everyone knew whose boat belonged to whom. And the names on the boats told their own story. Some were of wives or daughters, or sometimes something else close and precious to the watermen, like *Water Lady* or *See Ya Later.* They were a waterman's identity. It was said in a rather straightforward way that a waterman might take a wife, but his boat was his mistress. It's his boat that takes him out every day, no matter what, and they relied on those boats to bring them back home.

Nellie went out the back of the old shanty and sat down on its dock. Her legs dangled over the edge above the water as the sky began to break at first light. She was far from the rest of the world now, as far as anyone could get. She always believed time stopped out here and innocence began. It was an innocence the outside world could never understand. In cities, people lost their identity, but, here, you kept it forever. The boys grew up to be strong and decent and the girls were known for their charity and goodness. It was a different world, a world that used to exist everywhere. But now? So much had been forgotten.

Nellie was fortunate to have left to receive her education, but even those years now seemed a million miles away. She was content knowing she had a good-paying job out here and could continue to achieve for her people, but she wondered if she could really keep up the life of an island woman and maintain excellence in her job. She would have to, and that's all there was to it. She thought of the surprise and love in Denny's eyes when he had seen her, and how she had felt the same. Her place was next to him. They had loved one another since they were children jumping off the dock into the Bay. Now he was the man who would stand beside her forever and spend his life taking care of her, no matter what.

Her mother would be home soon and tell her of the adventure she'd had in Washington, although she knew her mother and was sure that whatever she set her mind to would turn out right. Nellie was sure every woman on the island had had doubts at one time or another, but they went on and did what women had done out here for hundreds of years: they survived.

But they didn't just survive—they thrived. And so would she.

As the sun peeked over the horizon and the first rays spread forth their magical light, Nellie sat on the old dock. Alone, thoughtful, she told herself she would never doubt her coming home again. She wouldn't doubt if she could handle it all and she would never doubt she loved her Denny more than anyone in this world.

Nellie was thinking; Denny was working. He and his partner, Lem Carter, had gone out especially early this morning. Not yet four o'clock when they'd pulled out, they had a long day ahead.

They had worked together for a couple of years now. Lem was a tall, sturdy fellow who wasn't a native islander but had always wanted to be. He came over from Somerville after high school to team up with a Tuckerton guy and live on this part of James Island. When someone had told him Denny was looking for help, he'd moved quickly and it had really worked out. They crabbed until late fall, and then Lem would return home and work at a nearby factory so he could get his health insurance.

Health care coverage was a huge concern for the watermen. There were no benefits for these men, and that fact alone took some families away from the island so the wives could work to get insurance while the men fished out of the mainland marina. It was a burden not to have health coverage so that, if something happened, they had to pay cash.

"Looks like we're goin' to have a good year, Denny."

"Can't always tell. Might change, but so far it's hopeful. Lots of crabs swimming around."

Lem had heard the gossip and couldn't hold back any longer. "Hear you're goin' to marry that pritty girl, are ye?"

"Yes, I am. I've waited long enough and thought she'd never come back from out there, but she did."

"Feel sorry for her marryin' the likes of you. When's the weddin'?"

"When she says it is and she hasn't said."

"Just so she gives ye time to get your suit and fancy shoes."

"Keep on pullin' those pots, Lem. We've put out a mess this year. If they come in good all season, it will be good money for us."

Lem laughed and said, "Then ye can pay for that fancy weddin', Denny."

Denny never looked up as he answered, "Keep pullin'."

As he watched the pots break out of the water, he wondered what Nellie was doing. He knew she wasn't quite settled about all this yet. He knew she loved him and that was the most important thing. Everything else would fall into place. She was always like that. In school, she was smarter than most because she had thought it all through. But Denny was smart in his own way. He knew charts, maps, the ways of the water.

That's what made him so good on the water. His father had known he would make a good waterman because he just had the feelings it took. Not all the men could go out on the water. To be a good waterman, you had to have it inside you, almost a spiritual thing. To live your life in freezing cold or sweltering heat, hauling up heavy pots and bringing up nets with oysters, wasn't a life for everyone. But Denny loved it. He lived it every minute of the day. That's what watermen did.

Whether Nellie and he could make a go of it would be up to how much they both wanted to. From the looks of it to him, she wanted it as much as he did. He knew she would come around to it.

The sun was way up in the sky when Nellie left the old shanty. She was settled in her mind and heart now. All was right and well in her world. She had worked it out and this was where she belonged.

CHAPTER 43

Rennie called to tell Prue he was on his way to see Charles. Prue knew this meeting was going to be entirely different from the last one they'd had.

When Charles came in, Prue told him immediately of the impending visit from his old pal, Senator Richardson. She could see in Charles's face that he was ready for this encounter.

Prue didn't want to say too much, but did want him to tell him something.

"Charles, whatever you say to Senator Richardson, know that he has this coming to him, and, that if he demands to know where this information came from, it would be nice to keep my father out of it. But, if he goes further, tell him."

"Thank you for saying that, Prue, but this is between the two of us. He has pushed me around like I was some new kid on the block, and he's taken advantage of his friendship with my father, too. But I called my father early this morning to discuss it this with him, and he was appalled. But not surprised really. This town gets to everyone if they need something badly enough. I hope that never happens to me."

"Then don't stay too long, Charles."

The door opened and Senator Richardson walked in.

"Good morning, Senator. Can I bring you some coffee?"

"No thanks, my dear, I've had my daily quota. Are you ready, Charles?"

Walking back into his office, Charles remained quiet. He was so disgusted with the man that he didn't even bother to say hello.

Before closing Charles's door behind him, Rennie, the ever-smiling southern gentleman turned and said, "Thank you so much for your help, Miss Prudence."

She smiled as she watched the sly fox walk into the chicken house and close the door. This time the fox was in for a big surprise.

"Have a seat, Rennie."

Rennie made himself comfortable in one of the plush club chairs in a corner and then crossed his legs, appearing warm and engaging. He liked to set the table in his own manner before serving someone up for the meal.

Charles sat directly across from him and waited for him to begin.

Rennie looked at him warily and then broke the ice. "I feel a chill from you this morning, son. What's on your mind? I came over here to set some of the record straight but it appears you have something on your mind, too."

Charles continued to stare at him with a detached look and then began to speak. "You're most perceptive, Senator. You have gravely disappointed me, and I had such hopes that you might see that people are beginning to see the positives in working together. I see now you will never allow that to happen."

"Oh, you do, do you, Charles? Didn't that island woman tell you I was ready to try?"

"You can quit the charade, Senator. I know what you think of her and all the people on the Bay. You think they're beneath you, uneducated, they don't count in this world, and that high-and-mighty politicians and lifetime bureaucrats are the only ones who can solve their problems. Oh, those poor, pitiful folk and how they want to trust you. But you aren't worthy of them."

"Now hold on a minute, son. Just what are you insinuating here?"

"I'm not insinuating anything; I'm telling you what I know. You have no intention of helping them, but you put on quite a little show for Miss Frances."

"Why, of course I want to help them, but they will have to comply with things the way they are. They can't make up their own rules while disregarding others. What you don't know, Charles, is that they don't play straight either. They do things that aren't right out there and they think they can get away with it."

"Do they take money for it, Senator?"

The senator pulled himself up to the edge of his chair and leaned toward Charles. "Why don't you just spit it all out, son, and then we can fight this critter head on."

"How much personal money over the years have you taken from Baywaters and other agencies? You're so into Baywaters that it stinks, and you'll sell the watermen out to give the work to the company run by the chairman of its board." Charles stopped himself from saying anything else. He was too mad.

Senator Richardson sat back and rubbed his chin with one hand. Then he said, "You can't prove that, son. I don't know where you got that information, but you can't prove it."

"I wouldn't count on that, Senator. I'm not one to pull things from midair. And I'm not your son."

Rennie clearly didn't like this new attitude. "So, where do we go from here, Congressman?" All informalities were now at an end.

"We go forward. I want a committee made up of all the parties concerned. No more waiting and putting it off so you can build more facilities for the oyster beds. We're not even sure they work. I want to have this group of people figure out how to move forward together, and I want the fees to stop rising and the damned EPA regulations to cease until we can clear the air and see what really hurts and what helps. Right now these folks are in a stranglehold with no way out, and that isn't the way America does business. Or, should I say, the way it should do business."

Rennie was incensed. "Who do you think you are? Moses, for God's sake? We can't stop the EPA."

"We can't? If we can't, and the Congress can't, then the President has to. This can't stand anymore. Some of these rules are so complicated that no one can understand them and others are just plain insane. "

"I've made promises, Charles. I can't go against them."

"Yes, you can, and you will unless you want a full-blown investigation of your financial dealings to come down on your head."

"Watch it, Charles. You're talking blackmail. Your daddy—"

"My daddy nothing. He's sick to his stomach knowing what he does about you and your activities."

"He knows all this? You told him? And just where did you get all your high-and-mighty information anyway?"

"Let's just say I got it. Now, do you go with me or not?"

The senator sat and fumed, barely able to keep civil. "I'll tell you what. You stop this madness and I'll make a deal with you."

"I'm listening."

"I'll help you form the committee, I'll call off my dogs—but that damned woman isn't on it."

"We stop talking right now then. Frances Evans is invaluable to this work. Period."

"I see. You want it all then and I really don't have a choice."

"No, you don't, Senator. You come my way or you don't come at all. I'm fighting for justice here, but, if we fail in our mission, we lose a whole industry on the Bay, which hits our economy. And we lose a people who can't ever be replaced."

"Nothing last forever, Charles. Their way of life is coming to an end anyway. Their kids don't want it like they did and times are changing. Can't you see that?"

"That has to be their choice, not their government's. I'm not going to be the one to run them out."

"There's no talking to you, is there, Charles? I see your mind is made up, so why are we even talking? Do you think you can last in this town by doing what you're about to do? You can't go up against everyone, including the EPA, and survive in this town."

"No one should be in this town forever, Senator. We should come and do our job and leave. You've been here too long and are a perfect example of what happens from too many years spent here. You didn't used to feel like this, but look at what happened to you."

"You really aren't going to see anything my way, are you, Charles? So I think we're done with this conversation."

"No, we're not, Senator. You're going to help me or else I will go against you with all I can."

"You're a puppy compared to me. Do you really think I won't be protected? People owe me a lot of favors. That's how we do things here."

"That's really sick, you know. How can you live with yourself?"

"Very easily. As I see it, I'm helping the economy by encouraging

241

projects that last for a long time and employ a whole lot of people. It's progress."

"And how about those you are hurting?"

"I've told you, they hurt themselves."

"Is there no honor in you, Rennie?"

"Not much, according to you, but, if you can promise me you'll let this go, I will walk away. I want to retire next year. Let me at least retire with honor and go back to our beloved Virginia and be adored as their senior statesman at home after a good run."

"You really make me sick. You are the embodiment of everything that's wrong with our government today, but I will promise you this, in deference to my father's long friendship with you. You will announce you're not running again and plan to retire by year's end and that will give the party a chance to prepare for an interim appointment. Do this, and I will consider that your commitment to this project. You will not mess with this anymore, and no more promises about anything, do you understand me?"

"You'll shake on this as a Virginia gentleman?"

Charles extended his hand and shook on it. He was angry that it had to happen like this, but he had to have this chance to try to make things change.

"Thank you, Charles. It appears your daddy raised a damned tough little boy."

"I'll accept that as a compliment. Good-bye, Rennie, and I'll be waiting to hear your announcement."

After he had left, Prue quietly walked into Charles's office. She saw a man totally drained.

"I see you're still alive."

"I hate this town, Prue. I hate what happens to good people over the years. We have to have term limits if we are at all to preserve this country. I remember hearing about that man and all the dreams he had when he came here, and now look. It's horrifying and I hated to have to do that to him, but I hate what he's become to others."

"He deserved that, Charles, and you did him a favor to give him the choice of leaving with honor or disgrace. That's no small favor."

"If this all works out, I will owe your father a great deal on behalf of the fishermen here and everywhere."

"You don't owe him anything. That's how it starts, Charles, with people thinking they owe someone something. He did that as a favor to me, so you're off the hook."

"You're something. You know, you belong in politics with that cool exterior."

"Well, as a matter of fact, I guess this is as good a time to tell you as any."

"Tell me what, Prue?"

"I'm going to leave you soon. I'm going home to run for Congress from Ohio. It's our family business and Father says I'm ready and I think I am, too. I've learned so much here with you, but this has been my dream and now is the time."

Charles stood, and looked at her in shock. "You can't go, Prue. I need you to help me get through this. You understand this passion and that that's what's driving us."

"It's not passion for you, Charles, it's respect. You respect others' rights and their freedom to pursue them. That's what you're fighting for. The outcome isn't certain, but you'll take a chance to do it."

Charles looked at his assistant from a new perspective. Absolute wisdom had come out of her mouth and she had made more sense than hundreds of others he had heard speak for hours.

"I'm proud of you, Prue. With that attitude, you'll make it."

"That's the hope. And then I'll be right back here with you and Willa."

"I assume she knows. When will you leave?"

Prue smiled tenderly. "She knows this is what I've always planned and she understands it's what I have to do, just like she has to write. To answer your question, I'm giving my two weeks' notice, but it's my hope to be back here after next November's election."

"All I can tell you is that I wouldn't want to be the one running against you. You're fierce. By the way, I really like your girlfriend, but maybe you shouldn't tell her that. She seems to be confused about her personal life right now, and I don't know if I'm even a consideration."

"You are, Charles, but she may not even know that right now. She has demons to face, like all of us, and, when she slays them, she'll know how she feels about you. My odds are with you, and, if I'm right, you'll make a splendid couple. But only time will tell."

"Well, until that revelation happens, I have a lot to do. As long as you're still working for me, could you please make arrangements for me to fly over to Somerville? And I also want you to charter a boat over to the island. I want to tell Frances we are on our way, and, that while there will be a whole lot of bumps in the road, we have a chance now."

CHAPTER 44

Frances was happy to be back home. Relieved actually. She had called Nellie from Somerville before she got on the boat back to tell her to drive the cart over to the dock.

Nellie wasn't all that surprised to get the call. She'd known that, when her mother was done speaking, she'd want to come back home. Frances was a lady of action and not one for leisure. And she wouldn't want to be away from Jimmy for that long; they were two peas in a pod. She knew he would be looking for her. Even though he was in good hands, they weren't his Franny's.

There was so much to tell, and, from the minute Nellie met her at the dock, Frances couldn't be contained. All the way through the fried chicken, green beans, and mashed potatoes Nellie had fixed, Frances kept going. Jimmy ate while Nellie hung on her every word.

Finally Frances came up for a breath, and Jimmy put down his fork.

"So what do ye think, Franny? Do ye think they'll really do something this time? Or will it just go the way it has in the past?"

"Hard to tell, Jimmy. Ye can't ever know what these scoundrels will do. They say one thing to yer face and then go ahead and do what they want to do. I can only hope. Congressman Lee seems to care, but time will tell if he can sway them."

"Did you hold yourself in check, Mama? I know how mad you can get at these people."

"You'd have been quite proud of me. Willa was there, and she said it, too."

Hearing Willa's name, Nellie wanted to know all about what was going on in her life. "How is Willa, Mama? I mean, really."

"She's fine. Better now, I think. She's writing again. Seems her mind has found a story."

"Oh, that is good news. Did she say when she'd be coming back over here? I know she won't be able to stay away."

"She said she'd come when she gets things underway. She's still got something bothering her, though. It's buried deep down. She says the island affects her in a good way, so she'll come. The island has a hold of her now. Happens that way to some people. We all take it for granted because it's been with us since we were born."

Nellie smiled. "There's magic in these waters."

Jimmy pushed back from the table. "Well, ladies, you'll have to excuse me. Crabs is in these waters right now. That's all I know about. They're swimming so pritty and they're everywhere."

"A good lick this year, do ye think, Jimmy?"

"I think so, Franny girl. Good to have ye home. What do ye think of our girl gonna marry that Denny?"

Frances smiled at Nellie and said, "About time that boy got to askin'."

Frances then looked at Jimmy, who seemed more tired than usual. "Go on in and watch some TV before ye get back to work. You look tired tonight, Jimmy."

"I am tired, Franny. Each year it gets harder for an old body."

"Maybe it's time to quit the water."

"Can't do that. You'd kill me hangin' around for sure, and I couldn't stand not being out there every day."

"Well, go on then. Nellie will help me here."

Nellie leaned over to her mama and whispered, "He missed you something terrible, Mama. I don't think he's feeling well."

"And ye think he'll do anything about it? He's one stubborn waterman."

"Still and all, I'm worried about him."

"Oh, he'll be all right. I'll keep an eye on him. Don't ye worry."

As they collected the dishes, Frances's cell phone rang. "Who can that be?"

"Hello, Frances? It's Prue. Remember me?"

"I sure do. What's goin' on? I'm surprised to hear from you. Is everything okay over there?"

"Yes, everything is fine, Miss Frances. Hope you had a good trip back. The reason I called was to tell you that Congressman Lee is on his way over there, as we speak. He'll arrive in Somerville in time to catch a charter boat. He should be getting there soon. I'm sorry it's on short notice, but it's been quite a day here."

Rather shocked, Frances said, "He's what? He's comin' here? That's kind of odd, isn't it?"

"I guess a little, but he wants to talk with you in person. Can you put him up for a night?"

"I sure can. Can you tell me what's on his mind or should I just wait?"

"He wants to talk to you face-to-face, Frances. I really am sorry for the short notice."

"We do short notice out here all the time, so don't ye worry, Prue. I'll meet him down to the dock when his boat gets here. Do you know what time?"

"He should be out there within the hour. Is there some way you can find out?"

"I'll find out. Ye say it's a charter? I'll get on it."

"You're the best, Miss Frances. Have a good time and a good evening."

When her mother hung up, Nellie said, "What was that all about?"

"You'll never guess. Congressman Lee is on his way over here. He'll be here within the hour. He's taking a charter. Only one I know of, and that's run by Pusey Wills. I'll call over to him down from your daddy's boat."

"Something big must be up for him to come all the way out here to tell you, Mama."

"Well, it's either bad or good, and we won't know until he gets here. So no use to wondering. I better make a plate for him. Go upstairs and make sure we have our extra room ready. Honestly, a congressman going to stay at my home. What's this world comin' to?"

As Nellie passed by the living room, she noticed her daddy fast asleep. *That's odd. He still has to go down to his shanty and check on things before he can go to bed.* That was the daily routine in season. The watermen ate their supper early, around four o'clock, went on down to finish their work, and then came home to sleep. Nellie would keep an eye on him when she came back downstairs.

This was a busy time of day. The women finished cleaning up from supper and then those who picked crabs would head on down to the Co-op to work while their men went back to their shanties to check on things. There had to be an order to the work out on the island or it didn't get done, and that meant you didn't make money.

When Nellie came back downstairs, she noticed both her parents had left. She was relieved to see her daddy had only been catching a quick nap and that he was up and away with Mama. He did look especially tired though. She decided to walk on down to the dock by herself. Odds were, her mother would come over soon anyway, once she had talked to Pusey.

Nellie loved this time of night. You could always hear a game of horseshoes being played in someone's yard and gentle laughter coming from inside the house, as people got ready to go to bed and then begin their routine all over again the next morning.

The sun was getting ready to say "so long" for another day. The moon was already in the sky waiting to take over. James Island was like no other place in the world, except maybe another island, and there weren't many inhabited islands left in the country. It was too hard a life for the women and children. There were so many things to think about when you were on your own, cut off from the land.

She thought about her daddy down inside his shanty, doing what all the others were doing. They worked so hard, but the men also had a strong fellowship. They were close. They had to be. No time for fussing at one another. They were a community and that meant they relied on one another.

They would talk about problems with their boats, and, if one needed help, one of the other men was only too happy to provide it because next time it could be his boat that needed work. It was a band of brothers as much as the women were a band of sisters. Everyone belonged to the other. And no one didn't know what was going on all over the island. It could get a little too close, but they had learned how to get along.

Just as she had expected, her mother was walking up the path as Nellie reached the dock. Frances yelled, "If ye turn around, ye should see his boat coming in now."

Charles had that great smile on his face as the boat made its turn and came aside the dock. Frances noticed how happy he looked. Could these waters really have magic in them?

CHAPTER 45

"Well, how ye comin', Charles?"

"I'm great, Miss Frances. Let me introduce Pusey Wills. He's been kind enough to bring me over."

Frances laughed. "Hi there, Pusey. Guess the good congressman doesn't know that we all know one another."

"Hi, Frances. How's Jimmy comin'?"

Charles listened to the two of them as he grabbed his small traveling bag. Did they all ask about one another with a "how ye comin'"?

"Jimmy's fine. Old, but fine. Ain't we all gettin' there? How's everyone over to your house?"

"Very well, Miss Frances." Then Pusey turned to Charles and said, "Call me when it's time to go back, Congressman."

Charles patted him on the back, as any good politician would, and said, "I'll do that. I don't know exactly if it will be tomorrow or when, but I'll call you."

"Nice meeting you, Congressman." Then with a wink to Frances, he added, "Don't let Miss Frances talk yer ears off."

"Go on, get going, Pusey, afore I come after ye."

"Hi to Jimmy for me, Frances."

Charles hugged Frances and Nellie, then said, "Okay, ladies, lead me onward."

Frances asked, "Do ye want to go out to the picking house? I'd love to show it to ye while the women are over there."

"I'm all yours."

Nellie yawned. "I'll take your bag on home. You'll enjoy seeing the Co-op, but I think I'll pass, if you don't mind."

"Not at all, Nellie. I don't think we'll be too long and I'll talk to you later."

"Have a good time, Congressman."

Charles turned to Frances as Nellie drove off in the golf cart. "How's it going for her?"

"Fine, really fine. This is where she belongs and she fixed it so can work out here. She was lucky she's good at what she does. This way she keeps her benefits and has an income, too. Now she can get married."

"Married? That was awfully quick."

Laughing, Frances poked him in the arm. "Quick? Those two have known one another since they were babies. To my thinking, it took an awful long time for that boy to ask her."

Charles enjoyed being with this woman and was interested in all she had to show and tell. "Now, my dear lady, tell me about where you're taking me."

"It's just a little ways over here. It's by the watermen's marina on the other side of Tuckerton. It's a picking house, but we call it the Cooperative. We started it so we could pick our crab meat under the law of the state. It's all certified and no problems from the state. It's kept up to standards and all. Took a lot to get it out here, but now the only hardship is that we don't have near the women to pick anymore. At one time, of a day or evening, we would have up to fifteen or more women picking. Now, that's all changed. They can't make a lot of money and the young girls have gone off and don't want to do it so much anymore. Everything is changing."

Charles listened as they walked. It was a beautiful walk, until something big bit him. "God, what was that?"

"Oh, those are the big flies that come in spring. They're nothing; wait until the greenheads and the skeeters arrive."

"That didn't feel like nothing, That hurt."

"Listen for the buzz and then swat 'em."

All of a sudden, paradise here was a little tarnished.

As they turned a bend, a big building with an official-looking sign stood in front of them. "Well, here we are." Frances opened the door and said, "Welcome to what we do."

The pounding of mallets on unseen tables could be heard the instant Charles walked inside. Lining the scrupulously clean white walls of the first room were pictures of women picking and visitors who had come through the years. Charles paused and looked at each one.

"Looks like you've had politicians out here plenty of times."

"Yes, we have. They came by the barrels when we first opened this up, but now it's not an *attraction* any more." Then Frances took him to another wall of pictures: these were of children, school-age children.

"Who are these children, Frances?"

"The Baywaters Commission has a program to teach youngsters about their heritage and so they come out through the year. This is always a favorite stop. They go around the island and people talk to them about all the things out here. They even get to see our famous island cakes made, and they stop by Floyd's store and eat a mess of crab cakes. It's a great time to see the children come 'cause they're going to learn and then take information back home with them."

"That's really neat."

"Yes, it is, Charles. There's a lot of good been done over the years, but it seems lately that things have changed for the worse."

"We'll talk about that in a little while, but first I want to meet the fine women working here."

Frances led him through more doors and introduced him. Alice, a pleasant-looking woman, asked him to sit down beside her. Then she showed him how to crack the crab, take the back off, remove the legs, cut across its underside, and pick the meat out of the body. Charles was mesmerized. She picked two of them so he could learn, and then laid out paper in front of him, and handed him one. Charles's eyes got as big as half-dollars.

Frances and the other women about died laughing. "Go on, Charles. Pick that sook clean."

He appeared to be in shock and was definitely overdressed for this occasion. "Do what?"

"Pick her up and crack into her."

Alice handed him her picking knife, hers all her life and as sharp as a knife could be. "Now be careful with this, but, go on. Give 'er a try."

He couldn't back down. His pride was at stake even if his hands were shaking. He took the crab and did what she told him. He really thought he'd lose it right there, but he had to go through with this.

Alice guided him through each step, and, by the time the first crab was picked, he was pretty proud of himself.

"Here, do another one."

"Oh, I couldn't really." However, Alice didn't take no for an answer. Charles took it, and, this time, picked it without instruction.

Alice grinned. "Looks pritty good to me."

Frances said to Charles, "Ye can go wash your hands off over there."

Relief swept over his face. "Thank you, Frances."

"Come on, Charles, we have to make one more quick stop before we go on home."

Alice smiled and said, "Ye come on back anytime. I think ye got the hang of it."

They walked out and Charles broke down laughing. "I must have looked like a fool in there."

Frances took his arm and said, "Can ye imagine how they would look sitting in your office?"

They walked around the back of the building and then down a short lane surrounded by tall marsh grasses swaying in the wind. Ahead was a long dock.

"So this is where the watermen dock up, huh?"

"You're catching on. Jimmy's boat is down there. I want to see if he's still here."

Along the dock, they passed shanty after shanty. "These are something, Frances."

"Yes, it's really peaceful out here at this time of the day. Different in the morning. Then the men are all buzzin' like bees to get out on the water and to their business."

"This is where it all happens, huh?"

"Yes indeed. They bring in the crabs and then put them in the long troughs in the back of the shanty. If they're sellin' soft crabs, then they're up all night watching for the shells to bust and then for them to shed. They got to get them up out of the water after they shed as fast as they can. Crabs start to grow their shells back on right away. It's quite a process."

"I never realized all the work. Do they sell them just as crabs? I mean not picked and not soft?"

"Oh yeah, but not so much here in Tuckerton. We pick 'em mostly, and then ship the lump meat over to the mainland in coolers to sell to our customers."

"It's a hard life."

"It's hard and tiring when the crabs start, but it's how we live."

CHAPTER 46

Jimmy wasn't at his boat.

"Well, time to head home. I thought Jimmy would still be down here, but I see he went on back home. Nellie didn't like the way he looked tonight so I thought I'd check on him, but I see there's no need."

Charles spotted a couple of deck chairs in front of Jimmy's shanty and sat down in one for a minute. "It's nice and quiet here, Frances."

"This is the quiet time when the sun goes down, the moon is out, and the day is done. Nice to rest."

"Well, now I can add crab picking to my resumé, just in case I need to look for another job."

"I surely hope not, Charles. You're a fair man and that's something that doesn't come along much anymore in our leaders. Everyone's fighting with the other and they all seem to have their own agendas."

"I know that's how it looks, but there really are some good people who try to do the job they are paid to do. However, once you get to Washington, or any higher position, the rules seem to change and it gets tough."

"Now, what's brought you all the way out here? Not to pick crabs, I think."

"You're a wise lady, Frances Evans. And one whose trust I want to keep. Well, I'm here to tell you that I had a rather interesting meeting with Senator Richardson. He came to me in hopes of intimidating me into going his direction with more government intervention on the Bay."

"I knew that old goat was up to something. He was just too nice, but, still, he's a Senator, and I wanted to believe the best in him. Thought maybe he had mellowed in his age."

"Not all people do, Frances. Well, anyway, our conversation got rather heated, and, as you know, thanks to Prue, I had sniffed out a few things on the good senator. I finally pulled the plug and laid it out to him. He wasn't really happy about that, but finally backed away. He knew I was intent on doing this. Now, I don't know if he really thought a little pip-squeak in Congress was up to the task of taking on a big shot senator, but I made him see the light. He said he was going to get ready to retire and so he wouldn't have the time to mess with this."

"I don't know what you said, Charles, but you had to have some pritty nasty stuff on that man to make him give up like that. I think his retirement may have been your idea?"

"No comment, Miss Frances. Let's just say he saw the light."

Frances laughed out loud and said, "The Lord surely works in mysterious ways. Not for me to question."

"That's not what I came to tell you. I want you to know that I understand the season you're in now, but this next step won't ever happen if we don't come together soon, and I want you to be on this committee. It's very important."

Frances sat there, speechless. So many thoughts ran through her mind. She had given so much of herself already to bring light on this life she was trying to save, but was she willing to do more?

"What are you thinking, Frances?"

Frances looked him right in the eye and said, "I think maybe I shouldn't be on that committee. It should be all watermen and not a feisty old woman."

"With all due respect, that committee needs a feisty old woman, Frances. You know this life as well as any, and haven't you told me that this is an equal partnership deal?"

"I wish you wouldn't listen to all I say sometimes, Charles."

"But I do and it's deeper than that. You really made a point with many of us when you talked about our history: the history of this country and where and how it began. The Chesapeake is the cradle that held the infant who grew up to be a nation. If the sum of its parts is in decline, or, worst case, the parts vanish all together, we've lost something so valuable to our intrinsic relationship to our beginnings as a nation, and that's something that can never be replaced.

"Do you want to be known one day only by some crab pots or oyster tongs sitting in a government museum? That's what will be left to this story. History will change, and it will never be known what the oyster and crab meant for and to the people, both native and the early explorers. It all grew out of a grand dream. The Chesapeake is a life-force in this great nation. That's why so many people are drawn to it and involved with trying to keep it alive and viable."

"Ye don't have to tell me that, Charles, but I'm glad you've reminded me of it. Ye sound like me when I was much younger and more active with my feelings. Ye have the passion for it, but I saw this coming—we all did—out here on the islands. We aren't alone. What's coming is hitting so many people all over this country. If we can just show that we can work through this here, and if we can get a break, we can hold back time. That's all we're asking. We don't want handouts; we want to fish."

Charles took her rough hand in his and said, "I think, Frances, you've just said yes."

They sat quietly for a moment. Then the peace was suddenly broken. Alice was running down the dock, yelling, "Get home, Frances. It's Jimmy."

The Lord did work in mysterious ways. Frances and Charles ran to the Co-op, grabbed Alice's golf cart, and headed the short way to the Evans home. The few minutes between places had Frances's head spinning. And the fact she had forgotten her cell phone this one time made it all the worse.

Charles insisted on driving the cart. That, unlike picking crabs, he could do. Frances was way too nervous.

By the time they reached the front step, neighbors were already gathering to help.

Frances jumped off the cart and ran inside. Charles thought it best to stay outside until they knew what was going on.

Nellie met her mother at the door, and took her back to the bedroom where Jimmy was on the bed. Frances took one look and knew this wasn't good. His breathing was labored. "Talk to me, Jimmy."

"Franny, I don't feel very good. I think it's my heart."

"Do ye have pains?"

"Yeah, and they're going up and down my arm."

Frances turned to Nellie and said, "Sit with Dad. I'm calling the doctor."

Calling the doctor meant their doctor on the mainland. When something like this happened, it was always a race against time. The doctor's answering service came on and Frances told them Jimmy had to get to a hospital. They agreed, given the symptoms.

Frances came back in and said, "They're sending a helicopter." She sat on the bed, rubbed his forehead tenderly, and leaned down and gave him a kiss. "Hang on, Jimmy. You're goin' to be all right. Just hang on."

Nellie went outside to tell the neighbors what was happening, and then waved Charles into the house. He felt awful and wasn't sure what he should do. He had just gotten there and now this. The one thing he didn't want was to be in the way.

"Nellie, maybe I should call Pusey and have him come back and get me."

"Don't do that yet. Let's take care of Daddy and Mama and see what happens. I'll stay over here for now. I have too many things to do, and Mama needs to do this by herself. You'll stay right here in our home. You came out here to do something important and you're not going to leave the minute you get here."

"Nellie, I've already done what I came for and this isn't the time for hospitality. It's the time for you and your mom to take care of your father."

"It's okay. I mean that and I wouldn't say it if it wasn't. If you go back tomorrow, then that's a different story. But, for now, you can help me."

"Okay, Nellie. Is it his heart?"

"That's what Mama said and she's usually right. All the women over here grow up with a sense of things when it comes to health and knowing whether it's bad or not. This isn't good, so he's going over to the hospital."

"How? By boat?"

"No, they're sending a helicopter over. It'll be here soon now."

Charles was getting another lesson in how difficult life was on an island. When you live near everything, it's so easy, but, over here, it was far from that. An emergency situation becomes a huge and dangerous event. He wondered how many people died before they could make it over to the mainland and how many got there but died because it took too long. This was like living on the frontier. You always had to have a plan.

He offered up a quick prayer and realized, for some odd reason, the only person he wanted to talk to at the moment was Willa. He seemed to sense she would make it better.

Nellie came out of the bedroom with tears in her eyes. Had Jimmy died? Charles didn't say a word. Just then he heard the blades of a helicopter, and, from the noise, it sounded as if it were going to land on the house.

Frances hurried out of the bedroom and ran through the kitchen and out into the open with her arms in the air. There was a large field next door and down the helicopter came. When two men got out, she brought them inside with their portable litter, and, within minutes, Jimmy was on his way to the helicopter and then to a hospital.

"Good luck, I'll be thinking of you both," Charles shouted as Frances disappeared out the door. Nellie ran after her with the pocketbook she was going to need when she got there.

Charles joined the rest of the gathering and saw again the intense concern this community had for one another. It could have been any one of them. Denny had come while the medics were in the house, and he was standing there with his arm around Nellie's shoulders. She belonged to him, even if they were not married yet. They watched together as the helicopter lifted off. Charles saw Frances's worried face staring out the window at her daughter. Then she smiled slightly and they were gone.

CHAPTER 47

Nellie went off with Denny. Charles decided he would call Willa. She would want to know what happened. He walked over to a bench looking out on the Bay and made the call.

"Hello?"

"Hello, Willa. I had to talk with you. I'm over on the island and—"

"You're where?" she interrupted. "Why are you over there?"

"It's a long story, but I had to call you. I needed to hear a friendly voice."

"What's wrong, Charles?"

"I came out to talk to Frances face-to-face about what's transpired since she's returned and I had barely got here and everyone's gone. Jimmy had a heart attack and he was just taken, by helicopter, over to the mainland."

"Dear God. Is he going to be all right? How's Frances and Nellie?"

"So far, he's okay. But who knows? Frances went with Jimmy. Nellie stayed here to do some things."

"I get the picture. You're alone with Nellie in Frances's house, and you're feeling very odd."

"In a nutshell. I won't leave until I know all is well."

"How did you get out there? Cap'n Tuck?"

"No, I asked Prue to arrange this on the double-quick and she chartered a boat out here from the marina in Somerville. The captain's name was Pusey Wills."

Willa couldn't help herself; she began giggling. "Pusey Wills? Are you sure it wasn't Pussy Willow?"

Charles started laughing, too. "I needed that, Willa. I knew you were the only person in this world who could make me feel better right now."

"So what's your plan, Congressman?"

"I don't know. Have any ideas?"

"Go fishing."

"That's two for you, Willa. However, it could be a day or two until I hear about Jimmy or see Frances, so it might actually not be a bad idea."

"What? To go fishing while Jimmy is in the hospital?"

"It's not that. But if I stay here—which I'm going to do—maybe Nellie's guy can take me out to see the real deal on the Bay."

"You know, Charles, that's not a bad idea. Sometimes I don't know how smart I am."

"Yep, you're one sharp cookie. Now you have to say yes and go to dinner with me when I get home so I can thank you."

She was enjoying the easy conversation between them and then it hit her.

"Charles? I'm coming over there. I'll leave early tomorrow morning and be there by late afternoon. I really want to be with Frances and Nellie. And maybe even you," she gently teased.

"Is that a halfhearted compliment, Willa?"

"Maybe, but I also can't sit here while Frances might need me."

"I think it's a great idea. They all really think the world of you. And I'll ask Nellie about setting up the fishing outing for me tomorrow. Can you call Prue and tell her what's going on out here?"

"Absolutely. I'll call her right away. I pray Jimmy is going to be okay. See you tomorrow, if you survive your day."

"Seriously, Willa, thanks. I'm really very glad you're coming."

"So am I. Bye, Charlie."

What was a small thing, meant a lot to him. She had called him Charlie.

Nellie came back home an hour later, and Charles was glad to see her.

"Have you heard anything yet, Nellie?"

"Actually, I have. Mama called and told me Jimmy did have a heart attack, but a mild one. They're pretty sure he's going to be okay. I'm so relieved. Daddy works too hard."

"Is there a way to work on the water not so hard?" Charles asked.

"No, not really. This life takes a toll on the men. *And* their wives."

"And you're willing to take it on with Denny?"

"No choice. I love him and always have."

"Speaking of Denny, do you think I could go out with him tomorrow morning?"

Nellie smiled and said, "You have to get up at three o'clock, you know. If you want to, I'll call him right now."

"Go ahead. I think it would do me good to get a firsthand look at this business."

"Maybe he can go out at four. Give you a few minutes more sleep."

He listened to their conversation and got the gist it was all right with Denny. He looked down at his Rolex; it was now nine o'clock.

"He said yes, so you better get to sleep. I'll wake you up. You'll smell the coffee anyway."

"Thanks, Nellie. Where do you want me to sleep?"

"Sleep upstairs. It's all ready for you. I'll show you. I'm going to sleep down here in Mama and Daddy's room. I'll feel closer to them that way."

"I understand completely. Do you think I can handle this?"

"If you can handle Washington, you can handle the Bay."

It didn't take five minutes after Charles's head hit the pillow and he was gone. Nellie, however, had a restless night, She was so afraid that, although her mother had said all was fine, something would go wrong. By three o'clock in the morning, she had hardly slept at all.

Charles never slept more than six hours, so, when he smelled the coffee, he was ready to get going. Thank heavens he had brought a pair of jeans with him and a sweatshirt. He was good to go. By the time he went downstairs, Nellie had his coffee on the table and food in a cooler.

"Wow, you're something,"

"Used to it and I've been taking care of Daddy, so it's my routine now."

As they sat there, Charles having coffee and Nellie finishing packing the cooler, Nellie asked, "What was it you wanted to tell Mama so badly that you came out here in person?"

"I wanted to tell her that all things are a go for the committee and that I wanted her to sit on it."

"She must have loved that. When does it begin?"

"Well, she wasn't too keen on it at first and it will meet in the early summer. I know that's not easy, but she has to be on that committee."

"She must have fought you some, but you're right, She's got more understanding about the whole picture than most anyone."

"Yes, she does, and now I've seen one of her projects out in that Co-op. It's amazing what all she has accomplished for a life she lives and loves."

Nellie looked away for a minute, then said, "Now with Daddy . . . she won't leave him, you know."

"Well, let's see what happens. There's still time and it sounds like Jimmy is going to be all right."

"How about Senator Richardson? I don't think he's going to back down."

"I took care of that and he won't be a problem."

Nellie got the message and didn't pursue it. Obviously Charles Lee was a tough man, too.

"You better get going, Charles. Do you want me to walk over with you?"

Not wanting to admit he'd get lost as quick as a wink, he said, "I'd like that, Nellie."

"You'll be back by twelve thirty or so. I'll have lunch waiting for you."

He looked at her and said, "Willa's coming over this afternoon. I called her last night, and, when she heard what happened, she wouldn't take no for an answer."

"Broke your heart, I'll bet." Nellie laughed.

"That obvious, eh?"

"Congressman, all men are that obvious."

By the time they reached the marina, Denny was finishing up loading the boat. He smiled at the two of them. "Morning, Nellie. Morning, Congressman."

"It's Charles, and good morning to you. Thanks for taking me out. I'll stay out of your way."

"Heck ye will. I figure if ye want to learn, then ye have to work."

Charles shrugged his shoulders and said, "You're on." Then he looked at Nellie and said, "What do you think?"

"I think you'll do just fine." Then she looked at Denny and said, "Take good care of him. We don't need any more trouble. I'll call you when I hear anything about Daddy."

Denny leaned over to kiss her, Charles went onboard, and the boat headed out.

She watched it make its turn and then head for open water. Suddenly, she felt so alone. Nothing could happen to her daddy. She couldn't bear it and her mama would break down for sure. They had been together all their lives. *All their lives. Just like Denny and me.*

Jimmy Evans was a quiet man, but a better man there was nowhere on this earth. He had always been there to cheer her up when she was little, and then, when she went off to college, he held her hand before she got on the boat and told her she could do anything if she wanted it badly enough. Right now, she prayed. If she really could do anything, it would be to see him get better and come back home.

At that moment, her phone rang. It was her mother.

"Good morning, Mama. How is Daddy?"

"He's comin' fine, Nellie. Slept most of the night and he's right here, wantin' to come home."

"Absolutely not, Mama," Nellie shouted. "Put him on the phone."

Nellie could hear him grousing a bit. Then, "Hello, Nellie girl."

"Daddy, you're staying put, do you hear me? Stay there until they say you can come home."

"How do ye know they haven't said that?"

"'Cause I know you and I know how you want to come home and go out on the boat, but you can't."

"Who says?"

"I do and Mama does, too. So you're staying and that's that."

"I can't stand it here, Nellie. They've given me medicine, and, if I can go home, I promise I won't go out on the water . . . for a while."

"I heard that, Daddy. Let me talk to Mama."

When Frances got back on, Nellie asked, "Do we have a prayer of keeping him there?"

"Maybe a day, but no more if he feels up to coming home."

"Then he stays. We outvoted him."

"But I'm coming home just for the afternoon," her mother said. "I have things to do."

"Like what? What's so important I can't do it?"

"Well, I run off on our guest for one thing."

"Our guest has gone off with Denny."

"He's what?"

"You heard me, so that takes care of that. And Willa is coming over this afternoon. Charles called her and she said she was coming. She is worried about Daddy."

"A whole house full and I'm over here."

"You're with your husband and he needs you, and right now he needs to stay put."

"Oh, all right, Nellie, but I'll still call ye later. Make sure ye fix food for our guests."

"Mama, leave me be. I can do this."

"I know ye can, but you know how I am."

"Yes, I do, and, if you don't stop worrying about everyone, there will be more than one person in the hospital. I think we have quite enough for now, don't you?"

"Love ye, Nellie."

"Love ye, too, Mama, and kiss Daddy for me."

CHAPTER 48

It took awhile to get out to the crab pots. Denny's territory was rather spread out, but, aside from the hideously early hour, Charles was enjoying the experience, including the hot coffee, the sounds of the spluttering diesel engine, and the sheer beauty of the Bay at this time of the morning.

"How ye comin', Charles?"

"I'm fine. Really better than I thought. It's so peaceful out here."

"Enjoy it now, 'cause as soon as we get out there we'll have plenty of work to do."

Charles sat back and watched Denny's mate, Lem, work on some of the ropes that had become frayed. They all sure knew what they were doing out here.

"How long have you been on the water, Lem?"

"Most of my life, but not full time with the crabs like now. I have another job in the winter in Somerville. I work on boats. I make more money doing that."

"You don't oyster?"

"Nah, Denny does that hisself. I need to pay for my own health care, so I do the boats, and so far the money's been good. They'd like me to go full time, but I can't give up the water and the island."

"Where do you live in the winter?"

"My family's over there on the mainland, so I put down there for the winter, but I come on out here on weekends when I can."

"Do you make boats or just do work on them, Lem?"

"I work on 'em, but I can make a workboat. Why?"

"Well, I'm thinking of having one made, or maybe buying one."

"There's a few nice ones for sale over in the boatyard, if you'd be interested. I could tell one of the guys to show them to ye."

"I'd like that. I don't know when I'm leaving here—maybe another day or so—but I could stop in on my way out."

"I hear you're a congressman. I never met a real important man before."

"Well, I've never met a real waterman until I came over here, so that makes us even. I think I'm not really important, but I think what you're doing is."

"Aw, come on. You have the power," Lem said with a self-deprecating tone.

"You give it to us. Some of us try to wear it better than others, that's all."

"Where you from? I hear a southern accent."

"Good catch, Lem. I'm from Virginia. I live in Charlottesville. That's the home—"

"—of Thomas Jefferson," Lem finished proudly. "I know. I studied my history in school. I like history and he was a neat man."

"Yes, he was. All our Founding Fathers were neat men."

Denny began to slow the engine. "We're here, Charles."

"Great. What do you want me to do?"

"We'll let you know."

Charles watched as they positioned the boat around the pot markers. Then Denny and Lem started pulling up the pots, full of crabs scrambling every whichway to get out.

"Wow," Charles said. "I've never seen so many crabs in my life."

"Yeah, they're trying to escape us, but it's a hopeless cause."

The first pot was dumped out, and, as Denny baited the empty one to put it back in the water, he told Charles to put on heavy gloves and start putting the crabs in the baskets after Lem sorted through them to throw back the ones that were too small.

"Looks to me like a lot can't be taken from this pot, Denny," shouted Lem.

"Well, this next one looks better. This isn't as easy as it looks, is it, Charles?"

"I should say not. These crabs are crawling and squirming all over the place. But I can get them into those baskets."

Charles was absolutely fascinated watching these two young men work. "Do you get men who keep them anyway, regardless of the size regulations?"

Denny smiled sheepishly and said, "Do ye think I'm going to tell *you* that?"

Charles laughed. "Good point. Protect the brothers at all costs."

"They'll fine our butts off if we take what's not ready yet. I can't afford to get fined so we take what's ours and leave the rest for another day."

"Good thinking, Denny. Tell me, what do you think of all the regulations?"

"Too many. And every years the fees go up and it's getting near impossible to make a whole lot of money. If we have a bad run, it's pretty hard on us. That's why so many my age leave and don't want to do this anymore. I hate to say this, but the government is in everybody's faces these days."

"I know that. You're not the only industry complaining, but you're the one I'm most interested in right now."

"Are ye going to help us, Charles?"

"I'm going to try. I can't change everything but I'm hoping to stop some of the ridiculous burdens being put on you."

"If you could do that, it would help us keep going for a while. Our world isn't going to be here for many more years. Too many things happening for us to make it."

"The world changes, and sometimes it's good and sometimes it's bad."

"Mostly bad lately," Denny said as he and Lem pulled up another pot and swung it over the deck.

Lem piped up. "Have you seen the paper work they want us to do? We want to fish; that's what we do. All the questions they ask are for some government people to look at, not for us. Makes us crazy."

"I've heard about it. We have to take a look at that."

Denny looked at Charles and said, "It's your turn now. Here come the critters."

After Charles sorted them, Denny yelled, " Now it's your turn to help me pull them up." Charles walked over, took his position, and waited for Denny to tell him to pull.

"Ready now, Charles. Your hands are are small compared to ours, but they'll work. Now lift."

Charles felt as if his insides were going to come out. The pots had to weigh a thousand pounds with the water pulling on them. "Good God, man. This is heavy."

"Can ye do it, Charles? Or should Lem come on over here?"

No way was Charles going to stop now, even if it killed him. Which it might. He wasn't going to be the topic of conversation when Willa arrived. He'd never live it down. He grabbed on to the pot and shouted, "Lift her up, Denny."

Denny chuckled, knowing that, by tonight, Charles wasn't going to be able to get up out of a chair. But he would know what it was like to be a waterman.

Nellie was waiting at the marina for Denny's boat to come in. She was worried that Charles might have jumped overboard when he found out how hard the work on the boat was. But, happily, when she heard the boat chugging, all three men were aboard.

"Hey there," she yelled. "You're alive."

Charles smiled, although she did detect a look on his face that was screaming, "Get me the heck off."

Lem jumped out, grabbed the rope, and tied the boat up to the dock. Meanwhile, Charles was wishing he could levitate. Seems his legs didn't want to talk to the rest of his body, so simply moving from the boat's bench was a major obstacle. Then he thought about the women in the post office and that did it: he wasn't going to have Miss Ida talking about what a sorry relative he was of Robert E. Lee for the rest of her life.

Nellie kept a straight face and said, "You look pretty good for your first time."

Charles took her hand as he got off the boat, slowly, every muscle killing him.

Nellie whispered in his ear, "It's all right to scream, Charles. We've all been there."

"But you weren't my age when you were there."

"I've got some good liniment back at the house. You'll feel better in no time."

"Have you heard anything from Willa? She's not here yet, is she?"

"Yes and no. Which part of that would you like to discuss first?"

"None of it right now. Do you have the golf cart with you? Please don't tell me I have to walk back to the house."

"Would work out the kinks, but I do have the cart over to the Co-op. You can make it that far, can't you?"

"I'm not sure."

"I'll go get it then." She looked at Denny and said, "You were supposed to take him crabbing, not kill him."

Denny smiled and said, "He's fine, Nellie. I have to say, he was great with those pots, but I think he underestimated how heavy they are."

Charles groaned slightly and said, "Just a little. Thanks for taking me out, Denny. And, Lem, please let me have those names about the boat."

Nellie looked at him, puzzled. "Do you want to buy your own boat and do this?"

"God forbid, Nellie, but I am interested in buying a boat or having one made."

"Well, Lem is the best one to talk to."

"Yes, I know. So now, what about Willa?"

"She called me on her way across the shore. She's going to stop in and see Daddy and visit Mama, which I am very grateful for, and then she's coming across with Cap'n Tuck. She'll be here around one thirty so you have time to get that rubdown on your legs and lower back. You'll be fine by the time she gets here."

"How's Jimmy?"

"Ornery as ever. He wanted to come back home, but I laid the law down to him, and to Mama. Those two don't like to be in those places, but he's really got to be careful."

"You folks are something."

"Are we a good something or bad?"

"The best!"

269

CHAPTER 49

Charles was so happy to get back to the house. Nellie hopped off the cart, helped him out, and then went directly to the bathroom cabinet and got the liniment. Within fifteen minutes of application, Charles had a strong smell about him, but he was a new man.

"What is this stuff, Nellie?"

"Our cure for all that ails ye."

He started laughing and then said, "I better go down to the dock to meet Willa. Can I borrow your cart?"

"Have at it. I'll have lunch waiting when you get back."

"Thanks." He hobbled out of the house slowly and wondered if he could even get into the cart, but, with one, good, courageous try, he was in. He was sore for sure, but better than an hour ago.

He looked at his watch and still had some time before the boat came, so decided to take his own tour. The peacocks were in full voice, making that haunting sound to one another. He loved it. They would make a beautiful addition to his home in Virginia. A reminder of the island.

The men were all coming back now, and he knew the women would have their dinners on the table. The water community ate dinner around one and then supper, a lighter fare, in the early evening. He thought back to how this had always been a southern practice, but now, in the suburbs and city, this wasn't the case anymore. Another change in lifestyle that wasn't necessarily for the better.

It was quiet, peaceful, and a place where contentment was found in the simple pleasures. Challenges were always there, to be sure, but, somehow, they were lessened by the slower pace and natural beauty. As he drove down one path and then another, each held an unexpected surprise with a story of its own. He saw very old homes and then some that were brand new. Many had been refitted for a more modern world and some were falling down, sad reminders that time really doesn't stop for anyone.

As Charles headed to the dock, he smiled as he passed the tiny post office. Just then, Miss Ida came out and he waved, thinking of the day he discovered he possibly had a distant relation to the island. He had made new friends in a world that doesn't particularly warm to outsiders.

When he saw the boat coming in, there was Willa, smiling at him. He was falling for her, no doubt about it.

Willa couldn't deny she was very happy to see Charles and be back to this small space that was taking up a large part of her heart. She felt like a little girl again, back on the small beach in Maine where she had spent so many happy days. Here, she belonged, and wasn't encumbered by what others thought or said. And here is where she sought her ultimate freedom from whatever it was that haunted her.

Tuck pulled in and Willa grabbed her small overnight bag and computer and got off the boat. Charles walked down the dock and, without thinking, hugged her tightly. It felt like the right thing to do.

"How was your trip?"

"Good, and I can report I wasn't scared of the water at all."

"That's great. See? Another triumph for the famous Willa Carpenter. I hear you went to the hospital."

"Yes, I did, but I'll save it all for when we get to Nellie's. Good news, though, and I hear you went crabbing."

Charles put her things on the golf cart without saying a word.

"That good, huh, Charles? Takes some time to get used to, I imagine, but you survived."

"Barely," he whispered.

"What was that? I didn't hear you." She giggled.

"Never mind."

When Willa watched him getting into the golf cart, she could see his maiden voyage hadn't exactly gone to plan, so she decided to skip discussing that until another time. As they left the dock, he said, "This is really such an extraordinary place, isn't it, Willa?"

"If I didn't know better, I would think you were falling in love with it out here."

Charles wanted to tell her he was falling in love with her, too, but decided he first had to be sure how she felt.

"I really do like it. You know, life's so weird. I could have told Frances over the phone about what was happening, but I couldn't wait for an excuse to get back here. I just wish things hadn't gotten so crazy."

"Yes, I imagine you were scared to death by Jimmy. Prue said to stay as long as you wanted. Nothing too important going on back in Washington."

"She's one in a million. I'm going to miss her."

Willa looked at him with shock. "What are you talking about?"

"Oh, come on, you must know. You two are so close."

"You know we don't talk about our work much, so what did she tell you?"

"Well, act if it's news to you, okay?"

"Promise. Now out with it."

"Well, I had just had a meeting with Senator Rennie Richardson and it was a rough one. We got into it, but I think I came out ahead and drove my message home to him about his financial activities and how we had to get moving on this Bay committee. He left the office, seething I'm sure, but understanding completely. I told Prue about it—as if she hadn't heard most of it through the door—and, when I was finished talking, she told me some news of her own."

Willa suspected what was coming, but wanted him to be the one to tell her.

Charles said, "She's decided it's time for her to go back home and prepare for a campaign of her own. I guess this is something she has wanted to do all her life. A little something she left out of her interview with me when she came on board as my office manager and right hand."

Willa smiled.

"I'm assuming from the look on your face that you've known about this."

"You would assume correctly. Prue and I are close and we share our hopes and our dreams and I've known for a long time she's wanted to do something big in Washington. But I didn't know exactly what, so, yes, I knew what her final outcome would be, but didn't know everything."

"It's in her genes and I know the man she will be running against. He's a fool, so I'm especially glad she's doing it. Do you think she can win?"

"Let me put it this way: Chester Harding is one tough man. I adore him, but I am Prue's friend and in no way a threat to their family business. If I were, I tell you I would be afraid. Very afraid. They have all the money they'll ever need and Chester has a lot of friends in and out of Washington. He must think she's ready and I guess she does, too."

"In this business, timing is everything."

"You've been a very good mentor to Prue, Charles. She thinks the world of you and respects your ability to see the problem and want to solve it, even if it's not what your party wants. It's a lonely place to be an honest and earnest politician."

He looked at her in a whole new light. If he had thought he was falling for her before, this only enhanced those feelings a million percent. "Thank you, Willa. Watch out, or a man could think you liked him."

"I do like you, Charles."

"What happened to Charlie? I distinctly heard you call me that when I phoned you."

She was too confused now, afraid to say anything he might misunderstand, so she teased, "It must have slipped out without my thinking about it."

"Sure, Willa, admit it: I'm quite a man."

"Oh, brother." Wanting to move the conversation away from this, Willa said, "We better get back to the house. Didn't Nellie say she was making lunch for us?"

"Yes, she did." As he drove on, they both grew quiet, lost in their own thoughts until they pulled up in front of Frances's house.

Nellie was waiting for them in the kitchen. She hugged Willa. "It's so good to see you again, Willa. How is Daddy *really* doing?"

"Let me put my things down and then I'll tell you. What smells so good? I'm starving."

Nellie asked Charles to put Willa's things in her parents' room and then come back and sit down.

The smell of crab filled the house. When Willa saw the skillet on the stove, she sighed in ecstasy. "Crab cakes? I was hoping you would make them."

"I got the crab meat from Floyd. Knew you loved them. C'mon now and let's eat."

Before any food was touched, Nellie bowed her head, signaling to Charles and Willa to do the same. After Nellie said the blessing, the food kept coming. When it was finally all on the table, she sat down.

"Now, tell us about Daddy. The real story."

Willa took a couple bites of the crab cake first. "He looks pretty good and he's counting the minutes until he can get out and come home."

"That's what Mama said, but is he ready to come home?"

"He must be, but the doctor said it would be tomorrow, but that's not a definite. And I might add, your mom's pretty worn out."

"Oh, boy. If he can't get out of there, he'll be a holy terror, but I don't want him coming home if there's any chance he could have another, bigger attack."

"They aren't going to do that, Nellie. I told them I'd give you all hugs and their love." Then she turned to Charles and said, "Frances said she's so sorry she isn't here for you."

"Well, she's sort of preoccupied," Charles remarked, smiling.

Nellie put her head down and then said quietly, "It's the money it's costing them."

"What did you say?" asked Charles.

"It's the money. They don't have health insurance, and, if Daddy can come home, he will. Mama won't let him come if she thinks he's still in danger, but, if he can come home, they'll come on tomorrow."

Charles hadn't thought about that and now here it was right in front of him: one of the big challenges for these men and and women. "How will they pay for it? I don't mean to pry, but what do people do when this happens?"

"They pay it off if they can, or they do it over time. It's a huge problem for us."

"That will be on the agenda for this upcoming committee, I can promise you. I don't have all the answers, but this just isn't good."

"It's another reason so many give up and go to the mainland to get jobs and never return to the water, even if it kills them."

Willa sat there, saying nothing. She was thinking and would talk to Frances when she got back. Finally she said, "Don't mind me, I'm being a pig, but can I have another crab cake? I swear these are straight from heaven."

Nellie smiled as she passed Willa the plate. "They're an old, old recipe from way back, and Mama has never given anyone—including me—the exact recipe. When I make them, they're good, but they don't taste like Mama makes them."

Willa took the plate, smiling. "Nellie, don't you know what that left-out ingredient is? It's love."

CHAPTER 50

Charles went to bed shortly after the sun went down. Willa and Nellie both noticeed he was in none too good a shape walking up those stairs. He looked like an old man, hunched over, trying to get his legs to work properly.

Willa poked Nellie and whispered softly, "Do you think he'll recover?"

"Not sure, but my bet is on the fact he really wants to get in that bed and forget today happened."

When he was out of sight and they had heard the upstairs bedroom door shut, Nellie burst out laughing.

"Took him all of five minutes to get up there, take his clothes off, shut the door, and hit the bed. What do you bet he's already in dreamland?"

"Not taking that bet. I wonder if Charles will ever go out crabbing again?"

"If he was smart, he'd go out tomorrow, but the odds are totally against that. Once is enough, but my guess is he'll try it again one day." Nellie added, "Willa, let's go for a walk. It's nice this time of the evening to do that."

"Okay. You sure can't go walking all around Washington at night without looking over your shoulder, so this will be a rare treat."

They pulled on light sweatshirts and went out the door. One of the nicest things about Tuckerton was that everyone knew everyone, and watched out for anything that looked strange, so there was a comfort not many people in this world experienced anymore.

"Something's on your mind, Nellie. What is it?"

"I could say the same thing back to you. You keep coming over here, so there's something here you need. What is it you're searching for?"

"I don't know, Nellie, but you're right. There's a feeling I get out here like nowhere else and it haunts me. If I could only dig deep, I might remember something, or a thought might come to me. But it doesn't."

"You're trying too hard. You have to let it come when it's ready. Could it be you're not searching for the right thing?"

"What do you mean?"

"Maybe it's something that's not buried so deep. Maybe it's something you have to do, not remember."

"I don't know exactly, but I do know, Nellie, out here is where I come the closest to true happiness."

"Everyone says that. I like to think the island is enchanted. Spirits from hundreds of years are here. They call to us in the night. Hear them, Willa?"

Willa closed her eyes and heard the faint sound of water lapping at the shoreline. A few geese were settling down for the night, honking quietly. Ducks were rustling in the marsh grasses.

"Yes, Nellie. What I hear are the sounds of eons of time out here, everything doing what has been done forever. The sounds are comforting and one could get lost in them."

"You do hear it then. Not everyone does. You seem to have a link out here with us. It happens, but not often. Outsiders can't feel the water, the marsh, the breezes. They can't taste the air, the mud that surrounds the island at low tide. It's all here and we've had it all our lives, but, to you, who has a sense of things, your experience is new, fresh, and alive. It teaches us not to take it for granted."

"Maybe you should be the writer, Nellie. There's poetry in your words. Your feeling for your home is poetry, pure and simple."

"You know, when I was speaking before Charles's committee, I was so out of place. I felt uneasy and words were hard for me to come by. There's no poetry over there."

Willa stopped, looked at Nellie, and then put her arms around her. "You sure have us figured out, don't you?"

"You're not like that, Willa. You don't belong over there. You belong out here."

"I don't think so, Nellie. I think this is a lovely dream for me, but I couldn't live out here all the time. I'm a city girl, and find my mojo there. But there's no getting away from it—Tuckerton is a part of me now. I was meant to discover it. Serendipity, I guess. From the time I just happened to glance down at that newspaper and read of your upcoming talk, my life changed."

"The good Lord does that to people. At the time, we have no idea what's on His mind, and then we go on this roundabout journey that leads us to someplace else. Someplace we never expected."

"And to someone else, too, Nellie. I look at you and Denny. You were off to the city, off the island, and into a world a million miles away from here, and look where your journey has led you."

Nellie smiled softly. Her young, pretty face reflecting the moonlight, she had the look of a true island woman. She was brave, strong, and alive.

"You belong here with Denny. He's your perfect mate."

"And who's yours, Willa?

"You think it's Charles, don't you, Nellie?"

"Wouldn't be a bit surprised. He's in love with you, I can tell, and you're falling in love with him. But you won't let yourself go into it. Something is holding you back."

All of a sudden, Willa wanted to be alone. She didn't want to talk anymore.

"Nellie? I don't mean to be rude, but can I ask you a favor?"

Nellie nodded, almost as if she knew what Willa was going to say.

"I need to be alone and walk in the darkness for a while. Would you mind if I did that?"

"Not at all. Maybe you'll find light in the darkness."

"Thanks for understanding."

Nellie hugged Willa and walked back to the house. Willa stood there for a moment and then decided to walk over to the dock and sit on one of the benches that looked out to the water. Yes, she needed to be alone, and think, and discover.

Charles was up very early and tried to be quiet; however, when he got downstairs, he was surprised to see Willa sitting alone, drinking her tea.

"I didn't wake you, did I, Willa? If I did, I'm sorry."

"No, you didn't, Charles. I'm afraid I didn't sleep much last night. I went out walking with Nellie and then she came home and I sat down by the dock for a long time."

"Did you find what you were looking for?"

"Why would you ask that?"

"I see a look in your eyes as if you've lost something and don't know where to find it."

Willa didn't want to answer him so she switched the subject. "I see you're walking better this morning."

Charles dropped his head and chuckled. "I tell you, Willa, this is a rough-and-tough life over here. It's much healthier. Better than sitting on your duff talking—or should I say arguing?—with people all day, but it does take a toll."

"Don't they both? I wouldn't do your job for a trillion dollars. Poor Prue; I hope she knows what she's getting into."

"Remember, you don't know anything."

"I won't betray you. But it would make for good blackmail."

"Funny, Willa." Suddenly he turned serious. "I'm leaving on the boat this morning."

"I sort of figured that out when I heard you up so early."

"Will you miss me?"

Without skipping a beat, Willa answered, "Yes, I will."

Charles walked over and pulled her out of the chair. He looked into her eyes and said, "Yes, you will, Willa Carpenter, and I'll miss you, too."

Willa's legs were trembling. He made her feel a way she hadn't ever felt before. She knew, if she looked up at him, they would kiss, and she wasn't ready for that yet.

He knew what she was thinking and didn't know if he should take the chance, but then—he did. He raised her chin up with his fingers, leaned down, and kissed her gently on the lips. Instant magic. The kiss didn't last long, but that wasn't the story of what was happening here.

Willa pulled away slowly and said, "We shouldn't, Charles."

"Why shouldn't we, Willa? It appears everyone sees it but you."

"I don't want to talk about this right now."

"You have to talk about it, Willa. The eight-hundred-pound gorilla has been in the room with us every time we're together. What's holding you back?"

Willa turned away, walked over to the sink, and looked out to the water beyond. The dawn was just breaking. "I don't know, Charles. I don't know. I feel like . . . like I'm betraying someone."

Charles walked over behind her, put his arms around her waist, and held her tight. "Who in the world could you be betraying? Is there someone else?"

"No, there's no one, but I know what I feel."

He moved her hair gently to the side of her neck and whispered, "I'll wait for you, Willa. I've never felt like this about anyone before. I'll wait."

Nellie had been about to walk downstairs, but she'd heard the two talking quietly. A smile had broken on her lips, as she'd quietly tiptoed back to her room. The words had finally been spoken, and now Willa had to find out what was holding her captive. There was no way back for her now.

It was time to leave and Charles had said all he was going to say. The moments they had just shared made for an awkward situation between them. It was a blessing when Nellie came down and made breakfast for herself. The conversation turned to Jimmy and Frances.

"Mama texted me and said they're on their way home this afternoon and the two of you are to stay put."

Charles said, "Willa possibly, but I'm on that boat this morning. Tell your parents I have to get back to Washington. I did what I came here to do and I'll be in touch with your mother, Nellie."

"She'll be sad not to see you, but I understand completely."

Charles looked at Willa and said, "Would you walk with me down to the dock?"

"I think I'll say so long here, Charles, if you don't mind."

Nellie didn't look at either one of them.

"Then good-bye, Willa. I'll call you when I get back to town. Take care of yourself over here."

Nellie said, "Hold on a minute, Charles. I'll walk down with you."

Willa wanted to go, but she just couldn't move. She looked at Charles and said softly, "Have a safe trip."

He smiled and then he and Nellie were gone. The moment Willa saw them disappear down the path, tears streaked down her face and she heard those voices in her head saying, "Love him, Willa, and don't lose him."

The phone in the house rang and Willa decided she had better pick it up.

"Hello?"

"Willa? This is Frances. How ye comin'?"

"The question, Frances, is how are *you* doing?"

"Well, Jimmy's 'bout dyin' to bust out of here, so when we have all the paper work done and they come round to see us again—which ye know can take hours—we'll be home this afternoon. You're stayin', aren't ye?"

"Yes, I am. Nellie threatened me if I leave. Charles just left for the boat, though. He had to get back but said to say hello to you two."

"I understand. We'll talk when I get Jimmy settled in. Did Nellie go on with Charles this morning?"

"Yes, she did. Do you want her to call you later?"

"No need to tell her; she will anyway. It'll be good to be home."

"Take care, Frances."

Willa hung up and decided she'd better get moving, too. She looked a wreck and she wanted to help Nellie cook and clean up the house. She went upstairs to where Charles had slept and found herself sitting on the bed. She pulled up the sheet and breathed in deeply. His scent lingered. She stretched out on the bed, holding the pillow close to her body, and wondered what it would be like to be here with a real man and in a real relationship. Not a fantasy one she had made up in her books.

CHAPTER 51

By the time Charles reached Somerville, the marina was already void of any boats. They had long ago left to go out fishing—something he was mercifully happy he wasn't doing today. He knew he would feel his time out on the water for days to come.

He had texted Prue on the way over to tell her he was on his way back but would get there too late for business today. She was to make arrangements for his return from the small airstrip in about two hours. There was something he had to do first. She had answered with a "be good, be safe" message.

Then he asked where the boatyard was and headed over. A few blocks up from the city pier he found the fascinating place. Boats were everywhere, in all stages of repair. He walked over to two men standing inside a huge Quonset hut.

"Hey, fellows. A friend told me to come here and ask you about building a boat or seeing some he said you have for sale."

"Who was your friend?"

Okay, they're not too warm and fuzzy .

"Lem Carter."

"How do ya know Lem Carter?"

"I went out crabbing with him yesterday."

One of the men laughed a little and said, "Don't take this wrong, but ya don't look like a waterman."

"I'm not. I was out on his and Denny Bradshaw's boat. I was a guest. Believe me, I'm no waterman."

They laughed out loud, apparently seeing he could take a poke or two. One then started talking with the shortest cigarette butt in his mouth that Charles had ever seen. How did he keep from getting burned?

"I'm Boyd. Boyd Crenshaw's the full name, but Boyd to all who know me. What do ya want the boat fer?"

"I'm Charles Lee, and, well, I'm not sure quite yet, but I'm interested."

"Do ya want it fer crabbin' or do ya want it fer pleasure?"

"Can you do both?"

"Ya can, but what I'm askin' ya is it mainly fer pleasure?"

"I would say yes. I don't think we'll be going out crabbing every day, that's for sure."

"Well, I've got a couple fer sale. One's a real beauty, but she'll cost ya. She's out back. Been workin' on her fer a few months. She'll be ready by summer."

Charles liked this man. He was no bull, totally to the point. Why couldn't there be men and women like this in Congress?

When they turned the corner of the building, there she was, right in front of him.

"Oh, she's a beauty, Boyd. Tell me what makes her purr."

Boyd seemed to be liking Charles, too, and he clearly loved this boat. "I been workin' on her fer a while now. She still has some to go, but she's fine, all thirty foot of her."

"Okay, tell me more."

"She's a Chesapeake deadrise. White cedar over white oak frames with white oak sister keels. She's powered by a converted automobile engine with a top speed of twenty-five mph. I'm paintin' her white, and you see she's got a red copper bottom. This lady never had a drop of blue paint on her."

Charles was trying to decipher all what Boyd was saying, but the last part really blew his mind. "What was the last thing you said about her? No blue paint? What's that about?"

"Not good fer a boat, unless yer 'specting bad trouble to hit her."

"Ah. Superstition?"

"Yessir, and one we don't mess with."

"How much?"

"Well, she'll run ya around ten thousand or a bit."

"A bit more or a bit less? And when will she be ready?"

"Not long now. When would ya want her?"

"I'm not sure, but I'll think on her. You can't sleep on her, can you?"

"Nope, deadrises are strictly for pleasurin' or going out crabbin'."

Charles got out his wallet, fumbled for his card, then handed it to Boyd.

"This is how you can reach me. If any other boats are available, let me know. I do like this one, though."

Boyd took his card, and, before looking at it, pulled one of his own out of the dirtiest shirt Charles had ever seen. Then he lit up another cigarette.

"Great," Charles remarked. "I'll call you in a couple of days if I'm going to take this one. I really am interested in her. She says everything Bay to me."

"I'll keep her fer ya until you let me know you don't want her." Then he looked down at Charles's card.

Charles got a kick out of watching Boyd's expression change.

"Well, I'll be derned. Ya are a real congressman?"

"Yes, I am. From Virginia."

Boyd shook his head as he grinned ear to ear.

"Ya kept that a secret. Usually politicians let ya know for miles down the road that they're a-comin'."

"Glad to meet you, Boyd. You sure know your stuff here."

"Don't ya worry none." He squinted at the card again. "Congressman Lee, I'll take good care of ya."

"I don't doubt you will."

Charles shook hands with him and left.

The minute Boyd was sure Charles wasn't returning, he called Lem to thank him. When Lem told him about the crabbing trip the day before, Boyd laughed himself silly.

"No wonder he said what he did about wanting a boat mainly fer pleasure. And he was kind of limping a little. I can still remember the first time my daddy took me out. Didn't move right fer a week."

Jimmy and Frances returned home in the late afternoon. He was tired, but so glad to be out of the hospital. Frances knew she was going to have her hands full, but she didn't want to stay at the hospital much longer either. As it was, this was going to cost more than they had, but her Jimmy was well for now and that's all that mattered.

Nellie had gone down to meet them, then helped get him in bed and settled down. Then she wanted to get out for a while and see Denny.

"Thanks, Nellie, for holding down the fort here while I tended to Daddy. What a time this has been."

"Thank the good Lord, it all turned out all right, Mama. It could have gone really bad."

"I know, Nellie. We'll have to watch him like a hawk. You know how stubborn he is, and, I swear, if he hadn't gotten out of that hospital today, he would have torn that place to pieces. I think they 'twarn't real sorry to see us go."

"How's his heart, Mama? Was there a lot of damage?"

"Some, but they patched him up pritty good. He'll be just fine. Don't ye worry. Where's Willa?"

"Last time I saw her, she said she was going over to Bradshaw's to get food for dinner."

"I want to talk to her. Think I'll go on over and meet her. We can talk while we walk back."

"Don't worry about Daddy. I'm here and he's not going anywhere. But I would like to go over and see Denny. I've been neglecting him the past few days."

"He'll get over it. It's your daddy and he understands those things."

Nellie hugged her mother and said, "Won't be long now and I'll be living in my own house."

"We have to talk about the wedding, Nellie. I have that committee to prepare for. I don't want to mess that up. Charles said he would let me know when the first meeting will be, in the early summer, I'm sure, and I'll have to be gone a few days then. You and Denny have to pick a date."

Nellie had a dreamy look in her eyes. "We will. I'm thinking September. It's so pretty then."

"Well, you tell me and we'll get working on it."

"Working on what?" Willa said as she walked through the back door.

"I was just going to walk over to the store to see you," said Frances. "What's for dinner?"

"No fair looking, Frances. I'm cooking tonight. It won't be the best dinner you've ever had, but it will give you all a break."

"Hi, Willa. You see the troops are home. I'm going over to see Denny. Be back later to rescue you."

"I'll be fine. Say hi to Denny for me."

Frances hugged Nellie and said, "I love ye, girl. Thanks."

Willa saw the love shared between the two. A pang of jealously shot through her. What she would give to be able to hug her mother. When would this pain end?

Frances put a pot of water on for tea and didn't look at what Willa unpacked for dinner. She loved this young woman, and so it wouldn't matter if it was good or bad—she would appreciate it.

"C'mon and sit down with me, Willa. I want to tell you why Charles came out here."

"I think I know, but I think he really came out because he's falling in love with it out here."

"I think he's falling in love with you."

Willa looked away and said, "Yes, I think so, too."

"Where does that put you in the equation?"

"Halfway in, halfway out."

"If ye don't mind me saying this, ye have to get on with life, girl. Ye got to set aside what's hurtin' ye."

"You sound like Prue and Nellie. Is it that obvious?"

"Only to those who love ye."

"Never mind that for now. What did Charles come here to tell you?"

"That he wants me to serve on this committee with the watermen. I feel kind of stupid doing that as it's men's business, but I agreed because he really wanted me to do it."

"He was absolutely right, Frances. You might be the only woman, but you don't know that for sure. What you *do* know is that you're a voice that needs to be heard. The wives live the same life and maybe harder. You raise the children, take on the worries about them, and, when the men are gone up the Bay, you're all alone to handle everything. You have to stick close and bear one another's burdens. Your role is immensely important."

"What ye speak is the truth. We have a burden to bear that is not understood. Our men know it and respect us for it. That's why I want Nellie to be sure she's not doing something she won't want to do for life. We don't divorce out here. We stay married."

"Is that one hundred percent true?"

"Pritty much. Oh, there's been an odd divorce or two. Or someone dies and remarries, but that's different. In order to be on the water, you have to have a mate who understands that way of life."

Willa reached across the table and said, "You're the most wonderful woman I've ever known besides my mother, Frances. You understand life. It's simple for you; no complications and fretting about things you know you can't have."

"We have dreams, too, Willa, just like any woman, but we understand the lives we choose."

Willa sat and thought about what Frances had said. The old woman was absolutely right. These women understood their lives. They weren't always looking for something else. The contentment they felt came from a well of unconditional love.

"Where are ye, Willa?

"Right here, thinking how much I respect all of you. I know you're not perfect, but your grasp of life is."

"Then write about that. Write what's in your heart and how you feel when you come out here."

Willa chuckled. "My publisher would love to hear this conversation. She keeps telling me I should drop a love story in this book I'm writing."

Frances never took her eyes off of Willa and answered, "Isn't this whole book filled with love for what you see and feel out here?"

Willa paused, taken aback by the rightness of what Frances had said. "You know, Miss Frances, I knew we would become good friends because you and I are so much like the gulls we both love. They're survivors, too, and we have learned from them. You are such a wise woman. If only you could bottle that."

"If I could, I'd be a rich woman and able to pay for Jimmy's hospital stay."

Willa snapped her fingers. "Speaking of that, I want to tell you something. I don't want you to interrupt me, Frances. I just want you to nod your head. Okay?"

Frances nodded.

"I'm going to pay for it all, Frances. Please don't insult my gift and tell me no. I want you to take it with the love I feel for you. I can well afford it, so it's no problem for me at all."

Tears puddled in Frances's eyes. She had never had such a gift. She remained silent.

"I'll take that as a yes," Willa said quietly. "All I ask is that I can stay with you a few more days and then I have to get back to town."

Sniffling quietly, with tears streaming down her cheeks, Frances did exactly what Willa had asked of her. She nodded yes.

CHAPTER 52

Things were looking up for the Evans family. Jimmy was getting stronger each day and planning on going back out on the water the following week. Nellie and Denny had decided on a late September wedding, Frances was busy picking crabs at the Co-op . . . and Willa needed to leave. She had stayed much longer than she'd expected, but had begun writing the book that had eluded her all these years. It was a love story, but about an old woman's love and devotion to her home and way of life.

"Do ye have to go, Willa? Ye know ye can stay as long as ye want."

"I know that, Frances, but it's time, and I've actually done more out here than I expected to."

Jimmy walked through the door of the kitchen to tell Willa he would take her to the dock. Willa was touched by his gesture. He was such a quiet man; yet, in his silence, he spoke volumes.

Frances said, "I have to go on now to the pickin' house and Nellie's run off to do her work over to the shanty. It seems that's her office now."

Willa hugged her tightly. "I'll miss you, Frances, but you know I'll be back."

"Got to, at least in September when Nellie and Denny get married."

"That's a definite. You have a good summer and stay away from those dreadful flies."

"They getcha, that they do," chimed in Jimmy.

"Well, I better get going. Thank you for everything."

Frances took her hand and said, "No, Willa, it's us who have to thank you for paying those bills."

"I just paid for the helicopter so far, so don't go thanking me yet. I called the hospital and told them to send their bill to me over in Washington. Turned out the woman who took the information was a huge fan of my books."

"Well, I'll be. Take care, girl, and come back soon."

"I will, Frances and call me and let me know what happens with the committee."

Frances began to walk out the door, then stopped and turned around. "Remember, Charles loves you. Love him back. It's that simple."

Willa smiled and said, "If you say so."

Jimmy said, "We got to be going, Franny. Let the girl get on her way."

"All right, old man, all right."

Jimmy took Willa straight to the dock, where Tuck was waiting for them and for the last kids to straggle onto the boat. This was the last week of school and they were an ornery bunch, but she knew Cap'n Tuck could handle them and anything else that came his way.

"Willa," Jimmy said, "before ye go, I just want to tell you how much I appreciate what yer doin' fer us. It's a real big thing."

Willa could see how hard this was for the proud man standing in front of her. She touched his arm and said, "Don't mention it, Jimmy. You're family to me, and, if I can't do this for family, what good am I?"

Jimmy nodded and said, "Have a good trip. See ye when ye return."

She stepped onto the boat, put her two small bags down in the middle section, and turned to look at one of the sweetest, kindest men in this world.

As the boat pulled away, Willa felt both good and sad, but it was how she always felt when she left the dock. She knew she would come back again, so there were no tears this time.

"What a visit ye had, huh, Willa?"

"You can say that again, Cap'n Tuck, but it all turned out just fine."

"Jimmy give us a scare. He's a hard worker and that's what takes us in the end."

"I guess that's not a bad way to go," Willa said. "Now what's new with you?"

"Well, not much, except I had a bit of excitement myself this weekend. Sad, too. Didn't turn out like yours."

"What happened?"

"Tommy James, cut that teasin' out, ye hear me?"

Willa stared as he disciplined one of the kids. They were all a tight-knit family, so it didn't matter if they weren't your kids—they got yelled at just the same.

"Now what was I sayin'? Oh yeah, the excitement. A mother goose had a young one and the nest was out by the dump in the water bushes. I been watchin' it since the young was borned. There were others, but a hawk or eagle must have got 'em. Anyway, the mother didn't come back for a day or two and the gosling was squawking and carrying on something awful."

"That's horrible."

"'Specially bein' the mother never did come back. I carried the gosling, all hissin' and fussin' at me, to my shanty. I penned her in and now it's been awhile and she's doin' okay."

"Will she be tame or wild?"

"She'll be tame, I 'spect, now she's been raised by the likes of me."

"That's so sad, Tuck."

"Be sadder if I did nothing and let the the birds come back and finish the job."

Willa lowered her sunglasses and stared at him in disbelief.

"Well, you know it would."

"I guess you're right, but it's the way you said it."

"What? Nature takes its course and it's best the gosling decided to save herself and forget about the past. Nothin' she could do about that."

Willa's heart almost stopped. It was as if he were talking about her. That baby goose was . . *her*. Suddenly, there it was, the deep dark pain of her past dragged up and laid bare on the deck of that boat. He kept on talking, but she didn't hear another word. Suddenly she couldn't breathe; her lungs gasped for air.

Tuck called to her, but his voice seemed so distant. Everything was muffled except for the pounding of her heart. Had the boat crashed? Was she drowning? She couldn't feel water, but it was the same feeling she'd had as a child in Maine as she'd gone under the waves, as she was dragged farther and farther down.

"Willa, are you all right?" Cap'n Tuck was shouting at her. He put a bottle of water in her hand. One of the older children had come to help him. Willa was clutching her chest and screaming for air.

A little girl, maybe seven, came over and took Willa's hand. Tuck tried to shoo her away but she just sat there with her and began singing. It was a familiar song Willa hadn't heard in years. It comforted her and began to bring her back. She wasn't drowning anymore. Her breath became gentle and easy. She removed her sunglasses and saw Tuck, who looked terrified.

"I'm okay, Tuck. Really I am." She looked down and the little girl was gone. "Where is she?"

"Where is who, Willa?"

"The little girl who was holding my hand and singing to me?"

Tuck stared at her, then quickly got up and went back to work.

He didn't believe her. "I tell you, Tuck, there was a little girl."

Tuck didn't answer her. He must have thought it best to let it go.

"I must have had a terrible anxiety attack. I haven't been scared out here once, and I don't know why I got so spooked today."

Tuck smiled and said, "It's okay, Willa. It happens sometimes when people are afraid of the water or they get kind of seasick."

Willa got up and walked to the most open part of the deck, took a deep breath, and noticed there wasn't a child on the boat anything like the little girl she saw. *Of course there couldn't be, because that little girl was me.*

She had been reliving that moment long ago when her mother had saved her. But her mother was as dead as the mother goose Tuck had told her about. And she, Willa, was the survivor left to live her life without both mother and father. Tears tumbled down her face like rain now, but, this time, they were tears of complete release. The tune she had heard was "This Old Man," the "knick-knack paddywhack" song she and her mother would sing when she needed to be comforted.

Willa looked up at the blue sky, realizing that what she was most afraid of was losing something she had already lost, and yet never let go. She had used her subconscious desires for her parents still to be with her to hold on to a past she could never again possess. Death had been too final for her, so she had tried to keep them alive in her constant thoughts. There wasn't anything wrong with this particularly, and many people did it for a while after loss. But it had gone way past a while now.

She finally knew what she had to do to lift the veil and see the joy in life. She had to tell her parents something. It would take all the courage in the world, but now was the time.

With tears flowing freely, she held on to the railing of the simple vessel and whispered, "Good-bye now. I will love you forever, but you need to go on and I need to be free. And I need to love."

She hadn't even realized that the boat had docked and the kids had gone on their way. Only Tuck was on the boat with her, and he stood at a distance, clearly knowing she needed a private moment.

Finally, she wiped her eyes, then turned around and said, "Thank you, Tuck, for the best ride I've ever had. I know I gave you a scare back there, but it's all right now. Everything really is all right."

Tuck, a wise old man, knew she wasn't talking about the ride. He looked at her, and, with the kindest smile, said, "No charge for the return trip, Miss Willa. This one's on me."

CHAPTER 53

Charles and Prue had worked on getting everything up to date when he returned from the island. Prue had also spoken to her family and she was getting things up to date for herself.

"Are you a little sorry the date for the committee meeting is in September, Charles?"

"Not really. The later date keeps us out of trouble with the watermen for the most part, and with Miss Frances. She's got her hands full now, so it's for the best."

Prue looked at him a bit sheepishly and asked, "Have you heard from Willa since she's back?"

"I didn't know she *was* back. When did she return?"

"A week ago, but she's changed somehow. I don't know what happened out on that island, but she came back different."

Charles looked a little confused and said, "In what way?"

"I can't put my finger on it, but she's happier and more settled."

Charles became slightly irritated and said, "Well, she obviously doesn't want anything to do with me, so I guess we move on."

Prue smiled. "Yeah, right. I know you Charles, remember? You're in love with that girl. You should know she's working like a fool. Made up with her publisher and she hasn't left her apartment. We had drinks over there the other night. She wouldn't even take a small break and meet me at the Scotch Bar. Now you know she's into this project."

"Trying to make me feel better? It isn't working."

"Give her time. Whatever went on over there, it got to her in a good way. She's not so sad inside."

"Probably found a waterman after I left."

"Hardly, Charles. She loves them, that's for sure, but she isn't going to marry a waterman."

He returned to the previous topic at hand. "Please make sure we have all the information out to all the committee members now that they've been identified. Frances was great to help us with the water community, and, I have to say, Rennie Richardson has kept out of it."

Prue raised her eyebrows and remarked, "By the way, I hear he's going to retire soon. Something about his family?" She smiled.

"Yeah, I heard that, too. I guess he's made it public now."

"Let's hope he doesn't change his mind. By the way, been meaning to tell you, I'm interviewing people for this job. I think I've found a fabulous young man."

Charles was in shock. "What? A guy?"

"Why, yes, Charles. He has excellent credentials."

"Guess I deserve this. I can't flirt with a guy."

"I don't think so. He's coming in tomorrow, so be here or be square. And be nice. I have to get on with my life."

"Did you tell Willa you're leaving?"

"Yes, I did, and I must say she did an Academy Award-winning performance of 'Gee, I'm so surprised.' I told her to knock it off. I figured you had told her. But then she hugged me and said she was so happy I was finally going to do what I had been born to do."

"Glad she at least tried to protect me with the element of surprise. I didn't mean to spill the beans, Prue, but we were talking and all . . . well, anyway, did you tell her your replacement will be a man?"

"I did tell her he was the best of the bunch. She laughed her head off. Said that would change things around here."

"I'll bet she had quite a time with that one." His cell rang. "Speaking of the devil, guess who's calling?"

"See you later, Charles. Say hi to Willa for me." Prue left the room.

"Well, hello, Ms. Carpenter. Hear you've been back in town for a week."

"Hello to you, too, Charles. Yes, I got back a week ago and I've been very busy, but I called to invite you to my apartment for drinks. Say six o'clock?"

"I'm in shock. Sure I can do that. I shouldn't, but I will."

Willa chuckled into the phone and said, "It's not personal, Charles. Really. I have something to tell you and it's all good. See you tonight."

Prue walked in again just as Charles was hanging up. She noticed the broad grin on his face and said, "All the information on the committee meeting has gone out, Congressman. Anything else?"

"You don't have to stand there staring at me as if I have egg dripping from my face. She asked me over to her apartment tonight, that's all."

"Oh, Charles, that's not all and you know it. Have fun, and I want a tell-all tomorrow morning."

"I have to go. There's a vote I have to cast on the floor. Behave, Prue—and I'm not going to tell you anything."

Charles had a busy afternoon and should have been tired, but, after a shower and change of clothes, he was ready for an evening with Willa. He had missed her, but he wasn't going to tell her that.

Willa had spent an hour picking out an outfit. She had never really thought about doing that before when she'd seen Charles, but tonight was different. She wanted to look extraordinarily good, and, by the time Howard the doorman called to tell her Charles was on his way up, she had succeeded. Simple was always best. Black tee with white slacks—though it was after Memorial Day. Not that anyone paid attention to that anymore. She pulled her long blonde hair back so the extra splash of wild turquoise earrings could be seen.

He knocked at her door, and, when she opened it, reacted as if it weren't just the flowers he was holding that looked gorgeous.

"Wow," he said. "You're a stunner, lady."

She smiled as he walked through the door. Within moments, the flowers were lying on a table and they were in each other's arms. When they came up for air, he whispered, "What's this all about, Willa?"

"It's a kiss."

Charles stepped back and smiled. "I know what it is, but what is *this* kiss about?"

"It's a kiss that tells you I'm sorry I've been so lost. I'm sorry I didn't answer you when you told me you were in love with me. And it's a kiss that asks you to give me another try."

Charles didn't say a word, but pulled her back into her arms. From that moment on, the night never seemed to end.

When the sun rose, they were still together, having talked and kissed all night.

"I never knew people could do this," Willa said, winking, as she stood up to make coffee.

Charles said, "I suppose in your books, things go differently, but that's not where we are right now. This was so nice. Want to go out for breakfast?"

"Nope. I'll make it here."

Willa went into the kitchen, started the coffee, and began to scramble eggs. Charles walked in and poured the orange juice. She giggled and said, "I hear Prue is protecting my interests and hiring a man for her position."

"That's one way of looking at it. If he's good, I don't care. She's going to be hard to replace."

"I don't know what I'll do without her."

"What do you mean? She's going to win that election next year and be right back here."

"Yeah, you're right." Willa stopped whipping the eggs and turned to Charles and said, "I miss the island."

"So do I. When do you want to go back?"

"Can't for a while. I have a meeting with Kit Winthrop, my publisher, and I'm going to finish this book before I head back out. So I think it's going to be this fall at the earliest."

"Isn't Nellie's wedding around then?"

"Yes, it was September, but they switched it to November. I'm sure we'll be invited."

He stood close to her and ran his finger up and down her arm. "Maybe by then, you'll want to marry me, too."

Willa turned to look directly at him. "Are you asking me to marry you? We really don't know one another that well."

"Don't we? We know all we need to know. We're in love and we aren't exactly innocent kids."

"Speak for yourself. Maybe we should take some time to think about this."

"Willa, what do we have to think about? We are alike, you and I," Charles said. "Think about it. Aren't we? You want to change the world and so do I. You do it through writing; I do it through laws."

She nodded. "You're right. I can't go on being scared to commit to you, I suppose."

"When did you figure that out?"

Willa looked at him and said, "You won't believe me."

"Try me."

"On the boat back over from the island, Tuck started telling me a story about a baby goose that had been left alone. Its parents had gone off or been killed. He took it home and it's surviving. Then something hit me, and, all of a sudden, I felt like I was drowning and couldn't breathe. It was awful, but, when I came out of it, I realized what's been grabbing at me all this time. I hadn't been able to say good-bye to my parents. I still wanted it to be like it always was, but it can't be. They're gone and I have to move forward. Or . . . or I may as well be dead, too. I stood there and said good-bye to them, Charles. They weren't going to leave me until I told them to go."

Charles held her tightly. He whispered gently, "Are you free now, Willa? Are you free to love me?"

Willa looked into his face. Her eyes were puddles of tears but they were joyous tears, not sad ones. "Yes, I am. That's why I called you. I had to tell you I was completely free."

Charles wouldn't let her go. For the first time in his life, he was completely and totally in love with a woman. Willa was his perfect match in every way, and he wasn't ever going to let her go. They stood frozen in place for a long time, holding on, completely lost in their own world.

CHAPTER 54

From the night Willa had told Charles she loved him and he had held her in his arms to let her know he loved her, they had been all but inseparable. A day didn't go by that they weren't together or on the phone.

Time seemed to fly by and Prue had stayed longer than she'd intended to, but now it was the end of August and she had to leave. The young man hired to replace her, Steven Allen, was a whiz. Charles really liked him and it didn't take long for him to accept having a male as his gatekeeper.

The meeting between the watermen—and one woman named Frances—the bureaucrats and agencies would take place in a few weeks. Charles had high hopes for this gathering. The stage was set.

"Prue, will you be staying until after the meeting or is it time for you to head out? I know after Labor Day your campaign begins, and then we won't see you until you come back here as a representative from Ohio."

"I'm leaving next week, Charles. It's time to let Steve fly. He's good and can go this one alone. He understand what's at stake here."

"Well, Willa and I will want to take you to dinner before you go."

"That's a deal, Charles. Willa's been working night and day on her new book, so she'll be ready for a celebration."

"She's going to miss you, Prue."

"She'll have you. When are you two going to get married anyway?"

"Some day. No rush right now."

"Don't wait too long, Charles. Willa needs someone to hold on to at night."

"I'll be there."

"Have you spoken with Frances lately?"

"I spoke to her last week. She's ready to go."

"Good. I'm counting on her and her strong convictions."

Charles said, "She will be an asset to the group, even if the men have to get used to that a little."

"I don't think that's going to be a problem. She's known among her people and they trust her."

"That they do. I just want to break through this ceiling and get something out of this really positive for the water community. I want to keep them fishing out there for a long time."

"Well, we'll see how it goes, Charles."

The Willard seemed a fitting place to say good-bye to Prue. Her favorite Scotch Bar was ready and waiting for the three of them to arrive. As soon as they did, the celebration began.

"Oh, Willa, how many times have we sat in here, drinking cosmos or red wine and solving the problems of the world?"

"A few, Prue. Some good memories here for us."

Charles said, "You two aren't the only ones. Many a high-profile meeting went on here. 'Til all hours of the night, I might add."

Prue smiled at him. "And you hated every minute of it, too."

"Well, sometimes I did, actually."

Charles leaned into the table and said, "Prue, what would you think if we made this more than a going-away dinner?"

"More? Why, what do you mean?"

Charles pulled out a small box and handed it to Willa.

"Charles, what's this?"

"Why don't you open it and find out?"

"You know, Prue, if I didn't know better, I would think you two were up to something."

Willa lifted the lid of the small velvet box and then Charles said, "I'll take it from here."

Willa appeared to be in shock. She clearly hadn't been expecting this at all. Charles slipped the ring on her finger and said, "Well, what do ye think?"

"Did you just say what I thought you did?"

"Yes, ma'am. I'm turning into an islander. Well, do ye?"

"You and Robert E. Lee." Willa laughed and looked at the rather large stone on her finger. "I can't believe how beautiful this is and how wonderful you are."

Prue started to cry. "I wanted to be with you when Charles gave you the ring. I hope you don't mind."

Willa leaned over and kissed her dear friend. "I wouldn't have had it any other way."

"Well, you accepted it, so I guess this means we just took another step forward on the way."

"On the way to what, Charles?"

"We'll stop here for now, Willa. Wear the ring always, with my love."

"Okay, you two, break it up. Let's toast."

Charles picked up his glass and said, "To good times, good memories, and happy tomorrows."

The meeting was nearing and Nellie was working like a fool. Her paying job with Global Waters Enterprises was taking a good deal more of her time than she had thought, but it would pay off for her mother and Charles's committee. She was working on the effect of regulations on the fishing industry, especially the Clean Waters Act. Interesting to be sure.

Frances and the five other waterman committee members that had been chosen were ready. They had met several times, though it hadn't always been easy at the end of crabbing season. They knew, however, that this was their chance, hopefully, to make things work on the Bay and surrounding waters. It would take time, but, if they could get off on the right foot, they might be able to work together this time for the sake of the survival of commercial fishing.

Charles and his new assistant Steve were piled in papers getting ready for this gathering, and Prue had been right when she had endorsed this man for the job: he was terrific. He was winnowing out what wasn't necessary and only taking what was. Charles knew this first meeting was going to make or break the whole attempt, and, if it failed, it would take years to put it all together again. It was in that light that Steve had named this Project Humpty-Dumpty.

Charles made one last call to Frances to make sure they were good to go.

"How ye comin', Charles? And how's that girl of ours?"

"Both are fine. I'll tell her you asked for her. The reason I called is to see if everything is set on your end."

"It is. Can't say we aren't a bit nervous, but we're ready to give it a try."

"That's all I can ask, Frances. This is important and I think you know that."

"We all do. And Charles? We want to do right by this. We want it to work."

"Then it will. Are Jimmy and Nellie okay?"

"Jimmy's back on the water, of course. Does that tell ye how he is? And Nellie is working night and day. She's been so helpful for us to get our information together."

"I know she has. It's better, you know, that she's not going to attend the meeting."

"I understand. One Evans is more than enough. I'll see you soon, Charles."

"See you, Frances. Be careful."

When he hung up, he sat a minute and thought of all the things he wanted to happen at this meeting. If he could get just a few, he would feel as though he had done his job.

The weather was perfect, the sun shining brightly as the boat with the six members of the watermen's committee arrived in St. Michaels. The meeting was being held at the Inn at Perry Cabin with opening remarks at the Maritime Museum. Frances was thrilled about this because both sites held a great deal of old history of both the water and the people who had lived here from the beginning.

Charles was there to greet them, and, after they disembarked from the boat, Frances hugged him and introduced the rest of the group. Then they went on in and met the men and women from the government agencies, Baywaters Commission, Global Waters Enterprises, and Steve, Prue's replacement.

All went well over coffee and introductory remarks. The tour of the museum was most impressive, and some had had no idea of the impact or the historical significance of the watermen and their work on the Bay. Things were looking hopeful.

The large conference room was set up with everything anyone might need for visual presentations or any other technical need. The meeting began. Charles stood at the front of the room and made his opening remarks, brief and to the point: "Let's get this done."

Each speaker had his or her own point to make and each had ten minutes, at most fifteen, with questions afterwards limited to another ten minutes. It was going to be a long day.

The meeting started at ten o'clock, and, by one thirty, everyone needed a break. Lunch was served. The seating had been arranged so everyone sat with someone from another committee or a member of the watermen's group. Charles and Frances were convinced this might help people from different backgrounds to talk to one another. Food was always a good icebreaker.

Frances sat at Charles's table but spent most of her time watching the others in the room. It was interesting to see that they were really communicating without loud words. Several of the watermen, especially the old-timers, seemed to have people asking them many questions. It was working.

During the afternoon session, a few of the government guests were contentious and wanted more rules on the watermen to protect the waters—they said. This wasn't well received, and all the good that had been done in the morning and over lunch seemed to be unraveling. Charles could see it coming and was clearly sick about it. He looked down at the agenda and saw that Frances was scheduled last, and last was coming after just one more speaker. *Good planning, Steve!*

The next speaker was from the Baywaters Commission and also a tight friend of Rennie Richardson's, He attacked the watermen from the start and went on to tell of every infringement they had on record. You could hear the rumblings and Frances was getting steamed, but she knew she was up next. Charles knew this was Rennie's way of saying good-bye on his way out. He let it go. He had faith in Frances.

Finally, Frances came to the podium. She waited a minute or two until everyone was quieted down. Then pictures she had brought with her were shown above her on the screen. She said nothing, but let people simply view the old photographs. Then the photos went from old ones to new ones. Now they saw the decaying buildings of Somerville and the enormous pile of oyster shells at the back marina that, by orders of state officials, were being held instead of being returned to the Bay. There were photos of James Island showing how the population was dwindling, and of old shanties that once had been home to many watermen, now falling apart.

She stood before them, and, when she opened her mouth, pure love flowed out like honey. Frances Evans spoke only ten minutes, but it made its impact.

Will the watermen survive or not? That's the choice we all have to make. It's not only the fault of regulations and fees, but they do hasten what's coming. We are all here to do something. Separate agendas won't work. We have to move as one boat gliding along in that Bay out there. To lose something so precious and so important to the state and to the nation would be criminal. It's a way of life for many of us who live here, and those whose businesses depend on what we do. It's the history of the cradle of this nation and it belongs to us all.

Charles sat there listening to this woman who didn't speak perfect English, but who spoke every word from her heart. You could hear a pin drop. They were listening. Maybe for the first time, they were hearing something that neither side had wanted to hear before.

In closing I leave ye with this thought. We are here today to try to come together. The watermen can teach ye ways that have been successful forever. Ye can teach them new technologies that will protect our ways and make it better. Lessen the burden of regulations on us and lighten the fees to allow us to make a decent living again. Help us get health care for our families so we don't have to go without or worry about it. We can all do this if we want to. And, if we don't, we will be as gone with the wind as any other vanishing peoples from the past.

Frances stepped down. As she walked to her seat, they stood up, first one and then the entire room. Through many misty eyes, they were clapping for a simple island woman with a simple message who had the courage to tell it like it is.

CHAPTER 55

November came and, this year, was milder than usual, perfect for Nellie's wedding. Charles and Willa had arrived a day ahead and were staying in a home they had rented for the weekend. Prue would be joining them but would arrive the next day.

Both Willa and Charles were so excited, but that couldn't compare to the comfort they felt coming back to the island. Her book was finished and she was satisfied. So was Kit, also celebrating Susan Crandall's success because she'd had a book picked up for a movie. Willa was happy for Susan—and she was very happy the book that was being optioned was an original, not a retread of one of hers.

Frances came to their rented house to check on them and knocked on the door. Charles opened it and gave her a huge hug.

"How's my favorite congressman?"

"I'm fine. And my favorite island woman?"

"Exhausted with all this wedding hoopla going on, but I've never seen Nellie so happy."

Just then Willa walked in, returning from Bradshaw's store, carrying some essentials for the weekend. When she saw Frances, she dropped her bag and hugged her dear second mother.

"It's so good to see you. It's been way too long."

"It has indeed. Charles, I wanted a few moments with ye before the festivities get going."

Willa picked up the bag and said, "I'll put this in the kitchen and make some tea. You two sit awhile."

Frances sat down across from Charles and said, "So what do ye hear? Anything?"

"I saved it to tell you in person, Frances. Your talk at the first meeting and your influence at the one after that has gone a long way to make people think about the future of the Bay and the watermen. The folks in Washington are working on the EPA to try to get them to review a lot of the regulations. That's the best we can do for now, but it's a start. Health care is on the agenda for Congress as fishermen all over have that situation, and they're talking about an independent plan for all the fishermen, but that will take time, too. Nothing is perfect to begin with and so much more needs to be done. But it's a beginning."

Frances smiled and said, "I hear from our men that they have been working with the Baywaters Commission on improving some of the oyster beds and are using the collected shells to dump back in certain places in the Bay. They're also learning about the aquifers and trying to improve the quality of the water. It's hard because the developers continue to throw trash in the canals and the runoff from the disturbed water tables continues to play havoc, but everyone is hopeful, Charles. The farmers are now trying to put forth an effort like ours to get the attention of the state government to help them with the tough regulations they're facing. Seems we've started something."

"That's how it goes, and I pray this is the start of something really big. The government can't sit on the industries so hard they can't move forward."

"You've been wonderful, Charles, and my guess is that ye have gotten a lot of heat."

"I'm a big boy, and a Lee."

Frances laughed as Willa called for them to come into the kitchen. "Yes, we know about the Lees."

Frances left, to take care of the million things she had to do for Nellie. But first she invited them to the big dinner down to the firehall. It was going to be the perfect start to a wonderful weekend.

The next day was mayhem, but, at three thirty, at the Tuckerton Methodist Church, Nellie Evans married her childhood sweetheart, Denny Bradshaw. Reminiscent of times past, the ceremony was simple and all about the vows of marriage.

The reception was back at the firehall and the whole island had been invited. This time, flowers adorned every table and food was overflowing. No alcohol was to be seen, as this was a dry island, and they were very strict about that. As the music began, Charles leaned over to Willa and said, "Come on, I have something I want to show you." They left as unobtrusively as they could, hoping no one would see them. But Frances did. She smiled, knowing where Charles was taking Willa. It had all been arranged awhile back, and she was so happy that no one had spilled the beans on his surprise.

The sun was low in the sky already as he led her down a path and then over to another one. Finally they arrived. In front of them was a big, old, weathered barn, one that had seen its share of change come to the island. Charles stopped and said, "We're here, Willa."

"We're where, Charles? It's a lovely barn, but what's this to do with us?"

"Open the doors, my love."

Willa opened the two large doors and couldn't believe her eyes. In front of her was a boat. She gasped when she saw it. "Is this your boat?"

Charles said, "Walk around the back, Willa, and take a look at her."

Willa smiled and said, "Okay, I'm walking." Then she saw the name across the back of the boat. She yelled, "What in the world?"

Charles walked toward her and said, "What do you think?"

"I think you've lost your mind, Charles Lee. You bought this for me?"

"Doesn't it have your name on it?"

"Well, sort of. I guess. She's a beauty all right. I can't believe it." She ran her hands along it, then stopped and bent to kiss the place it said *The Willa Lee*. "I guess you're sure I"ll be Willa Lee."

He embraced her and whispered, "Yes, I am, and soon, too."

"I love you, Charles, and this means we have to come over here often and take her out. She's so perfect."

"I had her delivered a couple weeks ago, and, thanks to Frances and Jimmy, we are able to store her here for the winter."

"You know, Congressman Lee, you've accomplished a whole lot this year."

"So have you, Willa. You let go of one world and found another."

"I suppose you're right. And I met a woman named Frances who taught me that life is found in the love of those who surround us."

"The culture of the watermen, Willa, is rare and precious. We dare not lose it or we lose part of ourselves."

Willa looked at the boat and said, "Are you going to tell me about this lady?"

With a mischievous smile, Charles opened his mouth, and, imitating Boyd, he said, "Well, Miss Willa, she's a thirty-foot Chesapeake deadrise, white cedar over white oak frames with white oak sister keels. She's powered by a converted automobile engine, with top speed of twenty-five mph. Painted white with a red copper bottom and she never had a drop of blue paint on her."

She realized he sounded just like them now. Willa laughed hard as she fell into his arms and said, "I'll love you forever, Charlie Lee."

THE END

A MAN AND HIS BOAT

by

Janice Marshall

A Boat is usually referred to as a SHE.
She is a high maintenance Lady.
He takes her places everyday. She doesn't go anywhere without him.
He trusts his life to her.
He shops for her and she's always pleased.
He tells her where to go and she goes and never talks back.
It's one Lady he can always turn on and get her going.
And two or three times a week she takes him for a roll on the Bay.

ACKNOWLEDGMENTS

Never are we truly alone when we write a story. It takes a circle of people and a basketful of appreciation to make it happen.

- To my editor, Kathy K. Grow, for taking my jumbles and making them a memorable story. How do we write without our editors? Answer: we don't.

- To the watermen who shared years of stories and information about what they do out on the Chesapeake Bay as they bring in those wonderful blue crabs and oysters we love to eat. I so appreciate what it takes to go out in rough water and in dangerous circumstances.

- To the women who share their lives as a team with their husbands. Nothing is easy about the life of commercial fishermen everywhere, including the watermen of the Chesapeake and the lobstermen of New England and the Gloucestermen of Massachussetts, all of whom earn their reputations for working at a dangerous job. The women raise the children, keep the home fires burning, and say a lot of prayers while their men go out on the water.

- To my friend Wilson Wyatt Jr. for the author photograph.

- To my dear friend Janice Marshall, who has influenced my life more than I can say. She was my inspiration for this story, and, through her poetry, we are invited to glimpse her world that she loves with a passion. She is a true icon of the Chesapeake woman and I am humbled to call her my friend.

~ To my dear literary friends of the Eastern Shore Writers' Association of Maryland, who are always in support of my efforts. Their strength is mine.

~ To my family, which supports my time away to write and discover new tales from this wonderful area of our nation. I appreciate it more than you know.

ABOUT THE AUTHOR

Anna Gill is the acclaimed author of four novels and a freelance journalist. Her writing reflects the love she has for the culture and rights of the fishermen not only in the Chesapeake Bay but all coastal and inland waters of the United States. Anna lives in Upstate New York. For more information, visit www.annagill.com.

www.ingramcontent.com/pod-product-compliance
Lightning Source LLC
Chambersburg PA
CBHW030640020726
47493CB00006B/1808